MY SECRET SISTER

LAUREN WESTWOOD

BOOKS BY LAUREN WESTWOOD

My Secret Sister

The Daughter She Lost

My Mother's Silence

Moonlight on the Thames

Finding Dreams

Finding Secrets

Finding Home

MY SECRET SISTER

ISBN: 9798455363566

www.laurenwestwoodwriter.com

AUTHOR'S NOTE

I began this book prior to the world-altering events of the Covid-19 pandemic, and have chosen not to address the issues it would have raised in connection with the events of this novel. Covid-19 has had a significant negative impact on many people who were receiving treatment for serious illnesses, and increased the physical risks for vulnerable people.

I would like to dedicate this book to the healthcare workers who put themselves on the front line so that people with serious illnesses could continue to receive treatment, as well as to all of the blood and organ donors who continue to give the gift of life.

I would also like to dedicate this book to anyone who is dealing with any of the real-life issues it presents. I may never meet you or learn your story, but please know that I am sending you my best wishes.

Finally, I would also like to dedicate the book to my family. You make my life worthwhile.

PROLOGUE

As I speed off in the ambulance holding my daughter's hand, I wonder how I could have been so stupid. I should have made the bargain, paid the price – anything to avoid being right here, right now.

"Her blood pressure's dropping; we're losing her." One paramedic pushes past me to adjust the fluid drip as the other scrambles to get out the defibrillator. Everyone seems to be moving in slow motion, backward almost. If only they could turn back the clock; they're trained professionals – why can't they turn back time so that this never happened?

But it's too late for bargains. Much, much too late. The grip on my hand loosens, then goes limp. I want to scream, but my throat is dry.

The paddles are placed on my daughter's chest. Her body jerks as the current racks through. Once, twice. I can't hear what they're saying. Black spots appear before my eyes – a flood of love, a torrent of regret. A voice whispers in my head that I can't silence. *This is all your fault. You killed her.* It's *her* voice, the one I hear in my nightmares. The woman who stole my memories, the woman who stole my life. And this time, I know she's right.

PART I

MARCH

2018

1

CLAIRE

I tack the letter to the fridge with a magnet. A plain white piece of paper, a few paragraphs of black print. I stare at it as the coffee burbles, and it seems to glow with an almost translucent hope. My daughter's hopes – her dreams – embodied in a few lines, a date, and a time.

Three months. The letter makes clear that no alternative date will be available. Such a short time for Jess to prepare everything that will be required: scales, syllabus piece, sight-reading. Such a short time to stay healthy and well, like she's been for the past few months. A short time… and yet, living day-to-day as we do, three months seems like forever.

As I read the words again, my mind leaps to the logistics. We live an hour north of the city, and even getting there for the audition will mean either Steve or me taking off work, which we can't afford. Then what happens if Jess gets in and has rehearsals, and…? I push all the doubts away. I picture the look on her face the day the letter arrived. Remember the way she smiled and hugged me and looked so happy. "Please, Mom! Please say I can do it! This is my big chance!" I hugged her back and whispered in her ear, "I'm so proud of you." Proud of what she's achieved. Proud of what she's survived.

I don't care if the audition is on the moon, the rehearsals on Mars; I will do anything to make sure Jess can fulfill her dreams. *Anything…*

The doorbell rings; my stomach clenches in a knot.

Even this.

I go to the door fingering the charms on my bracelet. I grip the Golden Gate Bridge and take a deep breath, steeling myself. This is just a test and an interview – no big deal. The fact that I'm going to be filmed for potentially thousands of people to see shouldn't make a difference. I glance through the peephole.

A tall blonde woman is standing outside. Despite the heat, she looks cool and collected. I visualize my house through her eyes: a typical eighties two-story box with a thirsty brown lawn, wheelie bins by the garage, a dead geranium by the door, and Becky's bike half-blocking the path. Dave Steiner, the CEO of *MyStory*, told me that they want "suburban"; they want ordinary people whose lives can be transformed by their services. They chose me for the program because they want *normal*. I pointed out that having one daughter who's sick, one who's practically a delinquent, and a marriage that can only optimistically be described as "failing" doesn't exactly qualify as normal in my book. Dave laughed at that and said, "Claire, you're perfect." No one else had said anything like that to me, even joking, in a very long time. How could I say no?

I arrange my face into a smile and open the door. "Hi!" I say, "I'm Claire. Come inside. It's a little cooler."

The woman introduces herself as Ashley, the producer. She looks down at my bracelet as it jingles against my wrist as we shake hands. I usher her into the kitchen and offer her a cup of fresh coffee. "Do you have any green tea?" she asks.

That throws me. She sits serenely at my kitchen table as I ransack cupboards, finally drawing out a squashed box of green tea that's a remnant of one of Becky's phases. I take out a desiccated tea bag, wondering if green tea goes off and, if so, whether it might cause Ashley any lasting damage. I decide probably not, so I heat some water in the microwave. By the time I set the cup in front of her, my heart is racing, and I don't know why.

"Thanks." Ashley's smile looks forced, and I wonder if she's thinking that my home is a little *too* suburban and ordinary, not to mention tired and cluttered, to be part of the program. And never mind the house – what about me? Forty years old. Ten pounds overweight (on a good day). My face prematurely lined, a few streaks of gray in my hair. Suddenly, I feel a crushing weight upon me. I really don't want to do this.

"I… um…"

The audition… Jess…

"Yes?" Ashley doesn't look at me. She opens her purse and takes out a thin white box. Inside are two swabs and a tube.

"Nothing," I say.

She takes out a pair of blue rubber gloves and puts them on slowly, finger by finger. The gloves match her light-blue top, and I wonder if that was deliberate.

"Open your mouth," Ashley says. "I'm going to swab both cheeks."

I open my mouth; she swabs. As the cotton bud makes contact with the inside of my cheek, I think how easy it is – how mundane. The building blocks of who I am, who my children are, and who my ancestors were – all in one little sample of saliva and skin cells.

"This is an exciting moment, isn't it?" She withdraws the swab and places it in the tube.

"Yes." My voice sounds small. I feel like I've survived a particularly painful dental procedure. "Very exciting."

She hands me a form, and I sign my name. With my DNA in that tube, I've officially embarked on my "Genetic Journey", as Dave calls it. I am now adrift on a vast ocean of possibilities and connections. One person in thousands – maybe even millions – who have taken the test. *MyStory* is the third-largest home DNA testing company in the state, and it's gaining market share all the time. Dave has grand ideas: he plans to build a global database that's bigger than Facebook. It is exciting, I guess. But there's also something daunting about being a tiny drop in that unknown sea.

"Now," Ashley says, "I'll take your sample to the lab for V.I.P. analysis. But first, I'll talk you through the rest of the schedule. The crew will move their equipment in today. We'll start filming tomorrow."

She talks. I stare down at the cup of green tea that she hasn't touched. It's getting cold, the snake of steam growing thin. Should I offer to heat it up? I don't know. Why don't I know?

Ashley stands up. I have no idea what she's just said. Have I missed something important? Why didn't she drink the tea?

Suddenly from upstairs, there's a flurry of musical notes. Each one is bright and pure, like a butterfly spreading its wings and taking flight. I feel a visceral sensa-tion of pride and a momentary loosening of the tension in my neck. Jess... my lovely, talented daughter. Most people go on a Genetic Journey to find out about their past. For me, this is all about her future.

Ashley looks at me with something like admiration. "Good luck," she says. "I hope we can help."

"Thanks," I say. "Me too."

I walk her to the door and close it behind her. I sink against it, the lightness of the music in counterpoint to the heavy weight of fear in my heart.

2

The first time I saw the bruises, I thought the worst. I mean, who wouldn't? Jess was eight and a half, and she'd started complaining of being tired at school. Sometimes when she came home, she'd fall asleep during her DVD, which was unheard of. She seemed listless, lacking sparkle, not at all like her usual self. I asked her what was wrong, and she said, "nothing." A niggle began to form in my mind. Was she being bullied? Did she not like her teacher? Was it something I was or wasn't doing?

Steve said it was nothing. School was important; Jess had to learn to toughen up. Steve had recently been promoted to health and safety manager out at the power plant, but there'd been a few lost-time accidents on his watch, and the job was stressing him out. I knew he was struggling, and yet his attitude towards the problem with Jess made me angry. We got in a couple of shouting matches at dinner, which made it worse. Once, when Jess got upset and ran off to her room in tears, I went in a few minutes later and found her sound asleep on her bed.

I took matters into my own hands and called the

school. Made an appointment with the teacher, the principal, the assistant principal. They were patient and calm in the face of my concern. No, Jess wasn't having any problems that they were aware of. Yes, she seemed tired and withdrawn. Was she eating well at home? Taking vitamins? It might just be a phase.

I left that meeting feeling frustrated and relieved in equal measure. I so wanted to believe that they were right. That Steve was right. That Jess herself was right. And then, one day, Steve was working late, Becky was out with her friends, and it was just Jess and me at dinner. I made her favorite macaroni and cheese and watched as she pushed it around on her plate. "What's wrong?" I asked her, frantic underneath.

"I'm just not hungry," she said. "Can I go do my homework?"

It was the end of my rope. I wanted to shout at her, shake her, hug and kiss her, and tell her that whatever was wrong, we could fix it. Instead, I sat back and stared her down. "Jess…" I kept my voice as level as a minefield. "Something is wrong. I want you to tell me what it is."

She gave me a huffy sigh and a well-practiced hair flick learned from her older sister. That was when I saw it. An ugly, purple-gray smudge on the side of her neck.

I jumped up. Swept her hair aside. She tried to stand up and duck away, but I was too quick. I got hold of her arm, and it was only then that I noticed the bruises there too, like an even line of malevolent fingerprints. My world began to swim with darkness. "Who's hurting you?" I whispered. "Is it someone at school? Or… Becky?" I hated myself even for having the thought. "Or…" Any other worse accusations died in my throat. Her dad? No – absolutely not. I could barely hold back the storm of tears and emotions. But this was not about me. I had to be the strong one: the one who could protect her. The one who *should* have protected her.

"God, Mom. Becky would never do that. Jeez." Jess turned away, but I couldn't let it go.

"Then who, sweetheart?" I moved in front of her and took her hands, forcing myself to look at the awful dark splotches on her wrists, each one surrounded by a pattern of tiny red dots.

"No one, OK?" She jumped up and ran out of the kitchen.

I felt like I was starring in a horror movie as I followed her upstairs. Her door slammed shut, the sign on it – "A Princess Lives Here" – juddering from the force. Her door didn't lock, but I didn't barge in. Someone had betrayed her trust very badly, and I needed to coax her back to me.

"Please, honey," I said through the door, "you have to talk about what's happening. That's the only way we can make it stop. It's not… your fault. None of it is your fault."

There was no answer. My heart was beating so hard that I was sure she could hear it. That she could feel the love I was sending her through the door that separated us – through whatever terrible truth separated us. I had to bridge the gap. I opened the door a crack.

Jess was lying in bed on top of the covers. Her eyes were wide open as she stared up at the ceiling. For an awful second, I thought she was dissociating, like victims of childhood trauma learn to do. She was so pale, her skin almost blue except for the dark smudges. When did she get like that? How could I not have noticed?

"Jess?" I said in a hoarse whisper.

"Leave me alone, Mom," she said. A tear rolled down her cheek. That tear was a lifeline. I knew then that I could break through.

"I know you're scared, Jess. But can you tell me what's

been happening? I promise I won't be mad. And that I won't do… anything—" I sucked in a breath "—without your permission."

"Nothing's 'happening'!" She sat up and crossed her arms protectively across her chest. "No one's doing anything to me, if that's what you're worried about."

I looked carefully for any hint of a lie. Would I even know it if I saw it?

Somewhere along the way, I had lost all the joy there was in being a mother. Life was so busy and relentless with work, and Steve's problems, and trying to get Becky to care about her future. Doing laundry, making lunches, worrying about money. Giving hugs and goodnight kisses by rote, living for the moment when the kids were up in their rooms, and I could plunk down on the sofa with a glass of wine and Netflix. Without even realizing it, I'd stopped delighting in every smile, step, and tiny accomplishment of my children. Becky was a drain on my patience, pocketbook, and sanity. Jess was my talented little princess, and I adored the idea of her. Yet, somewhere between nagging her about "fulfilling her potential" on the violin, grilling her over lost ballet shoes, and shouting at her to turn her music down, I had lost my appreciation of her. And now she was hurting. The pain tore me inside, sharp and white-hot.

"I *am* worried about that," I said carefully. "But if you say that no one's hurting you, then I believe it. So does that mean that you're…" I hesitated. She was only eight years old. *Eight. Years. Old.* "Maybe… doing it to yourself?"

She didn't answer right away. I rewound all the information stored away in my brain about self-harming. Becky was the queen of phases – anything destructive that it was possible to do, she'd tried it. Glue-sniffing, shoplifting, bullying, hate-texting. In junior high, she and her friends had experimented with scoring their skin with needles and inking their arms with pens. It only ended when one of the girls got blood poisoning. Following that incident (and five visits to a child psychologist that weren't covered by insurance), Becky moved on to a binge-dieting phase, the sharp objects forgotten.

Now, I tried to remember the cause of self-harm. Low self-esteem, bullying, abuse… all of it kept coming back to a single point. Someone was harming my daughter. And if she was doing it to herself, then someone must be the cause.

The violin. A creeping sense of dread engulfed me. She'd started lessons at age five and showed remarkable aptitude and promise. The teacher had recommended weekly private lessons. Jess performed in monthly recitals, and she loved it. But what if she was only pretending? What if I'd put her in a pressure cooker and this was how she was acting out? What if the *someone* hurting her was me?

I knelt beside her bed and traced the line of her tear. "You can tell me. I won't be mad, I promise. Are you hurting yourself?"

"I… don't know!" Her voice was high and strangled. "I don't know how the bruises got there. I don't know what I did." She put her hand over mine and squeezed my fingers hard enough to hurt. "I'm just so… scared."

Bruises or not, I engulfed her in my arms. Her thin body was racked with sobs. Her shirt rode up above the waistband of her jeans, and I saw bruises there too, each one surrounded by a constellation of red dots. And that's when the terror hit me. If no one was hurting her, and she wasn't hurting herself, then something must be seriously wrong. My baby. My blood flowed in her veins and hers in mine. We were two sides of the same coin – her the shiny bright side full of hope and promise.

Fear coursed through my body; my mind repeated a single thought in an endless loop.

Everything is fine. I must *make sure that everything is fine.*

3

The men are downstairs getting the house ready for the filming. I stay out of their way, wondering fleetingly if I should have warned Steve that his golf clubs are in danger of being "decluttered". Now that it's really happening, I wish they'd take everything away – all the stuff, all the memories – and create a clean, fresh space where we can start again.

Jess is still practicing. I go into the bathroom to listen. I want to go to her: tell her she's wonderful and that I love her more than anything. But I'm already in danger of becoming a smothering parent, overprotective and over-affectionate.

Instead, I focus on how grubby the bathroom is. After enduring Ashley's sainted presence, I see it through new eyes. When we moved into this house, Steve agreed to set aside some money to get rid of the 80s decor. Ten years later, it hasn't happened, and as our medical bills pile up, it probably never will. The floor is carpeted and smells faintly of mold, the walls are painted light green, and there's a wallpaper border above the mirror that's supposed to look like palm leaves but looks more like the gaping maws of a carnivorous plant. The border has started to peel off. I have a strong urge to rip it down: ball it up, throw it in the trash can. I let out a long sigh. When the men are gone, I'll find the glue and tack it back up. Make a temporary fix. Give it a transfusion…

I stare into the bathroom mirror and stick out my tongue. There are ridges on the side where I've bitten it hard enough to draw blood. When I close my mouth, a fine spiderweb of wrinkles takes shape around my lips. I reach up and try to smooth them away, but my bracelet catches in my hair. I manage to untangle it, but not without tearing out a clump of hair that I can hardly afford to lose. Against my sallow skin, the tiny silver charms look as bright and new as they did when they were given to me, one by one, over the years by my dad. I've been thinking a lot about Dad lately, and the bracelet reminds me how much I still miss him – just like I did when he went off on his business trips when I was growing up. I wish he was here now to give me a hug and tell me again that even though he had to go away, he'll always come back.

But he won't be coming back. Death has made a liar out of him.

Maybe it's the *MyStory* project, or maybe it's because this year is the tenth anniversary of his death. It still feels wrong not to be able to pick up the phone and hear his voice and his "Hello, Tiger!" Have him cheer me up when things are going wrong – and things have been going wrong, more or less ever since.

The music has stopped. There's a sudden clunk next door from Jess's room.

"Jess?" I call out. "Are you OK?"

There's no answer. Icy shoots of panic radiate down my spine. I rush out of the bathroom to her room. Even though she's twelve now, she still has the princess sign on her door that she's surely too old for. Every time I see that sign, I feel a mixture of relief and fear. It reminds me that she'll always be my princess: a perfect, healthy little girl in a sparkly blue Elsa dress. But if she got rid of it, then it might signal that she's got a future – that this isn't just a waiting game to the end.

She does have a future. I will make it happen!

I push open the door, half-expecting to see my daughter lying on the floor. My hand gravitates to my phone, ready to call the hospital to get a bed ready. And she is on the floor: she's kneeling in front of her closet, her ponytail bobbing as she ransacks the mess inside.

"Mom, have you seen my Converse?" She half turns to face me. "I can't find them."

My pulse jumps from terror to annoyance to relief in a split second. If it was Becky who couldn't find her shoes, it would have jumped directly to annoyance and stayed there. That probably makes me a bad mother, or at least, a normal one. Right now, I'd give anything to be "normal".

"I haven't seen them. Are they downstairs? The film crew is shifting stuff, so if they're down there you'd better rescue them."

"I'm sure they're here somewhere."

As she goes back to rummaging, I give her a quick once-over. Her skin is pale to the point of being translucent, with a bluish tint from the veins underneath. Her hair is chestnut brown, and she has thick bushy eyebrows, a long thin nose, and a rosebud mouth. She's what you would call a striking child: not cute and not beautiful, but who might one day blossom into something special. *Might* and *one day* being key.

She's wearing a short-sleeved T-shirt with "Mermazing" printed in pink and blue ombre letters. Underneath the fabric in the center of her chest, I can just make out the bump of the central line that is inserted into her vena cava. I want to reach out and pull her into my arms. But I'm also afraid to touch her.

"When did you see them last?" My voice is a masterclass in normality.

"I don't know."

In the old days, I would have been the annoyed, indifferent mom. The kind who would say, *"I told you to look after your things. To be more careful."* But now, I'm the kind of mom who spends her whole life walking on eggshells, running to Jess's room to investigate any noise or long silence, and driving her to hospital appointments so that she can be kept alive on regular transfusions of other people's blood. I need to appreciate every moment – I know that. But how can I, when all I feel is the fear of losing her?

"I'm sorry." I kneel down and help her move things, trying to reach the floor like an archeologist unearthing an ancient tomb. "We can—" *No… I'm not really saying this…* "—maybe get you some new ones. In a different color. Yellow ones would be nice, don't you think?"

"Yellow?"

"Or maybe purple." I'm sounding desperate to please her. Keep your room as messy as you want. Let me buy you some new shoes we can't afford in yellow *and* purple. In every color of the rainbow.

She's staring at me like she can sense that, underneath my calm demeanor, I am a raving lunatic. My helplessness seething below the surface is affecting our entire family. But how can I stop the way I feel?

I stand up, determined to pull myself together. "Or you can just wear your school tennies. Anyway, you'd better get going." This is sounding much better: much more like a normal mom. "I'm not paying for violin lessons if you're going to be late."

Her eye roll lifts my heart. Everything is fine. Everything is going to be—

There's dried blood underneath her nose – she's had a nosebleed. She's supposed to tell me these things. It could mean that her treatment has stopped working, which could lead to bleeding in her other organs or even on the brain. I check the trash can. Sure enough, it's filled with bloody tissues.

My breath shortens. I look at her; our eyes meet in an unspoken accord.

"Come on, Mom." Her voice is quiet but full of desperation. "I need to go to my lesson. It's… important."

"No. We need to get you checked out."

"Please, Mom. We can go afterward. I promise."

In the balance of our lives, I should be grateful that she's old enough to negotiate on her own behalf. An hour more or less – it could be the difference between making my daughter happy and having her be miserable. It could also, in the worst-case scenario, be the difference between life and death. Could I live with myself if I make the wrong decision?

"Fine. We'll go after your lesson."

"Thanks!" Her smile alone makes the bad decision worth it. "I'll get ready."

I bend down and give her a fragile kiss on the cheek. "I love you."

I leave the room and close the door. The princess sign clacks against the wood. I chalk one up for me and hate myself for doing it. I never got to say goodbye to Dad, and I'll regret that forever. But although I may make lots of other mistakes, I'm determined not to make that one again. Right now, my daughter knows that I love her. Right now, that's all that matters.

4

"If you're lucky, it will be cancer."

Each time I enter the hospital, I think of the doctor's words on that long-ago first visit, and I want to laugh – or cry. Sometimes it's hard to know which.

Jess walks beside me through the doors, her steps slow and heavy. After her lesson, I took her for ice cream and a burger. She wasn't hungry, and I ended up eating both her lunch and my own. The hospital is crowded with all walks of life. A depressing place, a hopeful place. Jess and I barely notice anymore. We both know the drill.

We proceed through the labyrinth of corridors to Hematology. I greet the nurse at reception like we're old friends. In the last few years, we've been here dozens of times, maybe even hundreds. We're definitely old somethings...

"Mom, I won't have to have a biopsy today, will I?"

"No."

Sometimes I wish I was a doctor. I wish I had the knowledge to cure my little girl, or at least reassure her that she won't have to have this horrible treatment or that one.

I'm her mom – I should be in control of the situation. But ever since the day I saw that first bruise, I have been in control of exactly nothing.

"Do you promise?"

"Yes." It's easier to lie.

Because we don't have an appointment, we have to wait. Jess reads a book on her iPad. I fiddle with my phone, but I can't concentrate on anything. I wonder if it's something I did in another life or earlier in this one that has landed me here again.

Following the incident with the bruising, Jess was diagnosed with Severe Aplastic Anemia. The diagnosis came after a battery of tests that left her even more bruised, exhausted, and in pain. The first time I saw her lying in a hospital bed with the flaccid bag of platelets that looked like chicken broth hanging next to her, I felt an uncontrollable surge of rage. I wanted to rip the tubes from her body and strangle someone. This was cruel; this was *wrong*. This really could not be happening.

But when I heard the diagnosis, my heart lifted a little. *Anemia* – that didn't sound too bad. I could give her iron supplements, stick spinach in her sandwich. Whatever it was, we would knock it on the head for good.

Unfortunately, I learned that her disease was much more serious than "just anemia". Her body did not produce enough blood cells. Those that it did produce were weak and of poor quality. At any time, she could get an infection or a virus and be too weak to fight it. I listened with my teeth clenched as the doctor spouted out gibberish in a calm and even voice, punctuated only by words such as "persistent" and "life-threatening". I could sense the tension and anger boiling inside Steve as he got in the doctor's face and said, "So what are you going to *do* about it?"

"She'll get a blood transfusion today," the doctor said. His frown was unreadable as he stood his ground and scribbled something on his clipboard. "And then, we'll have to wait and see. Take it day by day."

Day by day. My life started over from that moment. Gone were the usual moans and complaints about the mess in the house, the broken garage door, the neighbors' dog, and whose turn it was to take out the garbage. Enter a brave new world of just surviving. Trying to make sense of how things could have gone so wrong so quickly. Giving up trying to make sense of it all in favor of just getting through. Sleepless nights in a cold sweat of fear. Endless hours at the hospital, conversations with doctors, and second opinions. Arguments with my husband, calls with insurance companies, calls with the school. Getting behind with bills, getting behind with deadlines, getting behind with "just getting through".

My research demystified the doctor's comment on that long-ago first visit. Blood cancer – leukemia – is a terrible disease, but a more common one, and often a more treatable one. Jess's condition is rare, and although I did find a number of online communities and read and reread every heartfelt comment left by other suffering parents, I felt increasingly alone in the fight against this thing that I did not understand.

The doctor started Jess on a program of regular transfusions, blood tests, and medications. They inserted a central line into her chest to facilitate the treatments. From the start, she hated that line and got into a bad habit of scratching it until the skin got red and inflamed. The medications made her nauseous and dizzy and gave her headaches and a racing pulse. They turned my already skinny, pale girl into a wraith. Worse, they didn't work long term. Jess relapsed, and the next treatment that they tried was rabbit serum ATG. That treatment almost killed her. Sometimes, even now, I think that it's all a nightmare and I'm going to wake up. Four years on, I'm still waiting for that to happen.

"Jessica Woods," a nurse calls out. A reminder that it's all too real.

Jess's whole body slumps as she enters the consulting room. I believe she has a sixth sense; she knows what's coming. Unfortunately, so do I.

The nurse takes Jess's blood. Then we have to wait over an hour for the analysis. I make small talk, but Jess doesn't respond. I offer to let her play a game on my phone, but she refuses, staring instead at the poster of the human circulatory system on the wall.

Eventually, the doctor comes in wearing scrubs and a surgical mask. A nurse comes in with a rolling tray.

"No," Jess says before he's even said hello. She looks at me accusingly. "You promised."

"Come on, honey," I say. "You know we've all got your best interests at heart."

"No – you don't!"

It kills me that these words are coming out of her mouth. Jess is usually so positive, so "can do" about all of it – on the surface, at least. I also try to stay positive for her sake, keeping my persistent anguish under wraps. Both of us are very good at pretending – most of the time. But when the doctor confirms our worst fears – her numbers are dangerously low, she's in relapse, and they want to do another bone marrow biopsy – she starts to shake violently. I step in front of her like a human shield.

"No," I say.

The doctor eyes me askance. He proceeds to talk the talk, telling us that it's necessary to determine the next course of treatment.

"Maybe another day…" I stammer.

"No, Mom," Jess says. There's defiance in her voice – the only power she has against her illness. "Let's get it over with." My daughter won't look at me, but she stares the nurse with the huge needle dead in the face.

How long can we go on like this? The question claws at my mind. *Why can't she be cured?*

There's one simple reason. A bone marrow transplant is the only cure. But no one in the family is a match. I – her own mother – am not a match. Steve is not a match, nor is Becky, nor any of Steve's relatives. I coerced friends into being tested. No match. Jess was signed up for the registry where surely a match could be found. Surely! I'd read that for a person of white European ancestry, there was almost a 90% chance of finding a match. We were average people – the kind who would fall into a 90% category of almost anything. The test involved something called HLA markers. A perfect match required a minimum of six. Only six! How hard could it be?

"How hard can it be?" I asked the doctor that first time, feeling a little bit smug. This, too, sounded simple, easy. Jess would have a bone marrow transplant, and she would get better. End of story.

"Well…" The doctor had paused: that awful – evil – pause. "Have you researched your family tree? Do you have any non-European DNA?"

"What kind of question is that?" I had railed. "I mean, I don't know. Dad used to brag about being part Native American and part Eskimo; I thought it was just talk."

I watched him note down the words "mixed race?"

He went on to explain that the 90% statistic I'd been hanging my hat on actually was much lower for people with mixed ancestry. I just stared at him. "What are you saying?"

"There's no match for Jess on the registry. I'm very sorry."

"So…" The word hung out there like a body swinging from a pillory.

"So, more people are being added all the time. We certainly won't give up hope yet. But for now, it will be a waiting game. And if you have any more close relatives that we can test, then all the better."

"There's no one else." I'd stumbled out of the room. I missed Dad and his moral support. But I also felt angry with him. Was all that stuff about being part Eskimo and part Cherokee actually true? Was that why there was no match for Jess on the registry? I'd loved Dad so much, but I knew very little about him. If I'd asked more questions, would it have made a difference? It was stupid and point-less to blame him – or myself – but I had to put the blame somewhere.

It's been four years. There's still no match. We're still living day-by-day; we still have to *wait and see*—

The nurse rubs local anesthetic on Jess's lower back. As her gown gapes open, I can see each and every vertebra like a rare fossil in a museum. I try to take her hand, but she closes her fist.

"You OK?" The nurse prods Jess's back. "Everything asleep back there?"

Jess nods. Her eyes glaze over. The doctor moves in with the needle. It will travel through layers of skin and muscle and veins and tissues that I don't know the name of. He bends down. He is quick and accurate. The needle penetrates bone.

Jess screams.

5

The last thing I need is a film crew appearing on my doorstep. I've spent a fitful night dreaming of six-inch needles penetrating bone, sucking the contents into a syringe. My daughter in agonizing pain. A nightmare turned real.

After the biopsy, they sent us home with a new medication to "try". It made Jess groggy and nauseous, and I had to give her another medication for that. This morning, her back will be sore, and she won't be going to school. I should be there by her side – at her beck and call all day – even though she won't want that.

Instead, I need to be on top of my game.

They arrive just after eight-thirty. It's a small mercy that Steve and Becky are both gone by then. Steve is against the whole idea and thinks I'm living in cloud cuckoo land. Becky is Becky – if she was here, something would get broken or lost or posted on social media.

When the doorbell rings, I feel a flip of nerves, but also an unexpected something else – a tiny flash of pride. I'm a hassled, broke, suburban mom with a kid who's trouble, a kid who's sick, and a "barely there" husband. And yet, a film crew is here to interview *me*.

Answering the door is like opening the gates to a Trojan horse. Ashley comes inside, along with two cameramen, an assistant, and the assistant's assistant. I offer everyone tea or coffee, but by then, a table is set up in my living room with a spread of drinks, cookies, and snacks.

I'm corralled by a woman named Charlie who is in charge of doing my hair and make-up. I haven't been to a hairdresser in months, so she has her work cut out for her. While she's working her magic, Ashley tells me about the host of the show: a woman named Stella who will be conducting the on-screen interview. They want me to talk about my family and what I hope to gain from the process, or, in her words: "How exciting it is for you to be going on this journey!"

What I actually feel is more akin to panic. I wish that Dave Steiner was here to reassure me that I'm doing the right thing and that I've every reason to feel hopeful. But when I ask Ashley if he'll be coming over later, she tells me that he's in Washington, D.C. Instantly, I think of Dad – he was a salesman and spent a lot of time in Washington for work. I know that Dave isn't my dad – not even close. Still, I can't stop wondering what he's doing there. I can't stop the prickly feeling at the back of my neck like history is repeating itself.

Ashley frowns, seeming to have read my mind. "Don't worry, Claire," she says. "It will all be fine. Just be yourself. Have fun."

I have no idea how to do that. Maybe I used to be a fun person – I don't know. Once upon a time, in the dim and distant past – before marriages and mortgages, report cards and blood transfusions. Maybe in another lifetime.

"Time for eyeliner," Charlie says. "Look up."

My eyes start to water. Maybe it's the brush tickling my lower lid. Or maybe it's tears – I don't know anymore.

I first met Dave Steiner at the place where I've met most of my recent friends and acquaintances: the hospital. I'd just spent two hours at Jess's bedside holding her frail little hand until she fell asleep after her final dose of ATG. The treatment had initially put her into convulsions, and at one point, she'd actually flatlined for a few seconds. Though she survived all the doses in the end, every nerve in my body was a casualty. Steve arrived to take over, and I'd stumbled down to the coffee shop. I didn't even get as far as the counter. Instead, I collapsed at a table. All I could do was stare out the window at the cars in the parking lot and the people coming and going.

"You look like you need some coffee, and quick." A voice pulled me back from the brink.

He had one of *those* faces. The kind who might be a movie star or might be someone you've met at the school-yard gates. Maybe you've known him all your life, or maybe it's a chance meeting across a crowded room. Maybe a cheesy song will start playing, or maybe he's talking to somebody over your shoulder. In any case, I stopped staring out the window and stared at him instead. For a fleeting second, I wondered if I was seeing a reincarnated version of Dad. The man smiled. He had ridiculously nice teeth.

"I'm… sorry," I said. "What?"

"God, it's bad, then. What will be it be? Black coffee? A latte? Or… hmm… how about some hot chocolate?"

"Hot chocolate?" It came out as a question, which he took for an answer. The next thing I knew, he had conjured up a hot chocolate in a tall glass with whipped cream and sprinkles on top. It looked ridiculous: like something I would have ordered as a kid when we went to the ice-cream parlor. It looked delicious.

As I sipped the drink and its sweetness took effect, we exchanged introductions. His name was Dave, and it turned out that he lived only about ten minutes away from me but on the nicer side of town. His son, Jason, had broken his ankle playing soccer. It was a respectable, even boast-worthy injury. In contrast, having a daughter with a rare illness seemed grubby and unlucky, and I expected Dave to give the usual platitudes and be swiftly on his way. Instead, he stayed. He seemed genuinely interested in the illness and its treatment. Taking advantage of a sympathetic listener, I told him the whole story. He stopped me periodically to ask questions and was particularly interested in the HLA markers.

It was only after I'd told him about the registry and the fact that no match had been found for Jess that I began to wonder why he was so interested.

"Are you a doctor?" I asked him.

His eyes grew a little steely. "Not exactly. But something like that."

That put me on my guard. Years spent working as a freelance investigative journalist tend to do that. But as he started to tell me who he was and what his company did, I immediately felt a breathless excitement.

"Home DNA testing? Could that be used to find a bone marrow match for Jess?"

A drowning woman, reaching for a hand… Could this be the lifeline I'd been looking for?

"Well… it's a little more complicated than that. I don't want to promise anything I can't deliver. But I might be able to help."

Help. The tiny word meant everything. Just the fact that he was offering to help gave me more hope than I'd had in a long time. In one of our many fights, Steve told me that I'm jealous with my pain. It's what I have of my daughter, and I don't want to share it with anyone. I told him that he was full of it and that he had no idea how I felt. I didn't want to admit that he was probably right. But for some reason, I was willing to share it with Dave: to grasp the hand he was offering to pull me out of the quicksand. Dave went away and had some internal discussions with his people. The standard kit didn't test for HLA markers, but it would flag up potential relatives who shared a common ancestry. Long-lost relatives who might become new-found ones. And if any of them agreed to undergo additional testing, then maybe we'd come up trumps.

It wasn't exactly the silver bullet I was hoping for. But after meeting up for coffee a few more times, I got to know Dave better, and what's more, I got to trust him. In the end, I agreed to go on the *MyStory* program and be tested along with the other participants. They would interview me about Jess's condition, I would be paid to take part, and I would be allowed to write a series of articles about my experience. It seemed like a win-win situation all around. It *is* a win-win situation…

I just wish Dave was here to remind me of that.

As Charlie continues with my make-up, I wonder if I should just call the whole thing off. But that would be irrational and destructive – not something I can afford right now. Of course, I was hoping to see Dave, but he's hardly the reason I'm doing this.

Charlie finishes my eyes and brushes lipstick on my lips, dabbing it with a tissue. "OK, we're good to go." She holds up a mirror.

I stare at my reflection. The woman I see is unfamiliar. Not the one with the dark circles under her eyes who gets up five times a night to check that her youngest daughter is alive and breathing. Not the one who last got dressed up and had sex with her husband two years ago when he got drunk on his fortieth birthday. Not the one who dreads every call from her eldest daughter, fearing it might be her "one call" after she's been arrested for something. It's the woman I might have been if my life had been different. A woman who's going on a journey to find out the secrets of her ancestry; a woman who's going to make sure that her daughter gets to grow up, fall in love, have a family of her own, and follow her dreams. A woman that I get to be for the next hour or two.

I guess I can live with that.

6

MARIANNE

I feel nothing.

Nothing.

I can't allow myself to feel anything; I'm not going to allow it.

I'm not... under any circumstances going to...

The sob rises up inside me as I throw the bloody paper into the toilet and toss the useless plastic stick in the trash can. I'd like to say that my tears are those of relief. Relief that I've reached the end of the road, the end of an era. There will be no more injections, no more pills, no more awkward conversations with Tom. No more fighting against the implantation of hope and no more agony as hope slips away.

Life has judged me. This is the result.

I tear off exactly six squares of toilet paper and fold them neatly as the sobs rack my body, tears roll down my cheeks, and my nose begins to drip. I let them rack, roll, and drip. My tears are not those of relief. They are tears of pain, deep as the scars of a glacier. They are tears of wanting to hang on and keep up the fight. Tears of knowing that it's time to let go.

The words to a poem I wrote when the first embryo – Baby No. 1 – implanted, wrestle their way into my mind.

Spring has blossomed; the cherries are snowing white.
My heart is full of love, my body with new life.
I am walking on air, all of my dreams unfurled.
Counting the days 'til you arrive in the world.

When I'd showed it to Tom, he'd told me not to quit the day job (where I had a great maternity package). But I could tell that he was proud of me. I can still remember the feel of his breath against my belly as he'd whispered to the baby, "Daddy can't wait to meet you." He'd looked up at me with love shining in his eyes. I remember… and it hurts.

I use the six squares one by one. Nose, eyes, nose again. Then I throw the paper in the toilet and flush everything away. The water flows and gurgles. The bathroom is all shiny white and polished stainless steel. The cleaner is charged by Tom to keep it spotless and sparkling like the bathroom of a five-star hotel. In one corner, there is a large jacuzzi bathtub with a separate glass-walled shower and wet room. We had the bathroom redone after losing Baby No. 2. I'd been in a haze of sorrow at the time, or else I might have chosen to have a splash of color somewhere – a wall of blue glass tiles, maybe. The white seems cold, almost shockingly so. It reminds me of death.

The water stops flowing, and I reassemble my clothes. I've got a meeting for a round-two financing of an up-and-coming genetics company, and I need to make a good impression. I go to the sink, where my make-up bag is open on the counter. I stare at my reflection in the mirror. I'm tall, with long dark hair that is currently swept back in a French twist. I'm wearing a red suit from Saks, and when I get into the office, I'll change from my tennis shoes into my black Jimmy Choos. I dab concealer under my eyes and apply a new swoosh of eyeliner and a second coat of waterproof mascara. I put on lipstick in a red-brown shade called Mojave and pout my lips together. My looks and designer clothes are my armor against the world: my high siege walls that hide the mess inside. No one can see the rot and the death, the blood or the guilt.

I practice my smile until it becomes a mask that I can put on and off. Then, I turn away from the mirror. I should go out and face the music: face Tom. I should break the bad news to him and then get the 7:35 Metro. We'll wait on the platform together, and he'll hold my hand and rub my back. He'll lie to me: tell me that everything will be fine. After what we've been through, it's just easier that way.

I stay in the bathroom. Tom calls up, "Bye – see you later." The front door slams. I need to hurry: go downstairs, eat something, fill my travel mug with coffee. If I miss the 7:50, I'll be late for my meeting.

But when I go out into the hall, I am magnetically drawn to the closed door opposite the bathroom. My mother says that doors should remain closed to keep in the heat, or the cool, depending on the season. She was always big on doing those sorts of things right. I go to the door and put my hand on the knob, feeling a little like a child reaching out to touch a hot stove. This is stupid. I don't want to go into this room – ever – let alone now.

I go inside. The room is painted light green with a beige carpet. Sunlight streams in through the twin sash windows. There is a brass bed with a white matelassé bedspread and fluffy pillows. The room is one of four other empty bedrooms on this floor. When we first moved in, Tom and I used to laugh about the size of the house and about how we had so many guest rooms and hardly ever any guests. Then, we'd laughed about how we'd fill them all with children – so many that we'd have to convert the two rooms up in the attic to make more space. Then, we'd made love in all of the bedrooms, one by one, to try and make those children.

I chose this room to be the nursery. It has beautiful light and a leafy maple tree outside the window. Those first few months of the pregnancy were the best of my entire life. I scoured websites and stores for the best of the best. State-of-the-art strollers, antique cribs, the finest cashmere baby sleepsuits, wooden educational toys, organic cotton diapers. A designer maternity wardrobe for me, of course – nothing was too luxurious or extravagant. I tried to hold off buying too many baby clothes – Tom was adamant that he didn't want to know whether the baby would be a boy or a girl. But I was unable to resist. There were just so many lovely things: frilly dresses, sweet little overalls, Easter bonnets, tiny rainboots. Tom started to get a little worried, and my mother warned that I shouldn't count my chickens before they'd hatched. But I was so *in love* with that tiny life growing inside of me. I wanted to give it the perfect life. I checked off the weeks one by one. I knew precisely when the embryo went from being the size of a pea to that of a Brussel Sprout, the size of a turnip to that of a head of cabbage. (Tom and I found it uproariously funny how the books compared the growing baby to a different vegetable.) Week twenty-one; twenty-two; twenty-three...

Week twenty-four dawned bright and clear, crisp and autumnal. It was just after Thanksgiving. I went into work as usual and ducked out at lunchtime to browse the Black Friday sales. I found the most darling little baby snuggle blanket with the head of a squeaky elephant in impossibly soft fabric. I took it up to the register and paid for it. I felt a little twinge in my stomach like the Caesar salad I'd eaten might have been off. The clerk handed me the bag. I turned to leave. Then, there was a shooting pain between my legs and an embarrassing gush of blood. I tried to stagger out of the store, but I didn't make it.

When I woke up in the hospital, I felt so light that I could almost float away in my emptiness. The life inside of me was gone. I panicked – of course – but it was panic tempered by the knowledge that I was twenty-four weeks. Modern science was a wonderful thing. I had the best private health care money could buy, and my baby would be fine. It had to be. I simply would not accept anything else.

I couldn't move because I *hurt*. A half-remembered pain. Still, I looked around for the bassinet with a sleeping baby inside. I looked around for Tom, or my mother, or a nurse, or anyone.

I was alone. So deeply and desperately alone.

Baby No. 1 never even had a chance. The cord had got wrapped around his – for it turned out to be a boy's – neck. Instead of nurturing him, my body had suffocated him. Tom named him Adam, but in my mind, he didn't have a name. We buried him in the cemetery next to my maternal grandmother. My guilt has been suffocating me ever since.

I go to the closet and open it. Mercifully, most of the baby things I bought eventually found their way out to the garage. Now, the closet organizer is used to store extra towels and linen. I open up the top drawer. Buried at the back is the little elephant blanket. I fish it out and hold it to my face. It no longer smells brand new. It smells of nothing at all. The plush fabric, though, is still soft and absorbent. I use it to wipe away my tears for the embryo I've just lost: Baby No. 8, and all the ones that came before. The miracle sparks of life that my soul wanted to embrace, but my body has rejected. "I love you," I whisper. And then, I put it back again.

I go out of the room, pulling the door shut behind me. Calmly, I walk downstairs to the kitchen. I eat two bites of blueberry bagel that taste like cardboard and leave money for the cleaner on the table. In the hall, I look in the gilded mirror and reapply my lipstick. I must *never* allow the cracks to show. I put on my coat, pick up my briefcase, and head out into the cold morning air of early March. The buds are on the trees. Soon there will be a shower of cherry blossoms. New life, new hope, new babies.

But not for me.

Never for me.

7

I wait on the platform for the Metro. It isn't a long ride, but the train is always crowded, and it is a struggle to jostle for a seat. Today I don't feel like jostling, so I hang back out of the way of flailing elbows. My phone pings with a text message: *Everything OK? Mom.* I stare at the words as people push their way onto the train around me. It's as if my mother has telepathically read my thoughts and is sending a gentle prod through the ether that I need to continue with my day. Don't make things worse by doing something messy, like jumping in front of a train. Not that I would. My mother hates mess above all else, and as a result, so do I.

Fertility treatment is messy. Physically and emotionally. My mother knows about it, of course. Not long after Tom and I got married, *her* biological clock went haywire. She decided that it was high time that she had a grandchild. So she began a campaign of gentle haranguing: "a baby would make your life *perfect*"; and "I'm so proud that you've made all the right decisions in life. And now, you can have it *all.*" The chorus reached a fever pitch just after I was grieving over the loss of Baby No. 1. I had to tell her about the treatment just to silence her or else risk losing my mind. In her own way, she was sympathetic: to the injections, the cramping, the interminable two-week waiting period after embryo transfer, and ultimately, to the big fat negative results that are all I've achieved in the last few cycles. She's still sympathetic. But her words continue to ring inside my head. *"I know you'll do whatever it takes."*

To avoid answering the text, I get onto the train just as the doors are about to close. I try to elbow my way to a seat, but I don't manage it. Instead, I stand at the center of the car with my briefcase wedged between my legs. I grab hold of one of the ceiling straps and brace and jolt against the motion of the train with the others who are unlucky enough to be standing. In my direct line of sight, a woman sitting near the door gives up her seat to another woman with a huge pregnant belly. There is much gratitude on the part of the pregnant woman. The other woman reassures her that, "It's no problem. I've been there – I know how it is."

I turn away. The world divides itself into two halves: yin and yang, black and white. People with children and people without. People who will replace themselves and people who won't. People who will have loved ones to cry at their funeral and put flowers on their grave and people who won't. People who deserve to have these things and people who don't.

A man sitting nearby has to add his two cents. "Enjoy sitting down while you can," he says to the woman. "Because take it from me: once you've got a baby, you'll be run off your feet."

"I know!" the pregnant woman says. "This is my second. I can't believe I'm in for round two."

"Well, two is a good number," the man says. "That's what I've got – one of each."

"Ha, I've got four," someone else pipes in. "Oldest one is off to college."

"Lucky you."

I clench the strap, white-knuckled. Who knew that people on the Metro could be so friendly? So full of bonhomie? I look around, frantic for an ally of some kind: maybe a scary teenage hoodie or an old person. But no one else seems disturbed by the conversation.

"Yeah, studying law at GW…"

"Mount Vernon Preschool? – Seriously, you'd better call now to get on the waiting list—"

I can't take it anymore. I push my way down the aisle towards the far door so I can escape. The train stops again. Miraculously, a seat is vacated. I manage to scramble over to it. I sink down onto the dirty upholstery and put my briefcase on my lap. Small mercies.

But before the doors close, another pregnant woman gets on the train. At this end of the car, everyone is staring at their phones. No one seems to notice her. Her eyes meet mine, pleading. I feel a crawling animosity, a creeping envy. I should look away, check my emails – I've got a lot of work I could be doing. There are plenty of men around or other women who have "been there" and could give up their seats.

A man across from me looks up. Notices. Shifts. I practically leap to my feet. "Here," I say to the woman. "Please – take my seat."

The woman's hands go reflexively to her belly. "God bless you." She sits down, serene and smiling.

I claw my fingers into the handhold. I want to shout at her that God hasn't blessed me. Tell her that I want what she has but that I'll never be able to convince my husband to keep trying. Can I convince him? Should I keep trying? Am I giving up too easily? Tom and I *agreed* on eight rounds, and then we'd let it go.

But I can't let it go. I don't want to let it go. I'm a problem solver. There must be another way.

I smile back at the woman. "Thank you," I say. "You too."

8

Upon my arrival at the office, things do not improve. Thanks to a road closure, my taxi from the station got stalled in traffic, and I only have a few minutes to spare before my meeting. As I'm walking into the building, I realize that I've forgotten my key card and have to fill out a form at reception to get another. In the elevator, I get another text from my mother:

Hope everything is great. I've got a really good feeling about this time!

I feel like pressing the emergency stop button and going postal on the other three people in the elevator. Instead, I stab at the screen to delete my mother's text. The needy daughter in me wants to believe that she's genuinely concerned, but my cynical side suspects that this is just another way to make sure she stays in the driver's seat. My mother always has everything under control – something that I admire, envy, and resent in equal part. The only thing that ever happened to her that she couldn't control was my father dying. A decade later, she still resents that, I think. Still, for all of her lack of faults, she's my mother, and I love her. I *will* call her later, but for now, I have only one objective. I need to get through the meeting without anyone noticing that I'm off my game.

When the door pings open, I go immediately to my office. My secretary is standing in the doorway, looking concerned. "James has already gone into the meeting," she says. "Alan and Todd are sitting in too. The clients got here early, and they're chomping at the bit to get started."

Of course, they are. James Reiner is the firm's managing partner and my boss, and Alan and Todd are senior associates who are nipping at my heels to become Of Counsel. I hang up my coat and quickly change into my Jimmy Choos. The fact that I still care, even a little bit, what I look like must be how the human race has survived over the millennia. Today, my dreams of having a baby have died a final little death. I can never be the woman who has it all. In the past, Tom and I have had arguments over whether I should cut back at work, "take it easy", "put my feet up". I never did because I get a buzz from success. Usually. Some sports coach or other said that the league isn't won on the days you play well, but on the days you play badly and still triumph. I'm about to either prove or disprove that theory right now.

I hurry through the sea of open-plan PA desks clutching my briefcase. A set of stairs with a shiny chrome rail and glass balustrade spirals down to the conference room on the mezzanine level, and at the bottom of the stairs, there's a big window with views out to the Mall, the Washington Monument, and the Capitol. The whole thing looks very upscale and modern, the way a top boutique law office ought to.

All eyes are on me as I enter the conference room. I'm used to being the only woman in a roomful of men, and I'm not late, but I don't like the fact that everyone else is there before me. I know what some of them – the ones who don't know me – will be thinking. "She's late because she had to do the school run," or "her kid is sick, and she had to find a babysitter." Or, "she's just failed her last cycle of IVF."

But I must not let that affect me. This is a challenge, and I will rise to it. I take the only seat left around the long walnut table, below the projection screen that's already displaying the first slide of a PowerPoint presentation.

James cocks an eyebrow as I take my seat. "Sorry I'm late," I feel I need to say.

"Oh, you're not, don't worry. We're early."

I turn my head as a man addresses me from the middle of the table. I recognize him from the due diligence I've conducted on the company. Dave Steiner, founder, visionary, and 51% shareholder of *MyStory LLC*. He's in his late forties or early fifties, with sandy blond hair that's graying around the temples and a tanned, friendly face just a shade off handsome.

I introduce myself, but he seems to know who I am. He comes around to where I'm sitting and shakes my hand with a firm grip before introducing the others on his team. There's Fredrik Anderson – the money man – and three analysts whose names I don't catch. I make some small talk, asking Mr. Steiner about his flight. I find myself drawn into his deep brown eyes that seem to sparkle with amusement and intelligence. He's appraising me, and I'm appraising him. His half-smile gives nothing away.

We begin the pre-meeting. The commercial people go over the objectives for the financing and the valuation models. When I sneak a glance at Dave Steiner, I get the sense that he's a little out of place – like a mad scientist who is most comfortable in his laboratory but has to go through the motions of wooing banks and investors. A part of me likes that about him. But when he catches me looking at him and smiles, I look away.

As the bankers arrive and the finance people start to talk shop, Dave Steiner makes his move. He clears his throat, stands up, and goes up to the laptop that's projecting onto the screen. He clicks on a soft-focus slide showing a birthday gathering with multiple generations of a smiling, happy family. The caption reads: *MyStory – take a Genetic Journey today!*

Mr. Steiner turns to address the assembled throng. "Now that we're all here," he says, "I'd like to take a step back. You've all had a chance to study the numbers, and I'm sure that you'll have a lot of questions for us. But first, I want to make sure that you have a really good idea who we are and what we're about."

There's some uncomfortable shifting of backsides in chairs. Maybe Mr. Steiner didn't get the memo, but for the investors, it's only about the numbers.

"Because yes, we're looking for financing – that's why we're here. But with a business like ours, the prospects go far beyond the numbers. At *MyStory*, we are passionate about history and ancestry. We're providing a useful and valuable service to people. We're changing lives."

James gives me a look. Just about all of us around the table could rewrite the script for him: "The numbers aren't sound, but please invest in me because I'm a good guy." Or – "I've got a vision: of numbers written with my finger in the air." Maybe Mr. Steiner doesn't know how many people just like him there are out there and how many private equity investments ultimately fall through. Or maybe he doesn't care.

"I'm going to tell you a little secret," he says. "I want to create something big. A global network that's bigger than Facebook. Bigger than Twitter. A worldwide network of human relationships and connections." He pauses to let that sink in. "One of the limitations to the industry is getting everybody to take the test and onto the database. So we've got a unique business model to bust those constraints."

He looks at each person in turn. "We want everyone to be able to research their ancestry and find out where they came from. Everyone – not just people rich enough to gift a kit or two at Christmas. That's how we're different. We've been circulating the kits for free at universities and hospitals – get people to take the test. Then, if they want their results, they can log in to the website and pay for access to the database. The response so far has been phenomenal."

I am not a person easily swayed by a sales pitch. And yet, as Dave continues to speak, I sense an odd current in the room, as if everyone is being pulled in his direction by a strange magnetism. He could probably sell ice to an Eskimo – that's the kind of energy he's projecting. I want to be immune, but his manner is, admittedly, infectious.

"And just to make sure you understand exactly what our product is, we're going to do a little demonstration."

His assistant begins distributing little white boxes that gradually get passed down to my end of the table. Each box is sealed with a *MyStory* logo sticker. Despite the free-bies that end up bandied about the office, I always feel a little excited about opening a box with something unknown inside. A vestige of all those Christmases when my father wasn't around, but he'd sent a "special" – read, expensive – present from wherever in the world he happened to be at the time. When I think back on my mother's perfect life, with her nice colonial-style house in one of the best neigh-borhoods of Alexandria, I wonder how many of her friends knew how often my father was away on business.

Maybe the jewelry, the gifts, and the "reunions" were enough for her, I don't know. We never really talk about him. But I still feel that same flicker of curiosity as I did when I was a little girl, wondering what's in the box.

As the last box is passed out, I force all of my woes from my mind. Dave Steiner is standing only about two feet from me, and I can smell his aftershave. He's got his own white box, and he pops the sticker open with his thumbnail. "OK," he says, "get ready to do the honors."

There's a general popping of stickers and shuffle of box lids. I open the box. Inside are two long test tubes, two swabs, a form, and a padded envelope. My curiosity is replaced by a vague nausea. I've had my fill of tubes and medical forms. The fact that I've got to deal with this today of all days just seems cruel.

"Now, each and every one of you is going to get involved. Become a part of this. You may think you know who you are and where you come from. But I wonder—" he pauses for effect "—do you really?"

He sweeps his hand around the room and stops on Todd. "You, young man: do you know where your ancestors come from?"

It's kind of a bold move. Todd wears a yarmulke, so there's no prize for guessing that he's Jewish. Nor does one need to be a modern historian to know that asking Todd about his ancestors might lead to an uncomfortable answer. Dave Steiner, however, seems unfazed.

"My dad grew up in Israel." Todd's voice sounds thin and reedy after Dave's impassioned oratory. "And my mom's from New Jersey."

"Israel. New Jersey." Dave smiles gleefully. "Almost exactly where my relatives hail from. My mom's from Ohio. And my grandmother went to Israel after the war. She survived Theresienstadt."

There's more restless shuffling in chairs. A few people look interested. James, though, who hails from German stock in Wisconsin, is beginning to look decidedly uncomfortable.

"I could tell you her entire history," Dave continues. "Growing up in Bohemia, her parents were both teachers, and they perished in the war. I can tell you where their ancestors came from, and in fact, I can trace a genetic link all the way back to a burial site in Siberia that's been dated back to the year 33 AD. That's almost two thousand years."

I try to take this in, but to me, the man is more interesting than the cause. He's managed to hijack a dry-as-dust meeting for his own purposes. He's managed to ruffle James, and Todd appears to be hanging on to his every word.

"And that's just on my grandmother's side." Dave seems to sense the need to move on. "Let me just sum up by saying that it has been an absolutely *fascinating* and rewarding journey. And all of you can experience it too – courtesy of *MyStory LLC*."

He removes one of the swabs from the box and holds it up. "Now, please take out your first swab. I'm going to show you how easy it is."

Like a group of lemmings about to follow their leader off a cliff, we all remove our swabs from the protective packaging. There are a few whispers and a short laugh from someone down the table, but for the most part, there's nothing but rustling.

"And now, here goes nothing…"

Dave swabs his right cheek. We all swab our right cheek. Then, following Dave's lead, we all use the other swab to do our left cheeks. As I'm swabbing, Dave looks right at me. It feels oddly intimate, and I'm furious with myself for blushing.

"Good," Dave says like we've just mastered brain surgery. "Now, pop each sample in the tube and sign on the dotted line. My assistant will do the rest."

Part of me is expecting a big reveal. For someone in the know to stand up, clap his hands, and declare that this is all some kind of big joke. There will be talking and laughing and coffees all around, and then we'll begrudgingly get back to the numbers, all of us secretly thinking that Dave Steiner is quite the "Greatest Showman" and drawing our own conclusions as to whether that makes him more or less investable. When I look at him next, he'll be just another man in a suit, the bubble of charisma burst as if it had never existed at all.

The other people around the table sign their forms and seal their boxes. There's no big reveal. This whole three-ring circus, it would appear, is *real*.

Dave walks back to his seat. "I'd like to congratulate all of you for taking the first big step on your Genetic Journey. We'll process the results, and you'll get all sorts of interesting information." He gestures to his assistant, who begins collecting the boxes.

All but mine. As the assistant comes around to me, I keep my hand on my box. Now that Dave is no longer holding the room in thrall, I feel a strange reluctance to play along. Maybe it's because I've found out today that I won't be having a child – I won't be passing my genetics on to a next generation. For me, the buck stops here. Why look backward if there's no going forward?

"Why does it matter?" I say. My voice sounds shrill in the large room. "Isn't it just a parlor game? Does any good ever come of it?"

Dave turns the beam of his gaze on me. For a split

second, his Messiah façade wavers as he considers his answer.

"People are power," he says. "What are our lives about if not connecting with others? Sharing our lives with others?"

The other men in the room look bored like they want to get back to business, and my question is delaying the next best part of the meeting – lunch.

"Do you need a DNA test to do that?"

"Trust me." His eyes lock with mine. "Take the test, log on to the database, and see what happens. For some people, it's a novelty. For others, it's an eye-opener. But almost everybody is changed by what they discover. That is – if you want to be."

Do I want to be changed? Slowly, I remove my hand from the box and nod to the assistant to take it. Dave watches my every move. When I've finished, he lets out an almost imperceptible sigh of relief. I feel like something secret has passed between us, some sense of unspoken recognition – though I have no idea what it is.

"And now, for the next step on *MyStory*'s financial journey," Dave says. "I'll hand the floor over to Fredrik, who can take you through the numbers."

9

CLAIRE

It feels strange to talk about myself, my life spooling out before me as I answer the interview questions. The host of the show, Stella, is blonde, leggy, and casually dressed in skinny jeans and a cashmere sweater. She's like one of those friends that you dream of having but is probably out of your league. She's genuinely interested in my story (or very good at pretending to be). The camera is operated by a tattooed guy named Greg, who moves it around on a little dolly. Greg's assistant moves an umbrella-shaped shade around to get the lighting right. There is a vase of lilies on the table and two scented candles. My kitchen – my life – transformed.

We spend two hours talking about Jess's condition. After that, I assume that they'll want to call it a day, or at least take a break. But Stella sits back, takes a sip of her tea, and continues on with another question.

"So tell me more about your childhood."

I look down at my favorite "World's Greatest Mom" mug that was a gift from Becky and Jess. It's full of fresh coffee that I haven't touched. All my nerves return as I try to figure out how to begin. I recount the basic details: I was born here in Santa Rosa, the only child of Joe and Sylvia. Mom was a school librarian, and I grew up loving books and making up stories. I think that's one of the reasons I became a journalist.

Mom and I got along pretty well, but it was hard to get her attention. I remember her always surrounded by groups of children, working on a charitable committee, or singing in the chorus of some amateur Gilbert and Sullivan production. I often felt lonely, left behind in the wake of her energetic lifestyle. Even her death, when I was twenty-one, was swift and energetic. She developed a fast-growing malignant tumor and refused to have treatment. One day she was there, and the next, she wasn't.

"I'm sorry for your loss," Stella says.

Hearing her say that, I feel an unexpected bubble of anger float up inside of me. I do feel the loss of Mom but as something remote and detached. At the end of the day, I was always Daddy's girl. It's him that I miss when I sit alone in the hospital waiting room. It's his hand I wish I could hold as the doctor delivers another sucker punch of bad news. It's his loss that I feel every day, like the phantom pain of an amputated limb.

"Thank you," I say. The words sound inadequate, even a little flippant. I should tell her that I've had enough for now. But she's already on to the next question: "Tell me about your dad."

I lean forward, wanting to make her understand.

"Dad was special. I don't know how else to put it. He was so full of life and warmth." I catch myself smiling. "He had this natural charisma. But he was gone a lot." I can feel my smile fading into a twilight of resentment.

"Oh? Why was that?"

"He was a sales rep for a medical company. They were

headquartered back east. He was essentially a cross-country commuter." I reach for my now-cold coffee and take a sip. The charms on my bracelet jangle.

"That's a nice bracelet," Stella says.

"Dad gave it to me. He brought me charms from the places that he regularly traveled to." I touch them one by one. The Golden Gate Bridge, the US Capitol, a pineapple from Hawaii, a bucking steer for Texas, the Statue of Liberty, a dolphin from Florida. Most of the places I've never been to. "I guess he picked them up mostly at airport shops."

"How nice."

I want to take off the bracelet and throw it at her. Because put like that, it doesn't really sound nice at all. I want to make her understand that he was there for me even when he was away. I open my mouth to say it, but the words won't come.

"Yes," is all I can manage. "It was nice."

"And what about now? Does he live locally?"

"No." I purse my lips. "He died too. About ten years ago."

"I'm so sorry."

That word again. I've never realized before how impotent "sorry" is. Or maybe it's just my life that sounds pathetic.

"It was a boating accident," I say. "Off Point Reyes. He caught three fish – they found them in the boat."

I swallow back the lump in my throat and take another sip of cold coffee. Dad liked to cook his fish with butter and garlic on his mesquite grill. When I think of him and feel flooded by grief, I don't think of the funeral or the urn full of ashes. I don't think of the fact that it was all so sudden, and I never got to say goodbye. I don't think of how sorry I am that he never really got to know Jess, but that I'm glad he hasn't had to see her the way she is now. No – when I think of Dad's death, I think of those three fish.

"He… never got to eat them for supper." My voice cracks.

"What a fascinating story!" Stella gives the cameraman a quick glance. "Heartbreaking too. Your life is so interesting."

"No… it really isn't."

"What about your grandparents? Do you know anything about them?"

"Not much. I…" There's a dinging sound. My phone begins to vibrate. I look at Stella, worried that she'll be annoyed. But I never turn it off completely in case Jess needs me. Even though she's upstairs in her room, we use the phone like an intercom. I'm not going to apologize for that…

"Sorry," I apologize. "I need to just make sure Jess is OK—"

The screen is flashing. It's not Jess. It's the *MyStory* logo and the words: *New match found!*

"What's this?" I'm suddenly very aware that I'm on camera, and my nerves return full force.

Stella smiles. "Open it and see."

10

It's time to meet a newly-discovered "long-lost relative". In fact, you'll be meeting a whole village of them. Pack your bags. Your private jet awaits.

Somewhere through the fog of my brain, I know what I'm supposed to do. Stand up. Squeal and clap my hands. Gush: "Thank you!" and "This is so exciting!" and "I never thought I'd get to fly on a private jet!" That's the kind of person they're looking for; that's what is expected.

Instead, I just sit there staring at the screen.

Stella glances at me, then at the cameraman. She's going to say "Cut!" and it will all be over.

I fidget in the chair. The camera continues to roll.

Stella's voice is a little tight. "Your first DNA match on your Genetic Journey is to a community of people who live near Bergen."

"Bergen?"

This is getting worse and worse. That damn camera... *Bergen.* "Is that in Oregon? I don't want to go to Oregon."

I don't realize I've spoken aloud until Stella corrects me. "Bergen is in Norway."

"Norway!" My mouth drops open and closes again. The cameraman gives his assistant a thumbs up at my startled reaction.

"Obviously, you'll need some time to make arrangements." Stella beams a celestial smile. "But when you're ready, we're going to fly you to Norway to meet some of your distant cousins on your mother's side."

She spends a few minutes taking me through a complex chart of numbers, DNA markers, maps, and family trees. Apparently, my great-great-grandmother came to America from Norway, got married to someone called Larsson, and settled in Minnesota. I should feel excited, curious. Instead, I feel like I'm listening to the details of a life that belongs to someone else.

Most of all, I regret that I'll have to tell Dave that I can't go to Norway, knowing that he'll be disappointed with me. But it would never work. I've got a busy schedule with a lot of family commitments. I've got a sick daughter. On the other hand…

The letter on the fridge swims before my eyes. *Jess's audition. Three months' time.* The whole reason I'm doing this is to make these sorts of connections: to find long-lost relatives who might be a match for Jess. But equally, I can't afford a wild goose chase. It strikes me that this search might lead to connections with literally *thousands* of people with whom I share a distant ancestor. What's the likelihood that I'll find the one who is both a match for my daughter and be willing to help?

"Um… that's really fascinating," I waffle. "But it's going to be a little difficult for me to get to Norway."

Stella frowns. Are they going to drop me from the program? I don't want to lose her – or Dave – I need them on my side. But—

"Yeah, I live here. Is that OK with you?" A loud voice

filters in from the front of the house. Irritated footsteps. The camera pans to the door.

"Turn that off!" I say.

"Mom?"

Becky comes into the kitchen and plops her heavy bag on the floor. Instead of relief at the disruption, I feel a stab of annoyance. I might have been "in the zone" – in the middle of giving Stella a witty and insightful answer to one of her questions about my family history. But I close those feelings down. Becky is my daughter. She has a right to be here. She has a right to have me be a better mother to her. God knows I've tried – but somehow never managed it.

Steve has a theory that the friction between Becky and me is caused by the fact that we're too much alike. The first time he said it, I thought he must be nuts, as I can see few or no similarities. His theory is that, like me, Becky wants to grasp her life with both hands and throw aside any obstacles in her path: she's single-minded, committed, and goal-oriented. That description made me wonder if he knew me at all because it didn't ring any bells – not for me, and certainly not for Becky. I guess you could count my marrying young and having kids young as wanting to "get on with life", but in Becky's case, it seems to come down to trying out as many bad things as possible before she's even an adult – when many more will surely open up to her.

But once again, I'm being unfair. I try to picture her as a baby – just a little breath and fluff of life in my arms – so needy, so loving. Yes, she screamed a lot and never slept. Everything I did seemed to make her fuss or spit up or screw up her little face and wail. From day one, I was on the back foot, questioning every action I took as a mom because everything I did seemed wrong. I'd wanted to succeed with her – so much – because I loved her. I still love her. But even though we live in the same house, the distance between us has stretched to the size of an ocean. I have no clue how to bridge the gap. I wish there was something I could do to impress her or make her eyes shine with love the way they used to. It's a look I can only half remember. Was it ever even real?

"Hi, Becky." I wave her over. "Come see what they've found out." I lean in and speak to Stella in a low voice. "Is that OK? I'd… appreciate it."

"Of course." Stella looks less than enthusiastic. "It's about family, after all."

Becky makes a point of almost tripping over the cameraman's trailing extension cord on the floor. She grabs a Diet Coke from the fridge and comes over to the table. A few feet away, she stops, her eyes widening. "Wow, Mom," she says, "you look… different."

Her expression alone makes doing the program worthwhile. For once, I'm someone other than "just Mom" or "boring old Mom". I'm on a Genetic Journey, and right now, I look the part.

"Do I scrub up well?" I experiment with smiling at her.

"Not too bad."

"Good, so have a look at this. We're related to a village in Norway."

"Norway?"

"Yes, you know, like…" I rack my brain to think of a Norwegian actor or actress – someone that she might be able to relate to. But I draw a complete blank. All I can think of is: "… Abba. They were—" Dang, they weren't Norwegian "—from Sweden. That's next to Norway. Like a neighbor."

For that, I earn the famous eye roll. Definitely deserved. She sits down at the table and cracks open her Diet Coke, drinking from the can. She looks at the folder, then at Stella. "Norway," she says. "That's fierce."

"Really?" I say. A "fierce" from Becky is high praise indeed.

"I can explain what we've found out," Stella says.

If I wasn't already worshipful of Stella, I become a convert as she takes Becky through the family tree as we know it so far. Becky asks questions; she seems genuinely interested. Something I haven't seen from her unless she's on her phone watching the latest trending TikTokker. I stand up and begin wiping imaginary dust from the immaculately-staged kitchen counter.

Maybe it's time for a rethink. I started my Genetic Journey solely in the hopes of finding a donor for Jess, but maybe it will prove positive in other ways. It will be good for the kids to learn about the building blocks of their DNA. If Becky is interested, then maybe Jess will be too. Heck, maybe if I showed a little more enthusiasm, Dave might fly my *whole family* to Norway. Maybe what we've been lacking over all these years is a journey halfway across the world to meet some long-lost cousins in a small village near the Arctic Circle. Maybe this fresh, new version of myself could actually do something like that.

Somehow, the whole thing really takes off, and, before I know it, Becky's caught on to my idea.

"I'd, like, totally *love* to go to Norway," she's telling Stella. "We learned about Vikings in school. They even discovered America or something. Or maybe it was Canada."

"Yes, there is evidence that they had a temporary settlement in Newfoundland," Stella says. "Look, you see this marker? We can use it to trace back ancestry in places that the Vikings colonized."

"I guess they raped and pillaged a lot of people," Becky says in macabre fascination.

"Well, that's one theory. Though there is evidence that family groups were present…"

The new me can say something. Join in, show an interest. I can allow myself to feel happy that Becky is interested in her genetics – that we're on the same wavelength about something. I open my mouth… I'm going to do it—

But then I see the letter on the fridge. All the *reasons why not* start shouting in my head.

"Um, Stella," I hear the old me – the *real me* – saying. "I was just wondering… I mean, Norway sounds great and all, but do you think you could find us some Genetic Cousins a little closer to home?"

It's as if the air is sucked out of the room. I've done it again. Taken the little seed that might have germinated into a relationship between Becky and me and stamped on it, obliterating it to nothing.

"Sure," Stella says. "I understand. I suggest you talk it over with Dave when he's back from D.C. I know he wants to catch up with you. The journey's just beginning." Her smile is tight.

Becky gives a long sigh and stands up, not looking at me. "Thanks, Stella. Maybe we can talk more about it another time?" She glances sideways at me to make sure I've caught the unspoken "when Mom isn't around."

"Yes, Becky." Stella's enthusiasm towards my daughter now seems genuine, as does her growing coolness towards me. "We can definitely do that. You may want to go on your own Genetic Journey. When you're a little older."

"Definitely!" Becky gives me a look of pure defiance. Becky is seventeen, but soon she'll be eighteen and, for all practical purposes, an adult. Crossing the Rubicon, the invisible line. If I don't cement our relationship now, I might lose her forever. I swallow back a lump in my throat. I don't want that – of course, I don't. But right now, Jess has to be my priority. I hate that I have to choose between them. Why does everything with Becky have to be such a power struggle?

"Yes, well… fine." I don't bother to protest. Whatever I say, Becky's going to win in the end.

11

BECKY

I used to think I was adopted – sometimes, I still do. I guess lots of kids go through a phase of feeling like their parents are total aliens. I've been going through it for seventeen years. In the case of me and Dad, I accept that we might be of the same species, but I wonder sometimes whether Mom and I are from the same planet. I guess I'll have to go on my own Genetic Journey to find out.

As I go upstairs to my room, I wish that I could somehow rewind the last seventeen years of my life and start again, though I'd settle for the last seventeen minutes. Maybe then I'd know what I did or said that was wrong.

It's cool that Mom's doing a TV show (even if it is some kind of infomercial) and trying to find a donor for Jess. It's cool that we might have relatives in Norway, or North Carolina, or the North Pole – if one of them turned out to be "the match", then I'd be over the moon. And Stella was totally amazing – pretty, smart, confident. I mean, I would kill to be like her. If I was, then Mom would have to love me and be proud of me.

Dad says that the problem between me and Mom is

that we're too much alike. The first time he said that, I laughed in his face. I mean, *me*? And *Mom*? I know he meant it as a compliment, but how could it be? Mom's so anal. So unspontaneous. And she's got a chip on her shoulder the size of Alaska. The total opposite of me. I don't care about anything really, except my sister, and also about getting a car as soon as I can. I passed my test – second time! – and now I just have to figure out how to earn some money. As Grandpa Joe used to say, it's a "chicken and egg problem" – I need a car to get a job, and I need a job to get a car. They're paying Mom to go on her Genetic Journey, and I wish they'd pay me to do something easy like that – but I'd settle for babysitting or even working at fast food.

Jess is in her room, and I can hear her humming along to some music. She's had another awful biopsy, and right now, she's probably high on painkillers. I knock on the door and go inside. The sign on her door gets on my nerves, and her pink room – pink walls, pink bedspread, pink fairy lights on her headboard – is just so babyish, but her smile lights up the whole room, the whole world.

"Hey," she says. There's a fuzzy pink journal open on her bed, and she's holding a pink pen. She tries to pull the blanket up to hide them. I let her think she's succeeded.

"Hi." I go and sit on her bed. I give her a once-over check for bruises, my scan taking in her trash can. It's full of bloody Kleenexes; I wish I hadn't looked.

"You OK?" I say.

"Yeah, but Mom's mental," Jess says. "Have you seen downstairs?"

"Duh, just came from there." I want to give her a hug. Instead, I settle for sarcasm. "Apparently, we're from Norway. I mean, our genes came from there."

"And here I thought they were made in China." Her

delivery is so flat that I can't tell if she's making a joke or not. It's kind of funny, though, so I laugh.

"Good one," I say. "But do you even know where Norway is?"

"Do you?"

"It's where ABBA came from." *Mamma Mia!* is one of Jess's favorite films. This is going to impress her.

"Actually, they're from Sweden," she says.

"Well, Norway's practically a neighbor. It's where the Vikings come from."

"Vikings also come from Sweden, Iceland, and Denmark, not just Norway."

I roll my eyes. "Great, Jess. Whatever."

She shrugs. "Norway's cool. Or actually, it's cold."

I laugh again, but she just shrugs. She seems out of sorts. Not that I blame her – I mean, having a six-inch needle stuck in your back and totally feeling it when it breaks through your hipbone must be like everyone's worst nightmare. But, usually, Jess has a positive attitude about everything, even her condition, and tries not to act like it bothers her. I guess it's hard right now because it seemed like she was doing better – ever since they pumped her full of rabbit semen or something gross like that. All I know is that I hate seeing her like this.

"So…" I look down at the book peeking out from under the covers. "What are you doing?"

"Homework."

I turn my "Best of Becky" glare on her. Before she can react, I grab the notebook, stand up, and hold it over my head. "No, you're not. Liar."

"Give it back!"

I give it back. Even I, who Mom calls "The Queen of Bad Decisions", know better than to argue with Jess when she's ill. "Tell me," I say.

Jess leans back on her pillow with a sigh. "OK. If you must know, I'm working on my Bucket List."

"Bucket List?" I frown. "What the hell is that?"

"I think it comes from the phrase 'kick the bucket'. As in, it's all the stuff I want to do before I die."

I grab the book back from her, but I don't open it. The hot pink room suddenly feels chilly. I once had a dream of Jess lying in a coffin with pink ruffles all around her. She was wearing a pink dress and a big bow in her hair and looked like a china doll. Dead, lifeless. I press my nails sharply into my palm, trying to gouge the image away.

"Stop it, Jess. You're not going to die." I *need* to get this through her head once and for all. Out of the blue, I wonder if this is how Mom feels. That's like a major slap in the face.

"Mom says she's going to buy me new Converse," she says. "Purple, or yellow, or whatever color I want. A whole rainbow of Converse."

"Stop trying to change the subject."

"Maybe she wants options when it comes to choosing my funeral outfit."

I feel an almost uncontrollable urge to carve the word "STUPID" into my skin. Stupid Mom, stupid Jess. Stupid life. But I know that making another bad decision will not make things better.

"You're not going to die," I repeat. I should just leave it there – I know that. But curiosity gets the better of me. "What did you put down on the list?"

I hand her back the notebook, and she opens it to show me. Her handwriting is small and neat, unlike mine, which is fat and messy. I would have a zillion things on my list, but hers is much shorter.

1. Stand on stage at Carnegie Hall

2. Busk in Union Square
3. Audition for Youth Symphony
4. Get a million followers on YouTube
5. Dye hair purple
6. Kiss Taylor Compton

I look at her, stating the burning question. "Who's Taylor Compton?"

She giggles. "No one. Well… I mean… just someone."

"In your class."

"Yeah."

I lean in and give her a hug. "That's a sweet list. Should I Snap him for you?"

"No!" She pushes me away. "Don't you dare."

"OK, OK. How about some hair dye, then?"

"Mom will kill me!"

"Well, we'd better get started on the list before that happens." This time when I laugh, she joins in. There's a lot unsaid in that laughter, but the gears are turning in my mind. I'm saving up for a car, but maybe I should use the money to help Jess instead. How much would a trip to New York cost? How could I raise the money? How can I help Jess do as many things on her list as possible?

Jess stops laughing and closes the book. "It was just stupid, that's all."

"No – it isn't. It's a good idea. Now, you'd better put it away so Mom doesn't find it."

"Yeah," she says. "Thanks, Becky. You're the best."

"No. Seriously – I'm not."

But more than anything, I want to be.

12

Jess puts the notebook under her pillow. I get out the iPad and show her some cool TikTok memes I've found. I watch her watch them. Maybe I'm trying to imprint her on my memory, or maybe her comment about dying affected me more than I want it to. I think back over my life – and Jess's life – trying to remember every little thing, good and bad. Maybe my brain is too busy struggling with algebra and Civics and Spanish vocabulary all the time, but I know that I've forgotten a lot of my life already, which seems kind of weird.

I do remember the day I discovered my sister. Not like I didn't know I had a sister, but the day I became *conscious* of knowing her. It was kind of like excavating an earthquake site and finding a survivor in the rubble. It wasn't the day she was born or even years afterward. When I was four, Dad came home with a book called *Mommy, Mommy, What's in Your Tummy?* that was all about a boy whose mom got really fat, and he wondered what was inside of her: a soccer ball, a fire truck, a teddy bear? It turned out to be a baby. That was how it was with me.

One day, I was Daddy's little princess, ruling the roost with a chocolate-smeared face and a scream like finger-nails on glass, and the next, I was playing second fiddle to a tiny pink bundle with hands like sea anemones, fuzzy ears, and a sweet little gurgle. People came to see the baby, bringing gifts and saying how cute and beautiful she was like she was the baby Jesus or something. I was jealous of the gifts and thought she was noisy, smelly, and messy. Because of her, my life as Cinderella had turned straight into a pumpkin.

I felt that way for pretty much the next six or seven years. Jess was kind, pretty, and perfect. Her favorite color was pink, and she liked dolls and girly things. By then, I'd already been labeled a "tomboy" and a "problem child". I was the kid that made Mom shake her head when she talked to her friends. So I decided to *be* that kid: embrace her and own her. I made trouble whenever possible, prefer-ably involving my sister. I hid her ballet shoes, ripped up her homework, and committed little acts of sabotage that I tried to frame her for, and sometimes it worked. But all of that changed one unexpected night when she was seven and I was twelve – the night of her first solo concert.

I'd used my sister's violin for some of my acts of civil disobedience: hiding her rosin, loosening the tuning pegs, carrying it home from school and "accidentally" leaving it somewhere. In general, I hated the sound of the violin and hated the way Mom and Dad were so gaga over the whole thing.

So what changed that night?

I'd like to say that a lightning bolt hit me and I suddenly became nice. I'd like to say it was one magical thing, but the truth is, I don't know what changed. It was the night of the school talent show, and Jess was playing a solo. I, who had no talents, was singing in the choir. We were just coming off stage when I saw Jess standing in the wings. She was all alone and crying.

That was the moment when I put aside my meanness. I put my arms around her and asked what was wrong. All this stuff came pouring out: she was scared to perform, scared to let Mom and Dad down. What if she made a mistake? What if people laughed at her? I looked at her as if seeing her for the first time. She was so little. And at that moment, I hated Mom for putting her under so much pressure. I hated myself for how I'd treated her. Why had I never appreciated her before?

I'd like to say that I lifted her confidence with encouraging words, but the truth is, I gave her some tough love. I said that Mom was wrong to make her do this, and the only thing to do was to "show her." Get out there. Blow everyone away.

To be honest, I'm not sure if I wanted her to succeed or fail that night (though I can guess). She squeezed my hand just before her name was called and said, "Thanks, Becky. I just want *you* to be proud of me."

Wow. That was a total turning point. I sat in the audience as my sister took the stage. She looked small and nervous. The piano played a few notes.

And then, Jess put the bow to the string, and all of a sudden, something magical happened. The sound rang out loud and pure, spinning into the ears of everyone in the audience, into their minds and hearts. A light went on inside of me. This girl – I had known her all her life – and yet she was a stranger to me. She was *my sister*. The sound vibrated and echoed, and the notes came out faster and faster, whirling like restless spirits. And then, when the last note rang out, I got to my feet and joined the standing ovation. My sister. *We* had triumphed.

OK – full disclosure. Afterward, I was super jealous.

Everyone was talking about Jess and her triumph. No one was talking about me except in the usual way. But somehow, things had changed. I'd realized that deep down, Jess was scared and vulnerable; on some level, she needed me. I was her big sister – end of story.

After that concert, Jess and I became really close. We got bunk beds for Christmas so we could share the same room. We used to both lie in her bed, read by flashlight, and look through Mom's *Cosmo* magazines (we weren't allowed to, but I stole them). And we'd talk about all kinds of silly stuff. Clothes and hairstyles, CDs and doll accessories. For both of us it was "pre-boy", though we did read the articles about sex and "owning your orgasm" and things we didn't really understand that made us both a little uncomfortable. We'd talk about what we wanted to be when we grew up. I wanted to be Vice-President of the United States. (I mean, you get to be totally rich and famous and don't have to do any work!) Jess, of course, wanted to be a violinist. "Do you really like playing it that much?" I'd ask her.

"I don't know…" she'd say. "It's just what I do. I've never really thought about it."

That's Jess to a tee. She isn't plagued with self-doubt like I am. To Jess, things are the way they are. Things are good. Jess is a great sister and a genuinely good person. When I think of her, I sometimes think of that song by Billy Joel. "Only the Good Die Young."

I *seriously* hate that song.

When Jess got sick, I felt like my world had shattered. I didn't understand what was happening or what was meant by things like "prognosis" and "terminal". All I knew was that I had to *do* something.

By then, Mom had gone mental, and everything I did sent her into a rage or a long silence. So I approached

Dad, who was equally affected but was handling it in a more "dad-like" way. He told me that Jess had a disease called Aplastic Anemia. "Does that mean she's plastic, like a Barbie?" I asked, thinking it might explain a lot.

"Oh, Becky," he said and hugged me. That got me seriously worried.

Dad told me the bare facts. Her bones didn't produce enough blood cells. At any time, she could catch an infection and be too weak to fight it. Or her own immune system might attack the rest of her. I pictured a battle – little blobs of immune system soldiers with bayonets attacking her perfectly nice army of red blood cells, bursting them one by one. It just seemed so unfair.

But in a way, I was also relieved. Only a few days before her first hospitalization, Jess and I had fought over some stupid book or CD – I can't even remember now what it was. I grabbed her arm pretty hard and felt really bad when I saw the bruise afterward. I actually wondered if I had some kind of split personality – Good Becky, who loved my sister to pieces – and Bad Becky, who beat her up in her sleep or something. I definitely wondered if the whole thing might be my fault. Then, I wondered if it might be Mom's fault, but I kept that to myself.

Anyway, when I talked to Dad, I felt both better and worse. No one was hurting Jess. That was good news. It was also good news that when the nurse came over to draw Jess's blood, she'd bring a bag of colorful lollypops and let us both choose one. I liked the green ones best, but Jess preferred the cherry red ones. Sometimes if Jess wasn't feeling well from her medication, she'd offer me hers. (I'm not proud to say that I usually took it.)

The bad news was… everything else. I told Dad that I wanted to help. I said I could make her a card to cheer her up and use my allowance to buy her some new music downloads or something. Dad thanked me and said that, yes, there was something I could do.

The "something" involved getting my blood taken. I was a little surprised they let me near a needle after the incident with the fake tattoos when Mom crowned me "The Queen of Bad Decisions". By then, I was scared of needles, and I really hated watching my blood going into that tube. But I would have done anything – split open my vein and let Jess suck my arm like a vampire – if it would have made her better.

No one told me the results of that test, but a few nights later, I overheard Mom and Dad arguing. Mom was crying, and I heard her say, "It's just so typical. Becky is useless, absolutely useless!"

I froze there at the top of the stairs. I wanted to block it all out and go back to my room, but I couldn't move.

"It's a good thing she's not a match," Dad said. "I don't want Becky having that hanging over her head. Feeling like she has to be some kind of donor on tap for her sister."

"That would be the day," Mom said.

"And we'll test my brother too – hopefully, he'll be the one…"

Dad's brother wasn't the one. No one in our family was a match; no one on the registry in the whole country. So many times I lay awake in my bed (after Jess got sick, they wouldn't let us stay in the same room anymore) with Mom's words shouting in my head. *Typical Becky. Useless. Absolutely Useless!*

"Becky?"

I jerk back to reality. I'm in Jess's pink palace. The iPad is turned off, and she practically throws it back to me.

"I've had enough… OK?"

"OK…?"

She's turned her shoulder to me. I can't see her face.

She wants me to leave – I can see that. I stay right where I am.

"I want to go to bed – I'll see you tomorrow."

She digs frantically under her pillow. For a second, I think she's got something urgent to add to her Bucket List. But that's not it. She gets out a Kleenex.

I stand up and move around her bed. She tries to turn away, but it's too late. The blood pours out of her nose, down her face. Thick, red gore. It drips onto her white top and pink bedspread, like rose petals scattered at a funeral.

I grab the box of Kleenex on her desk, knocking over her music stand in the process.

"Here!" I take out a fistful and shove them at her. "I'm going to get Mom."

"No!" She jumps up from the bed and grabs me, staining my arm with little fingerprints of blood. "No, please, Becky. Don't. Mom will make me go back to the hospital, and I don't want to. Look – it's stopping. It's fine."

My pulse is pounding in my head as the war goes on between Good Becky – the one who wants to get Mom, and Bad Becky – the real me.

"It's stopping," Jess repeats. "Look." She puts the tissue down on the bed, grabs a clean one, and pinches her nose, keeping her head raised. I stare down at the used tissue. In another lifetime, I would be grossed out by the little polka dots of blood. But as she sets down the next tissue and takes a new one, I analyze the patterns, making sure that it's really getting less.

"One more," she says.

Biting my lip, I nod. I pick up the scattered pages of her music and hand her the trash can.

"Thanks." She gathers up all the tissues and throws them in. Bad Becky wins out. The nurse is coming by tomorrow to check on Jess and take her blood. That should be soon enough.

I put the trash can back by the desk, still hovering. "Do you need anything?"

"No… I just need to sleep." She sinks back on the bed, smiling at me.

I take her hand in mine. We both have olive-brown skin – the kind that tans easily. My skin is more tanned than hers because she spends so much time in this room. Her sanctuary. Her prison. Her… tomb.

"Are you scared?" I say.

Her eyes close for a split second, then she opens them again. They're the color of melted chocolate. There's a sparkle in them. Intelligence. Life. My stomach seizes up.

"Yeah. I am."

13

CLAIRE

In another lifetime, I would be looking forward to dinner – to celebrating the fact that I successfully got through the day's filming and have taken the first steps on my Genetic Journey. In reality, it's strange and strained. I'd been hoping that Jess would feel well enough to join us, and I've made spaghetti bolognese – one of her favorites. But before I'm done with the sauce, Becky tells me that Jess is sleeping. I swallow my worry and bark at her when she pushes aside the vase of tulips and the scented candles that I was hoping would "elevate" the meal, and spreads out her math homework.

"Sorry, Mom." She seems to be lacking the sparkle and enthusiasm from earlier, and I wonder if that's my fault.

"It's fine," I say through my teeth. Just then, the front door opens. Steve is home.

Becky goes to greet him – like me, she's always been a daddy's girl. There's an animated discussion between them over what's happened to Steve's slippers that he usually keeps by the door and the film people must have moved.

By the time he reaches the kitchen, I can sense the waves of stress emanating from him.

"Hi." I give him a quick kiss. "How was your day?"

"Not good." He goes to the fridge and gets a beer. "That OSHA inspection turned up a few red flags. We're meeting tomorrow to discuss 'lessons learned'."

Steve's job may not be glamorous, but it's stable and comes with good health insurance. When we met in college, I didn't give those things a single thought. Now, it's everything.

"That sounds… challenging. But you'll do great, I know it."

"Yeah." He glugs the beer down in one. "Thanks." He scrapes the chair back as he sits down at the table and checks his phone.

I stir the pasta and wait for him to ask me about my day. I've still got the last vestiges of make-up on from earlier, and I've changed into a long-sleeved black T-shirt that accentuates my chest. I was hoping to recapture some of the glow from earlier as well. But if Steve has noticed any transformation whatsoever, he's not letting on.

I set the table, clanging cutlery to get his attention.

"So… I had an interesting day," I say. *Thanks for asking.*

Steve sets down his phone.

"You're really doing it?"

"Yeah. It's kind of exciting. They've already identified some distant Genetic Cousins in Norway. Who knows what's next?"

"I hope you know what you're doing." The note in Steve's voice makes my hackles rise. "I mean, you're uploading yourself onto a database. Your DNA, your biological history. What if it voids our insurance?"

In the beginning, I had a well-thought-out answer to the "what if it voids our insurance" argument. Steve and I discussed the project at length. I'd hoped he would back me up: tell me it was a good idea and maybe even be tested himself. At the very least, I expected him to be glad about the extra money. We've had to pay for some of Jess's treatment out-of-pocket and already have a second mortgage on the house. But this argument is not really about the DNA testing. It's about the fact that we both feel trapped and helpless. And about the fact that Steve hates Dave Steiner.

"It won't," I say.

"I don't know what good you think it's going to do. I mean, it's like you've been taken in by some shyster."

I tip the pasta into the colander. The steam burns my wrist. I should just laugh off Steve's negativity. Instead, I feel a ridiculous urge to cry.

"Geez, Dad." Becky unexpectedly takes my side. "Don't be such a downer. I mean, Jess is already in a database, right?"

"And a lot of good that's done."

Silence descends like a poisonous mist. Even Becky keeps quiet. I know that Steve is hurting like I am. I know he wants the best result for Jess – and all of us. But knowing and believing are two different things.

I bring the pasta over to the table and sit down. My phone vibrates in my pocket. My instincts tell me to ignore it – I need to focus on getting Steve back on side. But Steve is intent on piling spaghetti onto his plate and pouring salt all over it. I take out the phone and check the name onscreen: Dave S.

I know it's wrong, but I experience a powerful flash of vindication. Things are strained with my husband, but I've got a secret someone. An ally and a friend. I'm glad to have Dave in my life. It might be petty and childish, but it feels good to have something that Steve doesn't.

I don't answer the call, but Steve has seen the screen. We are like two armies poised on the edge of a battlefield. Someone will blink and fire the first shot – it's only a matter of time. I wait for him to react. I *want* him to react so that we can end this standoff and make things right.

Steve reacts. He opens his mouth. He's going to speak. Any second he's going to look at me and *see* me – say something that will soothe the hurt and bridge the distance between us…

"Becky, can you please pass the garlic bread?"

"Sure, Dad. Here you go."

14

I fill the sink with sudsy water, fighting the urge to stick my head in and disappear. After the tense, awful meal, Steve has gone to the study, and Becky has decamped to her room. When I'm finished with the dishes, I'll take a tray up to Jess. Seeing her, stroking her hair, will be my one little present to myself.

I take off my bracelet and set it by the sink, feeling naked without it. Compared to my parents' marriage, mine seems like a complete failure. Steve and I met in college, had a whirlwind romance, and I ended up pregnant. I guess I was lucky that Steve was over the moon and saw me as his "forever girl". Before I knew what hit me, I had a ring on my finger, a starter home, and a baby. I later got a job at the local paper, which became my sanctuary from family life.

To be fair, Steve is a good husband and an amazing father. He was there for me through the darkest times: my mom's death, then my dad's. I was there for him when he lost his cousin in a car accident. We've been there for each other throughout Jess's illness. Maybe it's all the "being there" that's made me resent him. Maybe that's why my parents' marriage seems so rosy in comparison.

As I scrub the dirty plates, I think about how easy it was when I was a kid – an only child living in a happy little bubble. Dad's absences were like him going off to sea, sailing to strange and wonderful mist-shrouded lands full of exotic flora and fauna. I now understand that business travel is the worst kind, living out of a suitcase at one bland hotel after another, sitting in long meetings, and schmoozing with people one secretly despises. Mom never complained except when something went wrong with the house: a blocked drain or a leaking faucet, a dead pilot light or a flat car battery. Usually, there were neighbors who could help, and Mom learned to fix most things herself. And when Dad came home, we had a grand reunion that almost made his absences seem worth it. Almost. All in all, we were a close family, a happy family. I grew up and had my own family, and then Dad was gone.

I dry the plates and pick up the bracelet. It seems so shiny – so perfect – against my skin. Other than San Francisco, of course, and Hawaii on my honeymoon, I haven't been to any of the places where Dad regularly traveled. My ancestors, hailing from interesting places like Norway, would surely be disappointed. But it's not the lack of travel that I regret now. The pain of missing Dad is a physical thing, right in the middle of my solar plexus. I wish I'd spent more time with him and got to know him better. As he really was, not just as the knight errant that I imagined in my youth.

I leave the dishes to dry and make Jess a bowl of pasta. I feel the familiar fluttering of fear in my chest as I knock softly on her door and open it. Her room is lit by a soft glow of fairy lights on her headboard. It's like a pink cocoon from which she will one day emerge and become a butterfly. I have to keep believing. I tiptoe into the room. She's restless in her sleep, her brow covered with sweat. "No!" I hear her cry out. Her hand goes to her chest where she has the line inserted, and for an awful second, I think she's going to rip it out. I imagine her poor, oxygen-starved blood blooming onto the pink bedspread. My hand holding the bowl begins to judder. I set it on the nightstand and leave the room.

I take refuge in the bathroom. I may as well have a bath and wash off my make-up: slough off the trappings of the day and go back to who I was before. As I fill the bath and leave my clothes in a heap on the floor, I stare up at the palms on the wallpaper border, wishing that I could disappear into their leafy green darkness.

Just as I'm about to get in the tub, my phone rings again. This time, when I see Dave's name, I decide to answer it. Like a glass of wine after a long day, surely I'm entitled to something for myself. I turn off the faucets and sit on the edge of the tub.

"Hi," I say. "Where are you?"

"Hi, Claire. Sorry I couldn't make it today. I've been traveling, and right now, I'm in my hotel room. Drinking alone – vodka and tonic from the minibar. What a life – eh?"

"Poor you. Are you having a good trip?"

As soon as the words leave my mouth, it's like I'm a little girl again. When Dad called me from his hotel, I'd ask him about his trip, and he'd ask me about my day. "It's like I'm right there with you," he'd say. "Sitting in the classroom, raising my hand to get a bathroom pass." I'd laugh, and he'd laugh. He'd tell me what soft drinks he had on the plane and whether it was peanuts or pretzels. "It's like I'm right there with you," I'd say, though it wasn't true. Still, those conversations made it feel like he was part of my day and part of my life, even though he was far away.

"Yeah, it's fine. The hotel's nice." Dave's voice startles me back to the present.

"But it's been rough meeting with the lawyers and bankers. I hate that side of things."

"When are you coming back?"

"Tomorrow. I'll be tied up in meetings for the rest of the week, but when I get a free moment, I'll stop by and see you. Stella told me that you had some questions about the process. Maybe even second thoughts."

"I thought you were going to be there." I'm ashamed at how childish I sound. "It… would have helped to see you."

"Well, I knew you were in good hands. Stella's been with me since the beginning."

"Yes. She seems very competent." I'm being childish, and he's being evasive. This isn't about Stella, though thinking about her beauty and poise makes me feel like the ugly stepsister.

Dave lets out a long sigh. He's got my DNA chart – he knows more about me than I know about myself. Maybe he knows what I'm thinking too.

"You know," he says, "sometimes this job gets me down."

"Really? Why? You seem to love what you do."

"Oh, you know me. I like the people side of it. I like their stories and their excitement when they discover them. But today, someone asked me if it was all just a parlor game. Of course, I said no, and to me, it's a lot more than that – there's real benefit in making these human connections. But it got me thinking about you and Jess. About your family. How much it means to you. It's not just a pastime or a novelty, but a real matter of life and death. I guess that's why I feel so invested in your journey,

Claire. That, and because I really do count you as a friend."

"Right." I feel a little choked up. I know that Dave's a good salesman and that if he gets a result for Jess it will be good publicity for his business. But it's these little reminders of his sincerity underneath that make me value him even more.

"So remember to keep your eye on the ball," he says. "We both want a good result for Jess."

"I know. And I'm very grateful. It's just that… I'm not feeling very hopeful right now."

I feel guilty for my lack of confidence and vision. But with my daughter asleep in the next room when she should be texting, or watching videos, or begging me to take her to the mall, I find it hard to believe in anything.

"I do feel hopeful," Dave says. "We're making huge advances in our technology every day and testing more and more people. It's a numbers game – one that we're going to win!"

He's back in sales pitch mode, but I let myself be persuaded. I can almost visualize Dad here, whispering Dave's words into my ear…

"Anyway, Claire. Keep the faith. I'll see you soon."

I stand up and look at myself in the mirror. I run my hands down the length of my body, trying to picture myself as a Viking woman, scratching out a living in the frozen tundra. A woman… not just the frantic mom of a sick girl. The woman I could be again if my Genetic Journey leads to a result. The woman that I want to be…

"Thanks, Dave," I whisper. "I really don't know what I'd do without you."

I end the call. It's only then that I turn and see that the door is open a crack. Steve is standing just outside. I have absolutely no idea how long he's been there.

15

MARIANNE

"You did what? Seriously?"

Tom spears a bite of beef lo mein and gives me a goofy look like I've just made a joke. Normally, I would be proud and pleased to have been the one to say something funny – usually, it's Tom who's the life of the party and class clown all rolled into one.

Both of us work a lot, so this is a rare evening with just the two of us. I want to enjoy it – to enjoy *us* – the way I used to. But tonight, I'm on pins and needles. I need to tell Tom the news about Baby No. 8, or lack thereof.

It's different for men. They don't give over their bodies in the same way that women do. Losing an unborn child is devastating for them, of course, but it's more a theoretical loss than a physical one. Maybe that's why the distance has grown between us. Each time I lose a baby – and I see each and every embryo, implanted or not, as a potential baby – I'm ripped apart from the inside out. Whereas Tom seems to bounce back a little more quickly, like he's stopped believing that it was going to happen in the first place. The idea of telling him and seeing that look of pity on his face… I can't bring myself to do it.

Instead, I decide to regale him with the one candidate for "amusing anecdote" in an otherwise devastating day.

"Everyone had to do it." I keep the mood light. "Twelve lawyers and bankers around a conference table all doing mouth swabs. The CEO gave a great performance – you would have liked him."

As a theatre producer, Tom is used to dealing with big names and big egos. I am also used to big egos, though rarely are they attached to anything like charisma. I remember the spark of laughter in Dave's eyes and feel a little shiver in the dead place inside of me. The man definitely has charisma – in spades.

Tom continues to eat, chopsticks flying from carton to mouth. Obviously, my story hasn't interested him. I'm desperate to fill the silence with something other than the thing I need to say, so I default to "lawyer talk", which, in the old days at least, used to impress him.

"So the company will be needing a lot of capital to achieve their goals. They'll be a great client. If I lead on the file, I could make equity partner."

"OK…?"

I can hear the question in his voice. So much for keeping the mood light. We've had this conversation many times. The "maybe you should cut back, take it easy" conversation. The "you have to want a baby more than anything else in your life" conversation. As if *I* didn't. Yet, even without him saying anything, a familiar litany of doubts creeps into my mind. Maybe I failed to get pregnant in the last few cycles because I put my career first for too long. My clock was ticking, the alarm shrieking, and I didn't heed it. Maybe it was because I felt entitled to have it all – a great job, a great marriage, great kids – and I focused on all the wrong things. Maybe I should have been a housewife like my mother – my vision of a woman with the perfect life. How could I have fallen so short? I spear a piece of beef and shove it in my mouth, chewing and swallowing without tasting.

"Anyway," I say, "the test might prove interesting. I don't know a lot about my ancestors. It might be fun to find out more."

"For when the baby comes?" The smile Tom gives me is kindly, almost indulgent. "Maybe your mom can embroider a family tree and put it up on the wall in the nursery."

It's a joke – I should laugh. He means to be hopeful, not hurtful or malicious. But it does hurt – so much. My hand begins to quiver. A piece of beef falls from my chopsticks onto my plate. I stall for time, trying to re-spear it. It's not Tom's fault that he doesn't know. My failure to conceive is not his fault either. On paper, we are the perfect candidates for an IVF success story. Tom is not the guilty party here for what seems like some kind of terrible crime.

Which leaves me.

Tom cocks his head, considering me. He's used to reading unspoken thoughts on the faces of his actors and actresses. I try to picture him as the man I married – funny, irreverent, and smashing in bed – not the middle-aged man who's losing his hair and gaining inches around his waist and whose jokes now tend to have a bitter edge to them. I try to picture myself as the woman he married. Sexy, intelligent, driven, perfect. A woman who was different from the flakey, fly-by-night women that Tom dealt with at the theatre on a daily basis. I can still remember the way he used to look at me when I'd come home in my power suit, and how quickly that suit would come off. When was the last time he looked at me that way? Was it between Baby Nos. 4 and 5? Or was it as far back as Baby No. 3? It hurts that I don't even know.

"You're not pregnant," he says.

The words gouge themselves into my mind. You're. Not. Pregnant. Once upon a time – maybe between Baby Nos. 2 and 3 – that "you" would have been "we". An acknowledgment that we were in this together. That we were united in our grief and bound together in our hope. That love would see us through, and eventually, our time would come.

"No." I don't look at him. "*I'm* not."

He nods and resumes eating his food. I watch for a minute, fascinated by the action of hand to mouth, chew, swallow. The human body is so predictable, so mechanical. Usually… most of the time. It's so easy for other people. Why not us?

I push my chair back from the table.

"You OK?" he says.

Calmly, I take my plate to the sink, scrape the uneaten food into the waste bin, and put the plate in the dishwasher.

"Of course."

I leave the kitchen and go upstairs so that he can't see me. The *me* that's cracking on the surface, and especially not the *me* underneath. The joke that our lives has become falls flat and dies another death.

16

I lock the door to the master bedroom and lie down on the bed, staring up at the ceiling. The lighting is recessed, romantic, the shadows giving the room a boudoir feel. This bed has seen a lot of action in its day. For Babies Nos. 1 to 4, Tom and I used to make a point of making love on the days before embryo transfer so that it seemed like something natural, not just a medical procedure. For the last four, we haven't bothered. I think back to all the effort I've put in trying to make myself attractive: workouts at the gym, lunch hours at the salon, a drawer full of lacy underwear. A lot of it was gifted by Tom in the early days, but some I've bought myself, trying to remain sexy and desirable. I wanted to be everything to him – virgin, whore, wife, mother – a fairytale woman living her happily ever after.

Now, there will be no happily ever after. So what's left?

I know what's left – it's seething and bubbling like a glowing seam of magma looking for a way to the surface. I have to *do* something! The underwear... I swing out of bed. I throw open the door of my walk-in closet, wrest the drawer out of the built-in organizer, and dump everything onto the desk. Then I throw the drawer across the room. It hits the mirror but doesn't crack it. Too bad.

The rage courses through me as I go to the bedside table, where a few scented candles are tastefully arranged, and rummage in the drawer looking for matches. I can't find any, and that makes it worse. Though, it would be best not to set off the smoke detector.

I go to the desk and fling open the main drawer. Inside is a sharp pair of sewing scissors.

I pick up the first lacy bra and do my worst.

Destruction is hypnotic, addictive. Maybe it's the power of it – the only power I have at the moment. My body feels broken, bloody, useless, but the anger is life-affirming. I stab and snip, and the little pile of scraps of silk and lace begins to grow. I'm vaguely aware of Tom knocking on the door. He apologizes for having been insensitive and proceeds to offer some platitudes along the lines of "let's take this one in our stride… win one for the Gipper… that which does not destroy us makes us stronger."

I used to believe it. I don't anymore. I tune him out and keep snipping. Eventually, he pounds louder, saying that he's worried about me.

"I'm fine, Tom," I lie. "I just need a little time alone."

Once upon a time, maybe even up to Baby No. 6, Tom would not have gone away. He would have appealed to my better instincts, saying something like, "You may be fine, but I'm not." And I'd let him in. We'd cry together and vow to try again.

This time, he goes away.

A tear drops onto my hand holding the scissors. I wipe it away. I want the anger – not the tears. I want to wallow in my loss and cut up my underwear in peace. But I'm startled by my phone ringing. The tone is irritating, mocking. I can't bear the idea of speaking to anyone. The caller is persistent, however, and by the time I've reduced a red lace thong to a "barely there" pile of threads, the phone is still ringing. I take it out of my pocket, teeth clenched. My mother – I'm sure it's her. I have to tell her the news. In some ways, telling Tom was just a dress rehearsal for the real thing. But that rehearsal has taken everything out of me. I'm not ready to speak to her—

I look down at the screen. It's not my mother. Against my better judgment, I answer the phone.

"Hi, Marianne – it's Dave Steiner."

Dave Steiner. How odd that he should call just at my lowest moment. His voice transports me back to the meeting earlier in the day. I'm reminded of an old-time Baptist revival, with people fainting and babbling in tongues.

I challenged him. I ruined his show. I suppose he's calling to tell me that he's requested another lawyer on the file, maybe even taking his business to another firm.

Instead, Dave is a fountain of enthusiasm as he tells me the "good news". That he's just talked to James, and there's a meeting of the minds. He was impressed by me and wants me to be the lead lawyer. He wants me to handle all the documentation and negotiation with the investors. He wants *me*.

"That's perfect," I say, keeping up appearances. "I'm really looking forward to getting to know more about your business."

It's the wrong thing to say. Dave launches into a mono-logue, mostly repeating his spiel from the presentation. Outside, Tom is knocking at the door again. I stare down at the pile of silky scraps and wonder if I was possessed by aliens. I've destroyed hundreds of dollars' worth of designer lingerie. My favorite green bra that Tom bought me in Paris on our honeymoon. The pair of lacy underpants that Tom took off me under the table at the Toni Awards the second year he was nominated. The garter belt that I wore—

I push all of it out of my mind. My personal life is a shambles but dealing with clients is something I can do. I'm flattered that Dave has chosen me. I remember how at times during the meeting, I felt like he and I were the only two people in the room. We were complete strangers, but there was an undeniable connection between us.

"Do you have a family, Dave?" I ask.

I must have voiced the question aloud because there's actually a pause in the one-sided conversation.

"Pardon?" he says.

"They must be fascinated by what you do."

"Something like that." His laugh sounds a little forced. "Though right now, with the financing, things are pretty full-on. But it's a good question, and that's why I'm glad to be working with you, Marianne. You're a woman who cares about the big picture – you look at things from all sides. I could tell that much just from your question at the meeting today."

"Yes," I say. "I suppose I do."

"I like working with a woman with perspective. Vision." He gives a little laugh. "It will be interesting when you get your test results back. I know they're personal and confidential to you, but I hope you'll share them with me. I'm thinking… hmm… with your cheekbones, maybe Russian descent. Does that ring any bells?"

It's almost like a pick-up line – the strangest one I've ever heard. I laugh. The whole conversation is so ridiculous – so contrary to my current mood – that I'm almost enjoying it. "Maybe," I say. "I guess we'll see."

"Yes, OK. So I'll be in touch with the documents you need."

"Fine," I say. "We can meet up for lunch tomorrow at my office and discuss the terms sheet if you want."

"Well, that would be nice, but actually, I'm flying home tomorrow. So…" His pause is pregnant with possibility. "I don't suppose you've got time to meet up now – discuss things over a drink?"

I look down at the pile of cut-up underwear and come to my senses. It's already late – after nine – and I'm mentally and physically exhausted. My body is crampy and bleeding, and all I really want to do is curl up in a ball in bed and cry. Failing that, I really should have a conversation with Tom. I pick up a bra and pants set that still has the tags on it. Instead of cutting them up, I snip off the tags. Tom and I agreed on eight cycles. No more. But eight isn't a magic number. Maybe cycle nine will be the one, or cycle ten. I need to step back and think things through. I'm not a quitter – never have been. I've got a good life even if it's not perfect – yet. I need to keep hanging on for dear life.

Patch things up with Tom. Get him back on my side…

Another knock on the door.

"Um, sorry, Dave. I'm home now, so it's not really—"

Tom raises his voice through the door. "I'm going out for a little while. I need to clear my head. Don't wait up."

Don't wait up.

I know what that means.

"Marianne?"

"Um… actually…" *What am I doing?* "You're right, Dave. We should meet up before you leave. Now is absolutely fine. You're at the Conrad, right? I could meet you at the bar."

94

"That sounds great. It's always good to get to know each other in an informal setting."

"I'll see you in half an hour."

My heart is racing as I hang up the phone and put the scissors in the drawer. The emptiness inside… I just need to fill it up with some kind of distraction. I sweep the rest of the mess into the trash can and unlock the bedroom door. Tom is standing outside in the hall.

"Oh!" I jump. "I thought you'd gone."

His face is grim, and I can see that the news has affected him more than he wants it to. This is the moment – he'll take me in his arms, stroke my hair, kiss me the way he used to. I won't bother to call Dave back to cancel because I'll be lost in the loving caresses of my husband. Clinging on to what we have left.

"I thought that maybe we should talk." Tom does not take me in his arms. He does not look at me with love in his eyes. It's as if he's looking through me. Maybe that's my fault. There were things that I was planning to tell him, but somehow, the moment passed, and I never did. I kept myself hidden because I wanted him to see the beautiful, put-together woman in the suit, not the person I truly was. I was afraid I'd lose him if he knew the real me: the scared, ashamed, vulnerable me. Right now, I'm sad that even the fake, superficial me couldn't keep things from unraveling.

"I'm sorry, Tom. But I've arranged to meet a client."

"What?" His face is stony. "At this hour?"

"Yes, he's leaving tomorrow. So it's now or never."

Now or never.

"OK." Tom shrugs and goes downstairs. I go back into my room and change my clothes, putting on a black sheath dress, pearls, and a pair of high heels. Just because I feel terrible doesn't mean I have to look the part. When I go downstairs to the door, Tom is standing behind the sofa in the front room, flipping aimlessly through the TV channels. I go over to him and force myself to smile. I try to turn the lens backward and picture him the way he was. Hoping that maybe he'll see me the way I was. Right now, though, I can't do it.

"We will talk, Tom. But right now, I just need to do this."

"Sure," he says. Too quickly. I can almost sense his relief as he gives me a kiss on the cheek. His lips are cold against my skin.

17

CLAIRE

With our shabby bathroom as the dock, I'm put on trial with my husband as judge and jury. I look him in the eye and repeat that I am not now having, have never had, and do not plan in the future to have an affair.

"*I don't know what I'd do without you, Dave!*" Steve mimics in a high-pitched voice. "You're just so wonderful and caring."

"He's my friend," I protest, pulling the towel tight around me. "He's helping me."

"He's got you caught in his net of bullshit, hook, line, and sinker. He's using you, and at the worst possible time. Your daughters need you, but you decide to go off galivanting on some kind of 'Genetic Journey'—" Even his air quotes are sarcastic "— and to hell with the rest of us."

"I'm doing it for Jess." It hurts that there's not even any new ground to cover in this argument.

"You're doing it because you're bored," he snaps back. "Admit it."

I look at him, genuinely flabbergasted. "Bored? Are you kidding? I'm trying to save our daughter's *life*."

He shakes his head. "Her best chance is the bone marrow registry. Not some wild goose chase. I guess playing the waiting game is less exciting than focusing on your new 'friend' and his TV show."

I sigh. It's all just so exhausting. Anger, sadness, mortification – I feel them all – but through a fog somehow. My husband hates me. How did that happen?

"You said yourself that the bone marrow registry was a long shot. They can't test enough people or, in our case, the right people. We need to try something else, and I'm thinking outside the box. So I don't know why you're acting like this."

"Me? Why am *I* acting like this?" His laugh is bitter and tiny bubbles of spittle fly towards my face. "I don't know. Maybe because we're married. Maybe because we've got kids. Because once upon a time, we took vows. You know? For better or worse?"

I should be glad that he cares about our marriage – I realize that. When did I stop caring? *How* could I have stopped? And, more importantly, how do I make myself start again?

"I wish I could remember the better," I say. "Sometimes, all that seems left is the worse." I sit down on the toilet lid with my head in my hands.

"Then make it better," Steve says. "Start being more present. Stop this whole thing, and let's go back to normal."

"What is normal?" I turn on him. "Our daughter suffering? Being kept alive on other people's blood and cocktails of drugs? Because to me, that's a nothing sort of life. I want something better for her – better than what we have now!"

"A nothing sort of life? Is that what you call it? What about Becky? What about our marriage? Are you really willing to give up everything for your… boyfriend?" He fires the word at me like a weapon. Outside in the hall, I hear the sound of Becky's footsteps.

"Don't be ridiculous," I hiss. "He's not my boyfriend. If anything, he's more like – I don't know – a dad. I mean, he's a lot older than I am. And besides, do you think he'd want someone like me?"

"No." Steve's answer is quick and spot on. "No, I don't."

Steve's parting blow reverberates in the air as he leaves the bathroom, slamming the door in my face. I drain the water and get dressed, feeling like a wrung-out rag.

When I'm out in the hall, I can hear voices coming from Jess's room. She must be awake, and Becky must be with her. I should be glad that my daughters are so close, but their nighttime tête-à-têtes always annoy me. It's not that I worry that Becky's a bad influence – though she is, and I do – it's more that I wish Jess would confide in me. I'm her mother, but sometimes I wish I could be her sister instead.

I enter without knocking. The first thing I notice is the untouched bowl of pasta. Jess looks up at me like a deer in the headlights, her eyes flicking to Becky.

"Mom," she says, "are you and Dad going to get a divorce?"

I look at her pale, thin figure. So vulnerable that she almost looks like she'd need two parents to help her stand up and walk, let alone help her get through whatever awful medical procedures the future might hold.

"No," I say to both her and Becky. "Dad and I are just going through a bad patch. That's all."

Becky gives a little snort. "Yeah, whatever. Night, Mom."

She leaves the room, and I wish I didn't feel so relieved.

I let out a long sigh and turn back to Jess. My favorite times are when it's just the two of us, and I feel guilty for it.

"Can I go to Norway with you?" Jess says. "I mean, Becky says she's going. If I'm not sick, I want to go too."

"No one's going to Norway," I say. "Not right now. But maybe someday when you're older, you can go there. Meet your cousins."

"I'd rather go now," she says. "It would be nice to see the world before I… you know…?"

Die, die, die.

The unspoken word echoes around the room. A heavy yoke of despair settles over me. I hate it when she talks like this.

"Everything is going to be fine," I say.

I can't afford to lose it now; I can't show her how scared I am. Hesitation and weakness are the enemies here. Once we start down that rabbit hole, who knows how far we'll fall.

"But I'm not a match for anyone on the registry," she counters. "I'm not stupid, Mom. I've heard what the doctor says. There's no cure for me other than a transplant. And I'm not a match for… anyone."

Her logic is impeccable, but I'm not going to stand for it. I simply *will not accept* that it's the truth. I find a new spot inside my cheek to bite. I taste blood. My useless blood that is no good to my little girl.

"I need you to stay hopeful." I raise my voice. "Bear with me while I do this. I'm going to find all of our Genetic Cousins. And I'm going to speak to them, and I'm going to get them tested. And one of them is going to be a match. Then, you'll have the transplant. It will succeed, and you'll be able to live a normal life."

Jess looks at me with huge sorrowful eyes. "OK, Mom. I hope you're right."

I straighten up and give her a kiss on the forehead. I can't stand another second of this conversation. I *have* to be right. "Get some sleep," I say. "I love you, Jess – and your dad, and Becky. I love all of you. You're my family."

She snuggles down into her blanket with her old teddy bear, Mr. Tickles.

"I love you too, Mom."

I leave the room and go downstairs. I know I should try to work on my article, but instead, I make up the sofa bed in the spare room and crawl under the thin blankets.

Then I let the tears come. It feels like they will never stop.

18

MARIANNE

This is a bad idea; I just know it. I should turn the car around and go home – talk to my husband, face up to the reality that I will never be a mother, draw a line in the sand. Or… alternatively, I could tell Tom that I'm not ready to give up. That I want to keep trying. That I want *us* to keep trying. But what if he says no? What if he tells me it's over?

It might happen. Tom's record for fidelity has been dubious, at best. After Baby No. 6, I discovered some text messages from one of his ingénues who was "struggling to find her character". Around the same time, I also found an acrylic nail when I was washing his boxers. I kept my find to myself until after I lost Baby No. 7. Then I let him have it with both barrels. Tom broke down. He was angry with me, grieving over the situation. It was "just sex". He hadn't meant for it to happen, and it would never happen again. He loved me; he'd do anything for me…

I tuned it out. I couldn't focus on Tom's lies, what he was really doing, or who he was doing it with. All I had in my mind at the time was making sure that No. 8 – our last try – was successful.

It wasn't successful – so where does that leave us?

Bad idea or not, I keep driving. Across the river and into the city. I stop and go at each of the traffic lights. To say that fertility issues killed off our sex life is an understatement, but that's a loss I can't bring myself to grieve for right now. Tom will undoubtedly go out, and I'm out now, and maybe we ought to have stayed home and wallowed together in our sadness. Right now, though, that feels like an unbearable option. In fact, the further I get from home, the more the knot of tension in my chest begins to loosen. I push Tom out of my mind, push away the hurt I feel when I think about what we've become.

Instead, I focus on where I'm going and why. Dave Steiner. The *MyStory* financing.

There's quite a lot to discuss, but most of it can be done over the phone. This is supposed to be an informal "getting-to-know-you" meeting. A friendly drink and a chat. A diversion. That's all.

The government buildings are lit up and look beautiful. The Capitol, the Washington Monument, the Lincoln Memorial. I feel like I'm seeing them for the first time. Maybe it's because I'm no longer the same woman I was yesterday – or even this morning. It's like there's an electric charge in the air, just like earlier when Dave wielded a strange, charismatic power over the meeting. When just for a moment, our eyes had met, and I knew that he *saw* me.

Out of nowhere, a ridiculous little fantasy pops into my mind. Talking and laughing with Dave over a bottle of champagne in the bar, him still in his suit, his tie loosened around his neck. Riding the elevator up to his room, a delicious tension as he unlocks the door. Then a quick progression: my jacket shrugged off, the zip on my dress a whisper as he takes it down. For one perfect night – or even just a perfect hour – I'd feel his mouth on mine, my skin against his. I would experience that power: feed off it, take it for my own. Use it to move forward in my life. I will never be a mother. But I am still a woman.

I push the images out of my head, sealing them off like a ship in a bottle. In fact, the whole idea is laughable. Sex is the last thing on my mind – barely a blip on the radar screen of my existence. Tom might have used it to try and alleviate his suffering, but that doesn't mean it was the right decision or that it actually worked. Besides, I have made so many wrong turns in life – I *do not* need to make another one. I've cut up my underwear – I've done my destructive act for the day. This meeting is just business, and I'll keep it short.

I pull up to the hotel entrance and turn my car over to the valet. The bar is dark and swanky, with velvet sofas, chrome, and glass. The colorful bottles behind the bar are backlit like an old-fashioned apothecary. A soft jazz track is playing in the background. It's exactly like I pictured in my mind, and that makes me uncomfortable. I take out my phone. I should call Tom… The knot in my chest tightens again.

"Marianne?" A deep voice calls out from a booth at the side.

Dave is waving at me. There is no champagne and no loosened tie – he's dressed down in a polo shirt and chinos and drinking a glass of white wine. His hair is a little mussed, and, in the dim light of the bar, he looks years younger than he did in the meeting. He looks attractive. Instantly, I feel nervous. I smile at him because that's the best way to protect myself. I hope that I look less like a woman who has failed at IVF, locked her husband out of the bedroom, and cut up an entire drawer of underwear than I feel.

As I sit down opposite, Dave flags down a waitress. I order a glass of white wine, and he changes it to a bottle. Then he sits back in the booth, splays his elbows behind his head, and stares at me. I want to look away, but I can't.

"So Marianne," he says, "it's great to see you. Do you live close by?"

Small talk, getting to know each other. I can keep my answers pleasant, professional, and polite with a smile plastered on my face. *Yes, Dave – I live close by. I'm a friendly and sociable person. My life is great – everything is great.*

"No." I frown. "Not really."

"Well, I'm grateful that you made the effort to come here. Like I said, it's good to get to know each other. You intrigued me in the meeting."

"Oh? Why is that?"

"Let me tell you a secret." He leans in, a conspiratorial twinkle in his eye. I can sense him slipping back into Messiah mode. It rankles that he's using the same patter from earlier.

"You're right that a lot of people think I'm peddling in parlor games. I've worked hard on practicing how to talk them around. I'm a salesman, and I rely on the fact that most people are content to see exactly what they want to see." He takes a sip of his wine. "But the truth is that my job – my whole life's work – is revealing what's underneath. The foundations of who people are and why. So I'm always impressed by people who voice their true opinions. Those are the people I want to get to know."

I'm glad the wine arrives because I'm not entirely sure how to respond. He's still looking at me. It's my turn to say something.

"Maybe it was my true opinion," I say. "Or maybe I was just having a bad moment – a bad day."

"Maybe," he says. "Anything you want to talk about?"

My lips form an automatic "no," but I don't say it. He's wrong about me. I've never been one to put my true self on show. The opposite, really. I'm a person who says what I'm expected to say, does what I'm expected to do. Even with the people I love, like Tom and my mother. Especially with them. Some people say that it's easier to open up to a total stranger, but I've never tried it before. I'm not about to start now…

"My eighth and last IVF failed. I'm not pregnant. I found out this morning, just before the meeting. The baby… the embryo… I lost it."

Did I just say that? Oh my God, I think I did. I open my mouth and try to retrieve the words, suck them back. Instead, I hear other words coming out of my mouth. Describing the "trying", the failures, the miscarriages, the embryos that should have been viable but didn't implant or that didn't grow properly. All those tiny sparks of life that will never draw a breath or let out a cry. That will never know pain or love, or anything at all.

Part of me knows this is madness – I may not be the woman I was before, but this is inappropriate and beyond the pale. I watch his face, expecting to see a mirror of my own horror and shame. Expecting to see judgment.

Instead, he sits still for a long, silent moment. Emotions play over his face like clouds scattering across the moon, but I can't read them. Then, in a gesture that is entirely human, entirely caring, he puts his hand over mine.

"Marianne," he says, "I'm so—"

"Don't say it." I jerk my hand away. "Please don't say you're sorry. I can't stand people who are sorry."

"OK. So what should I say?"

"Nothing." I stare down at my glass. "I don't know. I just… wanted to tell the truth for once."

"Sure, I get it."

I should go. It was suicide to open up – and to Dave, my client, of all people. For a fleeting moment, I think of my father. Did he ever go to a hotel bar and end up having a drink with a woman who was completely unhinged? I push the thought from my head. I should go, but instead, I just sit there. The hole inside of me is too deep, too dark to escape.

"I was intrigued by you before," he says, "but I wasn't expecting you to surprise me."

I look up, my eyes clouded with darkness.

"The minute I saw you, I thought that you were more than just a beautiful woman. But if you're the kind of person who can face up to her worst nightmares and still show up for work – show up for life – then you're truly a force to be reckoned with."

Emotions bubble up inside of me, forcing their way to the surface. I try to imagine Tom saying the words that Dave has just said – believing that about me. I take a breath, bracing myself to start sobbing. Instead, what comes out is a laugh – too loud and too high-pitched. I laugh and laugh, and I can barely breathe, and I feel a strange sense of cognitive dissonance, like my emotions are all wrong. Dave sits there watching me, a little amused. Then, he laughs too. As I take out a tissue and wipe the tears from my eyes, I see something else in his expression. Desire.

It's been a long time since anyone has looked at me like that. A long time since I've felt that strange sensation, like looking over the edge of a tall building. I am in no state to do anything other than laugh it off, and then step back out of the wind…

He stands up. "Come on, Marianne. Let's go for a walk. I want to hear more about you. I want to know... everything."

Or...

He's a Messiah. It's his job to figure out what people need and give it to them, even if they don't know it themselves.

I stand up just as my phone buzzes and the screen flashes with a name: Tom. I turn off my phone and slip it into my purse.

... I might just decide to jump.

19

CLAIRE

The tulips wilt, the kitchen countertop loses its mirror shine, the film crew collects their equipment. Everything goes back to a fraught and grubby state of normal. Jess's new medication starts to take effect, and she insists that she's well enough to go back to school. Steve and I coexist in uneasy silences. Even Becky, who can usually be counted on to talk loudly and thoughtlessly at mealtimes, seems unusually subdued.

At first, I have an uneasy sense that something is happening behind my back that I know nothing about – scientists in their white coats testing my DNA, comparing it to charts, and entering it onto a database. Pressing a button to create a lightning network of connections all over the world. But as the week progresses, there are no more texts from *MyStory* about long-lost relatives in Timbuktu or even the lower fifty states. My sense of unease shifts to worrying about whether the process has ground to a halt. Or worse, that somehow my family is a tiny island floating in a vast sea of interconnections, isolated from the rest of humanity. I begin to wish that I'd agreed to go to Norway – anything so as not to feel abandoned. Another week goes by. There's no promised visit from Dave.

Eventually, Stella calls to schedule a few hours of follow-up filming. I spend a few hours the day before trying frantically to return the house to its show-home appearance. The morning of, I take the scented candles out of the drawer and arrange them on the table. I cut some camellias from the backyard and put them in a vase. But no matter how hard I try, the bloom is off the rose. By the time the kids leave for school and Steve has gone to work, I feel a rising sense of panic that I can't explain. I scrub the sink again, then the toilets.

The phone rings. My stomach gives a reflexive clench. Is it Jess's school – is she having a relapse? Is Stella calling to cancel?

No and no.

I feel no better when I see that the caller is my editor from the local paper. Over the years, he's provided me with a steady drip of freelance work, and he's expecting me to write a series of articles about the DNA testing. Inevitably, after a few minutes of small talk, he asks me how the first article is going.

"Great!" I say. *I haven't started yet.* "It's the best thing I've done."

"Can you get me a draft today?" he says. "Because the *Chronicle* might be interested."

"Today?" My mind races to all the reasons why not. Stella and her crew are due at three, and I was hoping to wash my hair first. But the *Chronicle*... if there's even the slightest chance of them picking up my article, then surely I have to take it.

"I'll need it by four."

"By four," I repeat dumbly. I hang up the phone and put my head in my hands. My bracelet jangles, and I stare at the little silver charms, hoping to draw strength from the love they represent. Then, I unclasp it so that I can type more easily and get to work.

I do a quick outline. I want to address the rise of the home DNA-testing industry and its transformation from novelty to "next big thing". My plan is to put a positive spin on it – the excitement of being a modern historian and genealogist from the comfort of one's own home. Bringing the past to life, giving our families a historical context. Finding out more about the people who may only be names on a gravestone or old photos in the attic, but whose blood flows in our veins. It *is* an exciting thing to be a part of.

But I also want to tell the other side of the story. The darker underbelly of what such tests and databases might mean for people's daily lives. I've already bookmarked a few accounts of the "DNA Horror Stories" that companies like *MyStory* would rather sweep under the rug. I note down accounts of anonymous egg and sperm donors who were found through DNA database hits. Not all reunions are welcome and happy. There are cases of people getting nasty surprises that their parents weren't really their parents or that their siblings were actually half-siblings. There are accounts of people discovering that they are susceptible to certain diseases, leading to fear and depression. And there are accounts of so-called Genetic Cousins showing up on people's doorsteps asking for money, or filing lawsuits to overturn inheritances, or generally making a nuisance of themselves through a claim of being "family".

Will I end up as one of the horror stories? I can't help but wonder as I make notes of sources and angles for follow-up. Meeting up with my Genetic Cousins, asking them to become bone marrow donors for my daughter.

What would I do if someone showed up on my doorstep asking me to donate a body part? While the bone marrow test is not evasive – a cheek swab or a blood test – the transplant procedure is major surgery. Bone marrow is extracted from the donor's hip bones using a needle and syringe. It can be painful for days afterward, and there may be other side effects.

The more I think about it, the more my search sounds not only ludicrous but parasitic. That certainly isn't my intention. On the other hand, I have to keep thinking about my daughter. There are many altruistic people out there who put themselves forward to be donors. I just need to find that one special person.

I shut down the bad searches and start writing my article, concentrating on the positives. Family, humans connecting with each other, Becky's genuine interest in our family's past. Putting our lives in perspective, seeing ourselves and our problems as part of a greater whole. Our ancestors have come through hard times, and we can too.

I spend the morning writing and produce a credible draft. It feels good to achieve something. I just wish I could stop now and step back from my own journey, focusing only on other people. But I know why I'm doing this and why I have to keep going, come what may.

It's almost one o'clock by the time I print out the draft. As I read through it, I realize that it's not quite as good as I thought. It's missing something… I can't put my finger on what. It niggles at me – but I need to prepare for the camera crew's arrival, and I still need to wash my hair. As I'm staring at the words on the page, the doorbell rings. My mind immediately jumps to fight or flight mode. I'm not finished with the article; I'm not ready for the crew to arrive early… My heart is racing as I rush to answer the door.

It's Dave Steiner.

Instantly, I go into self-assessment mode. Hair = messy. Clothes = frumpy. Make-up = non-existent. Self-confidence = zero. But then, Dave smiles at me like I'm the most beautiful person in the world. I lift my shoulders. I almost feel like I could take flight.

"Claire," he says. "It's so great to see you."

I stand there waiting for the bear hug that doesn't come. Of course, it doesn't. Dave is not a family member. He's a businessman trying to sell a product. Why can't I get that through my head?

"Nice of you to take time out of your busy schedule to stop by." I sound like a spoiled child.

"Oh, it's no problem." He grins. "I've been looking forward to catching up with you. Anything to escape the evil clutches of bankers and lawyers. I'm going to be doing a lot of flying back and forth to D.C. for meetings, but for now, it's nice to relax a little."

"Well, you'd better come in then." I can't help smiling as I usher him inside. I'm a person he can relax with. *Me.*

He follows me into the kitchen. I'm glad of my efforts to transform it back to a stage set – I hope he'll stay long enough to see me transformed by the make-up woman. I always wanted my dad to see me at my best, though it rarely happened that way. Usually, he was there when I was at my worst – messy, pimply, tearful. I guess it was good that he was there during the tough times, but I wish he'd seen a few more of my triumphs, small as they may have been. I decide that I'll show Dave my article. See what he thinks.

Dave sits down at the table. "Looking good," he says. "Though, I really didn't have you down as the scented candle type."

"I'm not."

"Should I have a word with Stella? Portray you as you really are?"

"No. Absolutely not."

I microwave him a cup of coffee, adding sugar and milk. Dave has a sweet tooth when it comes to hot drinks, hot chocolate being his favorite. This whole situation is weird enough without my knowing that.

"Can I show you my article?" I say as I bring his coffee over. "It's the first of the series. I'd be interested in your thoughts."

"Sure." Something flashes across his face. Boredom? Annoyance?

"I mean – you don't have to read it. If you're trying to relax."

"Let's have a look."

"OK." I wipe my hands nervously on my top. I'm not wearing my bracelet – maybe that's why I feel a little off. I rush to the study and clasp the bracelet back on my wrist. Instantly I feel calmer as if the tinkling of the charms has channeled Dad's spirit.

I give Dave the draft. He's already drunk most of his coffee. I swoop in to refill the cup. I add more sugar and more milk. He's reading my article… peering closely at the paper. I feel nervous – which is just stupid.

"Here's more coffee," I say brightly.

"Thanks." He sets aside the article like he's done reading it. It's taken me less than a minute to make the coffee. Has he read it that quickly? Or…

"That bad?" I say.

"No. It's… great. We should hire you to do our PR."

"I know there are some negatives in it. But you know I have to take a balanced approach."

"Sure. And you've done that very well."

I put my hands on my hips. "But…" I say, "there's a 'but…'. Come on, Dave, I can take it. I want the truth."

He laughs. "OK, Claire. The truth. I'm not a newspaper editor, and the article's good. You've captured the big picture – and you know I'm passionate about that. It's all about our children and our children's children. It won't take too many years before all of our genetic data will be uploaded and cataloged. Our great-grandchildren will be able to go to the library – or rather, access an online library – and trace their lineage back to the Stone Age. That's why I'm doing this."

"That's not why I'm doing it."

"Exactly! Got it in one. That's what's missing from the article, Claire. You!"

"Me? What are you talking about?"

"Your personal journey. That's what we're all invested in. When I read your article, I want to know why *you're* doing this."

"You know why I'm doing this." I'm flustered now. He's right, of course – he's identified the flaw.

"One of the problems we've both got is volume. If there were more people on the bone marrow registry, then your job of finding a donor for Jess would be easier. Same with me achieving my dream – I need to get more people out there taking tests. We've been handing out free tests to widen the pool, as you know. But lots of people still think it's a lark – a game. Families sitting around the table at Christmas dinner doing mouth swabs while they wait their turn at Scrabble."

"So…?"

"So an article like yours can help people see that it's more than that – or it could be. Yes, there are still some limitations to the science, but that's changing every day.

People need to get themselves on my database so that people like Jess have a chance."

I frown. There's a flaw in his argument that I'm not quite seeing.

"Someone out there is a match for Jess," he adds. "We just need to reach that person."

We. If I can cling on to anything from this conversation, it's that. I'm not alone in this.

"I know," I say. "But it just seems like such a long shot."

Dave chuckles fondly. "I like that you're a tough nut to crack. In fact, when I get up in the morning, look in the mirror, practice my pitches, and plan my press pieces, I think: 'What would it take to convince Claire?' Meeting you has been invaluable for that."

"Glad I could help," I say drily. I shouldn't feel flattered, but I do.

"Ah, Claire…" He reaches out across the table and covers my hand with his. It's such a caring gesture that I almost lose my composure. "I know that things are difficult for you. But you're such a strong person."

"No…" I take my hand away. "I'm not. I'm just doing what I have to do."

"Case in point."

"Anyway…" I shrug, eager to deflect the conversation away from me. "I think you've made a convert in Becky – or Stella has." I tell him about her interest in the Norway connection.

"I'm sure. For her generation, this will be commonplace. I'm happy to include her in the study."

"No way. She uploads enough stuff online to satisfy even the most elusive cyber-stalker. I don't need her uploading her DNA too."

"But that's what you're doing. Your DNA is her DNA."

"Yes, well… I know that." For a second, the horror

stories flash back into my mind. I don't want that for me – or for Becky.

Dave studies me closely. "Look, Claire, at the end of the day, this is your decision. You can walk away right now. I'll delete your profile from the database, send the film crew home, and we can call it quits. No hard feelings."

He's giving me an out. Surely, I should take it. A chance to stay myself, to keep my story to myself. Write my bland article and take my chances with the bone marrow registry. Be the same woman I was before I started this journey.

"I'm sure that a match will come up for Jess on the registry," he adds. "Eventually. In time."

I laugh miserably. "Time is a luxury we don't have. Every day that she's ill is one more day gone from her life. I've agreed to take a Genetic Journey – for a lot of reasons. And once I commit to something, then I see it through. Follow the yellow brick road and all that."

"That's another thing I like about you." When he smiles at me, he seems to take in my whole person, inside and out.

"Oh, stop." I blush.

"Sure." He immediately cuts the crap. He takes out his phone, pulls up something on the screen, and slides it over to me. "I'm glad we've got that straight. Now, since you're continuing on with your journey, it's time to step it up. I understand why you feel you can't go to Norway, so we've found you a few Genetic Cousins closer to home. Not as exotic a locale, but maybe a little more up your street…"

PART II

APRIL

20

CLAIRE

Two weeks later, I board a private jet to Austin, Texas, to meet my Genetic Cousins, Jeff and Jill Larsson.

I am leaving my family behind to venture into the great unknown. Steve was incandescent. Becky was indifferent. When I had to say goodbye to Jess, I lost it completely. Severing the umbilical cord all over again. I cried for almost two hours in the taxi to the airport. When the plane took off, I cried again. Tears of freedom. Tears of relief.

A camera crew films me getting off the plane (three takes of me going up and down the jetway stairs with my hair blowing into my mouth and the director barking: "look vulnerable!"). I meet the Larssons in a park by the river, at a kite festival. I'm not totally clear on the symbolism, but the film crew thought it would make a nice backdrop for the meeting.

Jeff and Jill arrive in a big Ford pickup, wearing big Stetson hats. In contrast, I feel sweaty and mousey in my navy striped J.Crew top and white linen trousers. My heart is pounding. I don't know these people from Adam. And yet, I *want* to like them and for them to like me.

The cameras are rolling as they walk over to me. I smile idiotically and hold out my hand. Instead, Jill throws her arms around me. "Claire," she says. "It's so great to finally meet you!"

I sweat in her embrace and then go to the outstretched arms of Jeff.

"Welcome home to Texas," he says.

"Um… thanks," I say. "It's… really hot."

"Oh, this is nothing!" It's only when Jill launches into a time-honored monologue about the weather that I come to realize she's nervous too. I like her for that. When she's done talking about hailstones the size of golf balls and weather hot enough to fry a rattlesnake on a rock, she leans in and whispers. "Sorry, dear. I'm rambling. I always find these first meetings hard."

"Me too," I whisper back. I like her even more.

There's a brief interlude where the film crew gets Jeff to fly a big "I love Texas" kite in the shape of a bucking steer. I make small talk with Jill until the footage is in the can (or the digital equivalent). Then we go to a dark little steak restaurant near the state capitol building, which is at least quiet and, more importantly, air-conditioned. There, I find out more about my Genetic Cousins. Jeff and Jill are brother and sister, both married, with kids and grandkids. Jeff's eldest son, Jeff Jr., is in the FBI missing persons division. His youngest son, Jonny J, is at Texas A&M studying American history. Jonny J got a free test handed out to him at his university. It was his idea to get the whole family tested, which they did at their annual Christmas gathering at the Larsson ranch in the Hill Country. ("Only two miles away from Lyndon B. Johnson's ranch – once we were practically neighbors.")

Since then, Jeff and Jill have met over a hundred of their Genetic Cousins, and apparently, new ones keep popping up all the time. I have a distinct feeling that I'm late to the party. Jill tells me about all the people they've met: doctors, pilots, ballroom dance teachers, truck drivers; in various locations: Texas, Wisconsin, Florida, and North Carolina being the Larsson hotspots.

"That was why Dave Steiner asked us to be part of his film," Jill explains. "He says that we're exactly the kind of people he's looking for. People who want to make the world smaller by making our world bigger." She stares straight into the camera as she says this, but I can almost hear the same words coming out of Dave's mouth. I feel a little annoyed, but I can't put my finger on why. Maybe because up to now, I've been pretty content with the size of my world as it is.

"It's just been so exciting," she finishes.

"I'm sure," I say. "I'm just starting my journey, so I guess I've got all that ahead of me."

"So what about you, Claire?" Jeff says.

"Yeah… um…" I take a breath. This is why I'm here. I tell them the basics: husband, job, two kids. The director gives me a nod, and I continue. "My youngest daughter is sick. She's got a condition called Severe Aplastic Anemia or SAA." I go on to explain Jess's illness. I feel like some kind of spokeswoman charged with educating the public or, in this case, the "family".

"That must be tough," Jeff says. "Jeff Jr. has a serious nut allergy. Once or twice in the early days, it was touch and go."

"It's not *exactly* like a nut allergy," I begin, then stop myself. "It's hard, isn't it? You just feel so out of control. Knowing that any moment, you could lose the person you love most."

"You hit the nail on the head," Jeff says. "And most people just don't understand. Why they can't pass him the peanuts at a baseball game, or why he's not eating the brownies they brought. That kind of thing."

I begin to feel a warm bond with Jeff. A solid connection based on more than a Great-Great-Grandma Ackerman who married a Larsson four generations ago. Jeff and I understand each other because we've both got children who have suffered.

"Jess loves playing her violin," I say. "She's got an audition for the San Francisco Youth Orchestra." Tears fill my eyes. I miss her so much. I even miss Becky. I almost… even miss Steve. "But she's in the hospital a lot. She needs regular blood transfusions. All the other treatments so far have failed. And as she gets older, it's not going to improve. In fact, it's likely to get worse. We're running out of options."

"Oh, honey." Jill looks distressed.

"The only cure for her illness is a bone marrow transplant. It's the only way she's ever going to be able to lead a normal life. Not have to worry about hospitals and germs, be able to go on school trips and hang out at the mall." I sigh. "But the problem is, she's not a match for anyone on the registry."

"So that's why you're doing this!" Jill claps her hands. "I *was* wondering. Don't take this the wrong way, Claire, but you don't seem like the others we've met who are doing it for fun."

"You're right," I say. "I'm hoping – but not expecting – that maybe someone out there…" I break off, shaking my head. "It's a long shot, but it's her only chance."

"So, what can we do to help?" Jeff says without hesitation.

Bless him. Deep down, I wasn't expecting to meet people who would actually take their role as distant blood relatives seriously and want to be *kind*.

"We can email all the Larssons on the master list," Jill adds. "If you want that."

"That would be brilliant," I say, tears prickling. "But I don't expect people to get tested for a bone marrow match. I mean, it's kind of like giving blood, so it's not difficult. But people have their own busy lives and—"

"We're family," Jill decrees. "And that's what family does – we help each other."

I think about this later when I'm back in my hotel room. *We're family. We help each other.* I feel uplifted by the fact that there are people out there who want to help, expecting nothing more in return than a Christmas card and maybe a batch of nut-free brownies. Will everyone I meet on this journey be as kind and unselfish? Am I the only selfish one, the one who needs something?

I open up a new file on the computer and begin writing a second article – a more personal one like Dave suggested. I'm planning it to be Jess's story, but the introduction, at least, ends up being all about me. I study the Texas charm on the bracelet that Dad gave me – a bucking steer with a cowboy on top. Whether or not the connection with the Larssons comes to anything or not, at least I've finally been to one of the places Dad visited. That seems like a milestone of sorts.

As I continue to write, I push the horror stories out of my mind. If everyone I meet is like the Larssons, then maybe my journey will be one of the happy ones. I just need to keep believing…

21

BECKY

My big chance arrives unexpectedly. Mom announces that she's going off to meet some Genetic Cousins in Texas for a few days. That's a big deal – Mom never goes anywhere. She and Dad have another shouting match, and I go up to my room and count my money. With Mom out of the way, it's the perfect time to start on Jess's Bucket List.

I've got exactly $82.62 saved up from babysitting and dog-walking. I also have some money in the bank from Christmases and birthdays, but that's my car fund. I'll need to find another solution for the big-ticket item – Jess's trip to New York. That's going to cost a lot more than I've got.

Dad used to tell me that I should focus on my strengths, not my weaknesses. But ever since the day the blood test results came back, I've stopped trying. Whenever I get an idea or an inspiration or think, "maybe I'll try this… or that…", I remember that I'm *useless, absolutely useless!*

Since then, I have found things I'm good at. I'm good at shoplifting, drinking, and binge dieting. My biggest claim to fame was when my so-called boyfriend sophomore year circulated a topless photo of me on Snapchat. Some people laughed, some people said nasty things, but everyone noticed me.

I wish that Mom would notice me, but in a good way, for once. I want to prove to her that I don't always make bad decisions. But the question is, how? It's hard to think about the future because I need to be here for Jess. When I think about what I might want to do with my life, I draw a complete blank. Right now, my dream job is to be a TV presenter like Stella. She's beautiful and put together, but smart too. When I met her, she didn't talk down to me. She treated me like an adult – an equal. Unfortunately, the smart/beautiful thing probably rules it out for me.

As soon as Mom is gone, I take twenty dollars and ride my bike to the drugstore. I'll start small – get the purple hair dye. It strikes me that Mom will probably be mad, and that makes me mad. I mean, if Jess gets worse and has to have chemo, then she'll lose all her hair anyway. I want her to have a chance to look glamorous and feel special before that happens.

I find the right aisle, but I can't find the right color. They have deep red and lilac rinse for old people, but they don't actually have purple. I end up finding some other stuff, though – some lipstick that's on sale, some hairspray that smells like mangos (no joke – it really does!), and some Red Vines, which are Jess's favorite candy.

I take everything up to the cashier, and it comes to $18.45. When I see the total, I come to my senses. If I spend twenty bucks on crap, then I'll never be able to afford the other stuff on Jess's Bucket List. I have to keep my eye on the ball – I can't afford a fail. So I smile sweetly at the cashier and say, "Oops, actually, I forgot my wallet."

She clicks her tongue in annoyance as I leave the entire bag of stuff behind and waltz out the automatic door.

When I'm outside the store, I feel good. I have actually *resisted* temptation and made the right decision. I figure the universe owes me one, so I go over to Stacey's house, and sure enough, her cousin knows somebody who works at a hair salon at the mall. We make Jess an appointment to get her hair dyed purple by a professional. It's going to cost $31.25 plus tax, but I figure it's worth it. We go to the food court, and I spend $8.25 on a teriyaki beef bowl, and then find that Stacey doesn't have any money, so I buy hers too. In the end, I've spent most of the $20 that I saved at the drugstore. So I'm not feeling quite so good.

But because I'm doing the right thing in helping Jess fulfill her dreams, the universe smiles on me again. On our way out of the mall, we run into a group of Jess's friends. It's kind of sad that Jess can't hang out at the mall with them because she needs to stay safe from germs, but if she could, she probably wouldn't be the same sister she is now. Anyway, I ask Jess's friend Carla who Taylor Compton is and what he's like. Carla's giggle says it all.

Turns out he's a popular, class president, future quarterback kind of guy. The kind of guy that all the girls like. He's probably out of Jess's league – and that makes me dislike him. "Do you have his number?" I say.

"No." Carla giggles again (which is really annoying).

"Can you get it?"

"Why do you want it?"

"Just get it." I text her my number. Jess is either going to kiss me or kill me. "And here." I give her the rest of the change from the twenty. "Go buy yourself an ice cream."

As we leave the mall, Stacey turns to me. "Are you sure you know what you're doing, Becky?"

I give her a long, level look. Now is the time to step up to the plate. Believe, achieve, succeed…

"Nope," I say. "Haven't got a clue."

———

I plan it as a surprise. Jess gets a transfusion on Friday afternoon, and the next day she has her violin lesson and is feeling well enough to go. Afterward, Stacey's mom drives us to the mall. Jess seems kind of preoccupied about her big audition – her lesson has tired her out, and she looks really pale. For a second, I wonder if it would be best just to take her home to rest, or maybe make her wear a surgical mask. (I bought her this really cute one with a cat's face and whiskers on it, but when I ask her about it, she says she's lost it.) But when I tell her we've got a surprise for her, I can see that she really wants to know what it is. Just before we get to the hair salon, I make her close her eyes. Then I lead her inside.

"Surprise!" I say, telling her what we've got planned.

"Um… cool." Her face turns a little green. "Does Mom know?"

"No! That's why this is the perfect time to make a start on the Bucket List!"

"OK…"

She's going to chicken out. I can't let that happen. This is her *dream*, after all.

"Look, I'll get my hair dyed too," I say. "Blue – my favorite color."

"Really?" Her face lights up like a full moon.

"Yeah, sure."

I arrange it with the hairdresser. All that's available is a trainee, but she'll have to do. Stacey sits on the stool laughing at us. Let her laugh. I haven't actually told her the second part of the day's plan. There's another item on Jess's list that I'm planning to make a start on.

This is going to be incredibly awesome – I have to keep telling myself that.

As the dye is rinsed out of Jess's hair, I give her an encouraging smile. There are bruises around her neck above the line of her T-shirt. Bruises that seriously shouldn't be there because she just had a transfusion! Her hairdresser has noticed them too, and she's stopped being chatty. Maybe she thinks Jess is being abused – which is what lots of people think before they know the truth. My stomach feels queasy. Maybe Jess should have gone for pink – something that's not the same color as a bruise. But it's too late now. Our two hairdressers turn our backs to the mirror while they do the comb-outs and blow-dries, so we'll be surprised (and happy!) with the final results. I keep up a steady flow of conversation – something that I'm pretty good at. I tell Jess how *outré* we are, which means "out there" in French. I think. I tell her how Mom's going to be so surprised (in a good way). Jess's face gets paler and paler. And then – it's time for the big reveal! The hair-dresser tells us to close our eyes. She spins us around. *Voila.*

"Oh," I say. *Oh.*

It's a disaster. My hair has turned a strange shade of blue-green, kind of like bread mold. Jess's hair looks like some kind of scary Halloween gone wrong. It's definitely purple, but with lighter strands of lilac and darker ones of black. With her skin so pale, she looks like a corpse.

Jess lets out a little scream. Then, the tears start.

I can't move. I feel shocked and embarrassed. "Um, looks great," I lie.

Stacey goes over to Jess and tries to comfort her, saying, "It's not as bad as you think." I stagger over to the counter and pay. With tip, it costs every penny I have. That makes me want to cry too.

And then I remember Plan B. *Oh God*. It seemed like a good idea at the time. Now, though… What have I done?

What I've done is WhatsApp'd Taylor Compton, Jess's crush, and set up a "first date" between them. I channeled my inner Stella and made up a story that I'm doing an interview for the *Roseville Reporter* – the high school newspaper – about up-and-coming future freshmen. He's the kind of boy (nice but a little full-of-himself) who agreed without too much persuasion. Jess knows nothing, and Taylor doesn't know that he's supposed to be meeting up with my newly transformed, glamorous, purple-haired sister. We've agreed to meet in front of Annie's Pretzels.

Jess rushes out of the salon. Annie's Pretzels is just across the way. I take out my phone, frantically trying to text him. Abort! Mayday! SOS!

I'm too late. Taylor Compton is right where he's supposed to be, right on time. I recognize his photo from WhatsApp. He's cute in that All-American Boy kind of way. Blond hair, blue eyes, braces, 49ers T-shirt, nice butt in denim shorts. I can see why Jess likes him. I can see why he's probably never looked twice at her.

I try to maneuver Jess past him, but it's impossible.

"Jess?" he says. "Is that you?"

My sister takes one look at Taylor Compton, and the tears turn into Niagara Falls.

"Taylor," I say, "thanks for coming. I'm afraid we're going to have to reschedule."

"What? Who are you?"

"I'm Becky Woods, Jess's sister." I look over to where Stacey is hugging my sister's shaking body. "I wanted… Oh… hell. Never mind."

Taylor looks at me like I have three heads. Then, he shrugs. "Whatever." He turns and walks off, right past Jess.

"Nice hair," he says with a cocky grin.

At that moment, I hate Taylor Compton. I hate Stacey and her hairdresser friend, and everyone else in this mall. I hate Jess's illness and the fear that I'm going to lose her.

But all of that pales in comparison to how much I hate myself.

22

"Becky!"

Dad's voice bellows up the stairs.

"What have you done?"

OK – I know it's obvious that Jess probably wouldn't have got her hair dyed on her own, but she was the one who put it on the list. Dad used to tell me that I shouldn't be afraid to "put myself out there" and that "it's OK to make mistakes." I made a mistake on this – I hold my hand up freely and own it. It's really far from OK.

Jess has barely stopped crying since we got home. I stood at her door, feeling like a blue-haired idiot, and watched as, in a grand gesture, she ripped up her Bucket List. If things had gone right, I'd had big plans for the second part of the Bucket List – buying bus tickets to San Francisco and running away for the day so that Jess could busk in Union Square. It would have cost about a hundred bucks. But now, I've got no money left and no hope whatsoever.

I go to my room and try to exercise mind over matter:

imagining a hole opening up in the floor that will swallow me forever. The one saving grace is that Mom is away, and Jess doesn't want to FaceTime with her. I have the strong urge to carve my skin with scissors: *What will Mom do when she finds out?*

In perhaps my only good decision of the day, I keep the scissors in the drawer. Instead, I try to think about how to right my wrong. I could make another appointment at the salon to try and undo the damage, but unless I beg money off Dad, I can't afford it. It all comes down to money in the end.

I wish Mom's DNA test might reveal a rich relative – like some kind of banker or CEO – like Daddy Warbucks. Then I could show up on his doorstep and say, "Hi! I'm Becky, your Genetic Cousin." And he would invite us inside his huge mansion with a swimming pool and servants and say, "Nice to meet you." We'd start talking, and then he'd agree to take me and Jess under his wing and transform our lives into something glamorous and special. We could go to the hairdresser every weekend and try all sorts of outlandish things. We could fly to New York for a weekend shopping trip and do one of those open-top bus tours that take in all the sights. We could go to a concert at Lincoln Center – Jess would love that. Best of all, she could take a tour of Carnegie Hall and stand on the stage. Maybe if they knew about her condition, they'd even let her take out her violin and play to the tour group or something. That would be beyond amazing.

But right now, there's no Daddy Warbucks. I don't have any money or any way to raise money. And all the money in the world won't make Jess better. Realizing that, I feel even more angry with myself. I wish I could turn the clock back twenty-four hours and avoid doing all the stupid things.

"Becky?" There's a soft thump on the wall.

"Jess?" My heart does a little star jump. My sister is reaching out to me. I may not be a good person, but she is. I get out of bed and go to her room. Everything's fine! I'm going to be forgiven!

But things are not fine. I know that as soon as I enter the room. Jess is lying in bed. Her skin is so pale that her face looks like a white flower petal in a sea of pink. The curtain of purple hair is shocking, garish. But the thing that strikes me most is how still she is. Like she's barely breathing.

"I'm cold, Becky," she says. "Can you get me another blanket? I'm just... too tired to get up."

This can't be happening. She just had a transfusion!

"It's not fair!" I say aloud.

"I'm sorry," Jess says.

"No – not you – don't apologize."

Her teeth begin to chatter. She curls up in a ball.

The fear chills me like an ice cube down my back. Is this my fault? Did she catch a virus at the mall? Is this the beginning of the end? I bound out of the room to get her another blanket. Dad is just coming up the stairs.

"Dad..." My voice shakes a little. "Come in and see Jess. I swear I haven't done anything. But she looks... bad."

Maybe, in another lifetime, Dad would have made a quip about our hair. But now, he jumps to attention.

"Thanks, Becky." He goes past me. "Jess? Are you OK?"

I stand at the door, holding the blanket before he turns back to me. "Call nine-one-one," he says. "She needs an ambulance."

"I want..." Jess's voice is barely a whisper, "... Becky. Can she ride with me?"

I thank the universe. I curse the universe. I pray to the

universe to throw us another lifeline. "Give me a chance to make things right," I whisper.

I'm not expecting an answer, and there isn't one.

23

MARIANNE

I wake up in a cold sweat, tangled in the sheets. A booming beat radiates through my solar plexus. My eyes are cloudy with a haze of smoke, my nose twitching from the sour stink of beer. I hear whispered words in my ear, and for a moment, they make me feel good. *Beautiful, special…* Everything I have ever wanted to be.

That part of the dream is nice.

It's been a long time since I've had the dream, so maybe I'm being punished for not communicating with my husband or using our shared grief to build bridges in our marriage. It's been just over a month since the last loss. Tom and I seem to have settled into a holding pattern, both of us relying on work as an excuse to circle around the issue of *what now?* For him, it's bona fide. He's in the final run-up to a big-name, big-budget production, and his reputation is on the line. I, of course, am flat-out working on the financing. Dave Steiner has been to D.C. two more times since that first meeting. I've mostly seen him at our offices or in group social settings. But ever since the night we met for a drink at his hotel, there is a murkiness between us, a blurring of boundaries. I find myself thinking about him at odd times and hearing his voice in my head.

Beautiful, special… I need to be careful. I'm not religious, but I do believe in a fundamental fairness, a balance of right and wrong. Once upon a time, I committed a monumental wrong… I've been trying to put it right ever since. I can't afford any missteps.

I lie in bed for a few minutes longer, trying to focus on the present. I will the dream to dissolve from my head, the way dreams do. This one doesn't, though, and I know why. First, because it isn't a dream at all, but a memory. Second, because it's a nightmare.

Tom is in the shower; the bedroom feels steamy from the heat of it. I've never told Tom about the dream. Maybe if I had, he would have understood why I am the way I am. It's my fault that despite our years of marriage and everything we've been through together, he's more of a stranger to me than Dave, whom I've known only a short time. With Tom, I've become like the grain of sand inside a pearl, lost inside a hard shell of scar tissue, anger, and regrets. Whereas spending time with Dave is fresh and liberating. Of course, I haven't told Dave *everything*. It's enough just to peel back a few layers and allow myself to breathe. That's all I'm doing.

I get out of bed and go to the walk-in closet to get dressed. I've made an appointment with the ob-gyn before work, so I need to leave early. I stare at myself in the full-length mirror, trying to reconcile the woman I am now with the girl in the dream. The girl I was at seventeen, with my whole life ahead of me. On the surface, I had it all: I was the straight-A student, the dutiful daughter, the teacher's pet. But even back then, it wasn't enough. All I could focus on was what I wanted but didn't have. I wanted friends; I wanted to be popular. I wanted people to look at me and see something other than an awkward geek.

When my father was around, he called me his "little butterfly". I liked the nickname because it felt like he understood that what I needed most was to emerge from my cocoon and spread my wings. I didn't need more hours spent studying; I needed time spent living.

My time came in the winter of my senior year when my mother let me go to the homecoming game. I went with my friend, Tammy, who was an "approved" friend because our mothers were both in the PTA. Tammy looked upon me primarily as a project. That night, she did my hair and make-up and made me change out of the plaid skirt and ironed blouse that I'd arrived in and into a denim mini-skirt and a tight T-shirt that would have scandalized my mother. She loaned me a pair of silver pumps that pinched my toes but made my legs look miles long. When she pulled me in front of the mirror, I didn't recognize myself. I was stunning! "You should dress like this all the time," she said, a proud Pygmalion unveiling a perfect statute-come-to-life, Galatea. It was the first moment when I saw myself as something other than my mother's daughter. I was a girl on the cusp of womanhood, a butterfly ready to break free of the cocoon. The realization was startling, frightening. It was electrifying.

As I sat in the stands shivering (the outfit was not so much "cool" as freezing), I drew looks from people who had never noticed me before. The Tomahawks beat the Raiders 24-3, which was cause for celebration. I thought we would go back to Tammy's house, eat ice cream, and maybe stay up late watching videos. Instead, Tammy told me that we were going to an aftergame party.

I wasn't sure I wanted to go. I had my SATs to take before Christmas and needed to stay focused. My mother might have tolerated a football game, but she would never have approved of a party. But when I saw how Tammy's popular friends were looking at the transformed me, I threw caution to the wind. My wings were itching to unfurl themselves and fly.

The party was noisier, dirtier, smellier, and hotter than I'd imagined. All of the football players and popular girls from school were there. A drink was put in my hand. It tasted like Hawaiian Punch. I lost Tammy in the heat and press of bodies.

An older boy from the junior college came up to me. His name was Hal, and he was from Rockville. He was handsome in that boy-next-door kind of way and seemed nice. I let him get me a second Hawaiian Punch, then a third.

The room got blurry after that, but Hal kept me steady on my feet. We ended up on a sofa in a spare room, and he started to kiss me. I liked the attention and reminded myself that surely, this was what butterflies did. And when he whispered to me that I was the most beautiful girl ever, and so perfect and special, I almost started crying. I kissed him back in earnest. I would have let him do anything at that point. Which he did.

Butterflies are weak and fragile. Not something I'd aspire to be.

"Marianne? Did you hear what I said about Mom's party?"

Tom. His voice startles me back to my senses. The mirror blurs before my eyes, the images dissolving. Who is that woman? Me. It's me. I'm here inside my own house, with my husband. I have a doctor's appointment in an hour, and then I have to get to work. A bad dream… that's all it was.

"Are you all right?"

Tom comes up beside me. His face morphs into the boyish face of Hal. He didn't leave me his phone number. Hal slipped away along with everything else. I never saw him again.

"Marianne?"

I'm clinging to Tom's arm, my nails pressed into his sleeve. Holding on for dear life. I couldn't hang on to Hal. I couldn't hang on to my father. I couldn't hang on to all the dead babies. Tom… he's all I have left.

"Sorry," I say, releasing my grip. "Really. For the way I've been lately." I force myself to brighten. "I've got an appointment to see Dr. Lena this morning. I… was wondering if you wanted to come along. We could get breakfast on the way?"

"I'm off to the gym now." Tom looks at me like I'm a suspicious stranger. "You didn't tell me there was an appointment today."

I try to read between the lines but draw a complete blank. After the home pregnancy test was negative, I went to the clinic to confirm the result with a blood test. I didn't tell Tom about that appointment as there seemed to be no point. Now, though, I wish we'd talked about it. I wish I felt like we *could* talk about it or that there was anything to say.

"Well," I say briskly, "I already had the appointment in case things had… worked out. So I might as well keep it. You know, closure and all."

"Sure, whatever."

My husband's indifference feels like a sharp sting. To him, it will be a waste of time. It *is* a waste of time.

I lean in and give him a peck on the cheek. I can't think of anything to say, so I settle for, "have a nice day."

24

"Mrs. Weissman? Please come with me."

My stomach somersaults with nerves as I stand up and follow the receptionist through the waiting area. I've been here many times, and yet the décor still looks strange to me. A doctor's office should be bland and sterile, with white walls, back issues of *Reader's Digest* and AARP magazines, and a fish tank to add a little color. Instead, Dr. Lena Oldberg's fertility clinic looks like it was decorated by Martha Stewart: chalk-painted furniture, shabby chic cushions, and wicker baskets filled with *Baby and Home* and *Good Housekeeping* magazines and the Pottery Barn catalog. They're going for an aspirational look. Idyllic young mothers with designer nurseries, space-age strollers, perfect babies, and proud fathers. The message is loud and clear: "Give us your money, and we will give you this life."

I've given them my money. Now where the hell is the life?

"Is it just you today?" the receptionist asks me.

"My husband had an important meeting that he couldn't cancel." I smile blandly. She doesn't need any more information. She doesn't need to know about Tom's early mornings at the gym and late nights at the theatre. She doesn't need to know whether or not I'm still entertaining a fantasy about seducing the CEO of *MyStory* even if I would never act on it. She doesn't need to know about my bad dreams or the balance of the scales of divine retribution in my life. All she needs to do is lead me to the comfortable consulting room with two green velvet chairs (the medical table is kept neatly tucked away behind a curtain) and more aspirational reading material. There, I can await the final consultation with my doctor. I feel like one of the children who found a golden ticket to Willy Wonka's Chocolate Factory. Veruca Salt, who was sent down the bad egg shoot. For me, there will be no grand prize, no inheriting the factory. It's not the clinic that has failed me, but I who have failed them.

"Dr. Lena will be with you shortly," the receptionist says as I take a seat.

I don't pick up any of the magazines. I don't look at any of the charts on the walls: the female reproductive system, a guide to healthy eating, stages of fetal development. Instead, I stare down at my hands and try not to think of Tom and the first time we came to the clinic – full of hope – and just a little smug that we were bound to be one of the success stories. I try not to think of my mother, who never had to bother with private fertility clinics. I try not to think about my DNA that is the end of the line and will not be passed on. I try not to think of what happened when I was seventeen that has indirectly led me here. I must be mad to still be clinging to a kernel of hope.

I'm so busy *not thinking* that I'm startled when the doctor comes into the room. I've been a patient of Dr. Lena for well over four years now. She's been my ob-gyn, my shrink, and my Dr. Frankenstein. But as she walks into

the room, I realize that she's also been my friend. I'm
going to miss this. The highs, the lows. The hope.

She comes over and puts a hand on my shoulder. Her
smile is full of compassion. Dr. Lena has been compassionate – to be sure – but also ready to prescribe a dose of
tough love. That's the thing I most value and respect about
her. But now, I sense that the tough love has turned to lost
love. She won't be cheerleading for me to "try again".
She'll be counseling me to let go. I wish I could knock that
compassion right off her face.

"Do you want to get a cup of coffee?" she says. "It
might be nice just to have a chat."

"Sure." A little light goes out inside of me. She's never
suggested coffee before. This *is* the end of the road.

She gets her purse, shoving in a few leaflets from her
desk drawer. I can't help but feel a tiny rekindling of hope.
Has she found something else that I can try?

We make small talk as we walk out of the clinic and
across the landscaped plaza to the coffee shop. Birds are
singing in the manicured trees. We find a table outside next
to an artificial brook burbling over perfectly placed rocks. I
offer to buy, but she insists that it's her treat. She goes to
the counter and brings back my skinny decaf latte and a
hot chocolate with whipped cream and sprinkles for
herself. An indulgent choice, I think, as she sits down opposite me. Her face has a rosy bloom to it. Instantly, I wonder
if she might be pregnant. I clench and unclench my fists
under the table.

"I'm sorry the results were negative," she says,
spooning off a mouthful of cream. "I know how much you
wanted it to work out. And it still could." She opens up her
purse and takes out the leaflets. The first one she pushes
across to my side of the table is on adoption. The second is
on foster parenting.

Instantly, I want to throw them back in her face. I should have known better – medical leaflets are never a good thing. I leave them on the table and take a sip of the too-hot coffee, glad of the pain when it burns my throat.

"You could start a whole new journey," she says. "Adoption or foster parenting."

"No." I cross my arms.

"Marianne, I know this is difficult…"

My anger is a coiled snake basking in the shadows. She's just stepped on it with bare feet.

"No, you don't, Lena!" I half rise from my seat. I want to blow the whipped cream all over her face. "You may see hundreds of women like me every year, thousands even. But don't tell me for one minute that you know what it's like. You're a fraud – with your chic office and your fancy hot chocolate. You're taking people's money and trading on their broken dreams. So don't talk to me about my *journey*!"

Calm – she's so calm. That's the worst thing. Her face reveals nothing, not even a flicker of upset. She's cold and heartless. Why didn't I see it before? Before I got paint samples and fabric swatches, before I researched cribs from Pottery Barn vs. Macy's, or strollers from Maclaren vs. Bugaboo? Why didn't I realize that this was all some sick hoax before I googled names that began with the same letter as Tom's grandmother's name to appease his Jewish relatives, and Christian saint names to please my mother? Why?

She eats the last of the whipped cream from the spoon. The compassion is gone from her face. People come and go from the café: women with fancy strollers, handsome doctors, a few couples well-dressed in smart casual. Talking, laughing, drinking coffee, enjoying the spring sunshine. I should walk out of here right now. Instead, like a kicked puppy, I sit down, still craving that dose of tough love.

"Marianne…" Lena's voice is even. "I know how you're feeling because I've been there, same as you. I've felt every bit as hopeless and angry. Every bit as… crazy."

Tough love. There, out in the open. The "C" word.

"You… have?"

"That's why I chose this specialization," she says. "When I was in my second year of medical school, I was diagnosed with ovarian cancer. My eggs were useless. All those potential babies, all those little lives… Gone."

I lean forward and take another sip of the strong coffee. I feel like I've been hit by a very large bus. All her words… all that tough love… She *does* understand.

"I knew I could never have kids the normal way. And, knowing that, I wanted them more than anything. It's because I knew what it felt like that I wanted to help other women. Women like you."

Women like me. The guilt is overwhelming. I wanted to have it all. My mother told me that I could have it all. I remember it all so clearly… her every word. I listened to her. I believed her. I did what she wanted. Told myself at the time that I wanted it too…

"But… you didn't help me." The words sound selfish and wrong.

"There are no guaranteed miracles in science. I told you that from the beginning. The tests showed that you were capable of getting pregnant by IVF. We went through all the options, and you knew the success and failure rates. We discussed early on whether or not you wanted to use donor eggs, which might have given you a better chance. You elected not to go down that route."

Donor eggs. I recall that, at the time, those sounded like dirty words. The idea of my husband's sperm fertilizing the eggs of another woman and implanted in *my* womb. It sounded hideous, wrong – a chimera created from spare parts. Even now, it makes me nauseous. It makes me—

"Are donor eggs still an option?" I say the words before I've finished the thought. "I mean, I understand that the child wouldn't be mine – not biologically – but still…"

A thousand reasons why it's a terrible idea enter my brain. Tom and I need to work on our marriage. Surely it's better to cut our losses and either divorce or adopt. I would have to go through the injections and the stress, the waiting and the losses all over again. When I'd vowed – and we'd agreed – that this was the last time.

I know all that.

But, suddenly, I am sparkling inside. The idea of having a baby growing in my belly seems of paramount importance. Because surely, I would be her – (I know in my heart that it would be a *her*) – mother. I would play her Mozart in my belly, see her heartbeat on my scans, nurture her by eating all the right foods, and simply *love* her. Or him. The baby would be Tom's – it would be *ours*. I could stop him slipping away from me and pull us both out of the pit of despair.

Lena is studying me from across the table. "It's your body," she says. "And as you're only thirty-eight, it's definitely possible that you might get pregnant with donor eggs."

"Definitely possible?" I say. "So, you're certain that what happened… before… won't cause a problem."

"Biologically, you are capable of carrying a child to term."

"That's great." Inside, the heavy stone of death lifts ever so slightly. I can't turn back the clock. I can't relive the past and make different choices. But I can make all the little sparks of life – all the little deaths – matter.

"But Marianne," she continues, "I have to ask you to consider it carefully. You seem – I don't know – a little unhinged. Perhaps you should leave it a while before making any decisions."

Unhinged! How dare she? Calmly, I push the leaflets back across the table at her. "Do you have a leaflet on egg donation?" I say. "Because I wouldn't mind having a quick skim through."

"I can email you something." Frowning, she picks up her phone again and takes a minute to scroll through. There's a swoosh as the email goes off.

"OK, I've sent it," she says. "But I really think you should take some time to think it over. In your current state, I really can't recommend it—"

"Thanks." I stop listening. Ideas are firing inside my head. I could *do* this. I could make this work. I stand up to leave. "I appreciate your candor. You've been very helpful."

"Don't you want to finish your—?"

Her email pings into my phone.

"I'll give you a call when I decide what I want to do."

25

CLAIRE

I'm in the taxi to the airport when the message comes in from Steve:

Jess is being rushed to the hospital. Where the hell are you?

I have a plummeting sensation, a drowning sense of dread. I immediately call Steve back, but it goes to voicemail. I want to fling my phone out the window; I want to scream at the driver to go faster, but we're stuck in a sea of SUVs, pickups, and brake lights. Most of all, I want to curse Dave Steiner – for organizing this quest that has brought me a thousand miles away from my daughter's bedside where I belong. Instead of cursing him, I call him instead.

Unlike my husband, he picks up on the second ring. "Claire," he says, with all the charm and jollity that deludes me into thinking that he was waiting for *my* call. "How did it go? I heard the Larssons loved you."

"I need you to step up the search," I bark. "The Larssons were great, but I need more. More matches, more potential donors." I tell him what little I know about Jess's condition.

"OK, Claire. Now, here's what I need you to do. I need you to take a breath."

I want to scream at him that I don't want to take a damn breath, not while my little girl is lying in a hospital bed. What horrific treatment will they suggest next? Horse serum ATG? Cyclosporine? Chemo? Some brand-new trial drug that will take forever for the insurance to approve? What will the side effects be? And what about the audition? Her one dream…

"I'll go over to the hospital now," he says. "They know me, so they might let me in even though I'm not a relative. I'll find out exactly what's going on. And then, I'm going to call my scientists. See if they've made any headway."

His words chink my armor. Dave is in my corner, on my side. He's got scientists on it; he'll make something happen. I don't care if other people think he's a charlatan who's selling magic beans or snake oil – I understand why people wanted to believe in those old-time remedies. I believe in Dave much more than I do my own husband, the doctors, or myself. I *want* to believe…

We finally arrive at the airport. Although I'm traveling by private jet, I'm told that the flight will be delayed due to ground fog in San Francisco. I yell at the pilot, though it's not his fault. I know that Dave can't control the weather, but my faith in him begins to waver. I just want to be with my daughter: to sit by her bedside and hold her hand. I want to stroke the hair off her forehead and whisper that everything is going to be OK. She can go to her audition – if that's what she wants – and then she's going to grow up, fall in love, get married, have children – do whatever her heart desires. But I can't do any of that right now. I feel so bitterly, so nauseatingly, helpless.

At last, the pilot announces that we can take off. Before we even reach the runway, the flight attendant has taken matters into her own hands and brought me two small bottles of red wine. I've drunk the first one by the time we're in the air. By the time we're out of Texas airspace, I've downed the second one and everything starts to blur.

As soon as we land, I check my phone. There's another missed call from Steve. Infuriatingly, he hasn't left a message, nor does he pick up when I call him. Dave, however, has arranged a car to whisk me away from the airport all the way home. That usually takes just under two hours, but today there's an accident on the northbound 101, which adds an extra agonizing hour to the journey. By the time we pass the blockage, I am hating myself. I vow that I will not be leaving my daughter's side again, no matter what happens.

We arrive at the hospital, and I jump out of the car. I run inside, so breathless and incoherent that I can barely even speak to the receptionist.

"I'm Claire Woods. My daughter, Jessica, is here."

It takes another eternity for the receptionist to type in the name and come up with the details.

"She's in the pediatric ward."

My mind plays a nasty little trick on me, and I hear it as the "morgue".

"No!" I cry. "She can't be…"

"Well, yes, that's where they put children." The woman sounds alarmed, like I'm the one who should be admitted to a different kind of hospital.

"What?"

"Pediatrics. The children's ward. Follow the blue line."

I snap back to my senses, noticing the tangle of lines painted on the floor like court lines in a gymnasium. I find the blue one and start to run. I go through nearly every corridor, up the elevator two floors, and finally, dead-end at a locked door with a buzzer on the wall next to an automatic hand sanitizer dispenser.

As I press the buzzer and wait for someone to let me in, I try and bargain with God – or the devil – with any higher power that might be willing to listen. I'll give up this ridiculous Genetic Journey and stay at home with my family 24/7 if only Jess can be all right. Alternatively, I'll follow the journey to the ends of the earth, personally meeting up with every person who shares even an iota of my DNA if it means that I can save Jess. I would gladly barter my life to save hers. Why won't someone take it?

The door buzzes open. I'm not sure if it's an angel or a demon that's been listening to my prayers, but the first person I see beyond the nurses' station is Dave Steiner.

"Claire!" He holds out his arms as I rush to him. "I'm sorry I couldn't call you. They've got a no-mobile-phone policy here." He shakes his head. "Ridiculous."

"Is Jess…?"

"She's resting now."

Instantly, it's like he's pressed the stop button on the roller coaster just before the car is about to fall. I may still be hovering in the wind at a great height, but now there's time to prepare for the drop. I cling to Dave with all my might.

"It's going to be OK." His voice is soft, near my ear. "I promise."

"I don't see how it can be," I sob. "Everything is such a mess. And then, Jess needed me, and I wasn't there for her."

In fact, I'm still not there for her. I'm wallowing in my grief and guilt in the arms of a man who is almost – but isn't – like my dad. God or devil? Angel or demon? Does it matter?

"I want to see her," I say. "Where is she?"

"She's—"

"Ahem." At the sound of the clearing throat, I know that I've made another big mistake. I tear myself apart from Dave.

"Steve." I force myself to smile into my husband's furious face. "I'm so sorry that I wasn't here. Where's Jess? Is she all right?"

For an awful second, I think that he's going to demand that I leave or else threaten to call security to escort me from the premises. Either that or commandeer a scalpel off a cart and slit Dave's throat. Or mine. It occurs to me that maybe it's a good thing he's jealous – at least he cares – and that must count for something.

He stands aside and gestures down the hall.

"Room six," Dave supplies for him.

There will be words, but right now, I have only one objective. I run down the hall to Jess's room and poke my head inside the door.

My baby is lying in the bed. I can barely see her through the jungle of drips and tubes. She's so small, barely a lump under the thin green blanket. Her skin is marbled and blue. And her hair… something is wrong with her hair.

"Jess!" I rush to her bedside, afraid to breathe for fear that she might blow away like a dead leaf. I try to memorize every detail of her face, every crease of her long fingers that are capable of coaxing such beautiful music out of the ether.

"Mom?"

She's conscious; she recognizes me! I take her hand, cradling it in mine. "How are you feeling?"

"I'm… just… tired." She sounds exhausted just saying the words. "And my head hurts."

"Your hair! What on earth did you do to your hair?"

"That was an accident."

The voice startles me. Another person I love but somehow failed to notice was in the room. Becky.

"Oh! Becky. Hi." I turn to her. "I didn't know you were there."

"No." Her eyes look big and hollow. "I guess you didn't see me."

Her hair also looks awful – it's the color of bread mold. I feel a familiar sensation of rising anger. "What did you do?" I say through my teeth.

Before Becky can answer, a nurse comes in to check Jess's vitals. The woman works efficiently, putting the blood pressure cuff on Jess's skinny arm.

"Please," I say to her, "I'm her mom. I just got here. Can you tell me her condition?"

The nurse gives me a look like she's wondering where I've been all this time while my daughter has been strapped up to tubes and machines and given someone else's blood. Seeing that flaccid little bag where the platelets have all but finished, my anger towards Becky dissipates, and my guilt floods back in. Jess now has someone else's blood cells in her body. Someone unrelated to her, whose identity she will never know. What will happen to those cells now? Will they be changed and become part of her? Or will they somehow change her, overlaying some stranger's genetic code over hers? Every night I pray for all of the people – all the saints out there – who give blood. People who have saved my daughter's life, time and time again. And yet, each time I see a bag of blood going into Jess's body, I can't help the thoughts that play in my mind like a horror movie. What if Jess gets the blood of a serial killer or a murderer and ends up running their programming? Because that's what DNA is, isn't it? A program for a person. How can my daughter fail to be affected by someone else's blood?

I'm pretty sure that's not how it works. A blood transfusion does not change DNA. But I'm so terrified by my own scenario that I don't even pay attention to what the nurse is saying. Something about the doctor – he's on his rounds and will be here soon. Which in hospital-speak means that it could be hours. I don't have hours, and right now, Jess doesn't look like she does either.

"Can I talk to him?"

She ignores me, focusing instead on taking Jess's blood pressure. Jess winces with pain as the cuff tightens around her arm. The awful dark color of her hair – is it supposed to be purple? – brings out the color of the bruises on her body.

"Please…" My voice breaks with a sob. I make the mistake of looking at Becky. To her credit, she doesn't meet my eyes. Her shoulders are slumped as she begins picking at her nail polish.

"Claire?" I turn again at the sound of Dave's voice. Steve is standing just behind, his eyes blazing with anger. But I can't worry about that right now.

"Do you know what's going on?" I say to Dave, increasingly desperate.

"What's going on is that you were out galivanting on some ranch in Texas in a private jet." Steve's voice is pure venom as he practically elbows Dave aside. "And this man shouldn't be here. He's not family. He's nobody."

The nurse stops what she's doing and looks at me. Becky looks up. Dave looks at me. Steve is too full of hate to look at me. And then, even Jess turns her head weakly to the side and looks at me. I am the eye of the storm. The cause of all this strife.

"We'll talk about this later," I say to Steve. "I just want to know what's happening with Jess."

"She fainted at home," Becky says. "I rode in the

ambulance with her. They gave her a transfusion and some antibiotics."

"Her blood pressure is still very low," the nurse says. "I'm going to check with the doctor. She may need some more platelets."

More platelets. More blood. My stomach roils, and I stumble against the wall. Dave steps forward and takes my arm. Steve turns away in disgust. He goes out of the room into the corridor, his phone in his hand.

"Thanks." I check that Becky's not looking and put my hand briefly over Dave's. Then, I have a terrible thought. I turn back to Jess. She's watching us. She's seen my hand. She's going to draw the wrong conclusion, just like Steve has.

I force myself to straighten up. "I really appreciate everything you've done, Dave. You've been a real help keeping me informed. But I think that maybe… I mean, it might be for the best if…"

"I'll go now," he finishes for me. He looks hurt. "It's all going to be fine, Claire. I just know it. I'm glad you made it back." He gives Jess a wink and Becky one of his winning smiles. "I'll work on that pool of donors."

A pool of donors. That's what I need. *We* need.

"Thank you, Dave." The words cannot express the gratitude I feel. "For everything."

"You're so welcome."

He takes a step away from me and gives a mock salute. "Talk soon."

I'm aware that both Becky and Jess are watching me. My face is heated and flushed. "Talk soon," I say to his back as he goes out the door.

26

"I want that man out of our lives."

Steve doesn't bother to wait until we're home and on our own before laying into me. Jess is staying overnight at the hospital, but they wouldn't let me stay with her. Steve's driving us home, too fast, in his work pickup. Him, me... and Becky. Becky is staring straight ahead out the window, her hands clenched in her lap. I want to reach out to her, but when Steve speaks, she nods in agreement. I hate that she's having to deal with our marital problems on top of her own issues. Even more, I hate that she's taken sides – with Steve – and that I can't blame her for doing so.

"I've already told you," I say, "it's not that simple."

"It is simple," Steve says. "Tell him to get lost."

My life flashes before my eyes. Pre-Dave, post-Dave, present. Things were simpler pre-Dave – I was alone with no one on my side. Since meeting him, I've grown as a person. I've made my world bigger and become less small. But now that has twisted and mutated again and become something ugly – even I can see that.

"We're just friends," I say. "I... look up to him."

Steve snorts. "Yeah, right."

"God," Becky huffs, "this is so perfect. Why don't you just split up and be done with it? Believe me, it would be better for everyone."

"Be quiet, Becky," I say, at the same time that Steve says, "shut up." I glare at him. In our household, that's unacceptable language. Being unkind, though, is still perfectly fine.

"Whatever," Becky tsks. "I mean, it's pretty selfish, you guys fighting like this. I mean, did you not *hear* what the doctor said? Is this really about you?"

Leave it to Becky to uncover the elephant in the room that's squashing the life out of everything. Because she's absolutely right. This is not about Steve and me. This is not even about Steve and Dave. This is about how we can possibly go on, given the terrible news we've just received.

"I'm afraid the situation is escalating." The doctor's words echo in my head. "She's stopped responding to her meds. There are some options we can try – and we will – but, I'm not going to lie to you…"

Lie to us, please, I'd wanted to scream.

I'd wanted a hand to squeeze. Steve's preferably, or Becky's. But Becky was already texting someone on her phone, her face a mask of shock. Steve crossed his arms and took a long breath. Then, he'd begun to rail at the doctor.

"You have to *do* something. I mean… pull your finger out!"

My head was swimming in a sea of despair, and I could barely focus on Steve's tirade.

"You're doctors, for Christ's sake!"

"Steve…" I roused myself enough to intervene. Maybe it's because I'm a people-pleaser, but I always make an effort to keep people who might be able to help onside. And avoid the corollary: don't alienate those people. I want the doctors to like us, to feel sorry for us. To know that we're good people who deserve help for our daughter. I tried to take Steve's arm. He threw me off.

"I mean, it's bad enough that her mom isn't even here when she ends up in the hospital." He glared at me, his words stinging like a poisoned arrow. "But you people have studied science and medicine." He turned back to the doctor. "There must be something you can do. What is it you want? More money? Is my insurance not good enough? Because if that's what it will take, then we'll sell the house; we'll find the money."

In a way, I was glad of his strength of feeling. At least there's one thing we both agree on. Jess is all-important. She's worth everything we have.

But as he parks the pickup in the driveway and orders Becky inside, I fear not only for Jess but also for my marriage. I need to make a much bigger effort to keep Steve onside. I need to keep my inner raving lunatic more tightly under wraps.

"I'm sorry you don't like Dave," I say, "but I don't know what else to do. You know he's helping me – helping us – find a donor. When I was in Texas, I met with people who were willing to help. Genetic Cousins who might be possible bone marrow matches. Isn't it at least worth a try?"

"Six months," Steve says, and I'm not even sure he's heard me. "They said that she might only have six months." When he finally looks at me, his eyes are full of tears.

Six months. Hearing him say it, it hits home. The fuse is lit on the time bomb that will blow our lives apart. *Six months.* Doubt and indecision whirl in my head. How am I going to spend that time? At my daughter's side? Or on some… wild goose chase?

"I hear what you're saying," I say. "And I don't want to waste that time. It's just that I'm trying to be proactive. I really hoped you'd see that. But…" I take a breath, "maybe you're right. Maybe I shouldn't go away again – if that's what you want."

Steve undoes his seatbelt. "Go, stay – do what you want." He opens the door. "I really don't care anymore."

His words have an awful finality about them. I know he does care, and I know that I want to save my marriage. But is that best accomplished by pulling together now and waiting for the end? Holding hands at the funeral of our daughter, hugging so tightly that our tears mingle together?

No.

I do want to save my marriage. But I want to save my daughter more.

"Fine," I say, making a monumental effort to keep my voice steady. "You go on not caring. But, in that case, I'm going to keep looking for a donor. And I'm going to find one."

"You've gone completely nuts." Steve gets out of the truck.

"Maybe. But at least I'll know that I've done everything I can. I'll be able to look at myself in the mirror once she's gone."

I let out a little gasp as I realize what I've said.

Steve gives a bitter laugh. "Good for you." He slams the door.

I go to my room, lock the door, and throw myself down on the bed. I should find Becky, make sure she's OK. She'll be as affected as any of us by the awful news we've received. But my whole body feels like lead; I just can't face it. I lie there staring at the ceiling, my life flashing before my eyes. I recall a day when I was eight or nine, and Dad was leaving for one of his business trips. It was just after my birthday. I'd had a party and eaten a lot of cake and opened all my presents. I guess it was that awful sense of "the party's over" that made me panic as he tried to go out the door. "I hate you!" I'd shouted. "I hope you never come back."

I was glad to see the hurt on Dad's face. I wanted him to react. I wanted him to shout at me – hit me, even. But almost immediately, he changed back to the Dad I knew. The one who called me "honey" and "sweetheart", who never had an angry or unkind word for anyone. The dad I loved more than anyone else in the world. The dad who was always leaving.

"I'll miss you, Tiger," he'd said, giving me his cocky, slightly lopsided smile. "You know that. And I'll bring you a nice present when I get back. Another charm for your bracelet, maybe."

"I don't want a charm," I'd said, even though I loved the silver charms he brought me. "I just want you."

"Well, you'll get me back too. I'll only be gone for a week. I promise."

That time, if I remember correctly, he was gone almost two months. He brought me the silver Hawaii charm. I dig my thumb into the rough contours of the little silver pineapple. It hurts.

Did I love Dad best because he was always leaving? Knowing that every time I saw him, he was on the way to somewhere else? Because now I'm in a similar situation. The person I love most in the world is about to leave me forever. The hourglass is cracked open, the sand pouring out. And just like with Dad, there's not a thing I can do about it.

"Oh, Jess." I bury my head under the pillow, but I still hear the phone vibrate as a text message comes in. Like Pavlov's dog, I pick up the phone.

It's Stella. I force myself to sit up.

Hi Claire, Sorry to hear about your daughter. We've had an interesting hit on a close relative of yours in Washington, D.C. We're going to rerun the test to rule out a false result. Keep you posted. S

Washington, D.C. I know for a fact that I don't have any relatives, close or otherwise, in that part of the country. But even as I reread the words, I feel an unaccountable chill. I finger the charms on my bracelet: the Golden Gate Bridge, the US Capitol. I write a text back. *OK. Let me know when you've got the results. Thanks. Claire x*

The text goes off with a swoosh. I can't take it back again.

27

BECKY

Part of me dies a little death each time Jess has to go to the hospital. I don't want to picture her lying in bed with her ugly hair or rewind the things the doctor said, so I focus on being mad at Mom and Dad. Usually, it's me against them, but seeing them against each other is even worse.

In theory, it's not my problem. I'm almost eighteen, and hopefully soon I'll be leaving home. But what about Jess? The idea of her living on her own with Mom and being smothered with love, or living on her own with Dad and not being smothered with love, is just so *wrong*. I mean, we've all been through so much – and we've been through it together. Surely that's got to count for something.

When we get home from the hospital and Dad sends me out of the truck, I think – "Yep, this is it. Over, done." I go straight up to my room and get my suitcase from the closet. Dad will be moving out, and I'll be going with him because there's no way I'm staying here with Mom. If that's taking sides, then I guess I've done it.

I start throwing clothes into the suitcase. I feel furious with both of them. Why is Mom winding Dad up with her so-called friend Dave? I mean, what does she see in him? I've never seen Mom idolize anyone, except maybe her dad, my Grandpa Joe, who's dead. Then, it hits me. Dave is a little bit like Grandpa Joe – a big talker who's everybody's best friend. Could that be what Mom sees in him?

And why is Dad getting so wound up? I mean, yeah, Dave is a lot richer than we are – he has his own company and probably has a lot nicer house and car and stuff. Dad's had to take a second job to "make ends meet" because insurance takes forever to approve Jess's treatments, and some of them are not covered. So maybe that's the reason. I feel kind of good having worked that out. Or I would if I didn't feel sick to my stomach every time I think about Mom, or Dad, or Jess or – anything really. Because I'm under so much stress, I've lost like ten pounds practically overnight. Every cloud has a silver lining, I guess.

When Mom and Dad come back inside, they aren't speaking – but that's nothing new. No one mentions a divorce, but I leave some things in the suitcase just in case. I'm like a refugee caught between two warring armies.

A couple of days go by. I run out of clean clothes, so I unpack a few things. Mom spends every day at the hospital, and some nights when she comes home, she looks so tired and worn out that it's like she's been in an actual battle. The doctors don't know what caused Jess's relapse, so they prescribe a bunch of new drugs. By the end of the week, they say that Jess can come home. That puts Mom in a good mood – sort of – and she lets me go to the hospital with her to pick Jess up. I get up the nerve to ask about her trip to Texas, which seems like a long time ago now. She tells me about some kite festival she went to (random!) and about her cowboy cousins who are going to get their bone marrow tested. All good. It made me hopeful that her Genetic Journey might actually turn up a match for Jess.

Then we won't have to worry about the Bucket List. While Jess was in the hospital, I fished the pieces of the ripped-up list out of the trash and taped them together for her. The problem still is that I'm too broke to help her do the things on it.

Secretly I'm still hoping that it will turn out that our DNA is related to someone rich and famous who will take me under their wing and make me their project. As soon as I can, I am *so* going to upload my DNA onto the database!

Mom's good mood does not survive the trip to the hospital. When we arrive, we're told that we have to wear masks. I'm given a hideous blue fake fabric thing that itches like crazy.

Jess is in her own special room, where they're keeping her free from germs. I got to hand it to Mom – she's a really good actress. She goes over and gives Jess a kiss through her mask and fusses over her, saying how much better she's looking. She seems hyper and stressed. I'm relieved when she goes off to talk to the doctor.

"What's up, girlfriend?" I say. I'm not as good an actress as Mom. Jess looks – in a word – terrible. She's pale and pasty, and her hair… for a second, I feel so angry. I almost wish they'd give her chemo, so it all falls out.

"I just… hate everyone," Jess says.

"What?" I look at her in surprise. That's a very un-Jess thing to say.

"It's bad enough that I have to be here," she says, "but now they're putting me on immunosuppressants."

"Immuno whats?" If Jess doesn't make it as a violinist, maybe she can be a doctor – she's good at all the big words.

"Immunosuppressants. That means I won't be able to fight any germs. I'll have to stay in my room, like a prisoner."

"Why would they give you that?" It sounds pretty dumb, but what do I know?

Jess launches into the why of it, most of which still sounds pretty dumb. "I don't want to do it, Becky. I mean, they're stealing my dreams. It's so unfair."

"Hey, that's not true. What do you mean?"

"Well, duh – Mom told me yesterday that I can't do the audition. We have to postpone it. It's like totally stupid. I mean, if I'm going to die, then why can't I do it? Why is it anyone's business? It's not like I'm contagious or anything."

"It is stupid." I feel like someone's punched me in the stomach. Jess has been practicing for the audition for months and months. If she's going to die, then I totally get why she wants her moment to shine. That said, I also understand why Mom wants to keep her safe – and alive. The longer she hangs in there, the more there's a chance of finding a match. Every second feels like sand going through a timer – like the one Mom bought to make sure we brush our teeth for two minutes. When the sand runs out, there won't be any turning it over again. I get why Mom doesn't want that to happen.

In the car, Mom goes over all the germ stuff. Jess sits stony-faced, staring out the window like a prisoner being transported to jail. When we get home, she crosses her arms stubbornly and refuses to go to her room. "I want to stay downstairs and watch TV with Becky," she says.

Mom's face looks like a plaster statue that's ready to crack. "Jess, we talked about this. You need to stay isolated as much as possible to avoid germs. You can watch TV upstairs on your iPad. And you can play your violin and FaceTime your friends and—"

"Stop it, Mom!" Jess puts her hands over her ears. "Just stop it. I'll go. But stop pretending, OK?"

"Jess, honey——"

As frail as she is, Jess manages to make a racket as she stomps up the stairs. I stand there, and honest to God, I experience a totally new feeling that I've never had before. I feel *sorry* for Mom.

Shaking her head, Mom goes into the kitchen. I should probably say something. But I don't have a clue what, and I'll probably just make things worse. I hover in the door-way, debating.

She goes to the fridge but doesn't open it. She just stands there. Her shoulders are slumped; she looks totally defeated.

Then, all of a sudden, she grabs Jess's letter off the door. The magnet skitters to the floor. She balls it up and throws it in the garbage bin.

"Mom?" I say, a little shocked.

She wheels around like she's just noticed that I'm there.

"What are you looking at?" Her face is grim and lined – I barely recognize her.

"Um…" *Do something! say something!* The voice of Good Becky whispers inside my head. I open my mouth…

"Nothing… umm… Sorry."

"I'll make spaghetti for dinner. It will be ready in half an hour."

"Yeah, sure. I'll go up and start my homework."

28

MARIANNE

I could still be a mother.

Not a half-mother of someone else's baby, but an honest-to-God biological mother of a baby. I feel completely revitalized with a new injection of hope. For so long, I've been treading water, waiting for pregnancy after pregnancy to fail. Allowing my marriage to fail in the process. But now, I see that there may be another way to achieve my dreams.

Since seeing Dr. Lena, I've done hours of research on egg donation. Everything I've read points to the fact that when a baby is gestating inside a woman's uterus, every cell of the baby's body is changed. It becomes, in essence, the biological child of the carrier. The rational part of me wonders if this could possibly be true, but the baby-mad part is ready to swallow this new information hook, line, and sinker. (There's a third part of me that wants to wring Lena's neck for not explaining all this before.)

Now my biggest regret is that I was too proud and pig-headed to explore this option earlier. I regret the wasted time and the fact that I've allowed things with Tom to spiral downwards. I regret… a lot of things. But I need to put all that behind me.

My first priority is to get Tom on board. After all, he's the other half of the equation. Surely once he knows the facts, he'll be as excited as I am. We'll be Tom and Marianne again – but better versions of ourselves.

I have to believe that it's possible.

A whole week goes by before Tom has a rare evening off from the theatre. I use the time to plan our reunion. I buy food to make us a nice dinner and leave work early to go to Victoria's Secret. There, I replace all my shredded underwear. It feels good to be rekindling the spark in my marriage and making an effort to show Tom how much I value him.

As I stand in the fitting room, I look at my body from all sides and angles. I'm fit for my age. Attractive – the kind of woman who can still turn heads. Sexy – though I've always hated that word. I channel that long-ago photo of a pregnant Demi Moore on the cover of some magazine, determined to look upon my body with new eyes. Not as a mothballed baby factory but as a safe little nest for nurturing new life. New life that may not have all my genetics but will be mine to love.

My phone rings as I'm standing in line to pay. Seeing my mother's number on the screen is a tiny pinprick to my positive mood. I've spoken to her briefly since the latest loss, but I haven't actually told her that I'm not pregnant. She doesn't know the exact timings of the last cycle, but by now she will have guessed the result. This can be a very quick conversation.

"Hello, Mother," I say as I hand the clerk my items. "Sorry – work's been really busy." I swallow hard. "And… the IVF failed."

The clerk's hand pauses in scanning my items. Her face

goes rigid – clearly, she doesn't know whether to show pity or horror or just ignore me. Suddenly, I don't care if the entire store overhears me. "But actually, I'm fine. Really."

"Um, do you have a loyalty card?" the clerk says.

"No." I meet her eyes, daring her to look away. I dare myself to keep listening to my mother's voice on the other end of the phone.

"Oh… that's so terrible!"

I give her the benefit of the doubt that what's terrible is the situation – not something I did or failed to do. With my mother, I can never be sure.

"Yes. But it's got me thinking outside the box. There may be another way. Egg donation." The clerk's eyes pop as I sign my name on the electronic reader and take my bag.

"What?"

"Dr. Lena says it's the best way forward. Voila! I get new eggs; I get a new baby."

"Marianne…" My mother's voice levels out. "You're going to think about this, right?"

I make an effort not to get angry: this whole concept is new to her, whereas I've had time to digest it. My clock, which I'd thought had run down, is still ticking wildly. But every minute feels like an eternity.

"Remember, you don't have to be perfect."

I stifle a laugh. That's rich, coming from her.

"Really, I know how much you want this – we all do. But at some point, you have to let go."

My good mood explodes like a bomb. All the negatives flood into my mind. Tom – I've barely even seen him; we can barely stand to look at each other. And here I am, holding a bag of underwear. I turn back to the clerk, frantic. I need to return everything. But she's helping someone else, and there's a long line and…

My pulse begins to race. I can't let my mother do this to me.

"I'm not going to let go," I hiss. "Not this time. I'm going to do *whatever it takes*."

"Marianne…"

I've made my point.

"I'll call you later," I say. "Or… tomorrow. Maybe. Bye for now.

I end the call, dart out of the shop, and make a beeline for a bench at the center of the mall. I sit there listening to the sounds of people milling around, the Muzak, the echoing voices. Eventually, I calm down. I even go back to feeling good. I've navigated the conversation with my mother. I've got a plan to seduce my husband and a bag of underwear for ammunition. Everything is going to be fine. I let out a little laugh. A couple of shoppers walking by look at me like I've lost the plot. I just smile, and they look away.

On my way out, I decide to pop into Saks, then Neiman Marcus. I buy two pairs of shoes and a slinky dress. Then, I hit the baby shops. There are so many lovely things on sale that it would be *wrong* not to invest in the future. It's all part of positive thinking. I am a woman on a mission, and this time, nothing is going to go wrong.

29

It all goes wrong.

When I get home, the lights are off, and there's no sign of Tom's car. But there is a car in the drive – my mother's. I bang my hand against the steering wheel. Why am I never on the same wavelength as her? I thought we were finished with our conversation, but clearly, she thought otherwise.

As soon as I park, she gets out of the car. I want to shove everything I've bought under the seat, but I *cannot* allow myself to be embarrassed about my decisions. Instead, I proudly hoist the pink bag of lingerie out of the passenger seat.

"Mother," I say coolly. "How nice to see you."

She looks at me for a long moment. Then, gingerly, she puts her arms around me, pink bag and all.

It's the worst possible thing she could have done. At first, my eyes tingle, then they prickle. And then, I collapse into a frenzy of sobs. She holds me tight. Strokes my hair. Whispers that it's going to be OK. She's my mother: of course, she's right.

So why doesn't it feel like it?

"Come on," she says. "Let's go inside. I'll cook supper."

I nod slowly, feeling like a small child again. I'd cried when I wasn't chosen to be a von Trapp kid in *The Sound of Music* and when I wasn't elected class representative. I'd cried when I didn't get a perfect score on my verbal SAT. Each of those times, my mother was there. My father flitted in and out, but she was always trying to lift me higher.

Too high. Because of her, my life went crashing to the ground. Weighted down by grief and regret that haunts me to his day.

I'm mortified when she picks up the pink bag. I wish she'd say something: make a joke. But I doubt she's ever worn anything more daring than a Playtex Eighteen Hour Bra in her life. That said, I do recall times when my father would return, and the two of them would snuggle up on the swing under the cherry tree. Once or twice I even saw them kiss. She tried her best to make everything perfect when he came home. Maybe my father was an underwear man – I don't know, and I don't want to think about it. My mother is old, my father is dead. I must regain my laser focus and put the rest out of my mind.

She puts the bag by the door. I follow her into the kitchen. Before I can let her get carried away making supper, I check my phone. Tom has texted: *Sorry, new Blanche is TERRIBLE! Need to rehearse tonight. Don't wait up. Tx Don't wait up!*

I have to grip the counter to steady myself. *Focus on the goal. I* must *focus on the goal.*

My mother hands me a glass of wine. "Thanks," I say.

"Now," she says, "tell me exactly is going on?"

"I told you already: the last IVF cycle failed, but Dr.

Lena says I might be successful with donor eggs." I stare at the wine but don't drink it. "Tom was supposed to be home tonight, and I'd planned a nice evening for the two of us. But now he's working late, and you're here, so that's not really in the cards." I struggle to keep the desperation from my voice.

"Also, I'm going on a Genetic Journey," I add before she can comment. "Did I tell you?"

She frowns. "A genetic what?"

I'm grateful that she's honed in on what seems like the least important news item. I tell her all about *MyStory* and the DNA testing kits wrapped up in neat white boxes. My mother likes crossword puzzles and board games, so I'm expecting her to be interested, maybe even supportive. Instead, her brow creases deeply enough to germinate seeds. It's a look I remember from my childhood: when I couldn't understand negative numbers or grasp the difference between a homophone and a homonym. Judgmental, accusing. Once, I would have done anything to avoid getting that look. Now, though, her reaction makes me curious.

"Are you sure you know what you're doing?" she says. "Surely, those tests can have serious ramifications. It's not just some kind of fun and games. Who knows what might come up?"

"That's it precisely. I don't know. I remember you said that my grandmother was from Schenectady and that her father fought in World War I, but that's about all I know about our genealogy. Maybe I don't have any kids to pass on a family history to, but it can't hurt to try and find out more."

"I doubt there's much of interest. My parents were American, and their ancestors came from England, Scotland, and Scandinavia. Like a lot of people in this country, you're a mix of things."

"What about Dad's side? Do you know much about that?"

"No." Her jaw sets in what I recognize as avoidance mode. "He was definitely a mongrel. Nothing to find out there. Frankly, I wouldn't bother."

"Maybe you're right."

My mother's indifference – or what she means to sound like indifference – is making the gears turn in my mind. Why have I never done any genealogy research? Why doesn't my mother want me to put it right?

As I'm about to ask her, she takes out her phone and checks the screen. Then, she begins gathering her things.

"Sorry," she says. "I just got a text from Mrs. Trisk. She's asking if I can host the book club tonight. Are you all right by yourself?"

"Yes, Mother."

Goosepimples prickle on the back of my neck. Talk of my Genetic Journey has clearly upset her, and I have no idea why. I'm not even sure I believe she got a text – but I can't very well accuse her of lying. Why would she lie?

I follow her to the door. "I'll call you in a few days," she says. "And I'd appreciate it if you would pick up once in a while. I do worry about you, you know."

"I know, Mother. Sorry."

There it is – my apology: the way most of our conversations end. Also, like most of our conversations, she doesn't let me have the last word. She pauses by the door and, to my mortification, she gestures down at the pink bag. "Next time you're going to Victoria's Secret," she says, "make sure you text me. I've got a loyalty card, and they're always sending coupons."

"Fine," I say through clenched teeth. "Next time, I will."

30

BECKY

It's kind of weird living next door to a prison. I guess like Mom, I kind of expected that Jess would get used to it. After all, she loves stuff like reading books and playing her violin. She's got friends she can FaceTime and an iPad to watch as much YouTube as she wants. But as the days slip by, I can almost feel Jess's anguish through the wall, leaking like radiation.

One night when I get home, I hear her shouting. A few minutes later, Mom comes down the stairs, her face screwed up like a prune. "Hi, Mom," I say. "Good day?" I don't actually mean to sound sarcastic, but that that's how she takes it. She gives me an eye roll that even I would be proud of. So I head upstairs and ask Jess if I can come in, but she says no, she's "busy". OK… I've got a math test that I need to study for, so I go to my own room.

But I can't concentrate at all. I stare down at the numbers on the page swimming in front of my eyes and think about what I can do to cheer Jess up. When I was fifteen, I had to stay in my room for two whole weeks because I got mono after making out with a senior at a school dance (he was all tongue – it's kind of gross now that I think about it). I was supposed to be reading *Moby Dick*, but, instead I spent most of the time messaging this other guy from my class, who was like my first real boyfriend. The whole thing ended when he forwarded that topless picture of me. But it was fun while it lasted.

Taylor Compton is obviously the key to making Jess feel better. I mean, if she's going to die (which she is not!), then she shouldn't do it without first having had a boyfriend.

But how can I make it happen? Well, it's kind of a crazy idea, but maybe I could actually write a feature for real on future freshmen for the school newspaper! I mean, *Mom's* a journalist, and she's no genius. But no… it would be a total waste of time and totally embarrassing even to try. I look at the math again, but it's just so boring…

Later on, I hear Mom bringing Jess her meds and saying goodnight. Then, she goes off to have a bath. The next thing I hear through the wall is crying.

I close the math book and go to Jess's room, not bothering to knock. Mom's got a bottle of hand sanitizer and some masks set up on a table by the door. I ignore them and go over to Jess, who's slumped down next to the bed. Trying not to breathe on her, I give her a big hug.

"Guess what I'm going to do," I say. I tell her about my future freshmen idea, minus the part about getting Taylor to message her. But then another lightning bolt strikes – I'll practice by doing an article on Jess! I mean, someday she's either going to be a famous violinist, or she's going to… well, either way, people should know about her.

To my surprise, Jess is up for it. I spend the next two hours interviewing her. I already know a lot about her illness and her dreams and stuff, but it somehow feels different when she tells me "her story". I try to write it down, but she talks too fast, so I record it on my phone.

"I mean, I love Mom and everything," she tells me, "but she's just so annoying."

This surprises me. Jess and Mom are really close. Mom idolizes Jess, and everything is all about her. When I mention that, she gets mad.

"That's exactly what I mean," she says. "Do you think I want that? Do you think I want to be her perfect little angel, always putting on a brave face?"

"I don't know."

"Well," she snorts, "no pressure or anything. I wish I was like you, Becky. You can be, like, your own person."

"Don't be like me," I say sharply. Which is kind of sad. I mean, this is my life. How have I already managed to screw it up so badly?

The list of things that Jess hates about Mom goes like this:

(1) That Mom still insists on seeing the doctor outside the room and not letting her hear what he has to say about her condition. Then, Mom lies and tells her that she's going to be OK when she knows good and well that if they don't find a donor, then she's going to die.

(2) That Mom saw Jess's Bucket List that I taped together and went totally ballistic. She told Jess that instead of taking silly risks like going to the city to busk, she needs to stay safe. But Jess doesn't want to stay safe – she wants to *live*.

(3) That Mom is constantly fussing over her: hugging and kissing her like she might never see her again. She's always trying to make sure that if Jess dies unexpectedly, then her last words will be "I love you." No fights, no harsh words, ice cream whenever she wants it, and full use of the internet with no parental controls. Jess just wants to be

normal – including having the occasional argument with Mom. But if Jess tries to say something – like about the Bucket List – then Mom's whole face crumples, and it's conversation over. Then Jess feels bad and goes back to playing the perfect angel with the brave face. It feels really fake and annoying.

When I read over the list, I actually feel a little sorry for Mom – totally the wrong reaction. I mean, it's hard to be the sister of someone who's sick, but it must be a whole lot worse to be their mom and feel responsible. I decide not to include the list in my article because Mom's only trying her best. That seems like a good decision, for once.

In the end, I stay up until 3 a.m. to type everything out. When I'm finished, I know that it's full of typos and that I'm going to fail my math test. But when I email it off to my friend Melissa, who works on the school newspaper, I'm actually thinking – *you know, this is GOOD!* If I could have a career as a journalist, then stuff like math won't matter. I'll be too busy meeting real people with interesting problems.

OK – full disclosure. I do fail the math test. I get the paper back a week later, and there's a big fat D- scribbled in red pen. But that same day, I hear back from Melissa that they're going to publish the article! And they want me to do more future freshmen pieces, including Taylor Compton. When I'm interviewing him, I'll put in a good word for Jess, and she'll be in with a chance. I mean, why wouldn't he want to go on a date with a girl who's going to be a famous violinist, even if she's got ugly hair now? It feels amazing to finally be doing something to help Jess. I even start wondering if maybe I should start my own Bucket List, and if I did, what would be on it? Not being such a screw-up, for one. It kind of threw me when Jess said that she wanted to be like me. Top of my list would be to become someone that my sister can be proud of. The next thing would be to get along better with Mom.

That one doesn't go so well. As soon as I get home from school, I can see that she's uber-stressed. It's obviously not a good time to tell her about the math test. I offer to make dinner – baked beans and hotdogs with tortilla chips. Then I tell her my big news about the article. "It's about Jess," I say. "They're going to publish it."

"That's nice," she says.

"Nice" is not the reaction I'm going for. It makes me mad, actually.

"And I failed my math test," I say.

"That's—"

Seriously, I think she's going to say "nice" again before she tunes in and hears what I've said.

"Oh, Becky." She tsks with disappointment.

I'm used to this. It's well within my comfort zone. I wait for her to get angry, suspend privileges, and then start lecturing me about my future. Instead, she just pushes the food around her plate without eating. She picks up her phone. Checks her texts. Frowns. Puts the phone down again.

"Mom, what is it?" I say. "You're acting really weird."

"Nothing," she says, too quickly.

"Is it Jess?" I feel a sudden chill. What does she know that I don't?

"No. It's not." Her voice is flat. "I'm fine. I'm just not hungry."

She gets up and takes her plate to the sink. Then, she leaves the room.

I'm actually starting to feel really worried. Something is majorly wrong. She's so preoccupied that she's left her phone on the table, and the screen is still on. I know I shouldn't, but I pick it up and scroll through her text messages to see if I can find any clues.

There are an awful lot of messages from Dave Steiner. I read the exchange from when Jess was still in the hospital.

Him: *I'm really sorry – I don't want to cause problems with you and Steve. Let me know if you want to stop.*

Her: *No! It's fine. Please, Dave, I need you.*

OK. I wish I hadn't read that one, but now the genie's out of the bottle. I scroll down to the latest message that's come in. It's from Stella.

The chain starts from just after Mom got back from Texas. Apparently, there's been a hit for Mom for a "close biological relative" in Washington, D.C. They did a retest, and now there's a new message – the text she received just now.

Claire – we should definitely meet. The results are certain.

I'm trying to puzzle out what the issue is when Mom comes back into the kitchen. I'm caught red-handed!

"Becky," she says, her voice low.

"Just curious to see what Stella had to say." I play the stupid card and push the phone across the table. "Great news about that close relative. I wonder who it is."

"Don't ever look at my phone."

"Yeah, sure," I say. "Off to go do some extra credit now."

I make a quick exit before she can even unclench her jaw enough to say anything more.

31

MARIANNE

The underwear sits in the bag by the door with the tags still on. With each passing day and night that Tom is working late and my seduction plans have to be put on hold, I have to fight harder and harder against the urge to take it all back to the shop. Or… to find another, more appreciative audience.

I try to practice mindfulness and use my alone time to heal. I imagine my body resetting itself after all the fertility procedures. Getting ready for a new miracle, a new embryo that will eventually be created and grow into something wonderful. I imagine how good it will feel to see hope on Tom's face – even to see his face at all for more than a blurry few minutes at the beginning and end of each day.

About a week after my trip to the shopping mall, I arrive home from the office after a tedious day of negotiations, ready to crawl into bed with a book. But I receive an unexpected text from Tom that he's taking the night off – for definite this time. In fact, he's already on his way home. All at once, I can feel the doubts gathering force, the whispers growing louder and louder. *Do I really want this? Do I want to continue on?* Tom and I agreed to stop fertility treatment after eight rounds. We were told that there was no magic number but that continuing on might prove destructive to our marriage. That part, at least, has proved to be true. But egg donation is a lifeline – I'm sure of it.

Yes. I need *this.*

As I retrieve the bag of underwear and go upstairs to take a bath, I feel an odd little itch to call my mother. Tell her everything – about how I'm feeling, about the problems with Tom, and most importantly, make her listen to what I've learned about egg donation and convince her that it's the right thing to do. Give her some hope that she might still have a grandchild. And maybe when I see her next, she'll take me in her arms and whisper in my ear that everything is going to be all right. Maybe she'll know the perfect thing to say, and I'll instantly feel better.

But as I slip into the too-hot water, I think about how strange she was acting that night when she showed up on my doorstep. It's also strange that she hasn't called or texted since. And then, another memory surfaces: not of her embrace or perfect, comforting words. I take a breath and lower my head into the water, letting the memories pull me under.

"You are a filthy, disgusting little slut. How could you do that?*"*

I can still hear the disappointment in her voice – the hatred, even – as she spoke those words. And then, she slapped me. I can still feel the phantom sting.

For weeks after the party, I hardly even knew what "that" was. I had only vague memories of meeting Hal. I remembered him telling me that I was beautiful and special, and I'd believed him. I thought that he'd get in touch and try to be my boyfriend. But he didn't. As time went on, I felt not so much beautiful and special, as angry and used. I rushed home every day, checked the answering machine, and then when there was no message, I'd go up to my room and cry. At first, my mother tried to comfort me. Then cajole, then threaten. I *had* to do well on my SAT retake to guarantee Ivy League. I *had* to pull myself together.

By then, I was no longer crying because Hal hadn't called. I was crying for myself and the dreadful fear growing inside of me.

My mother drove me to school on the day of the retest and gave me a bribe to do well – twenty dollars to spend as I chose. On my way home from school, I usually walked past a small corner mall with a 7-11, a Rite Aid, and a Pier 1 Imports. I'm not sure what my mother expected me to buy. Maybe some lights for my bed, or some new pens and stationery, or some make-up. Instead, I bought the most embarrassing thing a teenage girl can buy – and I'm not talking tampons. I went to the cash register wearing dark sunglasses and repeating silently in my head: *I don't need this; I don't need this.* The cashier was a middle-aged woman who smelled of cigarette smoke. She gave me a sympathetic look, and I almost lost it.

I shoved the "thing" in my bag and ran the rest of the way home. My mother had cooked a special dinner – not for me, but because my father had come home. Usually, I looked forward to seeing him. But his being there made me even more upset. All I could think about was the "thing". I thought about throwing it away or taking it back to the store for a refund (but I could *never* bear that humiliation). I repeated my mantra: *I don't need this. I. Do. Not. Need. This.*

As I took it with me to the bathroom, I tried to make a bargain with God. If only everything would be all right, then I would never do another stupid thing again. I would never go to another party, let a drunk boy whisper words that turned me to jelly, and let him take me to a spare bedroom and do what he liked. I would go back to being the perfect girl – my mother's daughter. The girl I wanted to be. *Please, God,* I whispered. *Just this once, let everything be fine.*

I followed the directions and awaited the results.

Everything was *not* fine.

I used my allowance to buy two more home pregnancy tests, though I was already sure that the worst had happened. The next worst thing was telling my mother. I don't know what I'd expected, but her calling me a *filthy, disgusting slut* and slapping me wasn't it.

Only a few days earlier, I'd got an acceptance letter for Princeton, my number one choice. My mother had tacked it to the refrigerator with a magnet – a big show of pride from someone who always kept an immaculate kitchen. I could only watch as she took the letter off the fridge and ripped it up, throwing the pieces in the trash. She told me I was a failure, a disappointment. I sat there numb, unable to fight back. But then, just as I was sure she was going to physically throw me out of the house, she relented and gave me an out.

"There is one way that we can put all this behind us."

I didn't ask how. I simply threw myself on her mercy and trusted her.

My lungs are ready to burst as I resurface. The water is still hot, but I begin to shiver. A door slams downstairs. Tom is home.

I must pull myself together and focus on my marriage and my baby. I can't let the past seep in, tainting every-thing. I rush to organize my thoughts, compartmentalize them. Shove the regrets back into my own miniature version of Pandora's box and slam shut the lid.

Tom. I will focus on Tom. My dear, quirky Tom. The man I vowed to love and cherish in sickness and in health, for richer or poorer. Thanks to our bad luck, he's not quite the man I married. But he's still *my Tom*. Or, he will be again. I get out of the bath and put on the new underwear I've chosen: peach satin. Not quite the white of our wedding night or the red that says "I'm trying to revitalize a marriage", but something that I hope is in between. I want this to work... so badly. It just has to.

I towel-dry my hair, give my teeth a quick brush, and put on a slick of lipstick. Then I go about the re-seduction of my husband the modern way: by sending him a text.

Hey Tom, I've got a surprise for you upstairs! M xxx

I go into the bedroom to wait. Should I have bought rose petals to strew on the bed? Or maybe chocolates... or... I don't know... ice? I've never been very creative at this sort of thing – I've never had to be. Tom and I went from having a healthy sex life to having no sex life at all, somewhere between Nos... No. I'm not going to think of the dead babies tonight. This is not about them, but about me giving them a much loved, *living* brother or sister. Righting past wrongs. Including my most recent wrongs... fantasizing about another man, a man who *sees* me... no. I cannot allow myself to think of anything but Tom – the man I want to be the father of my baby. I'm sick with nerves. I pace back and forth a few times, then lie on top of the bed. I get in the bed, then get up again.

Where the HELL is Tom?

My skin is prickling with goosebumps. I should have bought a new robe. My pajamas are in the drawer. I could put them on and then do a little strip tease or something.

God... Everything is such a disaster.

The door opens. Tom comes in. He takes one look at me, and his eyes widen. "Marianne? What's wrong?"

My lipstick has smeared, but that isn't it. I've started to cry. I wipe away the perfidious tear and jump up.

"Nothing!" Feeling for all the world like an idiot, I give a little twirl. "Surprise! What do you think?"

"Um…" He gives me his goofy grin. "What am I looking at?"

"I went shopping last week." I make my voice sound low, husky. "I thought that maybe, now that we're done with all the…" DO NOT SAY THE WORDS "DEAD BABIES", "… um… stuff, that maybe we could try again."

I take a step forward, praying for the smile that used to melt my entire body.

Tom takes a step back.

"You don't mean that you want to try and get pregnant again?" He looks absolutely horrified. "Surely you're not buying all that 'IVF didn't work, but once the pressure was off, we conceived naturally' crap?"

His words are like a slap in the face. Actually, I hadn't been thinking about that at all, though it does happen that way for some couples. The body, having been primed for pregnancy, manages to conceive naturally almost immediately after the previous loss.

"No…" I whisper. I can't look at him. I turn and make a beeline for the drawer with my pajamas. I take out the wooly top: light blue with white fluffy clouds, and put it over the awful peach bra.

"And why did you buy more expensive underwear?" It sounds like a joke, but he's not smiling. "You need something else to cut up?"

A sob rises inside of me. Surely, he's not so cruel as to keep punching me when I'm on the ropes. Is he?

"No, I don't." I swallow hard, trying to cling to my hope, to visualize the life I want. A life with Tom: two happy parents, a baby in a stroller. I can still make it happen.

"I cut up the underwear because I was upset," I say. "I

felt like a failure. I felt like I'd lost you. And maybe I have. But then, I sat back and did some serious thinking." I cross my fingers behind my back. "I thought about all the years we've been together. The good times and the terrible times. All that history. And I thought: I don't want to lose that. It's part of who I am. You're part of me, Tom. And I hope that I'm part of you."

He's staring at me, his face giving nothing away. The time has come to go "all in" and lay down my cards.

"So I thought that maybe we could try again with *us*. Tom and Marianne." I risk a half-smile. "We've been good together, despite everything. And I hope..." slowly, I take the pajama top off "... that we can be again."

That's it, I've said it. He hasn't moved. His face hasn't changed. My heart is liquifying, pooling around my feet. I want to bury my face in the pillow, my body under the blanket. Instead, I do what feels like the hardest thing I've ever done. I go to Tom and take his hand in mine, staring down at our entwined fingers – my skin white and creamy, his more tanned. "I love you, Tom," I whisper.

I have no idea if I've won or lost, if this is a beginning or an ending. I try not to think at all as Tom takes me in his arms and pulls me close. I breathe in his familiar scent and feel myself stiffen. I try to relax, to allow muscle memory to take charge of my body so that I can respond the way I used to.

Tom lifts my chin and kisses me. His mouth tastes of wine and cigarettes and smoky dark rooms. I wait for his hands to explore my skin, for my bra to end up on the floor trampled underfoot. *This is what I want*, I tell myself. But I can feel a creeping sense of dread. How many other bras has he removed in the last few years that were not mine? And when I lay awake at night imagining our reunion, why is it not Tom's face that I see...

No.

Tom's hands do not wander. Instead, he just holds me. I'm aware of the motion of his breath and the beating of his heart close to mine. Then, he takes a small step back. I'm not sure whether to melt or deflate as I feel his breath in my ear.

"I do love you, Marianne," he says. "But I've been… upset…by everything that's happened. And as a result, I've ended up hurting you." He runs a finger down my cheek, tracing the line where so many tears have flowed. "So can we take this slowly? Get to know each other again?"

I nod slowly: force myself to listen and see things from his perspective. There is still hope – lots of it. He still loves me. I'm playing the long game, I remind myself. Rome wasn't built in a day…

He lets go of me and picks up my pajama top. He drapes it around my shoulders. "Come on," he says. "Let's go to bed. I'm tired."

"OK." I make the monumental effort to look at him and smile.

I get into bed. The sound of Tom brushing his teeth grates on my nerves. Eventually, he gets in next to me and I lie with my back to him, spooning into him. I expect to feel his hands, his hardness. I try to make myself want it. But soon, I feel his breath, deep and even, on the back of my neck. He's asleep.

I let out a long sigh and roll out of his arms. I hate the relief I feel that tonight's "reunion" did not go to plan.

Tom starts to snore. I grip the spare pillow and hold onto it for dear life. My jaw is tight, every muscle in my body is tense. *You've taken the first step. Everything is fine.*

My phone on the bedside table vibrates with an incoming text. The voice of reason inside my head whispers that it will wait until morning. If I want to save my marriage, I should not look at it…

I pick up the phone and check the screen. It's a text with the *MyStory* logo and the words: "Match Found!"

There's an accompanying text: *Your results are in, Marianne! I look forward to meeting up again so we can discuss them!*

Dave x

I am white-knuckled as I grip the phone. How dare Dave Steiner insinuate himself into my bedroom, just as I was trying to put all of my transgressions, real and imagined, behind me. The fantasy trickles in past the barrier I've tried to build. Dave in the corridor of the hotel. Taking out his key and opening the door. Not a room, but a suite.

And then…

We sit on the bed. We… talk.

End of story.

My thumb hovers over the delete button.

"Dave? Who's he?"

I startle at Tom's voice. He's woken up and is staring at my screen over my shoulder. In fact, I've got a number of texts from Dave Steiner, and not all of them are about work…

I turn the phone off.

"Just a client."

"Oh." Tom rolls over and goes back to sleep. I turn off my phone and lie awake, staring up into the darkness. A chilling sense of dread prickles up the length of my spine.

That whatever small step forward I've taken tonight, the future is already spiraling out of control, and I'm headed for a fall.

32

It's still dark when I wake up the next morning with Tom snoring beside me. I lie in bed and take stock. Realistically, I'm as on track as I can expect to be. I've taken the first step to reconnect with my husband. Now I need to get him excited again about the prospect of being a father. Of being a family. Baby steps... literally...

In the meantime, I need to deal with Dave. Tell him that I don't want to get text messages from him in the night, see him outside the office, or have any sort of relationship beyond purely professional. He's been back home in California for the last few weeks, so it's been relatively easy to keep him out of sight, if not quite out of mind. But he's due to come back to D.C. in the next few days for another round of meetings. I don't want to feel any anticipation at the prospect of seeing him. I don't want to feel that his knowing the results of my DNA test gives us a kind of intimate connection. I must keep my mind on my mission and my eye on the ball.

I get out of bed and go downstairs. I like being up with the sun, feeling like I'm the first person crawling out of the primordial soup. I feel energized as I put on the coffee and eat a few bites of yogurt. While I'm waiting for the coffee to brew, I open up my laptop.

I feel a fragile, trembling sense of hope as I read through the articles I've bookmarked about egg donation success stories. I'm almost afraid to reread the article about the donor egg changing to become part of the host mother's body in case I've misunderstood. But the words are there in black and white. The human body really is a wonderful machine.

But, inevitably, I spy another article I've found about finding the best donor. I skim over it and then close the tab. It's a slow puncture to my good mood…

It's probably blindingly obvious, but the fact is that if the egg donor is a close relative to the recipient, then the baby will end up having the familial DNA. It will be all but indistinguishable from that of the mother's biological line. If I had a close relative to be a donor, then I could have a child that is biologically 99.9% mine!

But I don't.

I don't have a biological relative – close or otherwise – to be my egg donor. I have no siblings, and my two cousins on my mom's side are both boys. As the coffee percolates in the background, I feel a bubbling sense of frustration. Sometimes when I was growing up, I'd wished that I had a sibling – a sister. A guaranteed playmate, a confidant, a shoulder to cry on. Maybe it was my father's absences, or maybe my mother truly believed the party line that "only children do better in life" and wanted that for me. Whatever the reason, they never had another child, and I am alone.

Therefore, I must accept the facts. My child will not be a 99.9% biological match to me. It shouldn't bother me. It's only a few tiny percentages of difference between

99.9% mine and something less, like 85%. Only recently, I was looking at a long, drawn-out, childless life. Now, I have a new hope, a purpose again.

It *does* bother me.

I open my text messages. Dave's message is the last one I received. As much as I would like to derail my Genetic Journey, right now, I need to stay the course. The circles in my life are converging – all of this was meant to happen. My miscarriages, the failed IVF, the egg donation lifeline, and getting to know the architect of a global genetic database. Karma, Kismet. I'm meant to go on a Genetic Journey and meet my Genetic Cousins. I'll find the closest match I can, and an egg donor will appear. I have to believe it. Yes, there may be complications – like convincing someone to actually be a donor – but I will cross that bridge when I come to it. I am a businesswoman, a negotiator. I can make it work.

I start writing Dave a text when Tom comes downstairs. I put down my phone and stand up, pert and perky, and pour us both cups of coffee. "Hello, darling," I say. I let my robe fall open to reveal the lace of my bra. In my vision of the way things should be, Tom will come over, take me in his arms, kiss me, and whisper in my ear that last night was a perfect warm-up for the amazing sex we're going to have and that he's so glad that he's married to me. My skin tingles, waiting for him to come over and make it happen.

Instead, he rubs the sleep from his eyes and doesn't seem to notice my seductively disheveled state. He goes to the fridge and takes out the milk. He opens it and gives it a sniff. "This is off," he says.

"Really? It should have at least another few days."

"Well, smell it." He thrusts it towards me, clearly in a bad mood. I may live my life in my head before it happens, but Tom too has his expectations of how things *should* be. He takes his coffee with half milk and lots of sugar.

My insides drop like an elevator in free fall. I sniff the milk and feel nauseous at the sour smell. Still trying to smile, I pour it into the sink. It gloops out with large lumps of cream.

Tom sits down at the table. He puts his head in his hands and sighs.

"I'll… go out and get some more," I say. Fear of failure is leaching out and poisoning my every capillary and cell.

"Don't—"

Tom cuts off. I follow his eyes to the screen of my laptop. All my searches on egg donation – my shiny new hopes.

The look on Tom's face…

Oh God.

He stands up. "Jesus, you're crazy."

"No, Tom," I say, desperate to turn the clock back about two minutes. I follow him to the front door. "Let me explain. I'll tell you what I've found out."

"I'm going out to get some coffee," he says. "And then I'm going to the gym."

He picks up his keys and his gym bag. The door slams, and he's gone.

I throw another glass into the sink – the fourth one – and it shatters to pieces. But even the startling sound can't stop the flow of anger and hurt – and the fear that once again I've made an irreparable mistake.

Now, I'm late for my usual Metro. I sweep up the glass with my bare hands and throw it in the trash can, pausing only to suck on a thin red cut at the end of my forefinger.

With the evidence removed, I grab my coat and briefcase, and then I'm out the door.

Now that the orchestra of broken things has quieted down, I try another round of positive self-talk. I *will* do this. I will get Tom onside and convince him that he can be a father. I am not going to fail this time.

But the whisper of voices in my head will not be silenced. *You had your chance. You don't deserve to be happy.*

I get in the car and drive to the station. I'm so preoccupied that I almost fail to stop as a crossing guard steps out into the street with a group of kids. I slam on the brakes as she brandishes her stop sign in my face.

I grip the wheel to stop my hands from shaking as I refuse to meet her eyes. I drive to the next block and pull over. It's not the fault of the crossing guard. She hasn't done anything wrong. I'm the failure here. I'm the one who will never be able to live down the mistake I made. Me – and my mother. *We* don't deserve to be happy.

My mother made the appointment. Drove me to a gray, unassuming building in the ugly part of town. I didn't even know for sure what she had in mind until I saw the picketers. An elderly woman in a floral top, man-jeans, and flip-flops, and two younger, more militant-looking women, one of which had a bored toddler in a stroller throwing Cheetos into the road. The elderly woman waved her sign in my face: "Baby-killing is murder". My mother pushed it aside, her mouth set in a grim line. The two other women's signs read: "Choose life, not murder", and "Thou shalt not kill". *Baby killer.* I stopped walking. My mother took my arm, yanking it hard.

"*I know you'll do whatever it takes to put things right,*" she whispered in my ear. The other three women took up a chant: "Baby killer… baby killer."

"Shut up," my mother shouted at them. I looked at her

with a sickly fascination. My mother rarely used strong language. Other than towards me. *Filthy, disgusting little slut.* I felt every inch the part.

The women shouted back, but I didn't hear them. I hoped that they would rush the building and I could sneak away in the melee. My mother shoved me inside the door and pulled it shut.

Inside, they had made an effort to have everything look bland and clinical. As if you were just going in for a pap smear. I was numb as my mother went up to the receptionist and confirmed the appointment. I knew that I was here to be examined and be presented with the "options". Then I would have a waiting period to change my – or, in this case, my mother's – mind. I didn't want the exam, the options, or the waiting period. I would not be changing anyone's mind.

On the way home, my mother tried to talk to me. Tried to backpedal from her initial reaction, apologize for the names she'd called me. "I know it's difficult, but we'll get through it together. You're focusing on the future. You're doing the right thing."

Fleetingly, I wondered what my father would say. My mother had decided that we wouldn't tell him. But secretly, I was considering telling him the whole thing. All about the party, and Hal – who'd lied to me and made me feel special, when really, I'd been nothing to him. Telling my father would be like getting a second opinion, like one did when facing a medical procedure. Maybe he would disagree with my mother. Maybe he would share *my* view: that everything happens for a reason, and the life inside of me had a right to exist. That by making the choice my mother wanted, I wasn't focusing on the future, but destroying it.

But when I got home from the clinic, my father was

gone. I spoke to him that night on the phone when he was waiting at the gate for his flight. "Things are fine. School is fine. No, I don't need a present from California." He told me he was proud of me, and then boarding started, and he hung up.

To this day, I wonder if things might have turned out differently if he'd been there. Maybe I would have felt beautiful and special enough to stand up to my mother: to stand up for the life inside of me. But such speculation is pointless. My father wasn't there that night. The next day, my mother took me back to the clinic. The procedure was relatively painless.

The guilt was unbearable.

I don't blame my mother. She was unwavering in her belief that what I did – what *we* did – was the right course of action. Her vision was all about my perfect future. I would have a good career. I would meet a man and get married. And then, it would be a better time to get pregnant and have a baby. The right time.

I've never asked her if she has any regrets. I never told my father about what happened. I never told anyone what I knew in my heart: that the baby – Baby Zero – was a girl. I gave her a name. Lily.

I never named any of the other babies.

What was the point?

I swallow back a sob. In the rearview mirror, I can see children from the private school being ushered across the street by the crossing guard. The girls are dressed in neat white blouses and green and blue plaid skirts, and the boys have green sweaters and blue pants. The crossing guard's slicker is bright yellow, her stop sign as red as a lollypop on a stick. A veritable rainbow. I feel the familiar clench in my stomach. Usually, it's for babies, but babies become children, and children grow up. Lily would be twenty-one this year. Twenty-one! And if any of her siblings had survived, they might have been in the group of kids crossing right now. Or maybe they'd be going to St Clemmon's school, a few blocks over. The uniform there is even more stylish – red and white kilts and straw boater hats. I think they even have to wear white gloves.

God… I bang my hand against the steering wheel. I've got to pull myself together. Instead of wallowing in my misery and anger, I need to put it to good use and *do* something. I need to find an egg donor. As soon as possible.

A work email comes in from one of my colleagues about tax aspects of the refinancing. I don't read the email, but cc'd on the message is Dave Steiner.

I pull up Dave's text message from last night. It says that he has a Genetic Cousin for me to meet. Maybe this person who shares a DNA link with me will prove to be my savior. Or, if not them, then someone else. Rather than text, I decide to call him. I'll tell him the truth and then endure his calm, patient voice as he discusses the science and the options. I will listen, learn, and remain single-minded. I need a baby, and for that, I need an egg donor. The *right* egg donor. I need Dave to help me find her.

I dial the number. It rings for what seems like a long time. Then I remember the three-hour time difference. It's just after eight now, so that means that there it's…

5 a.m.

"Marianne?" Dave answers in a voice that's half asleep. "What's happened? Are you OK?"

"Hi Dave," I say. "Sorry to call so early." *Karma*, *kismet*.

"Well… that's OK."

"Great. I won't keep you long."

I'm planning to tell him about the egg donation idea. Get him on the case like a recruitment consultant. Set out my job spec and see what he can find. But before the words come out, I suddenly worry that that sounds too cold, too harsh. Going on a Genetic Journey should be about curiosity and connection, not about finding someone who fits a certain profile. Maybe he will see it as unethical and refuse to help. I can't take that chance.

"I just wanted to say that I'm glad you've found me a Genetic Cousin. I don't know who they are, but I'm sure it will prove to be an interesting journey."

"OK – so why did you really call?"

"No reason. I just... um... wanted to hear your voice."

There's a silence as he considers this. I sense that same crackle of tension between us that's been there ever since that that first meeting back in early March. I've been trying to deny it. It's one more thing that I've tried at... and failed.

"Well, it's good to hear your voice too." Dave sounds almost like he's purring. "I'll be flying back to D.C. tomorrow. Do you want to meet up for a drink?"

I think of my resolutions about my marriage. My last desperate hope. Tom's face when he saw my screen... the bag of underwear, most of it still with the tags on... *Beautiful, special...*

"Give me a call when you get here," I say. "And we'll see."

33

CLAIRE

"Call me when you've had time to digest it." Stella stands up, shoulders her Birkin, and moves towards the door. The innocent-looking manilla folder on the table is like a poisonous snake, coiled and ready to strike.

"No…" I mutter. "I mean – you're sure? You're absolutely sure that there was no mistake?" I keep asking the same question over and over again – why can't she give me a different answer?

"I'm sure." She gives me a sympathetic smile. "But it could be great news, Claire. Try to see it that way."

As she goes out the door, I give it an extra hard slam behind her. Then I collapse against it, my heart exploding in my chest.

It's human nature to cultivate and cling to a few constants in life. Eating the same cereal for breakfast, watching the news before bed. Waking up next to the same person, calling to mind a few cherished memories from childhood. It's the little things that form solid foundations, each component carefully crafted and fit into place like a jigsaw puzzle.

So what happens when you find out that everything you knew – or thought you knew – turns out to be a lie?

I watch as Stella gets into her car and drives off. She came here on her own, with no film crew in tow, and for that, I'm grateful. I want to convince myself that the whole thing is smoke and mirrors... showbiz. My Genetic Journey wasn't exciting enough, so Stella had to concoct something sordid and sensational.

My knees are liquid as I make my way back to the kitchen table, where the scented candles have been pushed aside, and a cup of tea is steaming. I want to believe in the power of tea to calm my nerves, fill the gaping black hole that has opened up inside of me. But nothing can stop the rot. I am hemorrhaging memories. The entire foundation of my life has cracked, and I am tumbling down to a dark place.

Mom.

Dad.

A… sister.

Stella had shown me a map. A hit on a database that the *MyStory* scientists found anomalous and looked at a little more closely. Like a cell infected with cancer, mutating into something ghastly, that pinpoint on the map is the epicenter of a wave of doubt that I couldn't have imagined. What does it say about me that I hadn't imagined it? How can I ever trust myself again?

Number, markers, charts. Science. Dad always used to say that you couldn't argue with science. Dad said a lot of things. Like "I love you" and "I'm so glad you're my daughter – my *only* daughter." Variations on a theme of: "I'm sorry I have to travel again for work"; "I'm sorry I'm going to miss your [school play, parent/teacher night, baseball championship], but I'll be back as soon as I can. I promise." Yes, if Dad had a chorus, it was: "I promise."

"I'll be there next time, I promise"; "I'll make it up to you, I promise"; "I'll be thinking of you non-stop and wishing I was there, I promise."

You can't argue with science.

It probably even explains the anger I feel. Some kind of chemical response to the realization that my world is not what I ordered, and I can't send it back again. I am powerless in the face of the truth.

My dad had a second daughter. A living, breathing person. She has a name.

Marianne.

Out of courtesy, Stella told me first, in confidence. It took a while for us to arrange this meeting because she's been doing other interviews for the program, and I've been focused on Jess. Apparently, even Dave Steiner doesn't know about this new match. He's been busy with his work and travels, and I haven't seen him since that day at the hospital. Stella said that it's up to me to tell him if I want to. In the meantime, she will assume that either I want out of the project, or I only want to connect with my more distant Genetic Cousins like the Larssons and their ilk.

She left me a printout of the information and made me a cup of tea. Left me to deal with the radioactive fallout.

Somewhere along the way, after Dad said his goodbyes and "see you soon"s, he went away and got another woman pregnant. The sibling – half-sibling – is two years younger than me. While my mom was at home dealing with a two-year-old, Dad was off on a frolic of his own.

Did Mom know? Her final decline was swift, but she had periods of lucidity. She could have told me – made a dying declaration. Except most of the time, Dad was there with me at the end. In the room, across the bed, holding one of her hands while I held the other. I want to cling to the memory. Dad loved us. She and me. This I believe to be an absolute truth.

Or do I? I take a sip of the tea, which is now lukewarm. Another law of science and physics that is immutable, some law of thermodynamics, I think. Hot liquids cool down. Even the universe will someday reach a state of heat death. The liquid tastes brown, if that's a thing. Stella didn't put any sweetener in it. I drink it down anyway. It is a tiny taste of sanity in my gone-mad world. I push aside the empty "World's Greatest Mother" mug, turning it around so I can't see the words.

As I withdraw my hand, the charms on my bracelet jingle. I have an almost uncontrollable urge to rip the thing off and slam-dunk it in the trash can. Instead, I stare at the charms one by one. The Golden Gate Bridge. A dolphin, a pineapple, the Statue of Liberty. The US Capitol… in Washington, D.C.

Where Marianne lives. *Marianne*. I could call her up. Surely, that course of action has to be considered. Talk to her, introduce myself – find out that it's all a misunderstanding, a hoax, even. Uncover the hidden camera that will reveal all. Marianne is a stand-in. It's all a clever, if not very funny, joke.

But what if it's not?

"Mom, where's the bicycle pump?"

I'm startled out of my ugly fog of thoughts by Becky coming downstairs.

"How should I know?" I barely even register her hair, which has turned a hideous shade of acid green.

"But my tire's flat. I need it."

The anger coils up inside of me like a tornado. *Becky*. Soon she'll be wanting to go on her own Genetic Journey. She won't have to wander very far down the yellow brick road before she spots the pin on the map. Alexandria, Virginia, just across the Potomac from Washington, D.C., where Dad's company was headquartered.

"What's wrong?" Becky is staring at me with an unusual amount of concern.

"Oh, nothing…" I hydraulically lift my mouth into a smile. Why am I lying? Becky is not stupid, and she's not a child. She's almost old enough that we should be reaching the friendship stage of our relationship. But even if she and I never get there, I wouldn't wish this on my worst enemy.

"OK," she says. "If you don't want to tell me, then I guess I'll just leave you here to stew over 'nothing'." She grabs a banana from the fruit bowl. If I don't speak now, the chance will be gone. Becky is my daughter: she deserves my confidence.

"It's the DNA test," I say. "I've just got some unsettling news."

"What is it?" She has a sly look in her eyes like she's expecting me to pipe up with a genetic link to Adolf Hitler or Attila the Hun. I wish…

"It's just that a relative has been identified that I didn't know about. A… close relative."

"Yeah, well, it's supposed to do that, right? Find your cousins and stuff. Is this the person in D.C.?"

"Yes," I seethe, remembering that she looked at my phone. "But I'm not talking about a cousin. You've got a new aunt."

"A new…" Her brow furls as she tries to work out the relationship. "You mean… wait a minute. What?"

I stare down at my hands folded on the table, trying to figure out if they – or anything else about my life – are actually familiar.

"My dad had another daughter," I say. "I have a half-sister. She lives in Washington, D.C."

"No!" Becky's mouth gapes open. "Seriously! That's wicked cool!"

Maybe we really are from different planets. I can't believe that anyone – even Becky – would have the gall to see it like that. I'm beginning to realize just how boring she must think I am now that my life has turned into an episode of Jerry Springer.

"So what was it?" she presses. "A one-night stand?"

"Maybe," I say. "Yes. Probably." Hearing her put it in those terms actually makes me feel a little better. I remember Dad telling me that business travel was boring and lonely. Maybe on one occasion, it all got too much, and he alleviated that boredom and loneliness by meeting someone in the hotel bar, and one thing led to another. He got stuck with the bill; she got stuck with a baby. Most likely, Dad didn't even know that he had another child. That doesn't make it right – far from it. But it explains the facts in a way that I can come to terms with… eventually.

"So, what are you going to do?" Becky says. "Have you emailed her?"

"God, no!" I *so* wish I hadn't mentioned it to Becky. "I might just let it go. I mean, I'm forty years old. I don't need or want a sister. I've got you and Jess and your dad, and… we're happy." I grin like a malformed jack o'lantern. "Right?"

"She's your sister." Becky sounds scandalized. "You can't just do nothing."

"Half-sister! And I can do whatever I want. I'm an adult. I'll make my own choices, thank you very much."

"But she could be the one." Becky's face clouds with anger. "The one that we've been looking for all this time. A match for Jess. Are you going to let Jess die rather than face up to this?"

"How dare you?" I hiss. "You don't know anything about what I'm going through. You don't care about your sister – don't pretend you do. She's just another toy for you to break. That's what the hair was about, wasn't it?"

"The hair was Jess's idea. I was trying to help her."

"Help her?" I snort. "That's rich. You've always resented her."

She laughs in my face. "Why would I do that? Is it because she's smart and talented and *easy* compared to me? Is it because she's so much sicker? Is that why you love her so much more?"

"I don't love her more than you. That's ridiculous."

"You're such a bad liar, Mom. I wonder if your sister is better at it than you."

"Get out of here!" I shout. "I can't take this – not now." I'm sounding like a toddler – hardly the strong role model I've always wanted to be but can't seem to manage.

"Sure," Becky says. "I'm going."

"Fine." *Just go.*

A text comes in from Dave Steiner. I delete it without reading it. For all I know, he too might be in Washington, D.C. – right this second. Which is just so… fitting.

"Good luck, Mom," Becky says breezily. "I trust you to do the right thing."

34

BECKY

Grandpa Joe had a saying: "Man makes plans; God laughs."

I didn't really get it when I was a kid. But as Mom storms out of the kitchen, I think I'm starting to understand.

To be honest, I haven't given Grandpa Joe a lot of thought recently. For one thing, he's dead, and for another, we weren't really that close when he was alive. When I was really little, I thought that he was a cool grandpa – the kind who always came over with candy or a little toy, and each time he'd kneel down and say, "No! That can't be Becky – she can't have grown that much!" Then he'd swing me in his arms, and I'd laugh and feel really excited. Then he'd put me down and go sit in front of the TV with a beer and watch baseball on TV. He was really into watching baseball – that much I remember. Usually, by the time the visit was over, the toy would be broken, and I'd have a tummy ache from the candy. I'd end up feeling kind of mad at him without really knowing why.

I began to find it a little weird, then really annoying,

how Mum changed whenever she was around him. It was like he was some kind of royalty who needed waiting on hand and foot, and she'd get all subservient and hero-worshipy like she was incredibly grateful that he was giving her his time. She'd fetch his beers, laugh at his jokes, and talk really quickly when she tried to tell him a story, like he might vanish at any moment. I didn't like to see her acting that way. (Come to think of it, it's kind of like how she acts around her friend Dave.)

When Jess was a baby, Grandpa Joe took all of us fishing once. I have only vague memories of that day, but I know that it was hot, and he told us some story about fishing in the Amazon, or maybe it was someplace in Africa. Anyway, I got the idea that Grandpa Joe lived some kind of mysterious life – like James Bond or something. When I asked Dad about it, he said that "Grandpa Joe likes to talk, but in real life, he's just a salesman. He has a boring job that he hates, same as everybody else. End of story."

But as it turns out, it's not quite the end of the story.

A secret sister.

That is *so* epic!

I kind of get why Mom's upset. I mean, even though I feel alienated from my family half the time and have seriously wondered whether I might have been adopted, if the answer had turned out to be yes, I would feel really betrayed. That's how Mom is feeling now, I guess. Grandpa Joe – the dad that she worshiped – isn't who she thought he was. I'm sure that must hurt.

On the other hand, she doesn't seem to see the upside – a very *close* biological relative is the person most likely to be a match for Jess. This is the whole point of her doing the test! Jess could have the transplant, and there'd be no more masks and hand sanitizer, no more transfusions, and no more drugs that make her sick. She could go to school, go to her audition, and become someone really great that Taylor would definitely notice. For some reason, as soon as Mom told me that she had a sister, I got this prickly feeling at the back of my neck. (Maybe I'm psychic!)

Anyway, it's no surprise that Mom and I don't agree on the whole sister thing – I mean, there's not much we do agree on. I'll let her run with it for now, but the whole thing prompts me to get out a piece of notepaper and write the words "Becky's Bucket List" at the top in big loopy writing.

I fill out the first few bullet points:

1. Stop failing math
2. Get an after-school job
3. Save for a car
4. Work on J's bucket list
5. Make sure new aunt gets bone marrow test

I stare down at the words "new aunt". I've never had an aunt before. What would she be like? She could be a celebrity or an ax murderer, an angel or a demon. But there are molecules in my DNA (or whatever DNA is actually made of) that must be the same as hers. That's kind of weird, but cool too. I add another number to my list.

I close the notebook and shove it under my mattress so that Mom can't find it. I'm not sure what she would make of my last item: (6) Get to know new aunt and welcome her into the family.

35

MARIANNE

"A what?"

I'm sure I've misheard him. Dave has caught me at a low ebb – at the end of a three-hour video call with the bankers. He's back in California now. Out of sight, out of…sight…

To be fair, I wasn't surprised that he wanted to talk in private after everyone else had dropped off the call. We haven't really spoken since meeting up the night after Tom saw my screen. I'm not really sure what there is to say – in some ways, words aren't important anymore. I certainly wasn't expecting this.

A sister?

Maybe he's just being funny – pulling my leg. Should I laugh? These days any kind of laughing might turn into crying, so it's best just to keep a straight face. *Think nothing. Feel nothing.*

"I know it's a shock, but I thought that you needed to know."

If he's being funny, he's doing a poor job of it. Instead of his usual charismatic self, he sounds like a boy who's just been caught by the teacher with his hands down his pants. Embarrassed. Like he'd rather be speaking to anyone else but me about anything else but this.

The initial results of my DNA test were, in all honesty, a little disappointing. The few matches that came up were mostly men. One match seemed more promising – a woman in Williamsburg, Virginia. I spoke to her on the phone, but when I discovered that she had a grandson who had arranged for the family to be tested, I decided not to meet her in person. She's too old to donate eggs, and I don't have time for lemonade on the porch. Maybe Dave was annoyed that I didn't show more of an interest in my Genetic Cousins and decided to shake things up. I don't know. In more ways than one, he certainly has thrown a curveball into my life.

"I'm really sorry to have brought this on, Marianne," he says. "But I'm afraid it's an occupational hazard. Most of the time, we give people welcome news. But we can't help the occasional skeleton in the closet."

Skeleton in the closet. Is that what it is? I have a feeling that my world should be rocking. It is rocking, of course. I should feel shocked and horrified. But do I? Tom always says that a lot of the time, my emotions are just plain wrong. That I don't feel things the way other people do. Sometimes I take things too hard, and sometimes things just float over my head like dandelion seeds in the wind. I sense that now is one of those times.

A sister. What would it be like to have one? A yin to my yang, a Bert to my Ernie. It seems a strange thing to have wished for when I was younger. But now that one has materialized, I feel… curious.

"Marianne, are you there?"

"Yes," I say. "Sorry. I'm just trying to take it all in."

"I get that," he says. "And I wish I was there to help

you through it. But I didn't want to wait to tell you. Because she... your... I mean, the other person involved... will also get an alert. In fact, I've been trying to reach her. As a courtesy, you understand."

She knows too – or she soon will. What does it all mean? I'm thirty-eight years old, childless, in a marriage that's balanced on a knife's edge. But I also have a plan. A plan that just ten minutes ago there seemed to be very little chance of implementing. Now, though...

There are possibilities.

"So, is she going to contact me? What happens next?"

"Well, to be honest, I don't know." Dave scratches his head. I can see from the camera angle that he's sitting at a desk in some kind of study or den. On the shelf in the background, he's got books, a couple of trophies, a picture of his wife and son, and a half-dead spider plant. "She's a journalist. She's doing a series of articles on her Genetic Journey. She's even being filmed for our documentary."

I have to laugh. Of all the people in the world that Dave Steiner chose to put on a Genetic Journey, he picked her – and me. They say that everyone is separated by no more than six social connections from anyone else. With the advent of Facebook, Twitter, and the *MyStory* database, maybe that's shrunk to three or four, or even less. In my case, less than one. A long-lost half-sister.

If I dwell on the implications, I'm sure that I'll discover my world tipped on its side. My father had another child. That means that my mother's perfect life was not perfect after all. I know it's wrong, but that makes me feel almost... good.

"There is absolutely no obligation on your part to contact her or to respond if she tries to contact you," Dave clarifies, switching to damage-control mode. "At *MyStory*, we respect the privacy of all of our subjects."

I laugh again. I even feel a little sorry for Dave – surely he can't believe his own spiel, which is clearly utter drivel. If my privacy was being respected, then my… sister… wouldn't know I exist. And vice versa.

"Marianne? Talk to me. Are you OK?" He sounds unusually frantic. "I'm coming back later in the week for the roadshow, you know that, right? We can talk more about it then."

"Sure," I say. I wipe the tears of laughter – or just the tears – from my eyes. "Let's meet up and 'talk' some more. But for now, in terms of the financing, I think we'd better have another look at your privacy policy. Just to make sure that you've dotted all those i's and crossed those t's."

"Good spot." He sighs as if he's carrying the weight of the world – instead of having just dumped it on me. "Under the circumstances, you're probably right."

———

Two hours later, I'm knocking on my mother's door. We've barely talked since the night she last came over to my house. Since then, my life has changed… considerably… in more ways than one. Whenever she's called to ask me how it's going, I've left it at "fine."

Now that I'm here, I'm questioning my motives. What good will it do to break the news that my father had another child from before they were married? Am I doing it to fuel my curiosity, or am I doing it to hurt her?

I am genuinely interested in the truth. Did the woman die? Did he abandon her? Or did she not tell him she was pregnant? It strikes me as either terribly twisted or hopelessly romantic – I'm not sure which. But will my mother be able to shed any light on it?

She opens the door wearing an apron, her graying hair lightly dusted with flour.

"You're early," she says. "I was baking scones."

She seems flustered. I wonder if I've done something wrong that I'm not aware of. When I was young, I was forever doing things that annoyed her. Leaving the back door open, dropping crumbs in the living room, tracking in mud, or playing the piano without the soft pedal down. It was better when my father was home because my mother was happy. When it was just the two of us, I was always living on eggshells. "I brought this," I say, handing her a bottle of chilled white wine.

"Thanks." She takes the bottle and ushers me inside. The house is immaculate, decorated in a tasteful colonial style with dark antique furniture and early American prints. The kitchen has a big Shaker table in the center, and there are sliding glass doors that look out into the backyard, showcasing the flowering dogwood tree at the edge of the fence. I've often wondered why my mother never married again after my father died. Maybe she didn't want to risk letting another man into her life who might leave the toilet seat up or shaving stubble in the sink. That wouldn't surprise me. Or maybe…

No. There's no way she could have known.

I get the bottle opener out of the drawer and two glasses out of the china hutch. She takes the tray of scones out of the oven.

"To what do I owe this pleasure?" she says.

I open the wine and pour it. I don't quite know how to begin. I take a long sip of the crisp golden chardonnay and decide that misdirection is the best course of action.

"Mother," I say, "do you still have Dad's things up in the attic?"

"Some of it." She eyes me askance. "I've given most of

it to charity. There are some papers, I suppose, like financial documents. I never know how long to keep those things for. I should probably just get rid of everything."

She brings me a scone on a dainty china plate and goes to the refrigerator for butter and jam. All of her usual little rituals – fussing over this and that – are starting to annoy me. As is her habit of doing a spring clean every six months and giving things away to charity. She's systematically wiped out most of my memories of this house, my childhood, and my father.

"I'd like to take a look at what's there."

"Why?" She frowns. "It's been there for years. Why now?"

"Something came up in connection with my Genetic Journey." I take a breath and jump in feet first. "A hit has come up on the database. I am a close genetic match with a woman in California."

"California?" She twists her apron string around her hand.

"I have a half-sister. Her name is Claire."

"No." My mother fires the word at me like a shot. "No. That can't possibly be right. It's a mistake on the test. It has to be. I told you those things were dangerous." She lifts her glass to her lips, but her hand is shaking so hard that wine sloshes down her chin. My mother is crumbling before me – something I haven't seen before. I feel a strange mixture of guilt, fascination, and fear.

"It's a ninety-nine point nine percent certainty."

"No." The glass comes down hard onto the table. "It's not right."

"The... other daughter... is two years older than me. So it might have happened before you and he even met. He might not have known."

"Yes, well, I'm sure he didn't." She closes her mouth into a thin line.

"Yes, Mother." I say the words by rote, but fireworks are going off inside my head. My mother ran her life – and mine – with an iron fist. So I've always thought…

"I'm going out tonight," she says. "Bridge. So I'll give you a call… another time."

My mother does not have bridge tonight. She wants me gone. Part of me wishes I could shove all the horribles back in the box and close the lid. To go on with pretending that everything in our lives is the same as before. Another part of me wants to understand where she's coming from. Maybe it explains nothing. On the other hand, maybe it explains a lot.

"I'm sorry I've upset you," I say. "Really. But I'm not sure it's something we can just sweep underneath the carpet. When I heard the news, I was surprised, of course. But then I felt curious. I mean, who is this person? Where did she come from? What is she like?"

"You need to go now," she says through her teeth.

I am defeated. My mother's walls are firmly up, the pretext of her perfect life kept intact. No bombardment with reason or compassion is going to batter them down. I put the cork back in the bottle and take my glass to the sink. I wash it out and then do what I'm told – I leave.

I probably don't have a right to feel angry, but I do.

PART III

MAY

36

CLAIRE

I book a ticket.

What else can I do?

Everything in my life is falling apart, but I can't focus on any of it – not until I get to the bottom of this deception.

Becky keeps asking me about her "new aunt". I tell her that I don't want to talk about it. Steve has got himself a second job to earn extra money – or to get away from the house – either way, I can hardly blame him. Jess is like a zoo animal – hating her cage and hating me. The drugs have stabilized her condition for now, but she has bad side effects like headaches, nausea, diarrhea, and a racing pulse. Secretly, I wonder whether it's worth trading my beloved little girl for the girl living in that room. I know that Becky is partially responsible for the tension between us – that and the canceled audition. Although I took the letter out of the trash, smoothed out the creases, and stuck it in the junk drawer, its absence is like a black hole sucking the life out of my relationship with Jess. The upshot is, that it's probably as good a time as any for me to go away.

Before I leave, I ransack the boxes of Mom and Dad's things that are up in the attic. I find old photos – happy memories of sunny days, pizza parlors, fishing expeditions, and Christmases past – and I cry over them. I take Dad's old clothing out of the suitcase. I hold his favorite sweater to my nose and try to breathe in the scent of him. But there's no smell left, and I dampen the wool with my tears. I look through his papers: pay slips, tax records, the documents from when he sold his house to buy a boat and a mooring. Letters pertaining to the modest life insurance settlement I got after he died. It was enough for us to buy this house, and for that, I will always be grateful.

At the bottom of the box, I find a blurry photocopy of his death certificate. I shed another tear at the black words in block print: accidental death at sea. I also find a receipt for an airport shop in Miami. It's dated a month before he died, and it's for a silver dolphin charm. I run my fingers over the contours of the tiny dolphin at my wrist and picture him in the shop, flipping through the charms on a rack before going to the gate. It feels pathetic and impersonal. And what was he doing in Florida anyway? When I got news of his death, it was such shock that I barely registered the fact that I hadn't seen him for almost three months beforehand. I guess in the history of our life together, there was nothing strange in that.

By the time I've shoved everything back where it belongs, I'm all cried out, and my anger is simmering. There's nothing to find – nothing to explain his life, or his death, or… my sister.

I hope that when I meet her, all will be clear. That this terrible ache inside will go away. Maybe it's God's way of giving me something in exchange for the gradual deterioration of my daughter. It's as if my life has reached some kind of awful, invisible line in the sand. Only by seeing this through can I figure out what to do next.

I pay for the ticket with my credit card behind Steve's back. I know that when I tell him that I'm going off on another trip, he'll be beyond ballistic. In the old days, if I got bad news, he'd be the first person I'd tell. But with our relationship at breaking point, I can't bring myself to broach the subject.

Instead, I go through the back door like a Trojan horse. I tell Becky. And let the chips fall where they may.

"So you're really going to go see her?" Becky says. She's just come home from school and has dumped her bag in the middle of the kitchen floor. She proceeds to make herself some kind of messy sandwich with tuna, mayo, lettuce, and ketchup that she sticks in the microwave.

"I've booked a ticket. That's as far as I've got."

"Wow, D.C.," she says. "You're so lucky."

"It's not a sightseeing trip. You know that."

"Yeah, I do. But it's good that you're going. I mean, she could be the one."

"I wish you'd stop saying that." I put my hands on my hips. "I'm not a match, and neither is anyone in this family. So there's no reason to expect that she will be."

"Maybe not. But that's why you did the DNA test, right? To find close relatives who will agree to be tested?"

"Right." I sigh.

"And anyway, I've got a good feeling about it." She pops a can of Diet Coke. Some of it fizzes out onto the counter.

"Like you did about the hair-dye?" I don't mean to say it, but it just comes out.

"Yeah." She takes her sandwich and skulks off. I feel even worse.

. . .

The chips fall that night at dinner. As usual, there is little conversation between Steve and me beyond "pass the carrots" and "is there any more sauce?" Becky adds to the tension by haranguing him about when she can get a car. Steve looks ready to blow a gasket. He tells her that she can get a car when she can get a job and pay for it herself.

"But Mom can afford a plane ticket to Washington, D.C.?" Becky looks right at me, knowing that she's dropping me in it. I just sit back and smile blandly. Little does she know that she's done exactly what I'd hoped.

"What?" Steve has to look at me.

"She's going to D.C.," Becky says. "*Didn't she tell you?*"

"No one is going anywhere." Steve pushes away his half-eaten dinner and gets up from the table.

"I'm leaving next week," I say. "There's someone that I need to meet."

Steve sits back down. Tension smolders in the room. "Becky," he says, "can you please go upstairs?"

"I'm eating," Becky says. She who hates vegetables makes a point of taking a second helping of carrots.

I put down my fork, rigid in my chair. Becky is enjoying herself. Finally, after chewing the last bite of carrot at least thirty times before swallowing, she gets up from the table. "Should I take a tray up to Jess?"

"She's sleeping," I say through my teeth. "I'll bring her something later."

"OK, whatever. Have fun, you two." She gives a mock wave. "Don't do anything I wouldn't."

It seems like a decade, an eon before she's finally up and out of the room. As soon as she's gone, I wish she was back. Because now I have to face Steve alone.

"I've got the name of a lawyer," he says. "I'm going to

go and see him. I seriously need to think about getting out of this marriage."

A glacial chill comes over me. Whatever I was expecting, it wasn't this. But now that he's said it, it seems obvious.

"Steve," I say, "will you at least hear me out?"

He shakes his head and then lets me have it, both barrels. "I just don't know you anymore, Claire. And what's more, I'm not sure I want to. I don't know if you're having an affair or if this DNA thing is just a passing fantasy, but don't tell me that it's work and that you're doing it for the family, or for Jess, or any other kind of absolute crap." His face is as red as a furnace about to explode. I need to do something and fast.

"I found out that I have a sister," I blurt. "A half-sister I didn't know about. She… um… lives in D.C." I can feel the hot prickle of tears beginning to form. I can't remember the last time I cried in front of Steve. Usually, I just get angry. But a lawyer… Jess… a divorce… A sister…

The tears come forth like a stream bursting its banks. Blinding, overwhelming. "Just when I think we've hit rock bottom, something happens to make it worse," I sob. "My life – our life – may be hard, but at least it's ours. But my past is all a lie."

Steve makes no move to comfort me, but he does visibly soften. "A sister?" he says. "You found that out on the DNA test?"

"Yes."

"Jesus." The wind is finally out of his sails. "And you seriously don't know anything else. I mean, is she older or younger?"

"Younger," I sniff. "She's thirty-eight."

"So that means your dad had an affair? Or a one-night stand?"

"Yes! I guess so!" I let anger take over. "Dad was only ever around part-time. A week here, a week there. Holidays – for the most part. But whatever he was doing, he somehow managed to father a child along the way."

"God."

"So whatever you think I'm doing – whatever you're accusing me of – then let me assure you, it's nothing like that. I'm definitely not having an affair! You may not believe it, but I just want my life back. I want Jess to be well and Becky to make something of herself. I want to be in a marriage with someone who loves me – not someone who can barely stand to look at me. And most of all—" I choke "—I want to be the person I thought I was two days ago. Yes, things were far from perfect – things are downright awful if you want to know the truth. But at least I knew the woman in the mirror. At least I had happy memories of my childhood and my life before everything went to hell. I missed Dad a lot, but it was because I loved him. He was my friend and confidant. I *trusted* him. And now, all of it is a lie."

As I gesture with my hands, the charms jangle on the bracelet. Suddenly, I can't stand it anymore. I unclasp it and throw it across the room. It ends up in a pile of fluff peeking out from underneath the fridge, a wink of silver that seems like it's mocking me.

A hand on my back. I jump. In the flow of my tirade, I haven't even noticed Steve coming over to me, turning me gently. And then, suddenly, I'm in his arms – somewhere that I haven't been for a long time and had given up ever wanting to be again. But sobbing against his chest, with him stroking my hair, I realize that this is where I belong.

"Sorry, Claire," he says. "I had no idea."

His chest is warm, and I can hear his beating heart.

"I'm the one who's sorry," I gasp. "For how I've been. But I wanted you to know the truth."

He lifts my chin. His lips, once so familiar, feel new as they brush mine. A lightning bolt shoots through my body. I haven't even dared to miss this closeness, this spark that was once between us. He deepens the kiss, and I move onto his lap. His hand reaches up beneath my shirt, and I shift on top of him until I can feel him underneath me. I want to cry out with joy – that whatever we've been through, there might be hope after all. He lifts me up, and I run my fingers through his hair and pull him to me. He fumbles furiously with the buttons on my blouse and then with the clasp on my bra. And then his mouth is on my skin, and I'm moaning with the sheer unexpected pleasure of it. His shirt comes off, and then my skin is against his, soft and slick. And just as I'm undoing the buttons on his jeans, I hear a noise and look up. Jess is standing in the doorway to the kitchen.

"Oh, God!" I cry, which Steve, whose back is to her, takes as a sign of my wanton pleasure.

And then, I push him away.

37

MARIANNE

I'm not expecting a card or a call. In truth, I'm not expecting anything at all, though I have been ruminating over plans of my own: gift basket? Champagne hamper? So when the email comes into my junk folder from a Claire Woods, I almost delete it. I don't know a Claire Woods, and I usually don't even check the folder at all. But I was searching for a password reset email, and that's when I saw it.

Claire Woods. A neat name. Eleven letters. As I open the message, I wonder if she has a middle name. Woods must be her married name. She's forty, so she must be married. Maybe she has kids. If so, then I'm an aunt.

I can't even begin to take that in.

Claire Woods clearly has no thoughts of sending a gift basket or a hamper. Her message is short and concise: *I understand that you've been told about the MyStory test results. I'm arranging to fly to Washington and was hoping we could meet. Please let me know. Best regards, Claire Woods.*

I respect that she's grasping the bull by the horns. I'm also impressed that there's so little for me to read into the message. It's like something that I might have written myself. Functional and to the point. Emotionally distancing in the event that I, the recipient, immediately hit reply and say: *Don't come – I never want you to contact me again.* Or, if I just delete the email, in which case it would be a waste of a plane ticket.

I look over her attached itinerary and hit reply before I can overthink the whole thing:

Hi Claire, it was good to get your message. Of course I'd like to meet you. My address is 5179 Ridgemont Road, Alexandria, Virginia. If you want to come over for dinner on Friday night, we'd love to have you. Yours truly, Marianne Weissman

I reread what I've written, delete "of course" in the second sentence, and add my phone number. Then, I press send, and the message swooshes off into cyberspace.

Immediately, I second-guess myself. Should I have invited her to stay? Offered to pick her up at the airport? If I had a sister who lived in California and was coming to visit, surely that's what I'd do.

The realization hits me like an oncoming train. I have a *sister*. She's coming to visit me.

I open up Google and type in my new favorite search after egg donation: Claire Woods. Of course, there are thousands of them out there. But I've narrowed the search down to California and journalist. I've found some of the articles that she's written. Most of them are local interest pieces. "Save the Redwoods" campaigning, and "The Real Cost of California's Wildfire Epidemic". She is clearly left-wing, intelligent, and opinionated. In fact, for a left-winger, her stance on the home-DNA industry, set out in a recent article she wrote for the *San Francisco Chronicle*, is a little surprising. She's a strong right-to-privacy advocate, and while she acknowledges that the tests may "yield some interesting results", she largely dismisses any claims of value beyond pure entertainment. Another article mentions the fact that she's agreed to take part in the *MyStory* program: "Genetic-testing Guru Hopes to Win Over Local Journalist". When I read that, I have to laugh. I can't imagine the article she's going to write when all this is over.

God.

In other spheres of social media, Claire Woods is a very private person. Her Facebook page is private, and her Twitter account is purely related to her journalism. My trolling does uncover a Becky Woods, aged 17, who seems to live in the same area, so it might be her daughter. Her Facebook photos are all of her friends and school – piercings and parties, dates and dares, homework and box sets. The only time she mentions her parents is talking about how unfair it is that they won't buy her a car until she can pay for gas and insurance. That sounds fair enough to me. I'm tempted to respond – to become a distant cyber-stalker who provides words of wisdom and a few home truths from across the miles. But I content myself with lurking – for now. It will be one less thing to explain away to Claire when she arrives.

This week.

I slam the laptop shut. I've wasted enough time. I need to make preparations. I've been so busy – with work, and avoiding Tom, and avoiding thinking about Dave – but now I need to focus on what's most important. I *must* decide what I'm going to cook for dinner when she comes. Does she have any food allergies? Should I write back and find out? No. I take out a pad of paper from my desk drawer and start making a list. I'll make risotto – that's my special dish. Surely, she can't object to that? And if she does, well… she's my sister: I'll make sure I buy enough wine.

In the middle of my planning, Tom calls. *Oh, God. Oh, God.* My stomach flips even seeing my husband's number come up. I've just about been managing to compartmentalize the cabinet of horribles in my life right now and keep everything separate. What I feel, what I've learned, what I've thought, what I've done, what I've not done. My plan of re-seducing my husband is all but off the table, and I'm petrified even to have a conversation with him. Luckily, he's so busy that this call is sure to be quick, and I can get back to planning Claire's visit.

"Hi," I say, a little breathless.

"Hi." His voice is flat. "I just wanted to check that you're OK to leave early on Friday to drive up to Mom's house for the weekend."

"What?"

No! This cannot be happening.

"It's her seventieth. Remember? It's the big dinner – please don't tell me you forgot."

"I forgot." I brace for turbulence. Tom and I are like two ships navigating in the fog, and I'm about to steer us onto sharp rocks.

"Oh, come on! It's been in your calendar for months."

I open my mouth to respond, but nothing comes out. Surely, under ordinary circumstances, I could be forgiven for an event involving my mother-in-law slipping my mind. For one thing, she's not my mother, and for another, she hates me. I can still remember the day when Tom brought me home to meet her, without having previously warned her that I was not Jewish, or me about the fact that this was going to send her into apoplexy. I know that she's an admirable woman: intelligent, educated, and an upstanding member of her community. A nice woman – just not to me.

"I thought we'd leave about four – try to beat the traffic. I can pick you up at your office. Can you get a couple of bottles of champagne between now and then?"

"I… can't go."

The silence is poisonous.

"I'm sorry, Tom, but something's come up. It's um… work. I just can't get away."

"What do you mean you can't get away?" he hisses. "I've moved mountains to clear my calendar for this. I told you it was important to me. You need to be there – you need to try and fit in with my family."

"Me? Fit in with your family." *Stop, stop!* A voice inside my head is shouting. I ignore it and rise to the bait. "That's just rich, Tom," I say. "Given that I've never been anything but a model daughter-in-law who's tried her best, and yet your mother treats me like I'm a wad of gum stuck to the bottom of her shoe."

"How dare you?"

This isn't the argument that we should be having. We should be discussing whether or not I should welcome my new-found sister into my life. Or, we should be unmasking the elephant in the room that's squashing the life out of every conversation – whether or not to try egg donation. I want to make an appointment for both of us to go and see Dr. Lena and get the process started. Failing that, we should be talking about our marriage vows and whether they still mean anything – to either of us. But all of these things need to be raised face-to-face. I haven't seen Tom to do it, or – more accurately – when I have seen him, I've been too afraid to bring it up. If I'm a secret agent on a mission, the time bomb is counting down its last few seconds before exploding in my face.

"Look, I'm sorry," I say. "Can you come home so we can talk about it? We could… go out to dinner. There's that new Japanese place on Third." I try to sound bright and cheerful, but I'm dying inside. "I feel like we've barely even seen each other lately."

"We were supposed to see each other this weekend."

"I… um… OK. I'll… cancel my plans." As soon as I say it, I feel relieved. My marriage has to come first. Claire Woods should have checked with me before booking anything. Surely, this whole situation is not my fault… Even if it feels like it.

"No. Don't bother. To be honest, it will be better without you there. I've got to go now. Don't wait up."

"No…" The word comes out as a tearful gurgle. "Please, Tom, don't say that. We need to talk. I… um… have some news."

"Frankly, Marianne, I don't want to hear it."

The call cuts out. I take the phone in my hand and throw it across the room. It hits the wall, falls to the floor, and the screen goes dark.

38

CLAIRE

This is a bad idea. How could I have been so stupid? My knees are shaking as I walk up the path from the street. The colonial-style house is painted white with black shutters. A large oak tree shades the front yard, its branches heavy and lurid green with late spring foliage.

A swing hangs down from the largest branch, creaking gently as it sways in the breeze.

A memory that isn't mine invades my thoughts. A little girl, her hair in pigtails, sitting in that swing on a warm summer's evening. A car pulls into the drive. She jumps off the swing, bubbling over with excitement. The car door opens; she's running now. A man gets out. "Daddy!" she screams as he scoops her into his arms, planting kisses on her head and hoisting her onto his shoulders—

No. I push the images from my mind. They aren't real, and I don't have to do this. I can turn back right now. Drive to the airport, drop off the rental car, get the next flight back home. The last time I went away, Jess got sick. I vowed not to go away again. So why the hell am I here?

A curtain twitches in the front window, but I can't see

anyone inside. My stomach is in knots; sweat is beading on my forehead. A few more steps, and I'll be at the door. The world feels like it's moving in slow motion. The ambient sounds of birds, crickets, and cars in the street are drawn and distant like I'm hearing them through water. I dig in my pocket and take out my phone. Dave's latest message is still on the screen:

Claire – Please call me back! Let's talk before you do anything!

I press delete. I haven't spoken to Dave or done anything other than delete his texts ever since Stella gave me the news. As far as I'm concerned, this isn't about him or his project. This isn't about tracing DNA links to a Viking settlement in Norway, a barrow mound in County Cork, or an Assyrian grave in Mesopotamia. This isn't even about finding a bone marrow donor for Jess, no matter what sort of guilt trip Becky might lay. This is about me, my dad, and the great big fraud that I need to get to the bottom of.

The door has a polished brass knocker, and there's a rattan welcome mat on the pristine white boards. There are no muddy shoes or blown-out flip-flops, broken bicycle pumps, or green waste caddies on the porch like there are at my house. This house is a *lot* nicer than mine.

I take a breath and slowly count backward from ten. I twist the bracelet around my wrist, fingering the Capitol charm. *So wrong.* Before I can talk myself out of it, I lift my hand and bang the knocker. The sound rings out, hollow and mocking.

No one comes. I stand there for a century, a millennium – probably less than twenty seconds. Someone is home; I saw the curtain move. And that someone…

Footsteps inside. The door opens.

She's there. Face to face, her dark eyes a mirror of mine.

The world spins and tips. I grip the doorframe.

"Hello, Claire," she says. "Would you like to come inside?"

My sister. She's taller and thinner than me, with high cheekbones and dark hair swept back in a twist. Her make-up is subtle but definite, and she's wearing a light summer dress and espadrille sandals. I feel dumpy in my jeans and long-sleeved striped cotton top. I feel like *a disappointment.* If I had a long-lost sister, I'd want one that looks like her, not me.

"Um, hi," I say. "Marianne." The name seems wrong somehow. Whimsical and a little wild. Once again, I wonder what her mom was like and how Dad met her. Met her – and got her pregnant – while my mom was home changing diapers and reading Dr. Seuss books. I want to put that out of my mind, but I can't do it.

She stands aside, and I walk into her house. It's immaculate – cool and airy with a parquet floor in the hall, Federalist-style cornice moldings, and a staircase with carved wooden spindles and a cream carpet runner. Opposite the stairs, there's a marble side table with a bunch of flowers and a gilded mirror, foxed with age. It's the kind of house that would make the film crew proud and their lives easy. How I wish that Stella would pop out from the cupboard under the stairs and say, "Surprise – we fooled you! All this is a big joke. Hope you're laughing."

I'm not laughing. My heart is beating so loudly that I'm sure *this woman* must be able to hear it. I dig the Golden Gate Bridge charm into my thumb, wishing it was sharp enough to pierce my skin.

"Come through to the kitchen." She indicates a door at the end of the hall. I follow her dumbly.

The kitchen is vast, beautiful, and shiny. Silver, granite, stainless steel, huge French doors leading to a backyard full of shady, mature trees. I feel like a toddler with messy hands, afraid to touch anything. The only saving grace is the two bottles of wine on the counter. One red, one white, both expensive. I want a drink more than I ever have in my life.

Maybe it's because we're both women of a certain age, or maybe, despite outward appearances, she's nervous too – but either way, I'm relieved when she goes immediately to the cupboard and takes out two crystal goblets. "Red or white?" she says.

"Red, please."

She pours me a large glass of red and half a glass of white for herself. If we'd been raised together, would I have taken her under my wing at legal drinking age and told her that it was cooler to drink red? Or maybe in her world, it's cool to drink white. Either way, why am I wasting time and energy thinking about it?

To avoid the rest.

"Here you go," she says.

"Thanks."

The silence is crushing. Normally, I'd use the old reporter's technique to let the other person fill it. But here on her turf, my principles go out the window. "You have a lovely house," I say. "It's just so…clean."

Her laugh is more awkward than warm. "Thank you. We like it here. Though, it's a bit big for us at the moment."

There's a lot in that statement that I can't interpret. "So um… you're married, I take it?"

"Yes." She invites me to sit down at the long wooden table that's polished like a mirror. There's a stack of coasters at the side. My hand is a little unsteady as I take one. She does the same. Then I have to violate another of my principles and take a sip of the wine before she does. If

I don't, it might slosh out of the glass, and the thought of damaging that table or the tile floor... I should have had white.

"My husband's name is Tom," she says. "He works at the National Theatre. He wanted to be here to meet you."

She blinks her eyes rapidly, which makes me wonder if she's lying.

"But unfortunately, this weekend, he's gone off to his mother's seventieth birthday party."

"Oh." I barely manage to maneuver the glass onto the coaster. "I hope my coming didn't spoil your plans." Though, what's a weekend when a whole life might be spoiled, I don't add.

"It was a relief not to have to go." For the first time, her smile seems genuine. "My mother-in-law and I aren't what you'd call close."

"That's too bad. Though, I suppose mother-in-laws can be tricky."

"My husband is Jewish, and I'm not," she explains. "So that's a problem. Plus the fact that she's a bitch."

The word seems like a stain on the stark white floor. *My sister* – if she uses language like that to describe her mother-in-law, then what must she be thinking of me? Luckily, I don't have to keep wondering because she gives me a few anecdotes of her mother-in-law's ill humor. It doesn't exactly break the ice, but it does fill the silence. I allow my mind to wander. If I was her older sister, would I be giving her advice about her marriage? Or would she play that role for me? If her mother-in-law is her biggest concern, then she's a hell of a lot better off than I am.

"I'm sorry." She takes a tiny sip of wine. "I'm rambling. It's all a little awkward, isn't it?"

"It is that." I drain half my glass. "And for me, it's been

a big shock. To be honest, I don't really know what to say or how to begin."

"How do you know Dave Steiner?" she asks. "I hear you're part of the TV program?"

I hadn't planned on divulging anything about myself until learning more about her. But I find myself telling her about how I met Dave Steiner at the hospital. He bought me a hot chocolate when I was at a low point, and the rest was… ancestry.

She listens without interrupting. And when I'm done recounting the story, I realize that I've opened up a can of worms. *Hospital, low point* – not things you'd broach with a stranger. I think back to my meeting with the Larssons – how open and friendly they were. How genuinely glad they were to have been reunited with a long-lost Genetic Cousin. Should I try to do some sort of bad acting job and try to replicate that atmosphere? Could I do it even if I tried?

No.

To her credit, she skillfully skirts around the subject. "So you're married and have a daughter, is that right?"

"Two daughters. Seventeen and twelve."

"How wonderful!" Her mouth tightens.

"Yes, well, you know how it is. Pros and cons. But what about you? Do you—"

I break off, embarrassed. I'm sitting in her kitchen; I'm seeing her house. No pitter-patter of tiny feet here.

"Sadly, no," she says. "Not yet anyway. I'm very busy with my job – I'm a lawyer – as you may know already."

I do, but somehow, the idea that we've Googled each other seems vulgar. "I'm sure that must be busy. Especially in Washington."

"Yes, it is. But I would like a baby, and the clock is ticking, you know?"

"I had my girls young," I say. "Which has its own drawbacks. But I don't regret it."

She looks at me for a long moment, and I wonder if I'm sounding judgmental. Again I think of the Larssons. This woman is their polar opposite – she's as closed off as a clamshell. It's not that she's being unfriendly, but I don't need my journalistic antennae in place to realize that this immaculate home is hiding something.

"I'm sure," she says. "Children are a blessing. Look at…our father. Blessed with two. On opposite sides of the country."

It's like she's lobbed a grenade over enemy lines. I'm relieved that our fragile little détente is over. I finger each of my charms under the table like a rosary. I'm beginning to feel hot and flushed, so I roll up my sleeves. When I next reach for my wine glass, the bracelet tinkles. I see Marianne looking at it. Her perfect face is marred by another slight frown.

"I'm forty," I say. "So it looks like I came first. But then he had you. I guess maybe he met your mom while he was on a business trip?"

She finishes her wine but doesn't get up to refill our glasses.

"I asked her, of course," she says. "She wouldn't talk about it. I've been assuming that your mother was an old girlfriend? Maybe your mother didn't tell him she was pregnant?"

"What do you mean?" My pulse begins to throb behind my ear. "Of course he knew. He was my… dad. Married to my mom."

"The whole time?" Against the stark white backdrop, her face looks a little green.

"Yes…?"

Slowly, she gets up. She pours us both another glass of wine. I am desperate for it.

"That's interesting," she says. "Because he was married to my mother too. The whole time."

"No," I say. *No. No. No!* This woman is lying. This is all some kind of sick joke. I can't accept what she's saying. I just *won't*.

"It's true, Claire," she says. "I'm so very sorry."

39

MARIANNE

The second I see the bracelet, I *know* the truth. That this is unbelievably messy, unbelievably *ugly*. As Claire sits in my kitchen and drinks my wine, I feel like a scab has been ripped off a gaping wound to expose the rot underneath. Suddenly, everything is stained and corrupted. Suddenly, everything makes a perfect kind of sense.

I think of my preparations. The food and wine buying, alienating Tom over the birthday party, getting the cleaner in, spending two hours on my make-up, and discarding outfit after outfit trying to get the perfect "meet the long-lost sister" look. As soon as she came in, I knew that I'd tried too hard, and worse, it *looked* like it. I'd tried too hard to show her that my life – without her in it – was perfect. Now I see that we've both been victims of a terrible deception. That should make me warm to her.

I feel very cold.

"So, what are you saying?" Claire's voice is high-pitched, frantic. "That our father was a charlatan, a fraud? That he had two families?" She downs the second glass of wine. "I mean, how is that possible? People don't *do* that."

242

"My father traveled a lot in his job," I say. "He was often away for long stretches. Weeks – sometimes a month or more."

The lines around her eyes deepen as the cold light of truth dawns. Claire is fighting, grappling with facts that are staring her in the face.

"My dad… did too."

If she was a stranger I met on the street, I'd want to comfort her. Reach out, take her hand. Failing that, I should open another bottle of wine. Put dinner on. But I sit still, feeling like a rotten plant with diseased roots reaching far down into the soil.

"How could he have kept everyone in the dark?" Claire is rambling now. "I mean, I loved him so much. I hated it when he was away. But I thought he was working. That he was doing it for me and Mom…" She sweeps her hand as if she wants my kitchen – my world – to go away. The bracelet jangles. *The bracelet—*

"I don't know," I say miserably. "I guess he duped us both."

My father may have had two lives, but it seems he spun us the same yarn. Claire and I share half of our DNA and more besides. That should make me feel closer to her. Instead, the opposite is true.

To avoid looking at her, I stare down at my hands. Nails painted a pearly pink. I really have gone all out for this meeting. Not only with the preparations but also with trying to visualize and imagine having a sister. If Claire and I had grown up together, we probably would have loved and hated each other as siblings do. As we got older, I'd like to think that we'd be close. Talking, laughing, WhatsApp-ing photos and funny gifs. Sharing secrets, sharing troubles. She would have been there with me through my fertility treatment, through my losses. And in my current situation, she would be first in line to help me out with the thing I need most. I wouldn't even have to ask.

Maybe if her mother had been an old girlfriend, or if my mother had been a one-night stand, we could have got there in the end. Maybe she could have been the answer to my prayers. Now, though…

God.

I stand up. "Would you like some more wine? I should start supper. I was going to make mushroom risotto. Is that OK with you?"

"Um… yes… I mean…"

I look at Claire. She looks at me. I can read her face, her feelings, almost like they're my own.

Claire stands up. "I'm sorry," she says. "But I just can't do this."

I keep my face neutral. We've both had a shock, but surely that will pass. Now is the time to consider what I want from this meeting. What she wants. Whatever I say next is going to set the tone of this relationship. *My sister…* A woman with the potential to become a friend, or a confidant – or much more. And suddenly, I do feel something. A deep stab of loathing and self-hatred. Just like our father, I am nothing but the worst kind of fraud.

I take a deep breath.

"Would you like me to call you a taxicab?" I say.

"Yes," she says. "I'd appreciate that."

40

CLAIRE

Back at the hotel, I raid the minibar, down a miniature bottle of gin, and call Steve. By the time I finally reach him, I'm drunk and a total mess.

"It was horrible! Worse than I ever could have imagined. So much worse."

I tell him what I've discovered. That all throughout my childhood, I was living half a life.

"I just feel so... betrayed." I grab at the word. "I mean, she *stole* my dad from me."

"Whoa, wait a minute." Steve is the voice of reason. "It's not her fault. Your dad's the one to blame here."

"You just don't understand! She was... I don't know... so cold. Yes... cold!"

"Come on, Claire. You can't have been expecting all sparkles and rainbows. It's a bad situation. But for the most part, it's in the past."

"It is not in the past! She's my... sister. She's in my life now, and I can't escape it."

"You're right – she exists. But it doesn't mean she has to be your friend."

"But I wanted her to be! Sort of." Instantly, I know it's a lie. "Anyway… I was hoping that some good could come out of it."

"Like what?" Steve sounds like the man he's been for the last few years – i.e., the jerk – not the reformed character he's become, ever since our heart-to-heart chat and spontaneous almost-sex.

"Like… you know!" I don't want to admit the truth out loud because it feels selfish and mean. I didn't go there with friendship in mind, and that killed our meeting. Right now, I don't deserve a sister at all. Not even… Marianne.

"You're still hoping to find a donor?" Steve says. "You're hoping that this woman will turn out to be a match?"

"Is that so terrible?" I sniff. "Jess is sick. I should be with her, but I'm not. Instead, I've flown across the country to meet… *her.*"

"Come on, Claire." Steve sounds like he's trying to soothe a madwoman.

"If there's any chance – any! – that I can find someone to help Jess, then I have to do it. I have to do something to clean up this awful mess!"

"So – did you ask her?" he says.

"What?"

There's a long pause and the sound of a minor tussle. A second later, Becky is on the line.

"So what happened, Mom?" she says, breathless. "Did you tell her about Jess and ask if she'll be tested? Did you tell her that she might be the one who could save her life?"

"No – of course, I didn't. Put your dad back on!"

"Why not? Come on, Mom – you have to do it!"

Right now, I hate Becky *and* Steve. Right now, the one person I wish I could speak to across time and space is

Dad. Not to accuse or berate him. Not even to have him tell me that the whole squalid mess is not true.

Just to hear his voice. Just once…

God, I must be completely nuts.

Steve comes back on the phone. "In that case, I guess you can come home early," he says. "I won't say that it's been a wasted trip, but—"

I end the call and throw the phone against the wall. Then I empty the minibar and mix a vodka and coke. I stagger over to where I've thrown the phone. My fingers are shaking as I try to compose a text.

Hi Marianne,

Sorry for how I reacted earlier. I was just overwhelmed, that's all. I'm really sorry if I've ruined your weekend. But I wanted to ask if we could meet up again before I leave. I mean, I understand if you don't want to. But now that everything's out in the open, maybe we could try again. Please let me know. Thanks so much! Claire

Gritting my teeth, I press send. My heart feels like it's going to explode. What if she deletes the text? What if she never wants to see me again? What if she… feels the same way I do?

I down the last dregs of the drink. Then I lie down on the bed, bury my head under the pillow, and begin playing the familiar game of *wait and see*.

41

BECKY

"Why doesn't she get it?" I yell at Dad. I wish I could magically reach my hands across the country and give Mom a good shaking. "Why can't she just ask her?"

Dad stares at the phone in his hand like he doesn't quite know how it got there. "I don't think we should get our hopes up." He pushes back his chair and gets up. It's been weird having dinner just the two of us. I cooked macaroni and cheese – one of Jess's favorite meals. Before dinner, I took a tray up to Jess's room. She took one look at it and shook her head.

"You have to eat!" I'd said, channeling Mom. It was then that I noticed the bad smell in the room. I am not good with bad smells, but I forced myself to look under the bed. There was a bowl filled with vomit and a balled-up sheet that I did not investigate further.

"Have you told Dad how bad you're feeling? Should I tell him?"

"No." Her eyes were full of fury. "Don't say anything, Becky. I'm serious. I can't take it anymore."

I shouldn't keep a secret. I should tell Dad. Right now,

I hate Jess, and I hate myself. But all of that pales in comparison to how I feel about Mom.

I stand up from the table and get in Dad's face. "Why shouldn't we get our hopes up? That's the reason Mom started this whole thing. And now, just because she's too scared, or too angry – or whatever – to ask her sister to take the test, we're supposed to just sit here and let Jess… you know…?" I want to throw my plate on the floor. Dad is mental, just like Mom. Or maybe he's just weak.

"No, Becky." He sounds defeated. "We just have to keep waiting for a hit on the registry."

"The registry!" I snort. "God. Like that's been any help. I'm tired of waiting."

He takes both of our plates to the sink. "Look, I can't be late for work. We're all doing the best we can."

"Then we need to do better!" The rage inside me feels like a firework exploding. I storm out of the kitchen and upstairs to Jess's room. She's asleep, but I plunk down next to her bed. I want to do something, but I've no idea what. I eat her entire plate of macaroni and cheese. That definitely wasn't the *something* that's going to improve things.

I stare at the things on Jess's bookshelf – mostly books and stuffed animals. But she's also got a mug that I bought her with some money Mom gave me for washing her car. It says: "I smile because I'm your sister. I laugh because there's nothing you can do about it."

Mom may not believe it, but my sister is so precious to me. I want that for Mom too. Ever since Mom told me the news, I've had this tingly feeling that it's important somehow. That it was meant to happen, and that our lives won't ever be the same again. Mom may be struggling with it, but to me, it's like we've found a four-leaf clover.

Seriously. Ever since I heard the news, my life was actually going better. My article about Jess came out in the school newspaper. I was all pride and nerves when I saw my name on the byline: "Future Freshmen – by Becky Woods". (I emailed it to Mom, but I'm not sure she's read it yet.) I also made an appointment to interview Taylor Compton. I'm planning to casually remind him that my sister is sick, and it would really cheer her up if she could go on a virtual date with a future quarterback, like over FaceTime or something. Hopefully, he's not dumb as a post and will get the hint.

At home, too, I was well on my way to righting past wrongs. I spent my allowance getting my hair dyed back to normal, and when Jess saw me, she gave me money to go to the drugstore and get a home hair color kit to do hers too. (It turns out that Jess has $123.45 in her piggy bank! – more than enough to bankroll her own Bucket List – especially since she can't do half the things on there.) I got the dye and did her hair in the sink. It's still a little too dark, but overall, it's a lot better.

I even thought that things were better with Mom and Dad – with the divorce off the table for now. In fact, Jess told me that before Mom left for D.C., she actually saw them about to do *it* in the kitchen – which is something that no kid should ever have to witness! If ever Jess had an incentive to stay up in her room, that would be it.

Anyway, I really thought our run of good luck was leading up to the best thing of all – Mom actually meeting her sister! I really respected her for making an effort.

I see now that nothing has changed.

"Becky, are you OK?"

I scramble up onto my knees. Jess is awake. Her hair is loose and stringy over her face, and her brow is beaded with sweat.

"Yeah, I'm fine. I just wanted to be here when you woke up."

"Did you have a fight with Dad?"

"No." I let out a long sigh. "I'm just – annoyed with Mom. Nothing new there."

"She hasn't called me. Is Mom OK?"

"Yeah, she's fine." I stare at Jess, and the truth dawns. Mom hasn't told her why she's in D.C. My anger spikes. "She's meeting her sister for the first time."

"What?" Jess scooches up onto her elbows. I tell her everything I know, watching the emotions flit across her face.

"Why didn't Mom tell me the truth?" There's anger in her eyes, but a sob catches in her throat. "She said she was going there for work. Why did she lie to me?"

Seeing Jess mad at Mom makes me question whether I'm doing the right thing. I don't want to ruin their relationship just because I'm upset. "She didn't exactly lie," I say. As one who is often accused of being "economical with the truth", I feel I need to point this out. "More like, she didn't give you all the facts."

"But why not? I mean, it's a good thing, right? It's cool to have a sister – like finding an instant friend."

It strikes me that Jess might be smart at school and good with music, but she's kind of dense when it comes to people.

"She's upset that Grandpa Joe had another kid," I say. "Plus, she doesn't want to get your hopes up that her secret sister might end up being a bone marrow match for you."

"I won't get my hopes up," Jess says. "But I still think it's a good thing. I mean, Grandpa Joe's dead. Now she has someone new to love."

"Maybe."

She shrugs. "I mean, I can't imagine not having a sister."

"And I can't imagine not having you."

We look at each other. We both know it's a lie. So many times, I've had to imagine it. I've lived those feelings even though it hasn't happened yet. How will it be when I see her lying there in her little pink coffin, her body a husk, her soul… gone? What will happen to the life that was her? All of her memories, all of her hopes and dreams…

I need to go. I can't let her see me cry. I stand up and lean over to give her a kiss on her pale, clammy forehead. "I love you," I say.

It's a relief to say it. To know that she knows.

.

42

MARIANNE

I reread Claire's message. The thing that annoys me – no, *hurts* me – most is the line about my weekend being ruined. I shared with Claire that I was happy to miss the party. She should have understood.

I stare at the message for so long that my screensaver flashes on. A happy hen sitting on a nest of eggs that star-bursts into a tiny Anne Geddes baby dressed as a chick. Corny, I know. It's a stark reminder that I should have found a way to break the ice with Claire. The meeting was too important not to.

I close the lid of the screen and check my watch. My mother is at her bridge club tonight. She won't be home until ten at the earliest. That gives me two hours to play secret agent, detective, and housebreaker.

I drive the short distance to her house and let myself in with my key. Coming inside, I look around as if seeing it for the first time. She's compulsively neat – always has been. I guess I inherited that from her. My mother also likes to keep her feelings under wraps to avoid emotional mess. She's not one to lose control.

And yet, she wasn't in control of her husband or her marriage. Or his second family.

I go into the living room. My mother has a few photos in silver frames displayed on the mantlepiece. There's one of me at my graduation, several of me as a baby, and one of my wedding. There are no photos of her or any with my father. I guess it's always been that way, though I've never consciously noticed it before.

Upstairs, I pull down the trapdoor that leads to the attic. It comes down with a shower of dust that I'll have to vacuum before I go. The ladder creaks as I climb up. The attic is dusty, but the boxes are neatly labeled. "Books"; "Marianne – swimming trophies"; "Back taxes"; "Paperwork".

I find the box I'm looking for: "M – bedroom". It's full of keepsakes that I boxed up before I left for college. I take it into the circle of light from the bare bulb and slit the tape open with my car key.

I sift through half-remembered things: CDs, old diaries, a pressed flower corsage from my prom. I don't know why I kept most of it – there were very few things from that time that I wanted to remember. Maybe my mother has the right approach: out with the old and in with the new. Maybe that was my father's approach as well. Except, he didn't do a very good job. He didn't manage to get rid of Claire's family. My mother may be a minimalist, but my father, it seems, was a hoarder of families.

At the bottom of the box is a small jewelry box covered in blue satin. It used to have a ballerina inside, but it broke off. I open the box. There's a black Swatch, a mood ring, a couple of old presidential election buttons, and the thing I'm looking for…

The charms tinkle as I pick up the bracelet – the Capitol, the Golden Gate Bridge, a pineapple, the Statue of

Liberty, a bucking Texas steer. I always found the thing annoying to wear – not my style at all. Apparently, it was Claire's style.

I fasten it around my wrist just to see how it feels. I have no idea what Claire's life is like because we didn't get that far. I got the impression, however, that she was closer to our father than I was. I notice that Golden Gate Bridge and Capitol charms are next to each other. The others all came later.

I keep the bracelet on and close the box. As I'm about to call it quits, I notice another box labeled "Old Photos". I open the box and flip through the album on top. I set it aside and open the next book, then the next. My hand begins to tremble, and the charms clink together. I grab my wrist to make them stop. All of the albums are the same. Half of my life, half of myself, obliterated and destroyed. Every photo of my father has been cut out or torn away. Only the rage in the act – creating his absence in negative space – shows that he was part of the family at all. I close the box and kick it back under the eaves with my foot. I wish I smoked or had thought to bring a lighter. I want to burn it, and maybe the entire house along with it. What-ever lies my father may have perpetrated, this one somehow feels like an even bigger betrayal. My mother *knew.* I don't how or when she found out, but she chose not to confide in me. The one person who surely had a right to know.

I go down the ladder and slam the trapdoor back up in place. I don't bother to vacuum or lock the door as I head back out to my car. I want to drive away and never come back, abandon my mother, my childhood home, and all my memories. I find my keys, start the engine, then turn it off again. I bang my forehead against the steering wheel, spouting every swear word I know. Every time I move, the bracelet makes a noise – an ugly reminder that this whole unsavory mess is real.

I sit in the car as the sky turns from deep indigo to murky black. The contours of the house are so familiar. My room faced the front, and I loved looking out at the trees along the street as their leaves changed to red and gold in autumn and a hundred shades of green in summer. I loved being the first one to see my father's car pull up into the driveway when he returned from one of his trips. He'd stand up, stretch, look at the house, and I'd tap on the window to get his attention. He'd pretend not to know where it was coming from. He'd check under the car, and in the trunk, and even go to the mailbox to look inside. It was our big joke.

By the time he came inside, I'd be downstairs, and we'd hug, and then my mother would come in from the kitchen, taking off her apron and fussing with her hair like some kind of 1950's housewife. That was what our life was like when my father was home – an old-fashioned existence plopped down into the middle of modern times. There were no mobile phones to interrupt or arguments to be had – not in my presence anyway. When my father was home, we'd play board games and cards, and it felt like the holidays with a long-lost relative coming to visit.

After he'd been home a few days, the magic would wear off, and I'd start worrying about the next time he'd leave. As soon as he was gone, my mother would withdraw from me, becoming sullen and irritable, and the walking on eggshells would begin. I used to think that if only I was *better*, if I *achieved more*, then I could make my mother love me.

Now, I realize that none of it was about me at all. She was unhappy with my father and the life that was so much less than the perfect façade she put forward to the world.

Unhappy with good reason. She might have had all of me, but she never had anywhere near all of him.

Eventually, her car pulls up alongside mine. She sits inside for a few minutes without getting out. My pulse begins to accelerate, my hands growing clammy. How much of the conversation are we already having silently, in separate cars, without communicating at all?

Finally, she gets out and opens the trunk of her car, removing her purse and a couple of empty muffin tins.

"Marianne," she says tightly, as I get out of the car. I don't offer to help her carry anything.

"You knew," I say. "All along, you knew. You cut up the photos that were in the attic. Obliterated them."

She shakes her head and walks past me to the door.

"Tell me why." I gesture with my hand. She notices the bracelet, pursing her lips.

"You should have left well-enough alone." She opens the door and goes inside. For a second, I think she's going to slam it in my face.

"Is that what it was to you? 'Well-enough'?" I push on the door and follow her inside. "I've spent my whole life trying to please you. I killed my baby because you wanted me to. So I could have a 'perfect' life like yours."

"Oh, please." She goes through to the kitchen. Opening the dishwasher, she slams the muffin tins inside. She puts in the soap and turns it on. I twist the bracelet on my wrist, making a red gouge mark on my skin.

"Were you even married to my father?" I say. "Or was that a lie too?"

"We were married."

"So he was a bigamist. Jesus!" I shake my head. "What would your charity friends have said if they knew that? What would they have said at the PTA? Or the church?"

"Shut up," she says. "Just shut up."

"No, Mother. I'm just getting started." I go and stand next to her, getting in her face. "When did you find out? *How* did you find out?"

My mother's shoulders droop. I notice for the first time how old she looks. Despite my anger, I have the over-whelming urge to comfort her. I try to put my hand on her arm. She jerks it away.

"I always knew," she says. "From the very beginning."

"From the *beginning*?"

"Yes. The beginning. He had another wife and another child. He wasn't going to leave them. But he wanted a life with me too. With us."

"But *why*? Why on earth would you have gone along with it?"

She turns and moves away from me. She sits down in a chair, staring at the blackness outside the French windows.

"I did it for you. So you would have a father. Every-thing I did, I did for you. I tried to give you a good life, a good home. I made him put all of the assets here in a trust so that in the event of his death, his... other family... wouldn't get any of it. And then, when his client called and told me that he'd died of a heart attack out in California, that's when I got angry with him. Angry for what he did and for the lies I'd been living. Angry that I could never tell you about it because you'd react just like you're doing now." Her shoulders rise as she takes a breath. "There was no reason for you ever to know. And if you hadn't taken that damn DNA test..." She closes her mouth in a thin line, shaking her head.

"God." It all sounds completely crazy and totally out of character for my cold, calculated mother. The only thing that rings true is that her story has now made me feel guilty. She did it for me – as misguided and damaging as that turned out to be.

"And as for the abortion—" her eyes are blazing underneath a sheen of tears "—that was the right thing to do at the time. I needed you to have a good career. To provide for yourself in case anything bad happened. Your father was no saint, not personally and not professionally. There were some dodgy things that he was involved with."

"Dodgy things?"

"Bad business deals, dirty money, risky people. I don't know the extent of it – nor do I want to. Your father was one thing on the surface and another thing underneath."

"Yes. A liar and a cheat."

"All those things and more." She sighs. "I knew that if you had a baby to look after, it would have ruined your life."

"The abortion ruined my life."

She shakes her head. "I did what I thought was best. I'm sorry if it was the wrong decision."

I feel like I've been flattened by a bus. My mother, admitting all of these awful personal things. Admitting that her life was as far from perfect as it could be. Making me believe that the surface of the water was placid while underneath, she was flailing and drowning. And I had no idea of any of it. Either I am a very stupid person, or else my mother is a very good swimmer.

"I… don't know what to say."

"Don't say anything," she says. "Just go and try to live a better life than I have. Get your donor eggs and have a baby. At least then you'll always have someone to love. That's all I want for you."

My eyes fill with tears. This time, I do put my arms around her. "I'm sorry, Mother," I say. "Sorry for what you've been through. Sorry that I didn't understand."

She feels insubstantial in my arms and, true to form,

moves away as soon as I loosen my grip. "Do you want me to make you a hot chocolate?" she says.

"No. I need to go home. But thanks for telling me."

She lets out another long sigh. "It goes without saying that I don't want this all spread around. It's no good to any of us. Can I rely on you to keep it to yourself?"

I recognize the signs. My mother closing all the doors and windows and bolting them shut, battening down the hatches. Protecting the lies she's lived with for so many years. Whatever intimacy we've shared, it's over and done with.

"Of course," I say. "You can always count on me."

43

CLAIRE

"Hi," I say, "thanks for meeting me. Sorry about last time."

"It's OK," Marianne says. "I understand."

Maybe she does. Today, she looks terrible. Her eyes have dark circles under them like she hasn't slept, and her clothes – cropped jeans and a floral T-shirt – look like something she fished out of the dirty laundry basket. Instead of meeting at her house, she came to my hotel and suggested that we take a walk by the river.

"It's just a little strange to find out at age forty that one has a sister," I say. "I don't really know how to act or what to say. I mean, is this it? Or do we send Christmas cards, or... I don't know."

She smiles faintly and gestures for us to sit down on a bench. The river is green and slow. Joggers and bikers whizz past us. People going about their business and their lives. They may all have their own personal dramas, but most of them probably know who they are and where they came from. Unlike me and... my sister.

"I went to my mother's house last night," she says. "To find this."

She opens her handbag and takes something out. Even as it jingles in her hand, something dies inside of me.

A bracelet. *My* bracelet.

She sets it on the bench between us. I swallow hard. If I had the urge to up and leave last time, it's nothing compared to now. I don't want to look, but my eyes are drawn to its silver glint in the morning light. We seem to have all of the same charms. Except, when I look more closely, I seem to have one extra – the dolphin. Who knows the how or why of it anymore?

"I also found the old photo albums," she says. "My mother had cut out every single photo of my father. Obliterated him, like he didn't exist. It turns out that she knew all along. She thought that as long as she kept up appearances, I didn't need to know."

I'm drowning in a pit of despair, but I have to face up to reality. "It's terrible," I say. "Because whatever your memories are, they're yours. And my memories are mine. Just because our dad was a liar doesn't mean there weren't good times." I want to convince myself that this is true, but the words sound insincere even to me.

"Doesn't it?" She seems utterly listless.

"No," I say firmly. "Our childhoods shape us. I loved my dad. So much. Maybe I loved a lie, but the emotions I felt were real. The good ones – like when he was around, and the bad ones – like when he went away. And ever since that awful day ten years ago when I got the call that his boat had washed ashore, and then his body was found, I've felt that a part of me was dead too."

Something flickers in her eyes. "The boat... Yes. He did like his boats..."

"They found three fish in his cold store." My eyes begin to tear up. "Did you know that? He never got to eat those three fish. That's... the thing I struggle with."

She shifts uncomfortably, and I get the idea that she didn't know about the fish. I feel a stupid little flash of satisfaction that I know something she doesn't.

"Did you go to the funeral?" she says.

"It was a memorial service. His body was in bad shape when it was found. So he was cremated."

She nods, frowning now. "My mother had a memorial service too. I guess if he died out your way, her urn was probably empty."

"Empty," I repeat, feeling a stab of fear. Dad's ashes couldn't have been in both urns – that's all I know.

She sweeps her hand as if to throw the conversation away. "Well, it's certain that he's dead – at least we know that. As for the rest, it's hard to say."

"Yes. And in spite of what he did, we didn't turn out too bad, did we?"

She laughs, and I regret speaking so boldly. I have no idea what she's really like beneath the façade or what her life is like behind the door of that beautiful house.

"Do you believe in Karma?" she says. "Kismet? Destiny? Anything like that?"

"Not really."

"Good. Because I can't say that my life is going too well at the moment. I'm hoping it's nothing I did in a previous life – or earlier in this one when I was making all those childhood memories. I used to think that you make your own luck. Now, I'm starting to think that it's more about atoning for past mistakes."

"I hope not," I say. "Because my life isn't going so well either." Taking a breath, I jump in feet-first. "My daughter, Jess, is sick. Seriously ill. She has Severe Aplastic Anemia, which is a rare disease. For the last four years, she's been living on blood transfusions and a cock-tail of medications. But recently, the disease has started to accelerate. She desperately needs a bone marrow transplant."

I'm half-expecting – and half-hoping for – the usual "oh my God, that's so terrible" reaction. The hug, the taking of my hand. Marianne, though, barely reacts. "That sounds... difficult."

"Yes. In fact, one of the reasons I did the DNA test was to find some biological relatives. Jess doesn't match anyone on the registry, and none of the known family members are a match. It's still a long shot, but family members make the best donors. There's less chance of graft-versus-host disease, which is where the body rejects the foreign tissue."

"And have you found any potential donors to test?"

"A few." I tell her about the Larssons. "They live in Texas. Five of them have agreed to be tested."

I can tell she's uncomfortable, and I instantly feel a strong sense of self-loathing. I'm here under false pretenses. Not because she's my sister but because she's a potential donor for my daughter.

"Please don't think I'm asking anything of you," I say. Everything that comes out of my mouth sounds like a lie. "Because I'm not. My tissue isn't a match, and there is no reason to think that yours would be either. I wanted to see you again because I wanted to apologize – not just for yesterday, but for everything." I crack a weak smile. "For... existing, I guess."

"And are you sorry I exist?"

"Oh God, no!"

She's so clever – I feel like I'm shoveling quicksand. "I mean, I hate what Dad did. But I've been an only child for a long time. It might be... nice... to have a sister."

She laughs then – not unkindly, but I have the uneasy feeling that my every thought is one she's had already. I hate being the one who wants something from her and has to pretend that I don't.

She stares out at the river, watching as two boats pass each other. I've lain my cards on the table and come up against the ultimate poker face. Marianne Weissman – my sister – has utterly confounded me.

"Children are such a blessing and a curse," she says finally. "Not that I would know. I've never managed to carry one past twenty-four weeks."

"What?"

"Eight rounds of IVF, a couple of miscarriages, all the rest failures. All in all, it equals eight dead babies." Her smile is sad and resigned. "So even though I don't have kids, I do understand, Claire, in some small way, what you must be going through."

"Gosh, I… had no idea."

Eight dead babies. And here I was thinking that she was the perfect sister, the lucky sister. How many more lies will I uncover in this horrible business?

"Luckily, most women don't know what it's like. The joy, the hope. And then, the endless, bottomless loss. It cuts a hole in your heart. Sucks out your life."

"I am so sorry."

Instantly, I regret the words. There is nothing more pathetic, more meaningless than "I'm sorry". I just wish there was something I could do or say to console her. But there isn't.

"Yes, well…" her tone is brisk again. "Now you know. It might have been nice to have had a sister when I was going through all that. My mother wasn't much help, I can assure you."

"My mom is dead, so she's not much help either." I feel like maybe we should laugh. We don't.

"Well, perhaps our father chose the same type of women, then."

I don't know if this is healthy or not. I feel like I'm walking along the edge of a razor blade. But talking must be better than silence. Knowing must be better than not knowing.

"Maybe," I say.

"In any case, it's all water under the bridge. I'm done with the IVF. At least, I'm done with using my own eggs and Tom's sperm."

I blanch without meaning too. If we really had been sisters at the relevant time, perhaps I would have been party to every detail about her and her husband's sex life, sperm count, and ovulation timings. But as it is, it feels like a very surreal sort of conversation to be having with a total stranger. I twist my bracelet. I *have to stop* thinking of her as a total stranger. She's my sister.

I *have to stop* feeling sick at the idea.

"Um, I imagine IVF must have been very tough. Especially with your job. I mean, being in law must be so demanding."

It's obvious that I'm trying to change the subject. For a second, her face flashes with a desperate pain.

"Life is demanding," she says. "Work, marriage, wanting something desperately that you can't have."

"Yes, it is. I feel the same way. I mean, I don't have a very demanding job. But Steve and I have money troubles, and Jess's illness has put a strain on our marriage and…"

I stop speaking. I cannot believe the words that are coming out of my mouth. It sounds like I've turned up wanting not only her bone marrow but her money too. If I was her, I would tell me exactly where to go and maybe take out a restraining order just to be on the safe side.

"I'm very sorry to hear that, Claire."

"Yes… I mean, I'm sorry."

Sorry, sorry, sorry! Will we ever be able to get past that?

"I… shouldn't be staying this stuff," I stammer. "It sounds like I want something when I don't and—"

"Yes, you do, Claire." Marianne looks at me levelly, without a trace of rancor or irony. She picks up the bracelet and shoves it into her pocket. "We're sisters. That's what the DNA test says. You want something from me. So it's best just to come out and say it."

"No… I…"

"That's why you wanted to see me again today. That's why you came here. Don't worry—" She smiles benignly "—I'm sure that if I was in your position, I would do exactly the same thing."

"Um… probably," I say.

This time we both laugh. It's not remotely funny.

44

MARIANNE

I haven't slept a wink. All night long, I kept thinking about my mother's story and the mutilated photos. I feel desperately sorry for her – of course, I do – but I'm also angry. In living her perfect lie, she made my life a lie too. Claire seems to blame our father for what happened, but my mother was just as much to blame. I feel shaken, and what's worse, when we meet up at her hotel, I *look* shaken.

It's clear that Claire and I have very different memories of our father. She grew up idolizing him and seems to idolize him still. Maybe that's how I ought to be feeling too. But when Claire comes out and tells me about her – our – father's death, I genuinely don't know how to feel.

Three fish. I consider this as she recounts the boating accident. How deep did the lies go, and who was telling them? I know that my father died on a trip to California, where he was supposedly going fishing with a client. But I've always been told he died of a heart attack, not an accident on the boat. Maybe the heart attack caused the accident, or maybe the little details don't matter, but it niggles that I might have been given misinformation. Most likely by my mother.

Why I don't mention it to Claire, I'm not quite sure. I guess it's because her mention of the fish make me feel like a younger sister – more ignorant and less worldly than she is. But then, out of the blue, my heart – and my hopes – take flight. Claire turns the tables on me. *"Of course, I'm not asking you to do anything, but…"*

That's the moment when I feel closest to her. Because I realize that there's a Crazy Claire behind her Sane Claire façade – it's not just me. I'm not the only one who wants something from this meeting.

I feel deeply for Claire and her family. She's obviously suffered in a different way than I have, but it's no less painful. I admire the fact that she's been strong enough to come here and ask for what she needs. Envy it, even.

Because when she comes clean with her true intentions, the moment for me to do the same comes and goes. She has to get to the airport; I have to go into the office. We agree to keep in touch. Of course, I agree to do the bone marrow test. Readily, willingly. "I'd love to help if I can," I say. I mean it too. I want to be the one who can save her daughter and make a difference. Maybe this is how I'm supposed to atone for what I did all those years ago and earn my own piece of good fortune. Then and only then will the moment be right for me to ask her for a *small favor* in return.

Claire thanks me profusely and begins telling me everything about Jess, who apparently is a prodigy violinist. I listen politely, all the while imagining a daughter of my own who is talented like Jess, though hopefully without the illness.

When we say goodbye in front of the hotel, we give each other a hug. I get the impression that she's "trying it out". Seeing how it feels to have a sister. For me, though, I view it as something deeper and more profound. A bond and a promise. Whether we want it or not, and regardless of what secrets the past may hold, it's there between us.

When Claire drives away, I put the bracelet on my wrist, trying to get used to the feel of it and the new direction that my life has taken. I stare out at the river – the water that is endlessly moving – flowing and pulsing like blood. I speak individually to each of Babies Zero through Eight. "I'm going to see this through," I say. "Everything happens for a reason, and I know why God saw to it that I found my sister, Claire. I think that finally, I've been punished enough."

There's no answer, but I do feel a kind of stirring inside my womb. A little nest, safe and warm, making a place for the baby that will come. Surely, it is written in the stars.

45

BECKY

The snow globe lights up. It has a miniature skyline of the Capitol, the Washington Monument, the White House, and the Lincoln Memorial. The snow is silver glitter. It's beautiful.

I want it.

"I saw it in the airport shop," Mom is telling Jess. "And I thought of all the places that you can go when you're older, once we've found you a donor."

Mom might be doing a TV show, but she's a pretty bad actress. Her smile lines look like cracks in an eggshell. I guess I should give her credit for trying to be positive. When I look around at Jess's room, it can't be easy.

The pink palace looks like it's been ransacked by police. There are wrappers and dirty dishes, clothes strewn everywhere, papers, books, and electric cords. It's like, overnight, she's turned into me. Her violin and music stand are nowhere to be seen – she's put them away in her closet. Her hair looks OK, but that's about it. Her eyes have a wild, strained look about them that I'm not just imagining. She stares at the snow globe; the yellow light inside makes her face look almost green. I can't tell if she likes it or if she's going hurl it at Mom.

I hope she doesn't.

Mom turns to me, not quite stifling a sigh. "I got you this." She hands me a rolled-up parchment. "Since you're doing Civics."

I unroll it. The US constitution is printed in calligraphy too small to read. It's cheap-looking and was probably made in China.

"Thanks, Mom," I say. I want to like it. I want to believe that she took as much care over choosing my gift as Jess's. I want to believe that she thinks that I, too, might someday be able to travel to interesting places and do exciting things. God knows – I shouldn't feel jealous of my sister. But when I look at the snow globe, I feel like something inside my head has been shaken up. All those beautiful white buildings. All that history. The pieces are floating around in my head like glitter. I wish Mom had got it for me.

She gives Jess a goodnight kiss and says that she's going to have a shower. I kind of wish she'd try giving me a goodnight kiss, too, even though I'd never let her. She meets my eyes as she goes out of the room. I can tell that the last thing she wants is for me to start asking her questions. I really should leave it for now.

But my head is still swirling with possibilities and unanswered questions. I have to *know* how things went. I follow her out into the hall.

"Mom," I say, stopping her at the door to the bathroom. "What was she like?"

"What? Who?" Mom sounds flustered and annoyed.

"Your sister."

The words hang in the air like the blade of a guillotine.

"Oh…" Mom waves a hand. "She was fine. Very nice."

This is seriously like pulling teeth. "So, did you tell her about Jess? Did you ask her to take the test? What did she say?"

Mom sighs. "Honestly, Becky, I'm too tired to talk about it. Even if she did agree to get tested, there's no reason to think that she'd be a match when no one else is."

I try to process this information quickly: "even if she did agree" sounds an awful lot like she hasn't agreed – not yet anyway. It could just be a turn of phrase. Or it could be important.

Mom goes into the bathroom. She turns back and gives me a tired smile. "Goodnight, Becky. Love you."

"Come on, Mom," I plead. "Can't you at least tell me her—"

The door slams shut.

"—name?"

46

CLAIRE

I should be feeling hopeful. I should be feeling that life is an open door full of possibilities. I have a new member of my family: a new sister. When I look at Jess and Becky together – so comfortable, so familiar – I see that all along, I've been missing something. A bond, a part of myself. Now I have the chance to open up my heart and make room for that missing piece, to welcome my sister with open arms.

So why does it feel so impossible?

The morning after I come home from Washington, I send Marianne one email. *Thank you for meeting me. It's all a lot to think about and take in for both of us. Please believe that I'm not asking you for anything or to do anything. But if you did want to take a blood test, I've attached the information they'll need to analyze the results.*

As I press send, I feel like someone on one of those daytime TV shows where people air their dirty laundry in front of the world, parading their dysfunctional families in the name of fame, free sandwiches in the green room, and a small fee for being on the show. It's one thing having to ask for something from a total stranger. The fact that the stranger happens to be my dad's secret daughter is just beyond the pale.

When the message is gone, I remove the bracelet I've worn for so many years and shove it to the back of my desk drawer. Over the years, the jingling of the charms has reminded me of Dad, summoning him like a medium calling forth a spirit. Now, it has become a symbol of his betrayal. He didn't give us each a bracelet in the hopes that someday we might find each other and learn the truth. He gave them to us because he was an arrogant narcissist – possibly even a sociopath – and fully believed in his right and ability to live two separate lives. Two lives, but what about his death?

Secretly, I have often cried over those three fish in Dad's cold store. To me, they were a symbol of the bright spark of his existence and how death cheated him not only of his life but of his fish supper.

I didn't see Dad's body. He was identified by his dental records. Steve took care of most of the arrangements, and I am forever grateful for that. We had the memorial service at the marina where he kept his boat. I remember standing on the edge of the dock holding the urn and thinking how light it was. How little there was to show for the life of a man so brimming with warmth and charisma. With love. The sky was mackerel gray, and the sea was a flat mirror that seemed to go on endlessly to the horizon. A thin fog was rolling in, like the white breath of ghosts. I opened the urn, expecting the ashes to float away on the breeze, becoming part of the great oneness – the sea of spirits and stars. Instead, the dust clumped out in the water and floated there, eventually sinking down into the unfathomable depths. I turned away. The dad I knew was gone.

The dad I never knew at all.

. . .

I spend the rest of the morning trying to come up with new ideas for articles. Every twenty minutes or so, I check my messages. It seems an eternity. By not picking up the phone, I've kicked the ball firmly into Marianne's court. I've made it my own waiting game.

Will she even respond? I don't know her well enough to know for sure. I replay every moment of our meetings in my mind. The huge revelations were painful and awful, but there's something else too – an uncomfortable little something that's niggling at me. Was it something she did, something she said? I can't put my finger on it, and eventually stop trying.

Twice I go up and visit Jess in her room. She's supposed to be homeschooling on the iPad, but each time I go in, she furtively closes down something else – a game, probably. It kills me that her violin is nowhere to be seen, but I decide to leave it be for the time being. I try to be cheerful, talking about the movies I watched on the plane. Tidying up the mess, folding clothes, pretending that the room doesn't stink of rotting food and unwashed hair. Pretending everything is fine when, underneath, my heart is splitting in two. She's so thin, and her skin has a yellowish tint, which means that the medication is putting a strain on her liver. Around noon, the nurse comes around to take her bloods. I stand just outside the door of the room, unable to bear the sight of any more tubes and vials.

When the whole awful procedure is done, the nurse tells me that Jess is looking pretty well under the circumstances. I thank her through my teeth, convinced that she's lying. As she's leaving, she takes me aside. "I can talk to the doctor," she says. "Give you a referral to see somebody."

See somebody. As in a shrink. I thank her politely and decline. I've spoken to shrinks before, and it's done absolutely no good. My daughter is sick. I'm entitled to feel the way I do.

Somehow we get through the afternoon. Becky comes home from school, makes the usual mess in the kitchen, and then goes upstairs. Even seeing her for a few minutes, asking her about her day, and getting the usual "fine" makes me feel guilty and angry with myself that I can't draw her out. I should be grateful to her. She's been an absolute saint when it comes to Jess. If I'm being totally honest, I'm a little jealous of their closeness – something I can't imagine ever having with Marianne.

When I next go upstairs to bring Jess a sandwich, Becky is tapping away on her computer. I'd like to think that for once, she's knuckling down. Doing some homework or studying to retake her SATs. But I know she's not. She'll be on Facebook or Instagram or some other time-sucking app that will get her exactly nowhere in life. Whenever I've tried to have the "what do you want to be when you grow up?" conversation, Becky always has some outlandish idea or hair-brained scheme, and it always ends in an argument. Now that I think about it, it's been a while since we had that discussion – a few years maybe. I regret the time I've lost with Becky. But what can I do? I've got a sick child who needs to be my priority, and talking to Becky is like talking to a brick wall. Still, it's my responsibility to patch up our relationship, and I need to do it urgently. But where can I even begin?

I knock on Jess's door. It feels strange not to be wearing my bracelet. When I go into her room, Jess hides whatever she's doing on the iPad. Instantly, I notice that the snow globe, which she'd put on the shelf above her desk, is gone.

Taped to the side is the little scroll with the constitution that I gave to Becky. It's a small thing, tiny and insignificant, yet it enflames my anger. When I gave Jess her gift, I saw the jealousy on Becky's face. That's Becky to a tee – she's not jealous of Jess's talent or her grades – she's jealous of a snow globe. And now, she's forced her sister to "trade".

Making a bargain – I'll be a good sister to you if you give me what I want.

I know I'm wrong even to think it, let alone allow it to bother me. Family members bargain all the time – being in a family requires constant negotiation. But it does bother me. A lot. My mind flicks to Marianne. I want something from her and have nothing to give in return. As a sister, I'm a poor bargain.

I mean to ask Jess how school's going and whether she wants me to get her violin out of the closet. I want to have another talk with her about the audition and reassure her that we'll reschedule it as soon as she's better. I want to keep cheerleading for her to stay positive and keep channeling hope. So many things I want to say…

But when I open my mouth, what comes out is: "Where's the snow globe I bought you?"

She shrugs. "Becky wanted it. So we traded."

"Are you OK with that?"

"Sure."

She seems totally listless.

"I can make her give it back."

She turns off the iPad and flings it to the side of her bed. "Why bother?"

I try to summon the usual lecture. *Must keep our hopes and spirits up. Must keep on going, keep on fighting.*

But right now, I just can't do it.

"You need to eat." I leave the plate with the sandwich on the nightstand and go out of the room.

I know what all the books and meditation websites say. In times of intense emotion, one should step back, take time to regroup. Take a breath, imagine a positive outcome. I ignore all of it and storm into Becky's room. She looks up when I enter and gives me a brittle smile.

"Hi, Mom," she says. "Did you read the article I sent you? The one I wrote about Jess?"

As usual, she's caught me off guard. "What?" I say. Now that I think about it, I do recall seeing an email from her. I haven't read it.

"It's about future freshmen. I'm doing a series."

My eye hones in on the snow globe sitting on her nightstand. The glitter is floating around the tiny buildings like she's just shaken it. I pick it up, staring at the miniature tableau.

"Why did you take this from your sister?"

She looks at me with the familiar hurt in her eyes. "I didn't. We traded."

"Do you not have enough… stuff?" I gesture around at the pit that is her room. The floor is covered with clothes, books, balled papers, electric cables, and discarded food wrappers. It looks like the cage of a giant hamster. "I mean, you have your health and your future ahead of you. Something that she doesn't have. Do you need to take her presents too?"

"No. Take it. It's no big deal."

"No big deal?" She's right, of course. It's no big deal. But the fact that she's backed down so easily only fuels my anger.

She sits up in her bed and looks at me. "Mom," she says. "Are you OK?"

"No. I. Am. Not!"

I throw the snow globe hard onto the floor. It bounces off the carpet and rolls under Becky's bed, adding to the chaos and mess that our lives have become.

47

BECKY

OK, maybe I should give it back. Maybe I've had it long enough. A week has gone by since Mom threw the snow globe under my bed, and we've barely spoken since. It's a talisman – I think that's the word – of how bad things are between us. But it's also become a talisman of my secret life that Mom knows nothing about.

I actually have not one but *two* ideas of future careers that I might be good at. First off is journalism. Not only do I call up Taylor Compton and interview him, but I also get a three-way video call going with him and Jess to get their ideas on other future freshmen to interview. I end up dropping off the call due to "bad Wi-Fi", and they talk together for a whole half-hour and seriously hit it off! (Maybe another possible career is online matchmaking – that's a thing, I'm pretty sure.)

The second new career is detective work. I've always been good at doing stuff behind Mom and Dad's back, but now I have actually *solved a mystery*. So Dr. Watson, Scooby-Do, Nancy Drew – eat your heart out. Here comes Becky Woods.

Actually, the mystery wasn't all that hard or complex, and I wasn't in any real danger (other than getting caught and grounded). But who cares?

This is what I do. I go to Mom's office and dig through the papers on her desk. I find her flight itinerary for D.C. printed out along with her hotel confirmation. That doesn't give me the information I need. But there's a notepad next to the desk. I do what I've seen detectives do in films – I get another piece of paper and rub over it lightly with a pencil. Some numbers come up and the letters "M" and "a". I start to get excited, but it's not a complete phone number or name. So that doesn't exactly work out, and I feel a little frustrated. I ball up the paper and slam dunk it in the trash can. That's when I notice that there are quite a few pieces of balled-up paper in the trash can. (Dad's supposed to take out the trash, but since he's started his second job, he forgets most of the time.) So I get down on my knees and go through them. It's kind of gross – there are also used Kleenexes and a sticky cup from McDonald's. I'm about to give up when all of a sudden, I hit the jackpot. A page from the notebook with a name and address!

Marianne Weissman. Her secret sister.

The next thing I do is look her up on Facebook. There are several Marianne Weissman's and MWeiss-man's, and the ones I look at don't seem the right age, but there are a few private profiles, so I figure it might be one of those. I send all of them friend requests. As Grandpa Joe used to say, you have to cast the net wide to see what's biting.

One of the MWeissman's bites.

She doesn't do it the straightforward way by just accepting the friend request. She spends a few days lurking. I'd posted a photo of me and my friend Melissa and her pug, Smoosh. MWeissman made a comment that "He's just so cute!"

The next day, she commented on another photo of me at my friend Liz's birthday party and asked if my dress was J.Crew or Ann Taylor. I responded that it was last season's Banana Republic from the outlet mall. The day after, she accepted my friend request. (Only three more friends and I'm at three hundred!)

I still wasn't totally sure it was her because two of the other private profile MWeissman's also accepted my friend requests. (Weird?) So after a few more days of trading comments with the first one, I decide, in true detective style, to set a trap.

When I searched Mom's office, I found something unexpected in her desk drawer – the charm bracelet that she always wears. (I guess I need to brush up on my observational skills because I hadn't actually noticed her *not* wearing it.) Grandpa Joe gave it to her, and the charms are from all the cities he traveled to.

When I held it in my hand and jingled the silver charms, it kind of hit home that this is a *huge* thing for Mom. I felt bad for her, but as I touched the little Golden Gate Bridge, I felt even worse for Jess. I thought if I gave her the bracelet, it might cheer her up. So I slipped it into my pocket.

OK – full disclosure. I haven't actually given it to Jess yet. I put it on my wrist and wore it to school. By lunchtime, all that dangling was annoying me no end. (Seriously – how can Mom, who is totally uptight, stand to wear it?) So when I came home and found that Jess was asleep, I put it in my own desk drawer. Now, I'm glad I did because I have an actual use for it.

I take a photo of the bracelet and then go up to the attic and find some old photo albums from when Grandpa

Joe was alive. The tape was off the boxes – a clue that Mom's been doing detective work of her own. I find a couple of pictures of the fishing trip we went on and one of him sitting in the bleachers at a baseball game, smiling and holding a giant bag of peanuts. There's also one of him in front of a small plane – he had his pilot's license, I remember. I guess he was flying off to live his mysterious life – or at least, his devious one.

I also find a copy of Grandpa Joe's death certificate, and his obituary from the local paper. I wonder if Mom wrote it because she was working for the paper at the time, and it seems full of love. It talks about Grandpa Joe as a big-hearted man with a kind, comforting word for every-one. Maybe it's because of what I know now, but to me, he just seems like a huge fraud, and I'm surprised Mom was so hoodwinked. I guess that's what family can do to you.

I take photos of everything I find and then post them, along with the picture of the bracelet, to my Facebook page. I write a few captions along the lines of: "Mom's on a Genetic Journey. These are some photos and mementos of her dad."

Naturally, my friends aren't interested, but I do get a response in only a few hours from MWeissman: "How thoughtful of you to share this. They look like a very happy family."

A happy family. Or half of one, as it turns out. In any case, I'm satisfied that I've uncovered the identity of my new Facebook friend. My secret aunt, Marianne.

So I decide to send her a message.

48

I'm happy to announce that I, aka Utterly Useless, aka The Queen of Bad Decisions, have made a major life breakthrough. I am not only a detective but also a builder of bridges – connecting with my new aunt in a few strokes of the keyboard. I jangle the bracelet on my wrist (I guess you can get used to anything) and read over the chain of messages from the beginning:

Hi, Becky. Yes, I am your mom's sister. I am so pleased that we've connected, and I'm so curious to find out more about you. Best, Marianne Weissman

To which I responded:

That's fine. I'm curious about you too. Sorry that Mom's acting so weird. But that doesn't mean that we can't get to know each other. If you want to.

Her response was almost immediate.

Yes, Becky, I definitely do.

I've hit the jackpot. My aunt has "taken an interest in me". Which is more than Mom's ever done. I end up giving Marianne my Gmail address that Mom doesn't know about. Already, I feel like my aunt and I have moved on to our own territory – we're keeping our correspondence and our deepening relationship safe from Mom.

Another week goes by. Every time I sit down at my desk, I feel a flurry of excitement. I remember hoping that Mom's Genetic Journey might turn up a relation who's famous or rich. But Marianne is better than anyone I could have hoped for. She's kind and smart, and she's curious about everything – even someone like me.

Marianne writes me a long email telling me about herself – she's a lawyer, happily married to a theatre producer (so cool!), and she works in downtown Washington. I look up her law firm and where she lives, and it's all so glamorous! I've thought about going to New York before, mostly because Carnegie Hall is in New York and that's on Jess's Bucket List. But until Mom got me the snow globe, I never really thought about how beautiful our nation's capital is in real life. I resurrect Becky's Bucket List and write "Visit D.C.!" as the number one thing. I mean, it's a natural place to visit – a total no-brainer!

Staring at the words on the paper, I allow my mind to wander further. Maybe I could look at colleges out in D.C. because it would be great to get far away from home. I get so carried away and start fantasizing that if I lived on the other side of the country, I wouldn't be able to get home for weekends and holidays, so I'd go to my Aunt Marianne's house instead. She sent me a picture of it, and it's totally beautiful. It's got a white porch and a big tree out front with a swing. It looks like something out of *Gone with the Wind*. I could totally see myself there, sitting on that swing, taking a selfie in front of the house. All my Facebook friends would be so jealous!

The one thing that's a little weird is that Marianne doesn't have kids. Maybe she's too much of a high-flyer and hasn't had time. Or maybe she doesn't want them. It's too bad, because if she did, then I could babysit and earn some money. I'd also be their aunt (?); no, cousin, I think. Or half-cousin. But Marianne is so nice that it doesn't matter that technically she's only my half-aunt. It would be even better if she could turn out to be a friend.

"Becky?"

The sound of Jess's voice from next door slams me back to reality. I close down the email I'm composing without even saving it to draft. I have a strong urge to carve "Marianne" into my arm just to let the flood of emotions ebb away with the blood. Because hearing Jess's voice, I know that all of my fantasies are never going to happen. First of all, I can't go to D.C. because I can't leave my sister here on her own. She needs me.

Second, I can't go to college in D.C. – or anywhere – because I'm too dumb to get in. Those schools back east would be looking for the next president or head of the FBI, or a future banker, doctor, or lawyer – not some ordinary girl with a juvenile record for shoplifting, low SAT scores, and hair that is still a little blue.

And finally, even if I skipped the whole college thing and just decided to go live in D.C., I could never in a million years afford it. I've got no money, no skills, no car, and no place to live. I'm, like, utterly worthless. I couldn't live with Aunt Marianne because I don't even know her. I'm sure she won't want someone like me hanging around, messing up her clean house, using her broadband, playing music, and bringing home boyfriends. I couldn't do that to her. She may be taking an interest, but that's a step too far.

Isn't it?

I give the snow globe a good shake so that all I can see is glitter. I wish I could just as easily erase my dreams – I'm never going to achieve them – and then maybe I'd be less angry all the time.

I hear Mom knock on Jess's door. "Are you OK?" she says, with the worried note in her voice that means she's going to put on a surgical mask and smother my sister with kisses.

"Yeah," Jess says. "But have you seen my charger?"

"No, of course not." The worried note turns into one of annoyance. That's Mom for you — she can do an emotional 180 in seconds flat. "You know you have to look after your own things, Jess."

"But it was here…"

I stand up. I've taken the charger because mine stopped working. I can't let Jess take the blame. I'll do it because that's my role in the household.

Aunt Marianne is a lawyer. She has a nice house and lots of money. She probably doesn't want a "new daughter". Especially not one who's a problem teenager.

But would it hurt to ask?

49

MARIANNE

I tell myself that what I'm doing is harmless. That I'm exploring a natural curiosity to learn more about my sister and her family. Claire seems reluctant to let me into her life – which, on one level, I can understand. Although she sent me a thank you email with the bone marrow test details, I sense that she wants to remain distant. I am trying to respect that. So I decide to go in through the back door. A wide-open door.

Becky contacts me. Not the other way around.

I introduce myself over Facebook, and we begin exchanging emails. Without my even having to ask, she sends me a photo of my father's death certificate and the obituary from the local paper, both of which confirm that he had a boating accident out at sea. At first, I feel hopeful – that maybe Claire and I are not related at all. But Becky also sends me some photos of Claire and her family with her father. *My* father. The photos confirm that the whole nightmare is real.

As we begin to correspond, I tell her about myself, making sure that it's a two-way exchange of information. It doesn't take long before I start getting a sense of Becky as a lonely, confused, and thoroughly messed-up young adult. The more I get to know her, the more I feel sorry for her. Claire has obviously neglected her, giving all of herself to Jess – the talented and vulnerable child. I'm sure that Jess has endured unimaginable pain and suffering that no little girl should be subject to, and I feel desperately sorry for her. But she's also the kind of girl who has it made in spades. A girl who, if she dies, will get a full-page obituary in the local newspaper: "Daughter's loss shatters local family". She'll have hundreds of people writing notes and reading out things at her funeral. And she'll never have to endure bad boyfriends, failed driving tests, terrible job interviews, shattered hopes and dreams. Jess is lucky. Becky may be less perfect on the outside, but inside, I sense she's more like me.

I ask her questions about herself – surely, there's nothing wrong with that. She tells me about her life in dribs and drabs. It's all a little bit rambling, but her deter-mination is admirable. I've never had much time for teenagers, nor had much contact with them. I'm desperate for my own child, but if I'm being perfectly honest, I've never visualized that child much past the baby stage. Becky is making me realize that children are complicated and messy – just like real people.

She seems especially curious about life in Washington, D.C. Her family isn't rich, and they're up to their eyeballs in debt, so she hasn't traveled anywhere. I play up the good: the cherry blossoms, the river, the historic sites; and de-emphasize the bad: the humidity, the traffic, the politi-cians. All of it definitely sparks her interest, and I respect her eagerness to change her life. I even consider inviting her for a visit.

But I fall short of doing it. Because deep down, I know

that in befriending Becky, I have a conflict of interest. Not to mention the fact that Claire might have a problem with it. That said, it's possible that in the future, I might be in a position to do Becky a favor and give her choices in life that she can't even dream of at the moment. In the meantime, I make an appointment for the bone marrow test – the ultimate bargaining chip. I have nothing to feel guilty about. This is a win-win situation for everyone. I am determined to keep believing it.

50

CLAIRE

Becky and I seem to have struck an uneasy truce, and that makes me nervous. I apologize to her over the snow globe incident, citing stress and jetlag, and she says it's no big deal. She keeps the snow globe. I say nothing more.

To be fair, she's actually spending time doing something other than Snapchatting or Facebooking or TikToking. She's actually writing articles for the school paper. She showed me one she wrote on Jess (it made me look like a bad mother, but not a terrible one, so I swallowed hard and gave her some praise) and one about some boy called Taylor who plays football and seems to be spending a lot of time FaceTiming Jess. I'm not sure how I feel about that, but Jess seems a happier inmate of her bedroom, so it can't be all bad.

Steve is working late most evenings at his second job, so most nights at dinner, it's just the two of us. There's always an awkward moment when we sit down together, and the invisible wall descends, and I have no idea what to say. My hand goes automatically to my wrist to touch my bracelet, and I feel a momentary sense of panic when I discover that

I'm not wearing it. I took it off when I got back from D.C. Where did I put it? In my jewelry box? Is it safe? I can't let it matter.

Becky is usually the one to break the silence. She's good at making small talk: a new series on Netflix, the speed of the broadband, new state fire control measures, whether Jess's charger has been found (miraculously, yes). We skirt around any awkward topics – school, her friends, the future – most things, really. Each time I successfully navigate a meal and a conversation with my eldest daughter, I give myself a mental pat on the back.

But one evening, a couple weeks after I'm back from D.C., we've just sat down to dinner when Becky ends the truce by lobbing a bomb in my direction.

"Mom, I want to go to college. In Washington, D.C."

I'm not proud that I laugh in her face.

"You need SATs to go to college," I said. "Not to mention money. If you want to do a course at the junior college here next fall, that would be great. Otherwise, you'll have to get a job."

"I could go to D.C. and live with Marianne."

I practically drop my fork. "What?"

"Your sister."

I've got a situation here – another one! – that's out of control. I don't know how or why this war began, but now Becky is using my half-sister as a weapon against me. It's almost like they've… been in contact. But that can't be. Becky doesn't even know Marianne's last name – I didn't know she knew her first name. She knows she lives in D.C. because that's where I went to visit her. Apart from that, there's no way that Becky could have got in touch with her on her own.

Did Marianne contact her?

Becky sits back in her chair, smiling her signature

"sweet-but-just-a-little-dim" smile that I sometimes find endearing but right now sets my teeth on edge.

"What do you know about Marianne? She hasn't contacted you, has she?"

Becky gets up from the table. "Of course not, Mom. I don't know anything. It was just another one of my silly ideas."

She takes her plate to the dishwasher. That's when I notice something silver on her wrist. A bracelet – *my* bracelet.

"Where did you find that?" I seethe.

"Oh yeah, sorry." She unclasps it, deliberately taking an age. "It was in your desk drawer. I was looking for the scissors. I thought maybe you'd misplaced it."

She sets it on the table. I watch as she leaves the room. I don't know my own daughter. I've seen her grow from a baby; I've seen her through all kinds of bad times. Loved her through those times. The one thing that always saw us through – and made early intervention possible – was that Becky was usually a terrible liar. Now though, all that is changing. If she can fool me, then maybe she really is growing up. Or maybe, I just want to be fooled.

When she's gone from the kitchen, I clasp the bracelet around my wrist. The charms make their familiar sound, but the weight of it seems wrong somehow. I get up and start pacing. Could they be in contact? Why does the idea bother me so much? The unexplained niggle that I've had ever since I got back tickles in my head like an itch I can't scratch. It's no doubt just my pure imagination.

I need to call someone, talk to *someone*. But who? It's times like this when I miss Dad most. The dad I knew – not the dad who really was. If he was still alive, I would call him. I can almost hear his bright and cheerful "Hello, Tiger," as a phantom voice in my ear. It brings tears to my eyes. Dad's betrayal is the worst thing about this whole mess. A second family, a secret sister. How could he have done that to me?

The fact is that Dad is dead. But there's also someone else that I can call – the person I want to trust in this situation. Someone that I've been avoiding for weeks now, though he's left message after message and clearly hasn't given up on me. The one person who can nip this whole Marianne thing in the bud because he was the one who planted the seed in the first place. I pick up my phone and dial the number.

"Claire!" Dave Steiner picks up on the second ring. "Long time no hear. How are you?"

I tell him. It doesn't make for pleasant conversation.

51

MARIANNE

"We need to talk. Can you meet me?"

I should not say yes. I am not at any man's beck and call. Not my husband's, and certainly not Dave Steiner's. I make a silent vow to myself – the same one I made last time and the time before that. Going forward, I will keep our relationship purely professional. It's much better that way.

"Do you mean now?" I check my watch. Of course, he means now. It's eight o'clock at night. Plenty of time for a "talk" and a "drink", and I can still make it home before Tom does. Why that still matters, I really don't know.

"Yes." The way he says it, I feel a melting sensation deep inside. His voice… that sensation…

Twenty minutes later I'm in a taxi. My stomach churns with guilt, which is well-deserved. Since meeting Dave, since finding Claire, all my carefully wrought plans – win back my husband, find an egg donor – things I thought I could achieve, and thought I *wanted* to achieve – have derailed in spectacular fashion.

There is no one root cause. I am still the same person I

was before, with the same goals and the same problems. Yes, a scab has been ripped off my past, exposing something stinking and rotten underneath. But that should not have a drastic effect on my present.

Yet, for some reason, I can't get over it. It's not only my past that's a lie, but my present too. My relationship with my mother is riddled with secrets and lies. My relationship with Tom – the same. He still hasn't agreed to see Dr. Lena and won't even entertain a conversation about egg donation. I hate him a little for that. I've been trying so hard to bail out the sinking ship of my marriage because that's what I do – keep bailing, keep trying – that I've never stepped back to ask myself "what's the point?" What the *hell* is the point?

My mother kept bailing. In the end, she got a nice house, clout with her friends, and half of my father. For her, it was worth it. But is it the same for me?

I might get to keep some part of Tom, who gave up on our marriage vows long before I did. I might get a baby, which would give meaning and purpose to all the losses that came before. I might get to be happy – because I'm certainly not happy now.

And the alternative?

I don't know.

Rain runs down the window of the taxi, blurring the lights of the city like red, white, and blue tears. *You could just let go. Jump off the cliff. Enjoy the free fall.* I can't silence the whispers.

I reach into my pocket and take out the charm bracelet. Claire is probably at home right now cooking dinner for her family. I wonder what she's making. Does she like cooking or find it a chore? Does she cook their favorite meals or just microwave some fish fingers and serve them with beans on toast?

I'm surprised to realize that I wish I knew those things about her. Is it too late to find out? Of course, it is. There's too much water under the bridge – or, in this case, too little. Claire wants me to be a donor for her daughter if I'm a match, but she doesn't want to know me. I can hardly blame her – *I* don't want to know me. But Becky does. The guilt inside me spikes. Becky is seventeen and caught in the middle. I remember all too well being that age and having no control over anything. Other people make choices for you, and you have to live with them forever. Time's arrow only moves forward – it's not possible to go back and right past wrongs. But is seventeen really old enough to make your own choices? I thought so at the time, but now I'm not so sure.

The taxi arrives at the hotel. I disembark under the wide awning and array of flags. The flags remind me of Dave's global vision. I genuinely believe that his intentions are honorable. He wants to bring people together and make positive connections. He wants to shine a light of truth on the hidden shadows – to open Pandora's box and see what's inside.

But what exactly is inside, lurking in the intricacies of those tiny chains of proteins and covalent bonds? Secret siblings, second families, unwanted connections with the power to destroy lives. But also potential organ donors who can save lives. I move my fingers from charm to charm. Claire has a dolphin that I don't have. When did our father give it to her? I'd like to ask her about it, but it's difficult given that we're not in contact. I shove the bracelet back into my pocket. Everything is back under lock and key – for now.

When I walk into the lobby and see Dave's tanned, smiling face and loosened tie, feel his arms around me, and smell his aftershave, I know that the pesky little box isn't quite shut completely. Pandora had to live with the choices she made, and so do I. Right now, I am choosing to make the same mistake yet again.

"Marianne," he says. "You look beautiful. Do you want a drink?"

"Yes."

We don't bother with the bar. Dave has a bottle of champagne on ice up in his room.

52

He kisses me with unexpected tenderness. As my own pleasure echoes through my body, I give in to the warm feeling of contentment. It only lasts for a moment until my inner glow is extinguished by the familiar itch of regret. *Free fall. Letting go.* It's exhilarating. It's terrifying. I pull the sheet around me and drink the dregs of champagne from my glass on the bedside table. Yes, my guilt is well-deserved. I am officially betraying my husband. I am officially having an affair.

Like most affairs, it wasn't planned. The first few times I met up with Dave outside the office, we really did just have a drink and talk. I tried to put my early fantasy out of my mind and made a point of ignoring the attraction between us. I would stay strong – I could have stayed strong. But that morning when Tom saw my screen, and his face was the ultimate rejection, something inside me just broke. Dave just happened to come to town the following night, and was willing and able to fix it. *Beautiful, special.* It's all I've ever really wanted to be.

Of all the things I thought would be different about

being with a man other than Tom, I find myself focusing not on the different sensations of touch, smell, and taste but on the curious fact that Tom likes to talk first, whereas Dave gets caught up in the heat of passion and is definitely a "talk afterward" man. I used to prefer Tom's approach because I felt like he accepted me regardless of what came out of my mouth. But as things are, Tom and I haven't talked or made love for a very long time. It's nice just to be with a man who wants me.

Dave spoons against me, his lips close to my ear. "We need to talk about Claire."

"Yes." I stifle a sigh. The price of being with Dave is that he doesn't just roll over and go to sleep. This conversation was always going to be ugly. I may as well just lie here and take my punishment.

"She was glad to have met up with you, and she was very grateful that you've agreed to take the bone marrow test. But she suspects you've been in contact with her older daughter. Rightly or wrongly, she's kind of upset."

"Let's be clear." I move away from him. "Becky contacted me."

"I get that. But Claire worshiped her dad – as you probably gathered. The fact that he not only had an affair, but a whole second family, has her feeling really conflicted."

"How is she conflicted?" I'm starting to get annoyed. "Claire also contacted me first. Not out of curiosity or even some kind of misplaced family duty. She's looking for a donor for her daughter, which I completely understand. But she doesn't know me and hasn't even bothered to try." My annoyance turns to anger. "I might be afraid of needles or hospitals. I might be anemic myself. And even if I am a match, the harvesting procedure is major surgery. It could cause me pain – maybe even cripple me – for weeks afterward. She should feel conflicted if she's asking me to do all that and then gets angry when I respond to her daughter's message."

Dave sighs. "She told me she hasn't asked you to do anything. Not even take the test."

I roll over on my elbow and run my finger over the hair on his chest. Light brown, with a sprinkling of gray. Tom doesn't have chest hair. I thought I liked that, but there's something masculine about a man with a little hair on his chest. Truly, I need to stop comparing the two.

"You seem to care an awful lot what Claire thinks," I say. "Did you have this heart-to-heart with her in a hotel room somewhere? She's my sister – we're related by our DNA. Where do we come down on the whole "nature vs. nurture" spectrum? Which one of us is better in bed?"

Dave shifts uncomfortably. Despite his charisma in the boardroom, his sense of humor in the bedroom is a little lacking. "Claire is just a friend," he says. "So there's no comparison."

"Isn't there?" I'm winding him up, but I can't stop myself. "My father had his first family in California. Then, he had his bit on the side – my mother – in D.C. Is it something in the water here that makes men stray?"

"Not the water – just the women." I feel him shrug. "But I'm not actually straying."

"Oh? How's that?"

"Sheila's filed for divorce." He gives a bitter laugh. "She says she's tired of 'playing second fiddle to my dream'. So I guess you could say that I'm carefree and single."

"Oh." The news sends a lightning bolt of fear through me. My goal in sleeping with him – if I ever had one – was to prove that I was still a desirable woman. The fact that we were both married seemed like a built-in exit strategy.

But if he's no longer in a relationship, and I'm ruining my future with Tom, then what exactly is supposed to happen? Dave already has kids. Whereas I want a baby. More than anything…

He tries to roll onto me again, and I push him gently away. It's high time that I end this before my life takes yet another wrong turn.

Dave takes the hint. "So what about you?" he says. "Are you really still trying to make it work with Tom? In my own humble opinion, he doesn't deserve you."

"Thanks. I think. I don't know what I'm going to do."

"I understand. But while you're considering, just keep in mind that I'm not like your father."

"I'm glad to hear it," I say. "Because at the end of the day, he's dead. He died two deaths, as a matter of fact."

"Two deaths?"

I've caught his interest now. I tell him about the information that Becky sent me. Two obituaries, two urns, two sets of ashes. Those things can be easily explained under the circumstances. But then I tell him about the three fish – and the two causes of death. One accident on the boat, one heart attack before he ever got on the boat. My mother reluctantly confirmed the latter. Dave's frown deepens.

"It could just be an error," he says. "It's a small discrepancy. Maybe it's not significant. Or maybe your mother got the information wrong."

I lean over and pick up my jacket that's crumpled on the floor.

"What about this?" I remove the bracelet from the pocket. "Is this significant?"

"That's Claire's, isn't it?"

I don't like the accusing tone in his voice.

"No, it's mine. There were two bracelets. Almost identical. Becky sent me a photo of her mom's bracelet. She has one extra charm that she received just before our father died. A dolphin."

Dave stares down at the bracelet. "Maybe you should come work for me. I can see you're quite the detective."

"Not really. I have no idea what it all means."

"Nor do I," he says. "But I think it does prove one thing."

"What's that?"

"Secrets are never a good thing. They're like worms. They have a way of eating through things. Forcing themselves out into the open."

I laugh and swing out of bed. I almost feel like kissing him again, almost regret my decision to end things. He watches as I get dressed, his face wistful.

"As soon as I get back home," he says. "I'm going to see Claire. Is there anything you want me to tell her? About… what we've discussed?"

I hook on my bra and give him a broad smile. "You can tell her that I've made an appointment next week to take the bone marrow test. And that I hope I'll be the one who can save her daughter's life."

It's Dave's turn to laugh, low and throaty. "Come on, Marianne. You may be a detective of sorts, but you're not a very good liar."

It's almost a relief that he's finally called my bluff.

"I just want to be happy," I say. "And to achieve that, I'll do *whatever it takes*."

"And what will it take?"

Secrets. They eat their way out from inside. It's high time that I tell Dave what I really want from my Genetic Journey – and from Claire.

So I do.

It's a win-win situation, after all.

53

BECKY

Me. Marianne.

Marianne. Me. I shouldn't have told Mom, even though it was almost worth it to see the look on her face. She doesn't want to believe that we're in contact. I'd hoped to give her a little clue that would annoy her but still leave a seed of doubt.

Another bad decision.

All of a sudden, parental controls are back on the computer. I can't talk to my friends, do any internet searches, or even do my homework without her knowing about it. She's like a pit bull with my leg between her jaws. My leg. Not Marianne's leg.

I think Mom's too intimidated by her sister to do anything.

After a few days of total irritation over the internet thing, I announce that I'm going to stay with Stacey for the weekend. Mom tries to stop me. She even goes so far as to call Stacey's mom and tell her that I can't go. I'm so humiliated. But I'm not going to let her win the war. I *need* to get in contact with Marianne. It's urgent – she told me in her last message that she's having the bone marrow test done! When she gets the results, I want to be the one who tells Mom that we've found a way to save Jess. Marianne already said that was OK – *if* she's a match. She reminded me that it's a long shot. But in my heart, I just know she's going to be.

When the day of the test arrives, I'm too distracted to pay attention in class. I'm wondering how Marianne is feeling as she goes off to the hospital to have her blood drawn. The "little stick" as the needle goes into her arm, her lifeblood flowing into the tube. It's so weird to think we're connected by that blood, even though we've never met. They should have the results soon – maybe even this week. It's so selfless of her to try to help – I really admire her. The more I think about it, the more determined I am to go to college in D.C. I so want to meet her in person!

When we do meet, I'm going to bowl her over with my politeness and good manners. She'll be so impressed that she'll invite me to stay with her and maybe even loan me the money for the plane ticket until I can get a job and pay her back. I can see it all so clearly like a red carpet rolled out at the Oscars. Maybe I ought to be a life coach. I can visualize how everything fits together, how it all plays out.

As long as no one else screws it up.

Like Mom.

When I get home, I force "Good Becky" to make an appearance. Dad's working, so it's just me and her at dinner. She asks me about my day, and I answer in complete sentences. I even manage to trot out a few facts about the bicameral system of legislation that we learned about in Civics. It's like we're both in no man's land, waiting for someone to fire the first shot. I want it to be me, but as she's setting the bowl of macaroni and cheese on the table, she beats me to it.

"Becky," she says, "I'm sorry about how I've been lately."

And the parental controls, and not trusting me… I keep hoping she'll add, but she doesn't.

"But you have to understand that things are really hard right now. With Jess and this whole thing with my sister. I'm feeling really destabilized. I could use your help – but I need to be able to trust you."

"You can trust me." It's pointless to say it, but I do anyway.

"I know, it's just—"

"What's wrong with Marianne?" I blurt. "Why do you hate her so much?"

"Oh, Becky." Mom sits down at the table and puts her head in her hands. I'm actually really shocked when I see tears leaking through her fingers. She's sobbing, and I have no idea what to do. I mean, Mom is usually so strong. What have I said or done that's so terrible?

"There's nothing *wrong* with her!" Mom says. "She was perfectly nice, perfectly polite. She has a good job and a nice house, and she seems… normal."

"OK—"

"But the whole situation is so creepy. My dad not only had an affair but a whole *second family*! He was the one person that I always trusted. But now, all my good memories of him are full of her. A woman I've met once, and I didn't feel any kind of bond with her. Not like the bond between you and Jess." She wipes away a tear. "I've never thought about having a sister before. But if I did, I'd want what you and Jess have. I wouldn't choose *her*."

"Why not?" This seems really important, and I want to understand where she's coming from. I mean, Marianne is so glamorous and successful. She's so perfect. Then it hits me. Mom is jealous of her.

I chew on this for a minute. Could it really be true? I'm used to having a perfect younger sister and looking bad in comparison. But Mom isn't used to playing that part. I'm proud of myself for coming up with that *hypothesis*. Maybe if I get good at solving other people's problems, I could be a therapist or something.

"I don't know." Mom takes her hands away from her face.

Her eyes look huge and haunted. I feel sorry for her and scared too. Mom may be many things – and lots of them I don't like – but she's a rock for our family. I don't want to see her this way. If jealousy is the problem, then what can I do about it?

"But you told her about Jess," I say. "That's a big deal."

"I did." Mom's tears evaporate, and I see anger on her face. "I felt like a door-to-door salesman. Some trailer trash on Jerry Springer. Like I'd found a long-lost relative – a sister – and then turned up at her house asking for something. Asking for her bone marrow to save my daughter."

"Which any normal, caring person would understand. You did what you had to do for Jess. I totally don't judge you, so why do you think Marianne will think less of you?"

"I just felt so ashamed."

"You're trying to save your daughter's life!" A therapist would probably know how to stay calm, but I'm getting angry. "I mean, Jess is dying. And you're worried about the fact that you've had to ask your *sister* to take a blood test? I mean, did you know that Jess is, like, rotting from the inside? She's throwing up all her food and shitting herself. She can't even type on the iPad because her hands are so shaky. She says that she's going to stop taking the pills. And I don't blame her."

Mom looks at me, horrified. I wish I hadn't said

anything. "Is… that true?" she whispers. "I mean, I knew she was feeling low, but… has she stopped taking the pills?"

"I don't know."

"I'd better go up and check on her."

I cross my arms. "I think you should call Marianne first."

Mom stares at me, her eyes full of fury. I'd like to think it's because she knows I'm right.

"You do know that Marianne had the test done today, right?" I check my watch. It's five-thirty now, which means that in D.C., it's eight-thirty. I'm itching to get on the computer and find out how it went. "She had an appointment and everything."

"She did?" Mom lowers her voice.

"Yes… isn't that great?"

"But you… you *know* that?"

"Yeah." My cards are on the table, so I may as well go all in. "OK – so I lied before. She and I have been in touch on Facebook. She wants to get to know me, and she wants to help Jess. But she thinks you don't like her." I glare at her for all I'm worth. "So she didn't want to do it through you."

Mom looks absolutely stunned, flabbergasted. Not in a good way. But I don't care. I've made the right decision to let Marianne into our lives. Mom's the one who's in the wrong.

"I'm not going to let Jess die just because you have a problem with Marianne," I add. "None of us want that, including Marianne. She's nice. Caring. I'm sure the whole sister thing was a shock to her too, but she's dealing with it. That's what adults do, isn't it?"

"I… just…" Mum shakes her head slowly.

"And if Marianne isn't a match, then it's not an issue. You don't have to have any more contact with her. And we keep on looking until we find a match. But she's my aunt. If I want to get to know her, then that's my choice."

I know I've won. I'm the one acting like the adult here. Mom opens and closes her mouth, but nothing comes out. I take her hand and squeeze it. "You know it's the right thing."

She stares down at our entwined hands. "I guess… you're right. I've been stupid and selfish. I'll call her – today. Thank her for what she's doing."

"Yeah, you do that. Then we get the results of the test and go from there."

"Go from there," Mom repeats.

As she lets go of my hand, I see a flash of silver at her wrist. I hadn't noticed that she'd started wearing the bracelet again. It reminds me of the snow globe (which I still haven't given back). Maybe I'm like one of those birds – magpies – that love shiny things.

"I wish I had a bracelet like that," I say. "I mean, I'd have a charm for me, and a charm for Jess, and a charm for you and Dad."

Mom stares down at the bracelet, fingering the Golden Gate Bridge charm.

"I guess that one's you," I say. "And the Capitol must be Marianne."

She looks up at me. I look at her. What have I just said, and what does it mean? If I had a bracelet, I'd have four charms. But there are more than that on Mom's bracelet.

"I don't think it means anything like that," she says. She tucks the bracelet back under her sleeve with a little shake of her head. I'm about to let it go, but then I remember something else that Marianne said when I posted the photo of the bracelet.

"You know what's weird?" I say.

"What?"

"Marianne doesn't have the dolphin charm."

"What?" She stares at me, then down at her wrist.

"The dolphin. She doesn't have that one. I don't know why. And also, her dad died of a heart attack – he wasn't on a fishing boat."

"What are you talking about?"

Her face has gone completely pale, and I wish I hadn't said anything. "I don't know. Maybe you should ask Marianne."

I can feel her anger rising like a wall of flame. "Sorry," I say instinctively, and leave it at that.

54

CLAIRE

I'm full of rage as I leave the kitchen. Becky – my daughter. Marianne – my sister. Why does the fact that they're in touch rankle me like fingernails on a blackboard? Becky lied, but that's nothing new. And Marianne? She's *family*, whether I like it or not. I must put it behind me. I need to check on Jess – make sure she's taking her medication and then call the doctor and make him give her another drug to relieve her symptoms. And I will do that. But first…

I go into the study, twisting the chain of my bracelet. I've got used to wearing it again – I feel naked without it and all the lies it symbolizes. Somewhere across the country, my sister has the same bracelet. The same, and yet not the same. One charm more or less – what does it all mean?

Becky is right. I need to keep my eye on the ball. There is only one thing – one person – who truly matters here. I started this journey for Jess, and I'll finish it only when she's cured or… cured. I can't accept anything else. I *will* call Marianne. I will welcome her into our lives and smooth things over.

When I turn on the phone, there's a text notification on the screen. I open it and find that it's from Dave Steiner.

Claire – we should talk. I think it's best if you don't contact Marianne for now. Can we meet in person to discuss? I'm in D.C. now and just about to board a plane. Back tomorrow.

I put the phone down on the desk and stare at it. There are too many things in that message to analyze and take in. Too much information – and too little.

I shouldn't call her until I talk to Dave. Dread pools in my stomach. Maybe this is how Becky feels before doing one of her many stupid things – poised on the brink of disaster and choosing to jump. *The only person who matters is Jess.* I dial the number.

The phone rings and rings. It's like she's taunting me. Three rings, five. She's not going to pick up. My anger is softened by relief…

"Hello, Claire." Her voice startles me back to my senses. Then there's a silence. One that it's up to me to fill.

"Hi, Marianne," I say. "Hope I'm not calling at a bad time."

"Of course not. Happy to talk anytime."

"Umm, great."

I should have written a script. I have no idea what to say. There is a lifetime of things that could and *should* be said. I stare at the photos on the wall of the study. The four of us on a beach in Monterey. Jess was five, Becky was ten. Steve is holding up a giant swordfish. He didn't catch it himself, but we saw the fisherman haul it in, and Steve begged a photo. At the time, it was a big joke. We are all laughing and smiling. Now, those smiles seem like as big a lie as the fish on the hook. All those smiles, all those moments of laughter. They might as well never have happened.

"So… I guess you met Becky? Online?"

God. Could I have come up with a worse opener?

"Yes, I did." Her voice is brisk. "I'm glad she told you. I was going to write to you, but then I was worried that you wouldn't want to hear from me."

I want to go for the juggler. Tell her that she had no right to cyberstalk my eldest daughter. Befriending her – grooming her – for what?

That's the big question. So far, Marianne's motives have only been good and honest. It's mine that are selfish and blurry.

"I should have been the one to introduce you. I'm sorry I didn't. It all still feels a little strange."

"That's very true."

I take a breath and steel myself. "Becky also said that you were... um... taking the bone marrow test. Is that right? I mean... like I said, you really don't have to."

There's a pause. "I wanted to, Claire. And in fact, it's already done. If I can save my niece, then I want to do it. Who wouldn't want to help if they could? To help out *family*..." she emphasizes the word, "when they're in a bind."

It's done! She's taken the test! She's done the selfless thing, the caring thing. I want to like her – I want to love her. She's my sister. Yet, her soft voice raises my hackles. She's so perfect – always saying just the right thing at the right time. She's just like Dad in that way. But just because he was rotten underneath doesn't mean that she is. But what about Dave's text? And what was it she said when we met up that bothered me? What does it all mean?

"I don't really know what to say," I stammer. "Other than thank you."

"It was just a simple blood test," she says. "We should have the result soon. Then, if I am a match, we can arrange the procedure. The nurse seemed to know something about Jess's disease. She told me that for a bone marrow transplant, she'll need a course of preparation. Some sort of chemo? To kill off her existing cells?"

"Yes. That's right." Jess will lose her hair, be sick for weeks, and be even more vulnerable to infection. Then there's the post-transplant risk of graft-versus-host disease. It will be a long and awful process. And yet, if she survives it…!

"Let's wait and see," I add. "I… don't want to get my hopes up."

"We'll keep our fingers crossed."

"Yes. I mean… thank you." It's all going awkward again. I want to end the conversation, but I haven't even asked her how she's doing.

"You don't have to thank me," she says. "But I was hoping you might do me one small favor."

I brace myself. This is it. She wants something. Dave is right. She's not what she seems on the outside. There's something about her that's just… off. I've known it all along—

"I told you that I'm working on the *MyStory* refinancing. I'm coming out to California next week for the closing. I'd love it if we could meet up. Just for a cup of coffee or a drink. Maybe I could meet Becky too if that's not too much to ask. By then, I should know the results of the test. We can have a pow-wow. A council of war – defeat Jess's disease."

"Yes, great." Reluctance creeps through every cell of my body. "That would be perfect. You could… come over for dinner? Meet everybody."

What the *hell* am I doing?

"Fantastic," she says. "I'm just dying to meet your family."

"Great. I'm sure they feel the same." My hand goes

reflexively to my wrist. The Golden Gate Bridge. The Capitol. And the others? Damn Becky and her offhanded comment. *The dolphin charm.* I could ask Marianne about that one. It probably isn't important. On the other hand…

"I'll give you a call when I know my schedule."

"OK." I can ask her about it *when she comes to visit.*

A sickly dread sweeps through me as I hang up the phone.

PART IV
JUNE

55

MARIANNE

I am the one.

The call came through from the lab last night as I was walking to the Metro. The conversation was a little rushed, and then the signal cut out. But the bottom line is that my HLA markers are a near-perfect match for those of my niece. I have a new role, a new purpose in life. I can save the life of Claire's daughter. I can help a little girl live a normal life: no more tubes and transfusions, drugs and side effects. I can redeem all of my previous bad acts and thoughts. I can do the selfless thing and not even ask for anything in return.

I want it to be that way.

As the plane leaves the runway, I stare out the window at the clouds on the horizon. We sweep out over the ocean before making a gentle arc to fly westward. In only a few seconds, we are surrounded by a bank of clouds. Somewhere down below is my house, my husband, the life I've always known. All the things I've ever strived for and wanted. Everything that I tried to cling to with an iron fist.

But now, the shifting sand has run out through my fingers. Before me is the great unknown.

I've been to California before. Tom and I took a vacation there the year after we were married. I spent a lot of my time working, and Tom was annoyed. It wasn't quite the romantic trip I had hoped for. We stayed in a few B&Bs in the wine country, a fancy hotel in San Francisco, and a seaside inn in Carmel. Back then, when Tom and I had sex, it was a haphazard, spontaneous thing. A romantic thing, with no expectations attached. I was even on the pill, actively trying not to get pregnant. Maybe if we'd started earlier, tried harder…

No. Even if we'd humped like rabbits in those early days, it wouldn't have made a difference.

And now?

Last night, I finally managed to corner him, and we had a short version of a heart-to-heart talk. I told him that I was hurt over his affair and devastated that we'd come to the end of the IVF road, which was why I'd been looking into alternatives. I even told him that I wasn't serious about egg donation – I'd been grieving over the loss of Baby No. 8 and felt like I had to take some action.

Tom held me in his arms and stroked my hair. He hadn't tried to have sex, and for that, I was grateful. I decided not to tell him that we were "even" because now we've both had an affair. I also didn't tell him the real reason why I missed his mother's party – that I was meeting my long-lost sister. A sister who needs me to save her daughter's life. A sister with healthy eggs.

Now that I think about it, most of the heart-to-heart chat on my part was all lies.

We left it that Tom would schedule a call with Dr. Lena. He'll get the facts, mull them over, and tell me what he wants to do. It had seemed like a good result at the time. Now, it feels like another little death.

The plane is turbulent for a few minutes, then suddenly it breaks through the clouds. Sunlight is blazing in a crystal-blue sky. The clouds rise up in mountains and valleys, a magical city in the sky. I wish I could go out on the wing and jump off into that fluffy, heavenly world. I wish… a lot of things.

I think of my father: all those business trips, all those airplanes. Two charm bracelets, two lives, two deaths. Presumably, he thrived on the clandestine nature of his twin realities. But did he ever stare out the window at the clouds and wish that it was all over – the complications, the struggle, the heartache? Did he ever regret his choices and wish that he could wipe the slate clean and start over? We might not have had the closest of father-daughter relationships, but still, on a human level, I wish I knew. At the moment of his death, did he regret not telling the truth? Or by then, was it all just too difficult?

As the plane levels out to cruising altitude, I take out my laptop. There's work I should be doing, but instead, I open up a blank document. I don't know who I'm writing to. Claire? Becky? Tom? My mother? Maybe the plane will go down and my laptop will miraculously survive. By then, it won't matter.

When I was seventeen, I went to a party and met an older boy. He called me beautiful and special, one thing led to another, and I ended up pregnant. My mother arranged an abortion so that I wouldn't "ruin my life". I knew it was the wrong decision – that the life inside of me was innocent and precious. A tiny butterfly in a cocoon that was mine to love and nurture. But I was too scared to speak up. Before I knew it, that baby – I named her Lily – was gone.

I have the overwhelming urge to delete the words. To crumple the secret up into a ball and toss it away. It all just seems so sickening, so ugly, and I feel detached from it – dissociated – as though it happened to another person. My fingers, though, betray the truth. I begin to type again.

My mother told me that my time would come. After I finished college, got married, got a job. Then it would be the "right" time for a baby. She had it all figured out, and I wanted to believe her. Wanted to believe that it would happen automatically, in its own time, despite the life I had already thrown away. But the universe is smarter than that. The universe has a system of checks and balances.

I read over what I've written. It makes me sound sad and naïve. Which is probably the truth.

My biological alarm clock went off when I turned thirty-one. It wasn't an earth-shattering kind of noise or even a ticking clock. It was more like a steady heartbeat, the gentle rhythm of breathing underwater. I woke up one morning, and the thought took shape. I am ready for a baby. I am ready to create a tiny life and feel it growing inside of me. Bubbling, flipping, rolling, kicking. It wasn't a mental longing so much as a physical one. I felt effervescent with excitement when I thought about what my *baby would be like. Would he or she have my hair or Tom's? My eyes or his? I could almost feel the grip of a sea-anemone finger, picture the soft, delicate pink of a seashell ear.*

Each month that it didn't happen felt like another failure. My guilt began to rise to the surface like an underground stream. We visited a fertility specialist and decided to try IVF. I got pregnant in the first cycle. I was overjoyed – life was smiling on me. I lost that baby at twenty-four weeks. The next one at sixteen weeks.

I don't know the words to express how it felt when those babies came into the world and died one by one. For that's how I saw them. All I knew was that I needed to keep trying. I needed to do it for Lily and all the ones who came after – to give meaning to the tiny sparks of life that were extinguished too soon. I wanted them – and me – to have a happy ending. To this day, that happy ending has never come.

A tear falls on my keyboard. The flight attendants are having a tête-à-tête, no doubt wondering whether to offer me a free drink or ignore me altogether. I ignore them. Now that the words are coming out, I can't stop.

All the losses changed me. How could they not? I clung to my marriage out of fear and desperation and ended up wrecking it beyond repair. My husband thinks I'm mad to want to try again. My doctor has advised me to adopt or foster. But neither of them understands. Deep down, I know that I am meant to have a child. It is etched into my soul like the path of a glacier. I will have a child of my own. I just need... a little help.

The doctor has advised that if I use donor eggs from a close relative, I will have a 60-80% chance of conceiving a baby and carrying it to term. To fulfill my destiny, to attain my birthright as a woman. I am thirty-eight years old. This is my last chance.

I hit save and slam down the lid of my laptop. I'm crying full tilt now, my eyes leaking like a tropical rainstorm. One of the flight attendants comes over and gives me a wad of tissues. "Thank you," I say, my voice nasal with tears. Another one braves my seat with a bottle of red wine. "You look like you need this," she says. I don't like red, but I nod my thanks and take it anyway. I drink it down, not bothering with the plastic glass. Then I turn and stare out the window, trying to lose myself again in that cloud universe just beyond the wing.

I'm not expecting it to work, and it doesn't.

56

CLAIRE

"She's… a match?"

My voice trembles as Dave Steiner takes my hand across the kitchen table. My heart is pounding hard enough to burst, but I don't care. A lifeline… I needed a lifeline, and one has appeared. My sister has come into my life, and now I know why. I want to laugh, cry out, dance around the room. I want to hug Dave because it's in large part down to his energy and vision that my daughter has a chance at survival. And not just survival, but a normal life! She'll be able to follow her dreams and achieve her potential. It's an answer to my deepest, most heartfelt prayers.

"Yes, she is," he says.

"But that's wonderful!"

"It is wonderful." He isn't smiling. "But…"

I stare down at our entwined fingers. This is a reset button not only for Jess's life but for all our lives. I might not deserve it, but I'm going to take advantage of it to the fullest. I'm going to be a better person, a more *present* person. I'm going to be a better parent to Jess *and* Becky. I'm going to be a better wife to Steve, a better citizen of the world. I'm going to become a cheerleader for *MyStory* and home DNA testing. Once Jess is out of the woods, I'm going to live every day to the fullest. I'm going to forgive my dad in my heart and feel grateful to him for providing me with this chance to save my daughter.

Most of all, I will welcome Marianne into my life and embrace her as a sister. I see now that I have completely misjudged her. When I met her, I had this feeling that although she was polite and perfect on the outside, she had some kind of hidden agenda underneath. I see now that I was imagining a reflection of my own desperate need. I don't deserve her kindness, her selflessness – not after the way I've treated her. I am going to make amends for that, first and foremost…

But…

Dave is still talking. I haven't been listening. I've been basking in Jess's moment, her salvation, but now I try to regain the thread of what he's saying.

"She's more than happy to help you out," he's saying. "But she's on her own journey too. I mean, think of it from her perspective. All those miscarriages and IVF failures. All those losses. She sees each and every one of them as babies. Potential lives that were never realized."

I stare up at him, wondering why the conversation has suddenly taken this turn. Hearing what he's saying, I grip his hand even harder, like I'm hanging on for dear life. I *feel* for my sister and the losses she's suffered. That desperate pain, that hollow emptiness. I've felt it too each time I've sat next to my daughter in a hospital bed. The dreadful toxic hope and the crushing, stifling fear.

"It's terrible what she's suffered," I say. "That's why I'm so grateful to her."

"The doctors say that donor eggs are her last chance. If she goes down that route, the probability of success is quite high. Higher still if she uses donor eggs from a close female relative, even one above the normal cut-off age…"

"What?" His words flash, disjointed, inside my head. "Donor eggs", "last chance", "close female relative". I've been floating in the clouds, and now I'm being pelted by thunderbolts. "What are you saying?"

Dave takes a breath like he's rehearsed this in his mind.

"She would like you to consider donating your eggs to her."

It all slams into place. Knocking me off balance, sending me into free fall. This is the tiny thing that's been bothering me, her words that I should have registered at the time. *"I'm done with using my own eggs and Tom's sperm."* Suddenly, I understand. It explains everything. Marianne's kindness, her selflessness even in the face of our dad's double life. Her willingness to take the test despite the way I've treated her. My sister can save my daughter, but she wants something in return.

"My eggs?" I whisper, dumbfounded.

"She's not asking you for anything," he clarifies quickly. "Just like you haven't asked her for anything. But I know that she would like you to *consider* it. She would, of course, cover all expenses involved. You could start the process immediately after the bone marrow transplant—"

"So let me get this straight." I feel short of breath. "She wants to trade her bone marrow – the one thing that can save my daughter's life – for my *eggs*. So she can have *my* baby?"

"That's not quite how it works. During the gestation period, the eggs undergo certain changes—"

"But why didn't she mention it before? She… should have said. I mean, it's just… wrong."

I stand up and back away, leaning against the kitchen

counter. Only minutes ago, I was feeling joyous, elated. But now… now…

"It's quite a common thing, actually."

A common thing. Of course, it is. Some women donate eggs, and some women use donor eggs – it happens all the time. I don't judge the woman on either side of the trans-action – not at all. An egg is not a baby. It often happens anonymously, or sometimes friends help each other. *Family* helps each other. Marianne said as much. But surely, she should have raised it before. She should have come clean and told me exactly what she was hoping to gain. A trans-action, a trade. Body parts for body parts. Bile rises into my throat. She didn't even have the gall to ask me directly. She went through Dave – the one person whom I thought was my ally in this whole awful business. And she waited to do it until after she had the test results – dangling my hopes in front of me like bait on a fishhook. Dave is wrong. What Marianne is asking is not normal. She's being manipula-tive, dangerous even.

She can save Jess. The angel voice that whispers in my head sounds a lot like Becky's. *Whatever she wants, give it to her!*

Dave is sitting back, watching me. He's too calm, too serene. It only fuels my anger.

"How do you even know about it?" I say. "Why would she tell you something like that? Whose side are you on?"

"I'm not on anyone's side." His voice is measured, even, like he's trying to talk a crazy woman down from the edge of a tall building. "I met her through the refinancing – as you know. She's been trying to identify close biological relatives who might be willing to donate their eggs. I've been helping her – just like I'm helping you. I guess you can say that we've become… friends." He hesitates. "Of a sort."

It flashes across my mind that I must be the sick, deranged one. Because the way he said "friends" made me immediately think that maybe Dave and Marianne…

"No," I say aloud. "Tell me that you haven't… with… her."

He shakes his head. "Friends, Claire. Same as I am with you."

That sends me even closer to the edge. Dave was *my* friend. *My* confidant. Now, Marianne has stolen him from me.

Just like she stole my dad.

"I want you to go, Dave," I say. "Now."

"Take some time to think about it. It would be a very selfless, beautiful gesture. Just like what she's doing for you."

"Selfless! Beautiful?"

I swoop over to the table. Steam is curling up from my "World's Greatest Mother" mug. What a crock that seems now – one more lie among many. I take the mug to the sink and throw it, hard. It cracks to pieces, the sound startling.

"Claire." Dave comes over to me. His hands on my shoulders are warm, solid. "I'll go," he says. "But I need to know that you're going to be OK?"

I whirl around and stare at him, my eyes burning.

"How can I ever be OK? A few weeks ago, I didn't even know that Marianne existed. But thanks to your test, she's come into my life and stolen – yes, stolen! – my childhood, my memories, my dad – even Becky. But that isn't enough for her. Now she wants—" I choke on the words "—my *eggs*."

I am way out of line here! My feelings are completely wrong. But my thoughts and words are lubricated by anger, and I can't stop them.

"She's looking for an egg donor that will give her the best probability of success." Dave sounds like he's talking to a slow child. "And that happens to be a related donor. Just like you want to find a close relative, she's doing something similar. It may seem a little… intimate… but I don't see that ethically it's a lot different."

"God, the ethics of all of this just boggle the mind! You'd better erase my footage from your program. The only way I'll be taking part is by writing is a letter to my Congressman and whoever else it takes to put you out of business."

He laughs, and I feel like hitting him. "That's what I like about you, Claire. You're such a worthy adversary. The sad thing is that I think you might have liked Marianne if things had been different. She's smart, conscientious, and compassionate. I'm sure you don't want to hear this, but you two are actually quite similar. Strong and put together on the surface, but so vulnerable underneath."

I think of Dad, ever the charmer, married to two women on opposite sides of the country. Women who seemed normal on the outside, and yet who had each settled for half a life.

"Is that what you like, Dave? Vulnerable women?"

He smiles his best Messianic smile. "Maybe."

I turn away, staring at the fragments of blue porcelain in the sink. My favorite mug – a gift from my children, and now I've smashed it to pieces. What would it feel like to pick up one of the shards and give myself a great big cut down the arm? Feel the sharp pain of the incision and then the blood dripping away. Go to the hospital and have someone take care of me for once.

God. Dave's right. I am the crazy one.

I take a long, deep breath. I've had my rant, broken something, and now it's time to pull myself together. Dave likes vulnerable women – so he's welcome to be friends with Marianne, but not with me. I'm stronger than that. On the surface *and* underneath.

"Jess's condition is critical," I say. "The doctors said she might only have six months - and that clock is running down. If Marianne is serious about the bone marrow donation, then that process needs to start now. I'll let Jess's doctors know and get the ball rolling. But if Marianne is a match, then there may be others out there. Can you please keep looking – and find them too?"

He frowns. "Claire, the answer to your prayers is staring you in the face. If I were you, I'd take the money and run."

He's right – absolutely right. But ever since that awkward conversation with Becky, a possibility has been growing in my mind like a monstrous shadow. I've tried – God knows I've tried – but I just can't vanquish it.

"Did Marianne tell you about the charm bracelet?" I lift the cuff of my shirt. I want to rip the damn thing off.

"Yes, she said you both had one."

"The Golden Gate Bridge charm is me," I say. "And the Capitol charm is her. So who are the others?"

"Pardon?" He looks perplexed.

I can stop right now. Keep the worms tightly sealed inside the can. That's what I should do. But my back is against the wall, and I have to make a choice. My eggs or my past.

"There were charms from Texas, Hawaii, and New York. Then, shortly before he died, Dad sent me a dolphin charm. It was purchased in Miami and mailed from Key West. Marianne doesn't have that one. So…" I take a breath, wishing that a hole would open up in the kitchen floor and swallow me. "Can you check if I have any Genetic Cousins in those places? Any close matches?"

"Claire… are you sure?"

"One family shame on him. Two families, shame on us. But why stop there?"

"You're very brave, Claire," he says.

"No. I'm not." I let out a hysterical little laugh. "I just want to save my daughter. Truly. But I'd rather do it without…"

What is wrong with me? What the *hell* is wrong with me? As the words leave my mouth, I feel a great, unbearable weight settle over me. She's my sister. Sisters help each other. What an awful person I am! What a parasite! All along, I've been asking for help, without being willing to give anything in return. My thoughts and feelings are unforgivable. But they're still… mine.

Dave, to his credit, recognizes my turmoil. "Take some time to think it over," he says again. "And if you still feel the same, then I'll let Marianne know that she'll have to keep looking too." He sighs. "She's not a bad person, Claire. Just a woman who's been dealt a bad hand. I mean, to want a child so badly and not be able to have one. To want your babies to survive. You know how that feels."

A sharp stab of pain hits me in the solar plexus. "I do know how it feels," I say. "And I will think it over."

"Good," he says. "For now, though, I'll get my people on that analysis. I'll cross-check you and Marianne to any matches in the places you've mentioned."

I nod miserably.

"And, in the meantime, give me a call if you want to talk further. Or else find someone else to talk to. And remember, don't take your eye off the ball. Jess really needs you to score a home run for her now. Whatever it takes."

Dave Steiner walks out of my kitchen. I stand at the sink until I hear the front door slam. I grab a paper towel and clean up the mess I've made, picking up the pieces of the mug and throwing them in the trash. But I can't stop the sinking, dizzying feeling that what I've set in motion is going to create an even bigger mess. My mind hisses the unbearable questions in a loop:

What have I done? What on earth *have I done?*

57

BECKY

The email makes me cry. It's titled "My confession". At the beginning, Marianne says that she wasn't planning on writing or sending it. But since we've grown so close, she thought that I deserved to know the truth. Me! And the truth behind her perfect life is just so sad, so tragic. It's like she's lived through my worst nightmare: drunk at a party, having sex with someone, getting pregnant. I guess things are easier nowadays because I could just get the morning-after pill. But it must have been awful for her back then. (Her mom sounds like a total control freak – even worse than mine!)

Now that I know her story, I respect her even more. She's a woman who was torn apart and tried to stitch herself back together again. But the stitches are jagged and uneven. She can't do it alone. But *I* can help.

A second email came in a little while after the first, and then a third email asking me to delete the other two. Of course, I'm way too curious at that point to delete anything, but I have a scary floaty feeling in my stomach. After rereading the second email, I use my fingernail to scratch numbers onto my arm. With each zero, I'm laughing, then almost crying. I am just so overwhelmed by what is happening. All my dreams are coming true. And what's more, I – clueless, useless, Becky – can actually help someone else's dreams come true also.

I feel for your family so much, trying to find a matched donor for your sister. Because I need to find a matched donor too. If I can get some eggs from a close relative, I have an excellent chance of conceiving a healthy baby. I would do anything for that. I think that egg donors usually get around $10,000 per cycle, but to me, that sounds ridiculously low. I was thinking that if I could find the right person, I would pay three times that. But I know that your mom would never agree to donate her eggs, and I don't have anyone else. Please don't say anything. I really shouldn't send this, but I just feel so close to you, Becky. I just wanted you to know what I'm going through. As I said before, I'll be in California for a few days, and I'm really hoping we can meet up. I want to see you. Get to know you. It may not be possible if your mom doesn't want to, but I hope that we can persuade her. I'm just so glad that either way – no matter what happens – I should be able to help your sister. I'll do another test when I get to California, but it's all looking really good. I would do anything to help out your sister and your family. I'm so happy, Becky, that you're part of my life now.

With love and best wishes, Marianne

She's a match! I want to jump up and down, pick up Jess and spin her around. We'll write her a whole new Bucket List – not of things she wants to do before she dies, but things she wants to do because she's going to live! I want to show Mom the email and watch her face light up with pure joy. I want Dad to clap me on the back and say, "We couldn't have done it without you, Becky. I'm so proud."

But Jess is doing her online lesson, Mom's at the supermarket, Dad's at work. But that's OK – I can keep the secret to myself a little longer, nurture my happiness inside my heart. In fact, maybe I ought to check all the details with Marianne first. Like the fact that she's written the right number of zeros and actually would pay up to $30,000 – Thirty! Thousand! Dollars! – for donor eggs. Not to Mom – Marianne's right, she would hate the idea – but to me. Me! I feel weak in the knees just thinking about it. I'll be able to fly Jess to New York, and we'll stay in the Trump Tower or the Waldorf Astoria. I'll book her a private backstage tour at Carnegie Hall, maybe even rent the stage for her to play her violin.

And, after that, we'll ride in the new car I'll be able to buy – maybe a Cabriolet or a convertible VW Beetle – and I'll be able to show her the apartment I'm going to rent in D.C. – downtown with a view of the Capitol! And then she'll fly home, and I'll start junior college, and I'll finally be able to make something of my life!

I think of all the different careers I've considered since Mom began her Genetic Journey. TV presenter, journalist, psychic, life coach, detective, therapist – all of them very worthwhile. But maybe instead I'll start a charity. Matching donors with recipients (for a small fee, of course). We'll do kidneys, and bone marrow, and eggs, and… I'll have to research what else. But it's an exciting prospect. In fact, I can't believe how exciting my life has become almost overnight! Marianne is my savior. Now that she's part of our family, nothing is going to go wrong. I'm not going to let anything ruin it.

I'm not going to let *Mom* ruin it.

I file Marianne's email in my secret Dropbox folder. Just thinking about Mom is like a bucket of cold water in the face. I feel so angry with her. Marianne has suffered so much, and now she's reaching out to become part of our lives. She's going to save Jess! Mom should be over the moon when she finds out, but I know her – she won't like what Marianne is asking.

When the message is off my screen, I sit back in the chair and try to think clearly. I need to speak to Marianne before Mom does so that I can arrange everything. Jess needs the bone marrow now. That will take a few weeks of preparation, with Jess having chemo and stuff. Then, after the marrow is harvested, Marianne might need a little time to recover. I'll be eighteen soon – so I just need to convince Marianne to wait until then. That way, Mom doesn't even have to know about the eggs. It will be better that way – way better.

It's not like it's a big deal or anything to be ashamed of. I want to help Marianne. Especially if she's a bone marrow donor for Jess. And once I'm living in D.C., and Marianne has the baby, then I could earn even more money by babysitting Marianne's child. Which would be my child too.

I guess that does sound a little weird. I sit back in my chair and stare at the snow globe. The baby would have the best of everything: a beautiful house, a big yard, all the latest toys and baby gadgets, a mother who loves her, and a… I rack my brain trying to work out exactly what my relationship would be. A half-mother and a half-cousin?

OK, that does sound *a lot* weird. Doubts begin to niggle inside my head. If I'm going to donate my eggs, maybe I should save them for Jess. Mom once told me that if Jess has chemo – which she'll need to do before the bone marrow transplant can happen – it might make her infertile. If I give my eggs to Marianne, will I be depriving my sister of her chance to have a baby?

I don't know.

But if Jess doesn't get the bone marrow, she won't grow up at all. Looking at it like that, it seems a total no-brainer.

Before I can do any more thinking, I hit reply. *Hi Mari-anne. I'm so thrilled about the news. A match! I am so grateful for everything you've done. You said you'd be here for a few days, so can we meet up? I was thinking maybe without Mom. So we can talk about the "other thing". If you tell me where you're staying, I can get the bus or something. I can't wait to see you. It's all going to work out and be great – I just know it!*

Love, Becky

I hit send, and the reply is almost instantaneous.

Sounds great, Becky. I can't wait to meet you! Mx

58

MARIANNE

The *MyStory* facilities are impressive and oh-so California. The offices are located in a business park perched on the edge of a promontory of land that juts out into the San Francisco Bay and has panoramic views of Alcatraz Island. On a good day – and two out of the three days I've been here so far have been good days – the city seems to materialize out of the morning fog, white and shimmering, like a half-glimpsed magical world. The complex is glass and steel with wide lawns, palm trees, tropical flowers, and even its own boat dock, foreshortening towards the horizon. Although I spend most of my time in meeting rooms, the view is intoxicating.

Dave gives us a tour of the conference facilities and the labs, where young, keen scientists in white coats go through the testing protocols. Everything is done onsite with state-of-the-art technology. All in all, it looks like a place where a business can be grown and nurtured and eventually become bigger than Facebook. When I walk the walk and talk the talk with the investors, lawyers, and key senior managers, I feel proud to be part of something that's growing, flourishing.

It's only in the other moments – alone in my hotel room or in a break between meetings – that my problems come rushing back. Small, first-world problems. But taken together, they are like a thousand tiny holes in the hull of my ship, and I am struggling to stay afloat.

Claire hasn't responded to my texts that I'm in town. Becky hasn't been in touch either after her initial acknowledgement of my emails.

Those emails. God. Did I really send them? To Becky? Have I really gone over to the dark side? Can I even be entertaining the thought…? I don't blame her for not responding. And yet, with every moment that goes by, I feel my future slipping away.

And what about Jess's future? When I arrived here, Dave arranged for another blood sample to be drawn and sent directly to Jess's doctor. I assume everything is fine, but no one has got back to me to confirm when the harvest can take place. I hate delay and this feeling of dread, like Macbeth's dagger hanging over my head. Because once the hospital gives the green light, I'll have to tell Claire – everything. The bargain I'm proposing. What I hope she will see as a fair compromise on both sides.

I wish I could confide in Dave. He knows about my secret desire, though not the steps I'm taking to get it. But Dave is keeping a respectful distance, and I have only myself to blame. On the first day of my trip, I pulled him aside and reminded him again that I didn't want to meet up for any more "drinks" or "talking". He said that was probably for the best. Not exactly what I wanted to hear, if I'm being honest.

Because the day after I arrived, Tom sent me an email.

A long one – a heartfelt one. He said that he talked to Dr. Lena, and she was very positive about egg donation and my prospects for getting pregnant. But having thought about it from all angles, he does not want to try it. He said we can talk more about it when I get back. Slamming the door shut and leaving it open at the same time. If anything, I hate him most for that.

So now, I am faced with a choice. My husband or my baby. I'm struggling more with the logistics than the grief. I've worked so hard to find an egg donor, and now I'll need to find a sperm donor as well. Or…I could just let go. Try adoption, try fostering. Continue my life with Tom, with my mother. Wake up each day and wonder – if I'd only followed my heart, exhausted every avenue – would things be different?

No. I'm not going to do that. I've made my choice and am hurtling down my chosen path. Or not so much hurtling, but slogging. Because as fast as my mind is racing and my world is crumbling, everything else seems to have gone into slow motion.

Three days go by, then four. The hospital lab leaves me a voicemail saying that I need to do yet another test. Niggling at the back of my mind is the fact that Claire must *know* by now that I'm a match, and yet, she hasn't called me. Did Becky say something? Or Dave? The more I think about it, the more resentful I become – which, considering I haven't told Claire the news myself, must be unreasonable. Now that I am so close to achieving my goal, every little thing chafes. I just can't bear the thought of anything going wrong.

The day before I'm due to return to D.C., I've had enough of my own waffling. This is my last chance. I've got to take the bull by the horns. I get the efficient *MyStory* receptionist to book me a rental car to be delivered to the complex the next day, after my final meeting. I begin making plans to go on a little road trip.

59

CLAIRE

Jess is practicing her violin. It's the first time I've heard her playing since I cancelled the audition, so I am beyond glad, beyond grateful to hear it. I know she's probably just bored of staring at a screen all day and wanted to do something else. But I want it to mean that she's turned a corner – that she's feeling better and wants to move forward again to achieve her dreams. I don't want it to mean that she's given up and is back to that damn Bucket List – trying to make the best of her last few months and weeks. It kills me that she's still so angry and distant from me. I may be her drug pusher and jailer, but it's like I don't know her anymore.

I go into the bathroom under the pretense of cleaning it. But really, I just want to listen to the glorious rise and fall of the notes spinning in the air. *Méditation* from *Thaïs*. That's what she's working on. A soaring melody that sweeps you away with its almost unbearable beauty. A piece that embodies all that is good about this life. Music that breaks my heart.

I wish that I could make this moment last forever.

Capture it, preserve every detail like a ship in a bottle. Relive it over and over and ignore everything else. My daughter. Her lovely music. I love her so much, and I'm so proud.

But would I really want to preserve *this* moment? I've got a toilet brush in my hand and so many other problems. I think of Marianne – all those lost babies, all of her dreams slipping away. I feel desperately sorry for her – really, I do. It seems unfair that she's lost so much but is also the one who can save Jess. For a small price…

My eggs. My sister wants *my eggs*. I've been reading up on egg donation, trying to convince myself that it's no big deal. I've discovered so many stories – heartfelt and full of gratitude. Many women become donors for the money, of course, but there are altruists out there as well. Family members, friends, people who just want to help spread miracles in the world. Dave's right – it's not so different than people who donate bone marrow. And as for the recipients, many are survivors of cancer – or chemo. If Jess has a transplant, she'll have chemo first to kill her existing cells. Someday she might be in Marianne's position right now.

So many beautiful stories… so much love. And now, I have a chance to be one of those women who multiply that love. One of those women who give instead of just take. So what's stopping me?

I scrub so hard that the handle of the brush starts to loosen. The beauty of the music is a direct counterpoint to my thoughts. Rightly or wrongly, I *know* what's stopping me.

Marianne deceived me – lied to me. I went to her beautiful home and told her my story and what I was trying to achieve. I was open and honest. She listened sympathetically and said that she would help. She led me to believe that her motives were purely altruistic. At any time, she could have told me what she wanted, but instead, she chose to keep her secrets. What kind of woman does that make her?

Her father's daughter, that's who. If Marianne has a baby with my eggs, she will be part of my life forever. A constant reminder of my dad's other life – or lives. One relationship built on lies and deceit is surely enough for a lifetime. The last thing I need is another.

Jess gets to a tricky measure, stops, plays it again. Slowly, one note at a time, and then over and over. When she was first starting out, she was always trying to play pieces that were too difficult, and she would get frustrated. She'd practice the same measure over and over again until it became effortless. It was a measure of her stubbornness, her indomitable will. Her teachers were amazed at her focus because most kids would rather just play the easy parts.

Gripping the toilet brush like a talisman, I listen to her struggling with the difficult intervals. *Willing* her to achieve it so that she can end the practice session and have a rest. Maybe that will be the moment that I go to her. Tell her the brilliant news. Watch her face light up with love, hug her frail body to mine. That will be the moment to preserve and treasure. The true moment of hope.

Because I know what my decision is.

I will donate my eggs.

Gladly, freely.

I will give Marianne whatever she wants. I will do anything – pay a price above rubies – if only Jess can be granted the time to perfect this one measure, this one piece, and all the others she wants to learn. I will do the kind, selfless thing and help my sister achieve her miracle.

I put down the toilet brush and pat my pocket for my phone. It's not there – I must have left it downstairs. I'll call Marianne now and tell her my decision: make it official – no going back. We can get the arrangements underway. I'll probably have to have some injections to stimulate my ovaries or something. The idea makes me feel a little sick. *It's no different than giving bone marrow*, I remind myself sternly. That, too, is an invasive process. I'd be a hypocrite to worry—

Everything has gone quiet. Too quiet. There is none of Jess's usual humming, no sound of the pages turning or the squeak of rosin against her bow. Just… nothing.

"Jess…" I call out.

But somewhere inside of me, I already know.

I run to her room. Jess is lying on the floor, her violin beside her. One of the strings is broken. A howl rises in my throat. Her breath is thin and raspy, her pulse racing beneath her impossibly pale, bluish-tinged skin. She is writhing around, struggling to breathe. It's almost like she's having… a seizure. Oh God, not that. One of the rare side effects of her treatment is life-threatening seizures. She starts to choke. "Mom!" she gasps. "I can't—" Her eyes roll up into her head. It's like I'm watching the last electrical impulses animate her body before they leave it for good. And I have no idea what I can do – what I should be doing to help her.

"Jess!" I wail. "Hang in there."

I rush back to the door. "Becky!" I yell. But Becky isn't home. Nor is Steve. I curse myself for leaving her even for a second, but I have to go downstairs to find my phone. I skid down the last few steps. I can't find my phone, but Becky's is lying on the table by the door – she's never without it, so she must have grabbed mine by mistake. I type in her code, but it doesn't work. Frantic, I throw it down and run to the kitchen to dial 911. By the time I'm done speaking to the dispatcher, I'm shaking and crying. The ambulance takes over twenty minutes to arrive. By then, Jess is almost completely non-responsive.

Please, please, I beg anyone and no one. *Please give me another chance. I'll do anything.*

The ambulance speeds through the rush hour traffic, but every second feels like an eternity. I know then that *anything* should have included inviting Marianne over days ago – as soon as she arrived in California on her business trip. I shouldn't have relied on the fact that Jess's meds seemed to be working. I shouldn't have relied on Dave to create a second miracle. It's my delay, my waffling, that has caused this to happen. As soon as I heard Marianne was a match, I should have been on the phone immediately. The fact that I wasn't is simply and utterly… unforgivable.

Two hours later, Jess is hooked up to five different machines and has been given a blood transfusion and a cocktail of intravenous medications. Steve has come and gone, having to return for his second shift. The doctor has come and gone, and nurses come in periodically to take Jess's vitals. The doctor has confirmed that Jess had a seizure caused by her new meds. There's damage to her liver, and she might also have an infection. They don't know the cause of her sudden decline. But one thing is for sure, it's bad this time. Really bad.

As I sit in the darkened room next to my daughter, I take out my phone to call Marianne. I need to find out if she will come to the hospital to get started on the harvest protocol. She's a lawyer – she might want me to sign something about the egg donation first. Which is fine. I'll sign anything… right now. Except… It's only then that I realize that once again, I've waited too long. It's after midnight.

If I were Marianne, I wouldn't want me calling her up in the middle of the night. On the other hand, surely she'll want the news about the eggs as soon as possible…

As I'm debating what to do, another nurse comes in and checks Jess's vitals.

"You need to get some sleep," she says. "It's the best thing for both of you. The doctor will see you in the morning."

It's like she's dismissing me, though we both know that I won't be going anywhere. I'll be staying here, in the heavy wooden visitor chair, all night.

"Thanks," I say as she leaves the bay. "For trying to help."

The staff here are very friendly, and the nurses and I know each other. But I would do anything… *anything*… not to have to see them again. If Jess can survive this latest setback and have a successful transplant, then she can be safe and eventually lead a normal life. *If*.

I need to approach this cautiously so that I don't make Marianne angry. I decide to send her an email saying that I'm dreadfully sorry for how I've treated her and asking her to call me urgently. If she's up, then maybe she'll call tonight. We can have the conversation we should have had before – the moment I found out that we are sisters. Maybe she'll help me, and I'll help her. We're family.

It's only when I press the button and my fingerprint doesn't work that I remember I've got Becky's phone, not mine.

I try her old code again. It doesn't work. *Think*. What would she use? Her birthday, our address? I try both. A message comes up that if I enter ten incorrect passwords, the phone will be locked. I try 0000 and 1234. All rejected. I try her birth year. Nothing. Two more attempts. My hand begins to shake. I try Jess's birth year. Nothing. One more…

Jess's birthday – month and day.

The home screen comes on. Success!

I let out a long breath, then pull up Google to access my Gmail account. But the phone is already logged in to another Gmail account. It's for Becky_L_Woods911. I know that Becky has a school email account, but this is the first I've seen of this one.

I should log in to my own account. Becky is almost eighteen – well past the age that her mom should be snooping through her emails. She needs her privacy, and I need to trust her.

But I don't.

I open the account. On the screen are messages back and forth between Becky and one other person.

Marianne.

Dark spots cloud my eyes. I knew about the Facebook messaging, and I was prepared to accept it. But this is something else. The two of them are as tight as two peas in a pod. The most recent messages relate to "Meeting up". My pulse starts to race as I read the exchange – apparently, Becky wants to meet her on her own because "you know how Mom is".

Anger floods my veins. Another message catches my eye. One that Marianne must have sent when she arrived at the airport. It's entitled: "My confession". I open it and read…

My mouth opens and shuts. The penny drops as if from a great height, leaving a crater opening up at the top of my head.

Marianne doesn't want my eggs. In fact, she doesn't

want to have anything to do with me. Why use tired old forty-year-old eggs? Not when she can have delicious, ripe, eighteen-year-old ones.

Marianne wants to save my youngest daughter. In return, she wants the eggs of my eldest.

60

MARIANNE

I should have called first. Let Claire know that I was coming. The satnav beeps, and I turn onto her street. I don't have to do this – I can turn around now and go back to Dave's offices, finish my work, then get my flight and go home. I nestle that thought inside of me, cradling its possibilities. I slow down so I can see the house numbers.

The street is an eighties subdivision of boxy two-story houses that have mostly seen better days. I pass houses with too many cars and pickups in the drive, sagging basketball hoops, faded American flags, and garages filled with boxes and garbage cans. There are no trees, and the air seems thick, maybe from the smoke of wildfires out to the east. Like many people, I usually think of California as a garden paradise without the heat and dust. I guess my father couldn't make his one life stretch to give both of his families equal footing in the world. Claire might have had more of his affection, but we seem to have had more of his wealth. Did he see that as a fair trade?

Claire's house is painted yellow with blue curtains in the front window. A wheelie bin is blocking half of the driveway, which is empty. No car. I've come all this way, and it's a wasted trip.

I pull over to the curb and park a few houses away. My hands feel clammy as I keep gripping the wheel. I'll pull myself together and then call Claire.

She is my sister; we are family. We are part of each other's lives now and likely to become an even bigger part in the future. Bone marrow, eggs. Helping each other, giving life, creating a divine balance. At the end of the day, I have done nothing wrong.

Even if it feels like it.

The house to the left of Claire's has a "beware of dog" sign in the window and a Dodge Ram pickup in the driveway. On the other side, the neighbor's lawn needs mowing, and two kids' bikes are lying in the driveway. Is Claire friendly with her neighbors? Does she like living here? I've increasingly begun to wonder about the little mundane details of her life. Maybe I'll find out those things if I have a child using Becky's eggs. The baby will, after all, be Claire's grandchild. The idea makes me a little sick. If I used an anonymous egg donor, there would surely be less *baggage*.

On the other hand, my bone marrow will be inside her daughter. I've read that bone marrow transplants can skew the results of genetic tests. Companies like *MyStory* will not guarantee results to transplant recipients. Jess will be receiving my DNA. So it's all going to be a little bit incestuous no matter which way you slice it.

I take a few deep breaths and take out my phone to call Claire. But before I can do so, the garage door opens. It's chock full of things and probably hasn't fit a car inside for years. Half of it has been converted into a workshop or man cave with a big tool bench and various gardening and woodworking tools around it. I notice all this only for a moment because just then, a brown-haired girl with a backpack comes out.

Becky.

I recognize her from her photos on Facebook, but seeing her for the first time in the flesh is still somewhat of a religious experience. Her hair is lighter than in her photos, pulled back in a long, lustrous ponytail. She's a little bit plumper than I expected, but it could just be her jeans, which end a few inches short of her ankles, and the unflattering plaid man's shirt. Her face is round and pleasant, her mouth upturned like she might start laughing at any moment. She's no particular beauty, but she has a youthful radiance about her. Someday she'll meet someone, fall in love, have children, and hopefully, a nice life.

Unless something happens to spoil it.

A dizzying wave of uncertainty sweeps through me. It's one thing corresponding with an emotionally needy girl on Facebook and another to see her in person. She looks so *young*. She says she wants to help me and that donating her eggs when she turns eighteen is no big deal. But is she even old enough to make that decision?

Right now, Becky's life and her future are ahead of her, swirling with infinite possibilities. But if she chooses to help me, those possibilities will crystalize into an action that she will have to live with forever. What will her choice do to her relationship with her mother? And when the time comes for her to start her own family, will she come to regret her decision? Will she come to resent me and... our baby?

I don't have to do this. I can walk away right now. Cut my losses and disappear the way my father always did. Maybe that's why he chose a double life: to have an escape route, an exit strategy. Maybe I should take a leaf out of his book.

Becky wheels out a ten-speed bike. She's leaving… It's decision time – now or never.

"Becky!" I say, getting out of the car. "Hi. Sorry – I should have called first."

She frowns quizzically like she's trying to place me. It takes her a few seconds. Not the sharpest knife in the drawer, maybe, but when her brain catches up to her eyes, her whole face lights up.

"Marianne?" She cocks her head. "Oh my God, is that really you?"

"Yes, Becky." I take a few steps up the steep driveway towards her, smiling.

She leans her bike against the side of the garage and comes towards me. She looks much prettier – almost beautiful – when she smiles. I made a mistake with Claire of being too polite, too standoffish. I'm not going to make the same mistake here. So I continue towards her. And then, I open my arms.

Her clothes smell faintly of sweat, her hair of shampoo. She's solid and muscular rather than plump, I note – athletic beneath the too-big shirt and too-small jeans. Suddenly, there are a thousand things I want to say, starting with "tell me everything" and ending with "I love you." Instead, when we end the embrace, I settle for, "Are you going somewhere? I don't want to keep you, but I'd love to see you – like we'd planned. I had a free afternoon, so I thought I'd come by."

"I'm sorry I didn't text you," she says. "I was going to, but Jess is in the hospital. That's where I was going. It's bad this time."

"I'm so sorry!"

I have no right to be here in this family's time of crisis. I've been angry at Claire and hurt by her not being in touch. When in truth, I have no idea what she must be feeling and going through.

"Yeah. But it's great you're here." She beams. "You're the one who can save her. So it's perfect timing."

"Yes," I say. I want to believe that it's perfect timing: that things are happening the way they are meant to. I come into town like Jesus entering Jerusalem, perform a miracle, and everyone is saved. But I can't stop the ugly whispers of doubt. Until it's done, there are still many things that can go wrong.

She looks at me like she's expecting more of a response. I gather myself and smile. "I could give you a lift to the hospital," I say. "And maybe we could get a quick coffee on the way?"

"Yeah, that'd be great. I'm starving. We can go to Jan's Bakery." She eyes me up appraisingly. I'm ultra-conscious of my gray pinstripe suit and three-inch heels that make me look tall and thin. "Unless you don't eat carbs."

"I eat everything." I smile. "Jan's sounds great."

"OK. I just need to leave a note for Mom. In case she comes back. She took my phone by mistake. I'll just be a sec."

She takes her pack off one shoulder and goes back into the house through the garage. Other than her clothing, she seems mature for her age. I guess between having Claire for a mother and a sick sister, she's had to grow up. I feel protective of her, which only increases my animosity towards Claire. For seventeen years, Claire has had this lovely child, whom she labeled a "problem" and "useless". Claire doesn't appreciate what she has, and from where I'm standing – and despite my own blurry intentions – that's unforgivable.

A car comes down the road. It slows and begins to turn. I quickly walk to the edge of the driveway, staying just outside the garage. Despite the dry heat, I feel a chill sweeping through my veins.

It's Claire.

I glimpse her face through the windscreen. She recognizes me immediately. Something Becky said flashes through my mind. *She took my phone by mistake.*

Once upon a time, I was Daddy's girl. He called me his "Little Butterfly", his "Princess". Even if he sometimes missed my birthday or my ballet recital, and if he wasn't there to lecture my date for the prom, I knew that he loved me. First, best. And somewhere out there, across the country, there was another little girl whom he loved first, best. A little girl who is now a big girl, and surely we can find some common ground in the fact that we're related, with the same DNA in our cells and the same blood flowing through our veins. Surely... that's the way it should be.

But at this moment, as my sister parks her car in the driveway and flings open the door, I know that "should" has no bearing here. She's found the message I sent to Becky. She knows that I want to help save her daughter and what I'm asking for in return.

Claire's eyes meet mine. They are positively murderous.

61

CLAIRE

She's there. Standing in my driveway next to my open garage door and my daughter's bike. I only came home from the hospital to have a quick shower and change my clothes, but now that I'm here, I see that I've interrupted some kind of get-together between my dad's secret daughter and... her egg donor.

"Hello, Claire."

If she's nervous, if she feels even the slightest trickle of conscience at being here – uninvited – at my house, she doesn't show it. Becky's phone in my pocket feels almost hot, burning my skin. I had come to terms with the trade – my eggs for her bone marrow. Having made the decision, I was more than willing to go through with it. Or, I thought I was. But now that she's here, I'm blinded by everything except the anger. This woman stole my memories; she stole my dad. I'm not going to let her steal Becky too.

"This is a surprise." I walk past her into the garage and take out Becky's phone. I could call Steve. I could call Dave Steiner. I could call 911. And yet...

Jess is lying in a hospital bed. This woman is the key.

She's a match.

I want her to be a match. But when I spoke to the doctor, he said it hadn't been confirmed that the harvest could go ahead. They still need to run another test. Although I want feverishly to believe that my prayers are answered, there's a seed of doubt in my mind. All the other leads have come to nothing. Then all of a sudden, Dave Steiner waltzes into my life and then Marianne – with her immaculate house, high-powered job, and charm bracelet that matches mine. At this moment, I'm seeing her for what she is. A fraud, an imposter. She's Dad all over again. She hid her intentions while worming her way into Becky's affections. I can't have her in our lives. There has to be another way.

I stop just inside the garage opposite Steve's work-bench. All of his tools are there. A vice, screwdrivers, hammers on a rack, a saw that he bought to fix the back-yard fence.

"Claire…" she says again, softly. "You heard that I'm a match, right? Everything is going to be fine now."

I turn slowly, teeth clenched.

"Why do you care?" I say. "Surely Jess is too young to donate her eggs, and if she has chemo, then they'll be no good anyway. But if she dies – which, as things stand, she's going to – maybe I can interest you in another body part? A kidney, maybe – or a cornea? Or maybe they will let you have her eggs once she's dead. I don't know – I've never asked."

Stop! – this is all wrong. I must stem the tide of awful, ugly feelings. I might be doing irreparable harm. *Jess*…

But Becky matters too. I think of her energy, her strong will, her desire to grab onto life with both hands. I love her. I have to protect her.

Marianne takes a step towards me *into* the garage. My

whole body goes rigid. I inch over to the workbench. There's a single hammer lying on top. I grab it – I should hang it back on the rack. I keep it in my hand.

"I want to help Jess," Marianne says, her voice tightening. "Did you hear what I said? I'm a *match*."

"It's too high a price. Becky's too young to make that kind of decision. I'm not going to let you ruin the life of one daughter to save the other."

"Claire," she says gravely, "I know you're under a lot of stress. I want to help."

"You can have *my* eggs." I look down at the hammer that I'm still holding. The smooth handle, the ugly iron claw. It's heavy in my hand. I need to put it down. "I'll give them to you – freely, gladly. They might be old and tired, but they were good enough to make two great kids. Take all of them. But I won't let you take Becky's."

"Let's just do the bone marrow transplant. We can talk about this another time. When Jess is well again—"

"Mom?" A voice comes from the kitchen door behind me. Small, scared. For a second, I almost think it's Jess: the way she sounded this morning when she woke up dizzy from the drugs. But this is not Jess. Even through the fog of rage and adrenalin, I know that.

"Go back inside, Becky," I say. "I'm dealing with this."

"Why are you holding a hammer?"

"Go inside!" I yell.

"No."

In a split second, Becky comes into the garage. Before I know it, she's got hold of my wrist and grabbed the hammer. I stare at her, her face morphing into something unfamiliar. Something strong and single-minded. I admire her for it.

"Stop it, Mom," she says. "Marianne is going to save Jess, and I'm going to give my eggs to Marianne so she can have a baby. It's totally the right thing to do. And then, I'm going to live in D.C. I'm done with this family. I'm done with all of this." She sweeps the hammer in front of her.

"Becky," Marianne says in a soft voice, "you don't have to take sides."

"Move out of my way, Becky," I say. "I want her gone from my house and our lives."

"No." Becky's eyes meet mine. But she is not the enemy here.

I step forward. I'm going to remove Marianne from my garage. I shoulder past Becky. I'm going to—

I blink. Once, twice…

It all happens in slow motion. Becky lurches to the side, but her bicycle is there on the floor of the garage. Her foot tangles, and she crashes to the ground. The hammer skitters to the floor. She falls onto it.

Marianne screams, but I don't see or hear her.

All I can see is the limp body of my daughter and the pool of blood that is slowly forming around her head.

62

As I speed off in the ambulance holding my daughter's hand, I wonder how I could have been so stupid. I should have made the bargain, paid the price – anything to avoid being right here, right now.

"Her blood pressure's dropping; we're losing her." One paramedic pushes past me to adjust the fluid drip as the other scrambles to get out the defibrillator. Everyone seems to be moving in slow motion, backward almost. If only they could turn back the clock – why can't they turn back time so that none of this ever happened?

It's too late for bargains. Much, much too late. The grip on my hand loosens, then goes limp. I want to scream, but my throat is dry.

The paddles are placed on Becky's chest. Her body jerks as the current racks through. Once, twice. I can't hear what they're saying. Black spots appear before my eyes. A voice whispers in my head that I can't silence. *This is all your fault. You killed her.*

We arrive at the hospital. The gurney is unloaded, and the medics push it inside almost at a run. I've been here so many times with Jess that it's almost become routine. Yet now, everything seems new and terrifying. I think of Becky when she was born: a tiny, red-skinned baby with a screwed-up face and a scream that made it her against the world. A difficult child, and although I loved her, I was too overwhelmed to appreciate her. I've never stopped being overwhelmed by her. I'm her mom – I should have done better.

Marianne is desperate to have a baby – to go through all the pain, joy, and bitter heartbreak that is parenthood. When she dreams of holding her own baby in her arms, she'll only be thinking of the joy. It's fallen to me, her sister, to show her the reality.

"Claire." Marianne comes up to me as I'm stumbling inside, gripping the wall, trying to make the world stop spinning. Becky is gone – I don't know which bay she's been taken to. Nurses and doctors rush past me like I'm invisible.

"I don't know what to do," I blurt out. "I've... I mean... oh God, what do I do?"

"You need to sit down. That's the first thing." She half drags me to the waiting area and maneuvers me into a chair. I sit, comatose. Around me, other people are living out their own tragedies. Someone is bleeding, someone is limping, a child is crying. An adult is slumped over in a chair.

Marianne leaves for a few minutes and comes back with a Styrofoam cup of steaming tea. My hands are shaking too hard to take it, so she sets it on the floor. She then goes up to the reception desk and talks to the person on duty. The tiny part of my brain that can think at all wonders if she's telling them that I pushed my daughter and ought to be arrested. Is that what's going to happen? Are police going to be involved? Am I going to jail? In a way, I hope I am. I deserve nothing better. My baby. My Becky. Through thick and thin, I've loved her. I think she knows that, but I can't be sure. I'm constantly telling Jess that I love her, but when was the last time I told Becky? When was the last time I went into her room when she was asleep, smoothed back her hair, and kissed her the way I used to? Why did I stop? How could I have given up on *us* so easily?

Tears are rolling down my cheeks when Marianne comes back over.

"They're taking her to the ICU," she says. "They need to check for bleeding on the brain."

I turn away and cry harder. Marianne sits down next to me. When she puts her arms around me, I don't pull away.

"This is all my fault, Claire," she says. "I wish I'd never taken that DNA test. I wish none of this had ever happened. I wish… a lot of things."

"It's not your fault," I sob. "I was the one who…" I can't say the word.

"It was an accident. That's what I told them. We were all in the garage talking together, and Becky tripped over her bike. I hope that's OK."

"You shouldn't lie on my behalf." I pull away. "I'm not asking you to."

"I saw it happen," she says firmly. "Becky tripped."

"I meant what I said. I'll give you my eggs. Or you can have Becky's if she dies." I slump into the chair and close my eyes. I wish that the earth would open up and swallow me. For so long, I've been fighting. For Jess, for my marriage, against Becky, against Marianne. Now, though, I've had enough. There's no fight left in me.

"No," Marianne says. "I don't want that. Not now." She looks stricken – the mask finally slipping enough so that I can see the grief that's behind it. I *see* her for the first time. I *see* myself in her eyes. All the fear and all the regrets. But the hope too, and the capacity for love. I wish I'd acted differently. I wish it was not too late to make things right.

Marianne goes off, taking charge of other things. Calling Steve. Calling Dave…

"Ask him to come here if he can." I gather all my energy to speak. "Please. I've asked him to look into something for me. It will probably come to nothing, but it might affect you too. I…" I shake my head, disgusted with myself. "I should have told you."

"What is it?" Her mask of calm is in place, but her voice holds a note of concern.

"The other charms on the bracelet," I say. "What do you think they mean?"

She frowns. "My father said they were from places that were special to him."

"Special to him?" I'm sure he never used those words when he gave me a new charm. "And the dolphin charm? Becky told me that you don't have it."

"Our father had two lives," she says. "But he also had two deaths. According to my mother, he died of a heart attack. That's what she was told. But there's no mention of that on the death certificate."

I nod dumbly, but there's no sense to be made of any of it.

"What have you asked Dave to do?"

I take a breath. "The last charm came from Key West, Florida. I've asked him to see if either of us have any close DNA matches there."

She stares at me. "So you think he had… another family?"

"I don't know," I say. "It's a long shot. All I know is that our dad might have been a liar, but the DNA test tells the truth."

"I just feel so… angry." She turns away from me.

"Me too," I say. "But I see now that there's no benefit in hiding from the truth. In fact, if I'd faced up to it sooner…"

The awful scene plays itself in my mind again like a horror movie. Marianne, Becky… the pool of blood. Saliva floods my mouth – I'm going to be sick. This… thing… my life… it's not a horror movie. It's real.

"Claire!" The vision shatters as Steve storms into the waiting area. His face is rigid with anger. I sense the bridges we've been building breaking up like matchsticks and floating away downstream. He doesn't know what happened, but already I can see an inferno of blame flaring in his eyes.

I am infinitely grateful that Marianne takes charge once again. There are introductions, explanations. She repeats her story about Becky tripping over the bike. I want to say something – to tell Steve the truth. I was trying to force my sister off the property. Becky got in my way, and I shoved her aside. It's all my fault.

I can't speak or move. Steve is talking to me, but it's like I'm hearing him through water. The room spins again. A doctor comes over. I hear a few words. "Critical condition", "Induced coma", "Wait and see".

But I can't *wait and see*. Not this time. The world tips and then, mercifully, goes black.

63

MARIANNE

I wouldn't wish what's happening on my worst enemy – or my long-lost sister. It all seems surreal, like I'm watching my own life unfold around me. Claire blames herself, but the fault surely lies with me. But what good is blame and fault in this situation? Life happens. Life can be terrible.

A nurse comes over to revive Claire when she faints. When she finally comes to, she's listless and unresponsive. Steve is clearly a man on the brink of total self-destruction – trying to demand answers from doctors and nurses who have none to give.

At first, I stay with them, trying to be supportive yet unobtrusive. But when Claire and Steve are finally allowed in to see Becky, I hang back. I have no right to stand with my sister at the bedside of her child, so I decide on a different course of action. I slip out and find Jess's ward. I flag down her doctor and demand that he speaks to me. I tell him that I'm a match and that I want to start the harvest procedure. Now. Today.

I'm expecting to be fobbed off – hospitals are busy places, and I don't have an appointment. But luckily, the doctor is switched on enough to make things happen. I'm ushered into a room where I'm given yet another blood test. We talk about tentative schedules and procedures, then I proceed to make some calls. I call work and tell them I need to take a few weeks of medical leave. I leave a voicemail for Tom telling him that I'm extending my trip – indefinitely. Last but not least, I call Dave. He's in a meeting, but I leave a message with his secretary about what's happening.

When eventually I go to find Claire and Steve again, I feel relieved that I've taken some action. I don't want Claire's gratitude or even her acceptance. I just want to be there in case she needs me. And I want to save her daughter.

The hours stretch on. Claire and Steve are with Becky, and I don't want to disturb them. I go down to the hospital store and buy some snacks and provisions. Then I return to Jess's ward. I'm hoping that I might be allowed in to see Jess – I tell the duty nurse that I'm her aunt. The woman frowns and asks me to wait. Then she makes a call. I'm surprised when a few minutes later, Jess's doctor comes down the corridor and over to me.

"Mrs. Weissman," he says. He puts on a pair of wire-rimmed glasses and looks down at his clipboard. "I'm glad to have caught you."

"Yes…" I say, suddenly desperate to make this happen. "Did you rush the bloods? Can we start the harvest protocol this week, like we discussed?"

"We confirmed that you are a match," he says.

"That's brilliant." Even though I know this already, I feel almost dizzy with joy. I can save my niece! I can make Claire happy. My sister needs me!

The doctor looks at me over the rim of his glasses. He does not look ecstatic. He takes a long time to respond.

Too long…

"Mrs. Weissman, I'm afraid that you can't do the harvest at this time. There's a… complication. That's what the blood test today confirmed."

"What?" The breath freezes in my lungs. That's the thing about giving blood – you do it for one reason, but you never know what they might find. Am I sick? Dying?

I don't realize that I've voiced my concerns aloud until the doctor shakes his head.

"You're not sick or dying," he says. "The opposite, in fact. You're… pregnant."

"No!" I shore myself up against the wall. "How long?"

"About six weeks. You'll need a scan to confirm the exact dates. But I'm afraid you can't donate blood or bone marrow while you're pregnant. It might be detrimental both to you and the baby."

Six weeks. I don't need to be a mathematical genius to do the sums. The last IVF failed. I haven't slept with Tom for a lot longer than that. It was around six weeks ago – mid April – that Tom saw the egg donation information on my screen. Around the time that I allowed another man into my life, if only for a short time. *Beautiful, special…* The baby is not Tom's. The *baby…* I place my hand on my belly.

The doctor is still talking. The words float over my head. Because suddenly, the elevator door opens. A man steps out into the waiting area.

"Marianne? Are you OK? Where's Claire?"

Inside of me, I feel *something* bloom like a firework.

"Hi Dave," I say. "I'm glad you came. I know it will mean a lot to Claire."

"Sure…" he looks at me, then at the doctor. "Now, what's going on?"

Maybe it's something in Dave's manner – the way he

puts his hand low on my back – but the doctor gives me a long, knowing look. "Good luck, Mrs. Weissman," he says. Turning, he walks off down the corridor.

I don't even realize that I'm unsteady on my feet until Dave grabs me by both arms. "Marianne?" I lean on him, and he helps me to a chair.

"I'm a match for Jess," I say, breathless. "But I can't do the harvest."

Dave sits down next to me. The fondness in his gaze turns cool. "Come on, Marianne," he says. "I know there are some things that need to be ironed out between you and Claire, but I really think you should reconsider."

"No. It's not that. It's a… medical complication. Something I never suspected." I take his hand in mine and look him straight in the eye. "You're a miracle worker, Dave. You've proved that time and time again. You've made me feel… well… let's just say that when you came into my life, you were exactly what I needed, right when I needed it. And I'll always love you a little for that."

His eyes widen and then soften. "I love you too. A little. You know that."

A tear rolls down my cheek. I let him wipe it away. But this is not about Dave and me. Before he can make any further move to draw me close, I hold up my hand.

"The thing is, Dave, that right now, you need to be working another miracle. Claire told me what she's asked you to do. Is there a result yet?"

"If there is," he says, "do you really want to know?"

"No – not really." I put my hand reflexively on my belly. "But tell me anyway."

64

CLAIRE

"I'm so sorry, Claire."

Each time someone says those words to me, I want to scream. This time though, I dig deep inside myself to come up with the right response.

"No. It's wonderful news. I'm so happy for you."

There will be no "eggs for marrow" trade. There will be no saving Jess – or Becky. I'm going to lose them both. I've spent my precious time worrying, complaining, getting through each day, and all along, it was written in the stars. All my hopes – the ones I had for Jess and the ones I should have had for Becky – are gone.

As their lives end, there will be new life. A miracle child for Marianne after all those miscarriages and failed rounds of IVF. I am happy for her. I focus my mind on that tiny green shoot of good in the world. What else can I do?

"No, Claire. This isn't right. I'm a match for Jess, and I told you that I wanted to help. I can consider… I mean…"

Her hand is on her belly. She looks stricken but determined. "A… termination." She practically chokes on the word.

"What?" I stare at her, sure that I've misheard.

"I've done it before," she says. "When I was seventeen. I got pregnant, and my mother forced me to have an abortion. It may not have been the physical reason for all my failures, but it was the psychological reason. This pregnancy will probably be no different."

For the first time, I see into her soul. I've judged her as being privileged and entitled. A spoiled woman who needs a child to complete her perfect life. But now I see what's behind it all. Guilt. Guilt that has changed her, shaped her over the years. Deep and indelible, like the scars of a glacier.

I push through my own cloud of pain and reach out and take her hand. Her skin is soft, her nails a little ragged like she's been biting them. My sister. I squeeze her hand. "It is different," I say. "This could be the one. It *will* be the one."

"But I promised." She wipes a tear from her cheek. "And I've been so selfish – monstrous! I mean, to have approached Becky! She's seventeen, just like I was. Just as vulnerable. I can't imagine what possessed me to do that – to turn into my mother!"

"You're not your mother," I say. "And you acted out of desperation. I know what that feels like."

"Maybe it's…" she sputters, "the only way to set the balance right."

"No," I say, leaning in close to her. The truth of what she's offering – and what I'm refusing – breaks through the fog like a beam of sunlight. "I don't believe that. And what's more, I will not trade a life for a life. If I've learned one lesson from all this, it's got to be that. We may share a dad and half of our DNA, but that's a line that can't be crossed."

She turns away, overcome by emotion. I can imagine

them all: guilt, relief, joy, sorrow. All the emotions of motherhood. Regardless of her mistakes, she's earned them.

"Dave can find another donor," she says. "He found me – there will be others."

"Yes." I don't bother to argue. We both know it isn't going to happen.

She squeezes my hand and then lets go. She's full-on crying now. I don't want to cry because if I start, I will never stop. But my eyes betray me, prickling, welling up. I feel her arms wrap around me, our tears mingling together, warm and wet. It feels so wrong and yet so right. It feels like we will never stop.

———

I sit by Becky's bedside, watching the rise and fall of her chest, the faint line blipping on the monitor. I hold her hand until the nurse practically drags me away. "Time for a break, Mrs. Woods," she says.

I nod dumbly. My break consists of walking to the end of the corridor and riding the elevator down two floors to Jess's ward. They've offered to move Jess and Becky to the same ward to make it easier for me. But I've said no. I need to keep them separate, like the two different people they are. If I didn't have that walk and ride on the elevator, I think I would be absolutely crazy. Not that I'd be able to tell the difference.

I stumble into the ward. Steve gives me a stony stare and gets up – his turn to sit by Becky's bedside. He blames me for what happened. *I* blame me too.

I go into Jess's room. Her little body is barely more than a lump under the green waffle blanket. She looks so small – she's deteriorating by the day. Her platelet regeneration count is almost zero. Her body is slowly shutting down, like candles on a birthday cake being blown out one by one. I brush the hair back from her face, feeling a blinding rush of love. I am so grateful for the time I've had her in my life. She came from my body, and she will return there, curled up not inside my belly, but inside my heart. There she will live forever, free from pain and death. I feel a quieting sense of calm knowing that.

I sit by her bedside, reach out and take her hand. She stirs at the touch, and her eyes flutter open. "Mom?" she says. "Are you OK?"

Given everything that she's going through, it hurts to hear her ask this. When her light goes out for good, what a loss it will be to the world. I swallow back another tide of tears. If ever I needed to be strong for her, it's now.

"I'm fine, honey. Did you have a good sleep?"

She nods. "Is Becky OK? Has she woken up yet?"

"Not yet. But soon, I hope." The lie is a balm. It soothes.

"Marianne came in to see me. She says she's having a baby. That's so great, isn't it? I'll have a cousin. Is that right?"

"Yes, that's right." I smile for dear life.

"I told her that if it's a boy, she should name it Daniel. Then he'll be strong, like a lion. If it's a girl, then Ruby. Red, like a heart."

"Did you? Those are good names."

Her grip when she squeezes my hand is surprisingly firm. "I'm so glad that you have a sister, Mom," she says. "It's the best thing in the world."

"Maybe. At least until you have a child."

"Yeah, when I'm older." Her smile broadens. "Becky said that if my eggs don't survive the treatment, then, someday, I can have hers."

"She did?" I sit back, stunned. My daughter – the one I never appreciated – is so caring, so selfless. Unlike… me.

"Yeah. Someday." Her eyes flutter and close, making small crescent moons. Her breathing evens out. In spite of everything, Jess still believes. Maybe… I can too?

From behind me, a hand rests on my shoulder. "Claire." Marianne's voice is soft. "Can I get you anything?"

"No."

"I'm getting you some tea. I'll be right back."

"OK. Thanks."

It's a strange feeling – one I never expected to have. My heart is cracked wide open. Because of that, there is finally space inside. For my *sister*.

65

In a way, Jess is right. It could almost be the best thing in the world. For the last few days – or maybe it's weeks, I've lost track – she's been here. Steadying me when the doctors bring bad news. Making me cups of hot chocolate and sweet tea. Calling Dave to see if there are any new leads, helping to smooth things over with Steve.

She endures my rollercoaster of moods and emotions. Sometimes I give her the silent treatment. Other times, I scream at her to go away. She occasionally leaves, going outside to the corridor until the storm passes. Then, she comes back, and I get up and beg her forgiveness. Maybe this is the pattern we would have followed if we had grown up together. But somewhere along the way, when she keeps refusing to leave – staying at my side, stalwart, when everyone else has deserted me – things begin to change.

In between my rages and silences, my agony and resignation, there is space for us to talk. She tells me about her childhood and about her mother, who seems to be an unhealthy mixture of traditional mom and overbearing control freak. She tells me more about the abortion that she's regretted every day of her life. And when she cries over all the lost embryos – which she sees as babies – I hold her like a sister. I stroke her hair, comfort her, and tell her that everything is going to be OK. I actually almost believe it.

On other occasions, she shares with me her memories of *our* dad. Good ones, like going to the beach at Chesapeake Bay and Newport News, weekend trips to Williamsburg, Mount Vernon, and Monticello. He usually was around for her birthday, the occasional 4th of July, and every other Easter. Marianne didn't idolize Dad the way I did, but his absences did make her heart grow fonder. She tells me about the bad times: missed school plays, missed graduations, missed Christmases and other holidays. She describes the rage she felt, the deep-seated ache in her stomach whenever he would leave. Of never quite understanding why he was there so little when she missed him so much. And then, the euphoric rush each time he came back…

It's like she's describing my life for me. I tell her my memories too – the flip side of the same coin. I usually had him at Christmas, and Easter wasn't a big deal in our house. I felt the same rage, the same euphoria. Her feelings are as familiar as my own reflection.

"Why do you think he did it?" I ask her the million-dollar question. "Was he just a thrill-seeker? Did he do it just because he could?"

"Maybe," Marianne says. "Or maybe it's possible to love two people – or more. To want to have two lives and not have to choose."

I close my eyes – I've been so long without sleep that I can barely keep them open – and consider this.

"Maybe. But most people have to choose. It would have been the right thing to do."

"If he had chosen us," she says, "then he would have been on the other side of the country from you. You wouldn't have had him half the time. Do you think that would have been better or worse?"

"I don't know. I mean, I loved him so much. It would have messed me up if he'd have left. But it might have been better for Mom. She could have moved on."

"My mom cut him out of all the old photos," she says. "I guess she would have been better off without him. But as for me... I'm not sure."

"The bastard," I say, cracking the first smile all day.

She laughs. "I'll second that."

I open my eyes as another thought occurs to me. "What about Dave?"

She gives a little start. "What about him?"

"Don't you think he's kind of similar to Dad? I mean, he's got that charming quality in spades. You want to like him. Or – at least, I do."

"Maybe... though I've definitely never seen him as a father figure." For the first time ever, I see her blush.

"I heard that his marriage is on the rocks." I study her closely. "I feel bad that he's always been there as a friend to me, and I wasn't there for him."

"Oh, well," she says breezily. "He's a grown man. I guess for his wife, living with a Messiah can't be easy."

"I guess not." I stare at her as her hands automatically move to her belly, cradling the life inside. There is something she's not telling me. I decide to let it go. I haven't earned the right to all of her secrets just yet. But I hope that in time, I will.

66

MARIANNE

I've never been a believer in strength through adversity, but the days I spend with my sister make me a convert. I get to know Claire, and what's more, I come to respect her. She's going through the worst time of her life – a lot of it because of me – and yet, once we start talking, I discover the depths of her pain and the heights of her spirit. United as we are in our desperation, I begin to see a hazy reflection of a half of myself that I didn't know existed.

It's not all plain sailing. Her moods and rages lacerate my self-confidence. It's clear that she hasn't forgiven me over my approach to Becky – and I can hardly blame her – I haven't forgiven me either. It also hurts when she gets resentful of my memories, and neither of us is going to get over the pain of our father's betrayal overnight. Most of all, she's on the brink of losing her babies: now Children Nos. 1 and 2. Despite my own suffering, I can't imagine that sort of pain. I would help bear the burden of it if I could, and when I offer to terminate my pregnancy to save Jess, I want to mean it. Abraham, when tested by God, was willing to sacrifice his son Isaac to atone for the sins of the world. I've always thought that God must have been a little horrified that Abraham would really go through with it. And when Claire, too, is horrified and tells me that she would never trade one life for another, that's the moment when both of us gain something unexpected. Each other.

All life is precious and unique. It's only now that I've met Claire that I truly realize it. Before, I had convinced myself that once I atoned for my mistake, I would be entitled to a child. Entitled to the perfect life that my mother envisioned for me. Now I see that I felt the loss of my embryos more as a failure than anything else.

Claire's ordeal has made me understand that motherhood is not about the mother at all. It's about bringing a tiny life, a new spirit into the world and loving and nurturing it for whatever it is, and for however long it blesses you with its presence. It's about being grateful for every moment, even when it's cut short. I know that Claire wishes she'd done things differently – felt differently, acted differently. She's staring down into a chasm of guilt, and I know how that feels. I'm beginning to see that it's those feelings that define motherhood. The darkness is a necessary part of the light.

When I lay my hand on my belly, I feel that sense of joy and fear in a new way. *My baby*. Yes, I've been here before. I've had embryos implant and then lost them. Embryos – because that's what they were. They were not babies – I see that now. They were tiny and precious spirits and sparks, but they were not babies. And as much as I don't want to tell myself that this one, conceived naturally with a man who is not my husband, is different, it *is* different. I don't want to hope, and yet, I can't stop hoping. That, too, is part of motherhood.

I haven't told Dave about the baby. Nor have I said anything to Tom. Tom and I had our chances, but those ran out years ago. I kept clinging to my marriage, like a limpet to a rock, in part because I didn't want to lose Tom the way I lost my father. Talking with Claire has also helped me see that. Although I haven't made any decisions yet, I'm now contemplating life without him. It's scary. It's liberating…

My focus now is on preserving the life inside of me – the miracle life. A unique and never-to-be-repeated combination of human DNA and stardust. A life that I didn't ask for and maybe one that I don't deserve. But I'll take it, just the same.

Dave sends me a few texts that I don't show to Claire. *We've been triangulating your results in Key West and also in Hawaii.*

The charm bracelet cities. Pandora's box is open. What will it reveal?

And:

Got a strong possible lead.

And:

Give Claire my love – thinking of you both.

Thanks, I will. I reply to this latest message. Claire is fond of comparing Dave Steiner to our father. Maybe I should find the idea disturbing, but I don't. I can see how our mothers fell for that kind of man. A man who's full of a rare spark of life – the kind who tears you apart when he leaves and lifts your heart when he returns. A man who could be the boy next door or could be a film star; you never quite know which. A man like that is also the father of my secret child. Dave may succeed in making a global DNA database that's bigger than Facebook – or, he may not. All I know is that he's given me a wonderful gift. His DNA. His ancestry. There's a kind of secret poetry in that.

Now, if only he can produce a gift for Claire too… That's what I'm hoping for.

A doctor comes into the waiting area. Jess has had another transfusion, but her organs are shutting down. The doctor tells Claire that she needs to prepare herself. Call Steve, get him here. Prepare to say goodbye.

Claire nods, but she doesn't cry. When I first met her, I might have seen that as a sign of coldness and lack of feeling. I know now that it's a sign of strength. She has a core of steel, but one that's glowing and warm. She feels everything just as deeply as if she was leaking tears right and left – like I would be.

I bow my head and pray for God to create a miracle and save Claire's daughters. But in the absence of a miracle, there is one last hope. While Claire is talking to the doctor, I take out my phone and send a text.

Come on, Dave. It's now or never.

67

BECKY

It's a beautiful dream. I'm floating on a warm, gentle sea with Mom's voice in my ear, telling me how much she loves me, how sorry she is, and how everything is going to be OK. She tells me that she's proud of me: proud of my energy and enthusiasm, proud that I'm always trying new things, proud that I tried to help out the family. Things I'm sure she's never said in real life. She tells me that I'm a special person and that I'm going to have an exciting future. I wonder if this is heaven because it can't be real.

"Please, Becky."

It *is* Mom's voice, high-pitched, frantic. Normal. The dream dissolves like a snow globe shattered on the floor, breaking into a million pieces. I am awake.

I hurt.

My head feels fuggy and heavy, but it's my body that aches the most. Like it hasn't moved in days. For a second, I wonder if this is a normal morning, with Mom spending an hour trying to coax me out of bed, going from calm and quiet, to busy and irritated, to full-blown yelling, depending on how long I take to get up. To be fair, it must be hard having to do that every day. It must be hard to feel like she can't trust me and has to constantly police me. I need to change all that. I should get up. Is it a school day or the weekend? Why don't I know? I *need* to get up and do something today to make someone proud, even if it's just me.

I hear a beeping sound and realize that I'm in a bed attached to some kind of monitor. This is not a normal morning. Mom is not telling me to get up for school. I'm in the hospital.

I start to wonder if this is all some kind of weird joke. That all along, it's me who's been sick, not Jess. Like that story where the man wakes up and finds that he's a cockroach. We read it in English class, but I forget the name. But no… I'm not the one who should be here. Memories begin to form like fragile soap bubbles.

A tall, dark-haired woman in the garage. Mom with a hammer. And then, the world starts to tilt.

The room comes gradually into focus. The fluorescent lights, the acoustic tiles. Voices, breathing machines, monitors.

And then, another sound. "Becky? Oh, Becky. My darling…"

Mom's voice again. I reach out, desperate to see if she's really there.

"Mom?"

My hand is heavy as she takes it in hers. She kisses it, sobbing. Mom so rarely ever cries. Is it my fault that she's crying?

"What happened?" I say. But as soon as the words are out of my mouth, I know. The scene in the garage – it was real. Marianne, Mom. Me. She tried to move past me. I fell.

"I've been so scared. So scared that you wouldn't wake up. That I'd—"

"It wasn't your fault, Mom," I say. "It was mine. I shouldn't have gone behind your back. I shouldn't have done something that made you hate your sister. I should have minded my own business."

"No." She squeezes my hand. "I was in the wrong. I should never have taken my eye off the ball. And I should have handled things with Marianne very differently."

"You were trying to protect me." The words surprise me as they come out of my mouth, but I know they're true. "Trying to keep me from doing something stupid that I would regret later. But you know I was doing it to help Jess, right? And Marianne."

"I know, darling. You were caring and selfless. I love you so much for that. And I'm so glad that you're awake. You're going to be fine." She shudders. "But Jess…"

I tighten my grip on her hand. "Is she going to be OK? Is the harvest going ahead? Maybe if I talk to Marianne – if we talk to her together – we can work something out. It can't… end… like this." Tears fill my eyes. I wish I was asleep again, floating on the sea. Away from all this. But right now, I feel very wide awake.

"The harvest can't go ahead right now." Mom's voice is barely a whisper. "Marianne has a… health issue that means she can't be a donor at this time."

"What?" I try to sit up, but it's like the breath has been squeezed out of me. "No. She promised. Let me see her. I know that she'll—"

"She's pregnant," Mom says. "They won't do the harvest now. And Jess doesn't have months to wait. She's slipping away."

"No!" I sink back onto the bed. I was so *sure* – that one way or the other, Mom's sister was the key.

How wrong I was. *Stupid, useless…*

"You were right about her all along," Mom says. "She's a good person, and she's family – my sister. I should have appreciated and celebrated that. She even offered to…" Mom lets go of my hand "… to not have the baby. To do the harvest instead. But I couldn't let her do that. You understand, right?"

I shake my head as a great sob wells up inside of me. Marianne… offering to do *that* after everything she's been through. To give up her dream and the life inside of her to save my sister. And Mom… refusing to let her do it. Everyone making choices – right or wrong – but the only choices they could make. And still, we've failed. Why is life so unfair?

"Haven't we suffered enough?" The words slip out of my mouth. I don't know who I'm talking to – Mom, or God, or the universe, or myself – maybe all of them.

"I don't think that's how things work."

"Oh, Mom." I know she's right. "I'm so sorry."

"Jess is still alive," she says bravely. "And so is Marianne's baby. And you know what they say?"

"Where there's life, there's hope?"

"Yes. There's still hope. That's why I wanted so desperately for you to wake up. Because Jess needs you. More than any of us. You've always been her champion. The one she looks up to. I guess maybe—" she turns away a little "—I was jealous of that. All I'll ever be is her mom. But you're her sister. That's a different kind of closeness – I'm starting to see that now. There's room for both of us in her life. So much room for all that love."

I reach out for her hand, lacing my fingers with hers. When I look at her face – really look at it – it's like I'm seeing her for the first time. The lines near her eyes and mouth, the strength in her profile, the kaleidoscope of emotion in her eyes. I feel the hope like a force field around us. Things really can be better between us. I want that more than anything. Well, almost anything…

"I'm sorry it's taken me so long," she continues. "Much, much too long. But as for Jess, if the end is near, then I know you'll want to be there for her." She stares down at our entwined hands. "You'll want to say goodbye."

"No, Mom. It's not time for goodbye. Not yet." It has to be *true*. "But you're right. I do need to get up. I want to see her now. Spend as much time as I can with her."

"I can call the doctor. See when you're allowed to—"

"No." I withdraw my hand from hers. "I'm getting up. Now."

"But Becky, you can't—"

I push through the dizziness and force myself to sit up.

"At least let me get you a wheelchair or something."

"You'd better do it quick."

I don't know where all this strength is coming from. Maybe I needed to be in a coma to finally catch up on my sleep, or maybe getting a good knock on the head has made the "real Becky" come forward, stand up, and be counted. Now that I'm awake, it's like a fog has cleared from my mind. I'm going to turn my life around. I'm going to be a whole new me. Mom and I are going to be a whole new *us*.

And Jess isn't going to die.

The "new me" deflates. What am I going to do if Jess dies? I just can't fathom life without her. And the Bucket List! I can't fail at that too! My head is pounding. I probably should lie down again. But what if she's dying right now?

Mom comes back with a wheelchair. She's obviously

taken it from some corner or corridor somewhere because there's no nurse with her.

"I shouldn't be doing this." She confirms my suspicions that she thinks this is another one of my bad decisions. "You need to rest."

"I *need* to see Jess." The old Becky rises up inside me. I won't take no for an answer.

"OK. I know you do."

Every muscle of my body hurts as she helps me into the wheelchair. My head is throbbing, and I can't take a full breath. But if Mom is taking this much care over me, then things must be nearing the end. I chase the thought from my head. Things *are* serious. But this could also be the first step in our new relationship – one founded on love and respect. With everything that we've been through, I have to believe that it's not too late.

The ward is quiet as Mom wheels me through. I guess if anyone notices I'm gone, they'll raise the alarm. We reach the elevator without anyone stopping us.

"I'm just so glad you're awake," Mom whispers as we get in the elevator. "So glad that you'll get to see her before… the end."

"And there's really nothing else to be done? I can't believe that with modern science, they can't do *something*."

"She needs a transplant. It's a simple as that."

"And Dave can't help?"

"He's doing everything he can. I told him about the bracelet and—" she purses her lips "—my suspicions. Dad had two families, but he might have had more. Marianne said that the charms were from his 'special places'. Dave is focusing on all the people who have taken tests in those locations. But until his vision is realized – until everyone is on the database – then it's all potluck."

"I know, but—" I hate feeling this helpless.

"I think Dave feels guilty about how things turned out," she continues. "I know he's trying hard. But I don't want to get my hopes up."

"Sorry, Mom."

"No, don't be. I was going to say that I don't blame him for anything. In fact, I'm very grateful to him. He found Marianne. And of all the people I know – other than you – she's the one who has refused to give up. She won't let me sink away into grief. She's been like a hand reaching out to me in quicksand."

"I'm so glad." I was right about Marianne! Me – right!

"Well, it's still early days, and finding her was a shock. The last shock, I hope. I don't think I could take another one."

"Yeah. Me either."

As Mom wheels me off the elevator, the other elevator opens. And speaking of the devil, it is Dave Steiner.

Mom's face turns red. "Hi," she says, "thanks for coming." She leans in and gives him a kiss on the cheek.

"Claire," he says. "Um…"

I notice at the same time as Mom that he's not alone in the elevator. There's a tall, dark-skinned girl who looks a little older than me and a man with thick white hair.

Mom stares, her mouth gapes open. Of all the shocks we've suffered, this eclipses all others.

"Hi Claire," the man says.

They step out of the elevator. It's me who breaks the impossible silence. "Grandpa Joe? But you're… dead."

"Hello, Becky." His brown eyes twinkle. "Good to see you – my, how you've grown! And, as you can see, I'm very much alive."

68

CLAIRE

I stare at the man in front of me. A volcano opens up inside of me, ready to erupt. Rage, disbelief... delight.

"Dad?"

He holds up his hand as if to stave off an imminent attack. "Now, before you say anything," he says, "I can't stay. It's complicated, and I'm not supposed to be here."

I sense rather than feel Marianne coming up beside me, her shock mirroring mine. Our *dad*... Alive. I don't know how it can be. I don't know if I even want it *to* be. But I can't deny what I see with my own eyes. My heart is leaping inside my chest. I reach out and grab Marianne's hand as Dad continues to speak.

"I came in person because I wanted to introduce you to Alannah." He indicates the young woman standing next to him. "Your... sister."

Sister. I sway on my feet. To my surprise, it's Steve who comes up and takes my arm to steady me.

"You bastard," he says to Dad.

"I'm sorry, Steve. But like I've said, it's complicated. I

know that I haven't been what I seem, and for that, I'm sorry."

"Dad?" Marianne's voice is small and girlish.

"Oh, Marianne." Dad goes to her and opens his arms. "I'm so sorry."

"I… don't understand." Tears begin to run down her cheeks. He folds his arms around her. Seeing them like that, I don't know how to feel. I look away from them – directly at Alannah. She's a beautiful young woman who looks to be in her early twenties: a few years older than Becky. When she sees me glance at her, she immediately looks at the floor like she's hoping the room will swallow her up. As much as I want that too, I give her the faintest of smiles.

She looks up and smiles back. It lights up her whole face.

Dad and Marianne separate. Dave, standing by, clears his throat. "Joe," he says. "I think they deserve some explanation. Don't you?"

"Sure." Dad looks briefly at Alannah, then back at Marianne and me. "When you two were growing up, I was a salesman – like I said. But I was involved in other things too. Things – and with people – that I'm not proud of. A few years ago, I decided that I'd had enough. Enough of the lies and constantly having to look over my shoulder. You were all grown up and didn't need me. I wanted to be there for Alannah – and her mother." He hangs his head. "My third wife, Alison."

Marianne and I both look at him with horror.

"Third wife?" I practically choke.

"Yes, well… anyway… By that time, things had escalated. I was involved with some unscrupulous people that I couldn't extricate myself from. I had to disappear."

"So you faked your own death?" Marianne now sounds like the tough lawyer.

"Not exactly," Dad says. "I was a witness, giving state's evidence for a federal money laundering prosecution. I got a new identity, and I had to disappear. But not all the bad guys were rounded up – they never are. That's why I shouldn't be here. I'm taking a risk."

"You?" Steve snorts. "That's a good one."

"You might see me as one of the bad guys," Dad says. "And I'm not denying anything. I may have betrayed everyone I love. But I still love them."

I stare at him. "You don't know what love is. How can you?"

"Maybe I don't know how to give it, Claire, but I still know how to feel it. I feel it for you and Marianne and for my granddaughters. All I ask is that you don't visit the sins of the father on the daughter. Alannah is at the University of Florida. She took the DNA test quite innocently." He looks at Dave. "One of the free ones you handed out. I still don't know how you pulled a rabbit out of that hat."

"It was the bracelet," I sputter. "The charm you sent me from Key West."

"Ah," Dad says. "Yes." He glances sheepishly at Marianne. "I wanted to send both of you something to remember me by before the end. But the person – let's call him a client – who was helping me bungled it. He almost gave the game away by calling your mother too early, before we'd sorted out all the details. In the end, I couldn't risk sending you the last charm." He hangs his head like this is the greatest of his transgressions. "I'm sorry about that."

To her credit, Marianne doesn't react to the hang-dog look. "And the other charms?" she says. "Were they... your families too?"

"There were no kids from any other relationships."

Marianne looks at me. We both realize that the question hasn't been answered – or maybe it has.

"But they were special places to me," he adds.

Once again, my effervescence turns to rage. "How could you?" I clench my fists.

Dave steps between Dad and me, his body like a human shield. "Alannah has taken the test," he says. "She's a bone marrow match for Jess. Not perfect, but close enough."

"I want to help," Alannah says. Her eyes rest on Becky as if sensing an ally. "If I can."

"It's been hard on Alannah, too," Dad pipes in. "I've told her and her mom everything. No more lies. Not to my family, at least. So whatever I've done and whatever you think of me, it's off my chest."

"Good for you." Steve's voice is laced with sarcasm.

Dave turns to him. "Come on, Steve," he says. "Let's go find the doctor. Get the ball rolling."

For a second, I think that Steve is going to deck him – or Dad – or both. I can hardly blame him. Instead, he exhales sharply. "OK. Let's do it."

He lets go of me, his support immediately replaced by Marianne shoring me up. I feel like I am submerged in water. All of my thoughts are heavy and slow.

"Alannah," Marianne says. "I'm… so glad to meet you."

The relief is palpable. I don't know how Marianne does it or why my genetic make-up seems to include only the angry, comatose genes. But either way, I'm grateful to have her here. Her… and Alannah.

"I need to go," Dad says. "And I won't be able to contact you again. But Alannah's going to stay until the transplant is done. Dave says she can stay with his family."

"So... that's it?" The words tumble out of my mouth.

"Claire." He speaks the word softly. Hearing his voice... his beloved voice... The next thing I know, I'm in his arms. I breathe in the smell of him. I'm crying, and he's crying. It's messy and ugly, and I hate him, and I love him so much. I never want to let him go.

His arms loosen. He steps away, clearly overcome. Yet, somehow, he manages to give me that shining, utterly charming smile. There's not even a hint of apology in his face. Well, maybe a slight hint...

"Goodbye, Dad," Marianne says. "And good luck. I'm glad you're..."

But Dad has already stepped into the elevator. The doors close, and he's gone.

69

CLAIRE

"Mom?"

I am awakened by a movement, a sound, a word. Startled out of the nightmare that dissolves the minute I open my eyes. Light is streaming in through the window of the hospital room. Pure light... my daughter...

But Jess is not pure light. She's a girl. A girl who is getting her life back – today!

And suddenly, I want to stand up. Rip off the tubes, pick her up, whirl her around. But all being well, I'll have years to do that. Right now, we need to get through Day Zero. I will be with her for every moment.

"How are you feeling, darling?" I say.

"Good. I'm ready."

Jess is all eyes, alabaster skin, and bow-shaped mouth. Yesterday morning, her hair fell out in thick clumps after the long and arduous preparation that included chemo. Before the chemo, we arranged to have some of her ovarian tissue harvested in case she develops fertility issues later in life from the treatment. It's something that would never have occurred to me if it hadn't been for Becky and Marianne.

At this moment, she is very vulnerable. I am the only family member allowed into the room with her and only suited up in protective clothing and a mask. Her blood counts have bottomed out at zero. From here, however, we will be moving slowly but steadily upwards. This is something that I *know*.

The door opens, and a nurse wheels a stand into the room. "Look what we've got here!" she says. "Let's get this party started."

There is a plastic bag on the stand. It is yellow like chicken broth – like platelets. So ordinary, so innocuous. But that little bag contains the gift of life.

Over the last week, I have got to know Alannah. A lovely, warm-hearted young woman. I don't see her so much as a sister yet, but more as a lifesaver. The harvesting process was not easy on her – it's given her joint pain and headaches – but she's borne everything with a good spirit. Of course, I questioned her about Dad, but she couldn't tell me very much. When she was young, he used to travel a lot. Then he quit his job and now works as a dive boat operator. He's a good dad, but when he told her that he had other daughters who thought he was dead, she realized she didn't really know him. I told her not to be angry with him. I don't know where that came from, and I haven't had time to process my feelings. But the fact that Alannah is here – right now – is enough.

The nurse takes Jess's vitals. The doctor comes in and gives the green light. I grip Jess's hand tightly as they hook the tube up to her port. Together we watch as the life-giving fluid goes down the tube drop by drop and disappears inside of her.

There's a tap on the window. Both Jess and I turn to look.

Marianne is there, and Alannah, and Steve, and Becky, and Dave. All of them are grinning, all of them giving a thumbs up. I know that this is the beginning of the journey, and Jess will have a long road back. But this is the first step…

We are all taking it together.

EPILOGUE

ONE YEAR LATER

MARIANNE

"Look at him – strong as a little ox. I think he'll be flipping over and crawling soon. Then you'll be in trouble."

Dave Steiner pats your head with the fondness of a favorite uncle. Which, for all practical purposes, he is.

"I wonder if he gets it from his dad or from me…" I muse, a hint of a smile on my face. We're sitting on a picnic blanket by the water. It's a hot day, and the Potomac is a cool shade of green. There are lots of people around, some swimming, and some trying to launch canoes and kayaks. You are a big baby, and you hate being on your tummy. Dave's right – you probably will be flipping over soon so that you can lie on your back and see the world.

"You'll have to get his DNA on the database," Dave says with a smile. "Then, by the time he's old enough to know any better, he'll be able to connect with all of his cousins. It will be a different world by then, mark my words."

I pick you up and hold you close to my heart. I want to protect you from all of that as long as I can. At the rate *MyStory* is growing, it won't be long.

"Is your DNA on the database, Dave?" I say, offhandedly.

"Sure it is." He winks at me. "A man in my position has to practice what he preaches, right?"

"Right."

I look down at you, beaming a shining ray of love in your direction. I suppose that, eventually, your DNA will end up on the database. You'll want to know your story, and where you come from, and the stories behind the people whose blood flows in your veins. And when that happens, the CEO of *MyStory* will be in for a big surprise. But not yet. For now, you and I will keep our secret.

I haven't told Dave that you are his son. Dave has his own life, and he and his wife are apparently in the process of a reconciliation. I have my life, and now that I have you, I don't want to deal with things like paternity tests, custody arrangements, and settlements. I'm on my own now – as soon as Tom found out that I was pregnant, he announced that his "girlfriend" (of acrylic-nail-in-underpants fame) was also pregnant. Apparently, neither Tom nor I were infertile, just incompatible. I still think of all the other babies – your dead brothers and sisters – and feel the tears well up from the bottom of my soul. I lost them. But then you came along, my surprise baby and the love of my life. I have finally discovered for myself that life and motherhood are two things that were never meant to be perfect. They are messy, complicated, ugly – sometimes smelly, usually stressful, often lonely. They are truly and deeply a blessing.

"Argh! It's so cold!" Dave and I both turn towards the bank of the river. Two girls in bikinis are trying to get into a two-person kayak, and they've ended up capsizing it. Becky and Alannah, our new "family". When I count my blessings, they are near the top. The two of them are sharing an apartment a few blocks away from my house for the summer. Alannah is finishing up her last year at the University of Florida, and Becky is currently my part-time helper and will become your full-time nanny when the time comes for me to go back to work. The two of them are almost like sisters, and it's been lovely watching their friendship blossom and flower out of what, only a year ago, seemed like an impossibly twisted situation.

Someday, I'll tell you the truth of everything that went on. The things that were said and not said, the truths that are known, and those that still remain a mystery. What matters most is that we've gained a large extended family, and we love each other.

Claire came to visit twice in the last year, and Jess was well enough to visit once. We saw all the sights here and then went up to New York so that Jess could have a tour of Carnegie Hall. It's her dream to one day play her violin as a soloist there – a big dream – but those are the best kind. Jess is a lovely girl and so talented. I hope that someday you'll get to know her and love her as much as I do. Once, before you were born, Jess was very sick. I couldn't help her because you were growing inside of me. But Alannah came onto the scene, and now she's almost as much of a daughter to Claire and me as she is a sister. And if that sounds a little strange, let's just say that none of us are focusing on the past and where we came from. Just the present, and most importantly, the future.

We've met more of our DNA cousins, too. Some are related to all three of us by blood, and others to me and not them, and vice versa. But all of us share one thing in common. We are family in the ways that matter. We may not always see eye to eye, and we may hurt each other, but we help each other, too. Without asking and without demanding. Each of us *belongs* to something greater than ourselves. Together, we are more than the sum of our parts.

"You look tired, Marianne," Dave says. "I'll watch Daniel while you have a little rest. Then, I'll take you home so you can pack."

"Yes," I say. "I still need to do that." All of us are flying to California tomorrow for a special family celebration. *Family…* who ever would have thought?

I give you a kiss on the forehead and hand you over to Dave. He takes you with tenderness and care. With love, even. And at that moment, I wonder if perhaps he does suspect…

I lie back on the blanket and watch the clouds drifting overhead in the bright blue sky. "Thank you," I say to him.

"For what?" He gives me that cocky grin that takes years off his face. He may be a film star; he may be the boy next door. But most important of all, he's your father.

"Oh, nothing."

Smiling, I repeat my thanks – this time to you. *Thank you* for existing. For making my life perfectly imperfect. For finally making me complete.

CLAIRE

"OK, Jess, time to go. You all ready?"

I know you are. All morning long, you've been bouncing off the walls asking me when we're leaving. If I was in your place, I'd be a nervous wreck, but your energy is all hard-won and well-earned excitement.

"Yeah! Finally!" You bound down the stairs with your violin case in hand, looking sophisticated in a black dress with your hair swept up in a twist. My heart shifts inside of me with pride and love, and as ever, that little shadow of fear. I'm your mom, and all of that goes with the territory.

"So, do you have everything? Music?"

"Check."

"Rosin?"

"Check."

"Extra strings?"

"Check."

"Instrument?"

"Yes!" you cry. "I'm *so* ready!"

"You so are. Let's do this."

Jess goes off, but I take a minute to compose myself

403

before leaving the kitchen and following her. There's a new piece of paper tacked to the fridge where the audition letter once hung. It's the latest email from Becky that I've printed out. Although she's living on the other side of the country, she's here with me always, curled up inside my heart. And also – I check my watch – she's due to arrive for a surprise visit that Jess doesn't know about. Right about now. I glance at the letter, rereading her words, feeling my heart begin to open and bloom.

Dear Mom,

D.C. is amazing! I am having the best time ever (but not in a bad way). Alannah is great and totally inspiring. I like my job at the café, and I've got lots of time to study for the extra credits I need for college. I think I'm going to study journalism, or maybe psychology. Or maybe I'll become a life coach, or an entrepreneur – in other words, I still don't know. For now, though, it's nice just to have options. I'm also loving looking after Baby Daniel. He's so cute, and while I was a little scared to hold him at first (he's so tiny!), I've got used to it. He's smiling now and sitting up. I swear that his first word is going to be "Becky!"

Marianne is great, and we're both enjoying her maternity leave. We've gone for lots of walks by the river and in the park, and we went to Mount Vernon and lots of other cool historical places that I probably should have heard of – but anyway, I have now. It may sound weird, but she's kind of like my friend. I hope you don't mind. I really miss you and Jess and Dad, and I know that FaceTime isn't really the same. But these few months have been just the thing I needed to really learn to stand on my own two feet. I can't wait to see you again. And tell Jess that she's going to kill her audition! I just know it! I love you so much, and I'm glad that I can finally make you proud.

Love always,

Becky

.   .   .

"I love you," I say aloud. Finally, I believe that she knows it's true.

Steve is already outside in the car waiting for us. It's an hour-hour drive to the city – one that I'll be doing twice a week once you join the Youth Symphony. It will be almost a year later than we'd hoped, but better late than never.

Back then, I'd stared at the audition letter on the fridge and wanted this for you more than anything. It took a journey – one that involved not only untangling strands of DNA but also exploring the deepest, darkest parts of myself – that got us here today. A journey that required me to test my limits, make impossible choices, and discover my true capacity to love, heal, and forgive. I'm still on that journey every day, and some days are easier than others. Today, the sky's the limit.

As you get into the car, I'm proud of your quiet energy and poise, as if you were born to do this. Maybe you were. There are no famous musicians in our family, even among our distant Genetic Cousins. You are a totally unique being with your own sparkle and magic. We can all put our DNA on a database and find our relations, but numbers and markers don't capture our essence as human beings. That's a good thing, I think.

I turn on the CD with your accompaniment. As we drive off, I marvel at the beauty of the music and feel a rush of joy. I think of all the people who have blessed my life and how close I came to losing them.

One year ago, I sat by your bedside and got ready to say goodbye. I had reached an all-time low, having both you and your sister in the hospital. I tried to prepare for the ultimate loss. Then, a miracle happened. A stranger entered our lives – several strangers, actually, because my dad is still the biggest stranger of all. In the span of only a few months, I went from having a staid but solid childhood to finding out that I'd been living a lie and was the daughter of a man with not one, not two, but three families. Three daughters, three half-sisters. One liar in the middle.

After the transplant, the full force of my anger, confusion, and disbelief took hold. Despite having counseled Alannah not to be angry, and despite the information she gave me, I knew that I needed to look for answers. I called the police and Jeff Larsson's son, Jeff Jr., who works for the FBI. They couldn't tell me much, so I poured through newspaper clippings, microfiche, and federal court transcripts of money laundering cases. I spoke to Marianne's mother and people who knew my own mother. I called up Dad's employer and learned that he hadn't worked there for years before his alleged retirement and so-called death and had left under a cloud of financial irregularities. That was largely all I could find out. If there was one thing that Dad was good at, it was slipping in and out of lives, appearing and disappearing without a trace. In the end, I stopped looking. Dad is out there, and I have to respect his wish – for whatever his reasons are – not to be part of my life.

It's taken me a long time to put my anger aside, and some days I still feel it. Marianne has proven to be a blessing, and she's made Becky happier than I ever did or could. She's given her a place that feels a little like home and a lot like an opportunity. Becky is spreading her wings. I miss her a lot, but I'm very, very happy for her.

Marianne is experiencing her own becoming – learning the ups and downs of motherhood and coming to accept that it's not possible to be perfect, either inside or out. I'm so glad that she now has her son Daniel. And if I have my suspicions as to who his father might be, I'm keeping them to myself. Marianne has lost things just as I have. But what we've gained, I hope, is infinitely more valuable.

Because you, my darling Jess, are worth any sacrifice. You are worth all the love and heartbreak that I've felt through the years. Though your transplant was successful, it took months in the hospital for you to heal completely and regain your strength. The days and weeks in the immediate aftermath were harrowing, as we had to *wait and see* if the bone marrow implanted. But the day that your numbers began to rise, the day the doctor declared the transplant a success, the day they removed your central line, and most importantly, the day you came home – these were powerful and defining milestones in our shared life. I would not trade them for the world.

Now that you're "cured", I'm still finding my own healing process difficult. I still wake up every morning with the instinctive worry honed over many years, and each time I see a bruise on your skin, my stomach plummets in free-fall. You, on the other hand, take everything in your stride – with patience, strength, and resilience. Maybe that's the way it's always been, and I'm only just realizing it now. Or maybe a little of Alannah's serenity, calmness, and infinite kindness is now part of you as her blood flows in your veins. When you came home from the hospital, you told me that Taylor had asked you to a movie when you were better. You also removed the "A princess lives here" sign from your door. It tore at my heart a little because I realized that you were growing up. On the other hand, I also felt a strong sense of hope. It's a signal that, finally, you are here to stay.

We arrive at the audition, and you are calm and collected as you sign in and disappear inside the vast concert hall. Steve grips my hand, and the next hour seems like an eternity as we wait, much more nervous as parents than you will ever be playing your violin – the thing you were born to do.

And when you come out of the room, a huge smile beaming on your face, I sweep you into my arms and hug you as hard as I can. Because although you are still my little girl, you are no longer as fragile as you once were. You are growing up and becoming strong enough to face your own love, pain, and heartbreak. Once, I would have spared you that pain, but now I realize that it's part of living. I want you to experience it all.

"Now, what's this surprise you keep talking about?" you ask, a little breathless from my hug, followed by Steve's.

"We've got a reservation at the Top of the Mark," I say. "It's the most famous restaurant in the city. You'll love it – and for once, there's no fog."

"Wow, OK. Cool!"

"You can order anything you want," Steve says. "You deserve it. Because we're celebrating not only your audition but the one-year anniversary of your transplant."

"Oh, is it?"

I'm happy that it sounds like you've forgotten.

My stomach is fluttering as we arrive at the Mark Hopkins Hotel at the very top of Nob Hill. We ride the elevator up into the sky.

"You OK?" Steve says, rubbing his hand in a circle on my back.

"Yeah." I smile at him. Your dad and I may have our ups and downs, but Steve is a good man. An uncomplicated man. And take it from me – that's the best kind to have in your life.

The elevator pings, and we step off. The restaurant is a dazzling jewel of glass and beaux-arts decadence – not to mention the view, which is to die for. But neither of us are looking at the view…

"Surprise!" I say.

You run to Becky, whose face is glowing with the love she feels for you. Next to her is your new aunt, Alannah, who looks stunning in a leopard print dress. Marianne comes over too, and the next thing I know, I'm holding my nephew, Daniel, in my arms. He's so adorable and warm, and I feel a rush of love for him (even though he needs a diaper change ASAP). I'm so glad that they've all arrived safely and that we could all get together.

Dave is here, of course. The program he made has already aired on television and is now streaming on the *MyStory* website. Our story is only a tiny part of it. (Unsurprisingly, they chose only to use the good parts.) One thing's for sure – our lives have been changed by our Genetic Journey in ways we could never have imagined. Dave and I are still friends, and I suspect that his involvement in what Marianne and I went through gave him an incentive to fix his marriage. He's no longer doing as much traveling as before, and while he's still the visionary, he's managed to delegate a lot of the nuts and bolts of running his company to others so he can focus on the personal stories. He comes up and gives me a quick kiss on the cheek. "It's good to see you, Dave," I say.

"Wouldn't miss it for the world."

Steve lets out a little cough. I ignore the thin current of cool air flowing between him and Dave. Men... enough said.

The maître d' leads us to a table with a stunning view of the city, the Bay, and the Golden Gate Bridge. Glasses are passed around, and champagne is poured. My bracelet catches the light as I raise my glass and propose a toast.

"To family," I say. "The ones we know, and the ones who are still out there to find." I look at Dave with a wink.

Marianne raises her glass and smiles at Alannah and

me. "To my secret sisters," she says. "Two in a billion stars."

Becky raises a toast too. She looks at you, her face still glowing. "To the future," she says.

Everyone raises their glasses. The sound of crystal echoes through the restaurant as the lights of the city begin to wink on, one by one.

"To the future!"

I look at you – at my family – and smile. I'll definitely drink to that.

A LETTER FROM LAUREN

Thank you so much for choosing to read *My Secret Sister*. I hope that you enjoyed the book as much as I loved writing it. If you did, please can you leave a rating or review. This is so important as it helps readers to find my books. If I can touch just one person out there with the stories and characters that I've created, then it is worth it to me. Your review may make the difference as to whether someone affected by the issues in the book finds it or not. Let's create a chain of hope together.

If you want to keep up-to-date with all my latest releases, please sign up at the following link. Your email address will never be shared and you can unsubscribe at any time.

https://www.laurenwestwoodwriter.com

This book was very special and personal to me, as it caused me to look deeply into my own experience of motherhood, especially during the pandemic. We all want our children to have great lives, and there is always a tension between keeping them safe and letting them spread their wings.

I wrote this story with the intent of exploring and validating the many conflicting feelings and emotions that arise when people are faced with serious issues and difficult choices. Until we are faced with situations of life or death, we never know for sure how we will think, feel, or react. Whether you love or hate the characters and the choices they make, hopefully their journey has proved rewarding and thought-provoking. Ultimately, I wanted to send a message of hope to anyone out there who might be affected in real life by these issues.

I have tried to be accurate with the facts behind the issues explored in this book, but inevitably, in a work of fiction, it is necessary to take some liberties with the timeline and details. While a novel tells a story with a resolution of sorts, these problems are not so neatly tied up in real life. I have spent many hours reading the heartfelt stories of people affected by infertility and Aplastic Anemia, and while some of them are inspiring and miraculous stories of success, there are just as many gut-wrenching accounts that do not have a happy ending. I have tried hard not to trivialize or sensationalize the issues explored in this book and the lasting scars that they leave. I have tried to present the story with a positive intention and a good spirit. I apologize for any errors I have made.

This book also touches upon the brave new world of home DNA testing, which I find particularly fascinating in our "do-it-yourself" modern era. I have also taken some liberties in regards to the use and testing methods of these kits. For people of my daughters' generation, uploading profiles of DNA—the essential building blocks of our individuality—onto an online database will likely become commonplace, and only time will tell what the implications might be. Following ancestral journeys can be a fascinating and rewarding experience, but as this industry continues to grow, we can only hope that an adequate ethical and legal framework will be put in place to prevent misuse.

Finally, I would like to note that I began this book prior to the world-altering events of the Covid-19 pandemic, and as such, I have not dealt with them here. Covid-19 has had a significant negative impact on many people who were due to or in the process of receiving treatment for diseases like Aplastic Anemia, not to mention increasing the physical risks for people who were already so vulnerable.

I would like to dedicate this book to the healthcare workers who put themselves on the front line to ensure that people with Covid and non-Covid-related illnesses could continue to receive treatment, as well as to all of the blood and organ donors who continue to give the gift of life.

I would also like to dedicate this story to anyone who is dealing with any of the real-life issues it presents. I may never meet you or learn your story, but please know that I am sending you my best wishes.

Finally, I would also like to dedicate the book to my family… we are in this together!

I love hearing from my readers—you can get in touch on my Facebook page, through Twitter, Goodreads or my website. I look forward to hearing from you, and learning your stories…

Thank you so much,
  Lauren

- Facebook: @Lwestwoodbooks
- Twitter: @lwestwoodwriter
- Web: https://www.laurenwestwoodwriter.com

ACKNOWLEDGMENTS

Writing this book posed many challenges for me, especially as it was conceived and written during the pandemic. I would like to thank all of the people who have believed in me and given me support. In particular I would like to thank my writing group: Ronan Winters, Chris King, and Francisco Gochez who have been my friends over many years. I would also like to thank the members of the Savvy Writer's Snug. Special thanks goes to Sophie Hannah and the Dream Author program for coaching me through the challenges of being the "first believer" in this book. I am also indebted to several amazing women that I will probably never meet: Brooke Castillo and Elizabeth Gilbert. Their work has helped me through my darkest moments of self-doubt and given me the courage to put my work out there into the world.

I would like to thank Donna Hillyer for her keen editing eye and insight. The beautiful cover is by Emma Graves. Finally, a huge thank you to my family: Suzanne and Bruce Remington, and Monica Yeo. Most of all, thanks to Ian, and to my wonderful daughters, Eve, Rose, and Grace, for your continuing patience and love.

Loved My Secret Sister?

Discover your next great read today.

My Mother's Silence and **The Daughter She Lost**
by Lauren Westwood

30899711R00247